TROUBLE LURKS

ELISABETH JOY

TROUBLE LURKS

ELISABETH JOY

STORYLIGHT PRESS

Published by StoryLight Press

This is a work of fiction. Names, characters, places, settings, and incidents are the product of the author's imagination or are used fictitiously in the telling of this story. Any resemblance to true events, locations, or persons, living or dead, is used fictionally.

ISBN: 9781967640010 (paperback)
ISBN: 9781967640027 (ebook)

Cover design by Rhys-Marie Whitnell
Cover art © 2024 by Lucy Peterson
Edited by Cate VonNostrand and Katja Labonté (https://katjalabonte. wordpress.com/)
Formatted by Abigail Kopp

To KDWC, without which this book would never exist
(And I'd have never met my best friends.)

CONTENTS

PART ONE
OF DOVES AND DANGER

CHAPTER ONE
TROUBLE LURKS AHEAD

"*Truth was never the problem.*"

Perched on the overstuffed chair in a corner of the Chandler Public Library, I stare down at the opening line of the book, the stark black letters weaving a riddle of confusion. "Well, then, what is? The lies?" I mutter to Secret, my allergen detection service dog, who settles calmly at my feet.

This book shouldn't exist. My father's name should not be printed on the cover, the bold "Dallas Caineson" standing proud under a shadowy city illustration.

Frowning, I flip to the back of the book, leafing through the pages until I reach the author bio. It's Dad's face that stares out from the black-and-white photo, concealed behind sunglasses and a cowboy hat.

Dad, who always let me help create his stories. When I was little, I'd sit cross-legged on the floor in the study, listening as he read his newest chapter aloud. When Lady Shadow discovered the secret to the air vent in the Hollingsworth Heritage Museum's basement, I was the first to know about it. When Jane Dodofmis destroyed the world's leading kombucha plant using her wily villainous schemes, I was there, making sure Dad kept the family of marmosets living under the plant safe.

I've never seen *The Freesia Guard* in my life. But its existence is proved by the solid weight in my hands, the smoothness of the paperback cover, and my father's name, stark against the shadowed background.

"Dad—" I can barely choke the whisper out, but I'm in a busy public library; I can't cry now. Instead, I blink up at the ceiling like it holds the answer to why I've never even heard of this book before. Once the tiles over my head no longer swim in my vision, I take a deep breath and examine *The Freesia Guard* closely. The starry sky is at odds with the city background on the front cover, across which a boy sprints with a small gray cat at his heels. The illustration stretches to the back of the cover, with the city fading into the stars, but otherwise, it's blank. There's no blurb, no ISBN—not even a library barcode.

This doesn't make sense. None of this makes sense. It doesn't even look like a library book, although I'd found it tucked between books 3 and 4 of The Misadventures of Lady Shadow series—the slightly shorter and fatter *Freesia Guard* out of place between Dad's most popular middle-grade novels.

Cueing Secret to stay, I pace to the end of the aisle, peeking out into the main section of the library. It's crowded for a Friday—little kids just out of storytime, parents milling about, even a couple of teens mucking around in the corner by the DVDs. The librarian's desk has a line stretching to the computer station. I frown and retreat to my chair. "Yeah, no help there," I mutter to Secret as I pick up the book again, turning it over in my hands. So I do the next best thing: open it to the first page and begin to read.

The plot follows a magical flower that can tell the future and the people who guard it: a group of children who call themselves the Freesia Guard. Five chapters pass, and the main character, Timmy, has been kidnapped, held captive in a train headed to an undisclosed location—all because this second-rate villain decided he needed the Freesia to take over the world, and Timmy tried to stop him.

"Ready to go?"

I jump, sticking my finger between the pages to keep my place. "Aunt Patience! Why do you always sneak up on me like that?"

Aunt Patience raises an eyebrow as if I'm somehow the one at fault. "Aren't you supposed to be quiet at the library?"

Sure, but that doesn't mean she has to give everyone heart attacks. I push to my feet, re-coiling Secret's leash, and grab the book. I swear, Dad's sister *enjoys* sneaking up on me, especially when I least expect it... like when I'm preoccupied by a book whose entire existence is news to me.

"Find anything good while I was losing the battle with inflation and watching my paycheck vanish?" Aunt Patience falls into step behind me as I head towards the checkout desk. The post-storytime crowd is mostly gone, and the library is quiet again.

"Maybe." Stopping at the end of the aisle, I eye *The Freesia Guard*, and after a second of hesitation, hold it up. "Have you ever seen this before?"

She squints at it before slowly shaking her head, tucking a strand of wayward dark hair behind her ear. "No. Should I?"

I hand her the novel. "Look closely."

"What am I..." She trails off, eyes widening as she stares down at it. "Dallas."

"And it was published last year," I add in an undertone, the unspoken "when he was already gone" hanging in the vellichor-infused air.

Perplexion makes itself known in the creases of Aunt Patience's brow, and she taps the cover, the dull thud somehow making this oddity more real.

Glancing down at Secret, who sits next to me, the 20-pound poodle all handsome in his red vest, I shake my head slowly. *There must be a mistake.* "Maybe it's a typo or something?"

Aunt Patience hands *The Freesia Guard* back with a shrug, though wrinkles still mar her brow. "Could be."

Folding the book under my arm, I start for the desk. "You don't believe it?"

"Just never seen it before," is her clipped reply.

I glance back over my shoulder, and the word that pops into my mind at her drawn expression is "troubled." And... is that *fear*? Unease stirs in my gut.

"May I help you?" The librarian's eyes pierce me through her old-fashioned spectacles as I reach the desk, and I nod, setting down the book.

"I'd like to check this out, but it doesn't have one of those barcodes."

"I see." The chain for her glasses jiggles as she pulls the book closer and flips it open to the back.

"Where'd you get it?" I ask, fingering Secret's lead as I watch her.

She closes the book slowly, peering at me through steely blue eyes. "May God be with you, dear. Take it."

I blink. "You mean... to keep?"

"Yes." Her gaze is steady, her eyes unwavering, and I shift uneasily.

"Really? Uhm, thanks! Thank you."

With a gnarled hand, she picks up *The Freesia Guard* and holds it out. I reach to take it, but she doesn't let go, her expression solemn.

The moment seems to stretch on, my unease growing with each second.

"Go with God," she says at last, voice grave as she fully extends the novel.

"Yes, ma'am." I don't know what else to say. "Thanks again."

When I turn, book in one hand and Secret's leash in the other, I catch sight of Aunt Patience watching from where I'd left her at the end of the juvenile fiction aisle. Something I can't name flickers across her face, but it's gone by the time she reaches me.

Questions swirl in my mind as I follow her out into the sunny Indiana afternoon. I squint against the brightness, trying in vain to make sense out of everything that's happened since Aunt Patience dropped me off while she picked up a few groceries.

"Go with God." What kind of librarian says that when they hand you a book? Is it *cursed* or something?

When we reach Aunt Patience's truck, I methodically latch Secret's crate before slipping into the passenger seat, mind still whirling. Curses are the stuff of fairy tales. Dad wrote some light fantasy, sure, but not much magic; his niche was spy fiction. Action. Normal people in abnormal situations, and abnormal people in ordinary places.

I stare at the cover of *The Freesia Guard* like if I try hard enough, I can see the answers that lurk just under the surface. *Dramatic, Tirana.* I shake my head. Dad would've said I was a real poet.

"This is a... rather interesting development," Aunt Patience murmurs, turning out of the library parking lot.

"What do you mean?" I have the feeling that she knows something she's not telling me, and I don't like it.

She glances at me, the look on her face almost searching, then wordlessly shakes her head. "I'm sure it's nothing."

That's a lie if I ever heard one. I bite my lip, letting my gaze drift to the trees blurring past my window. *What in the world is going on here?*

CHANDLER, INDIANA

"DALLAS CAINESON WAS BORN WITH A PROFOUND LOVE OF WORDS. Growing up, he and his sister wove intricate tales of impossible situations and intrepid heroes, whether they were cordial pirates, blathering dragons, or hounded spies. That fire of inspiration never burned out, and today, Caineson is the author of the much-acclaimed Misadventures of Lady Shadow series and its sequel series, The Odd Exploits of Baby Shadow. His stand-alone Sunglasses in Disguise *won the Barliman Award, and his work has been featured in* The Disparu Gazette, Columba, *and* iSpy.*"*

I bite my lip, running my fingers lightly across the page. My other hand clasps my locket, the medal warm against my palm.

"I don't understand, Seek," I mutter to the dog who's curled up, donut-style, on the foot of my bed. He doesn't answer, of course. It's not like he'd even know why Dad never told me about *The Freesia Guard*, even if I could find some alphabet soup that'd make Secret talk.

With a sigh, I drop my locket and flip to the front of the book. I've never heard of Underhill Aphrodite Press, which is the name printed on the copyright page. Underhill—a reference to *The Lord of the Rings*? My eyes wander to the framed map of Tolkien's Middle-earth hanging over my bed.

I was nine when Dad and I redecorated my room, painting the walls tan, adding that map... And we'd both been so excited to find the deep green rug, which matched everything perfectly. My nose stings, and I turn back to *The Freesia Guard* before tears can join the ache in my heart.

"Why, Daddy?" I half-whisper, staring at the publication date. It's a full *year* after he died. Who publishes a dead person's manuscript?

I would almost believe that this isn't Dad's book; that some scoundrel stole his name and bio and picture and writing style. But the dedication on the opposite page, which I've been purposely ignoring, proves otherwise.

"For my daughter: never be afraid to take the road less traveled."

Almost unprompted, my hand travels back up to my locket, and I trace the words engraved on the smooth back: "*Take the road less traveled.*"

This book is for me... but why? And how?

Leaving *The Freesia Guard* on my desk, I pad over to my bookcase, running my hands over the shelf of Dad's books. There's the tall picture book *Lulu Doesn't Like Apples*, and the sequel, *Don't Give Lulu Grapes*; the YA spy-suspense *Sunglasses in Disguise*, and the picture book based on it, *Eggplants in Sunglasses*... And, of course, The Misadventures of Lady Shadow series, followed by The Odd Exploits of Baby Shadow.

The Lady Shadow books are paperbacks, too, but they're thinner, whereas *The Freesia Guard* is nearly an inch thick. More useful for inflicting physical damage, I suppose, although I don't know why I'd ever need to hit someone over the head with a book.

You're getting paranoid, Tirana.

Maybe I should be.

I grab the first Lady Shadow book, *Lady Shadow's Premiere*, and return to my desk. After starting up my laptop, I type "freesia guard dallas caineson" into the browser's search bar. Dad comes up, but there aren't any books titled *The Freesia Guard* listed under him.

I'm familiar with the publisher for Lady Shadow, but Underhill Aphrodite Press doesn't seem to exist. The browser just comes up with an entirely unhelpful "No results found."

I frown, chewing the inside of my cheek. It's beginning to look like none of this exists... which is impossible, because it's right in front of me. It feels like the time in *Tesla's Attic* when the principal refused to believe his student existed because the kid wasn't in the paperwork. But like in that book, there has to be a good explanation for this situation, too.

"Maybe it's some sort of present for me, huh, boy?" I glance over at Secret, who lifts his head, sleepy mocha eyes watching me.

Dad could have written this, published it through a different press, and worked out a way to surprise me. It would be just like him. And it would explain the "Underhill," too—it's all a joke. A *Lord of the Rings* reference from the time Frodo went undercover.

"I bet Aunt Patience is in on it, too." That would explain everything.

Sufficiently less creeped out, I turn back to the book in question. It's probably the last gift from Dad I'll ever get, and suddenly, I want to savor it, keep the bittersweet feeling tucked in the pristine pages. But that's never what Dad would have wanted. "Books are for reading," he'd say, "not eye candy." So, taking a deep breath, I open the book to where I'd left off in the library.

Some time later, the call of "Dinner's ready!" jerks me out from Timmy's crazy world of palantir flowers, talking cats, and a quest to rescue the captured Freesia Guards. I reluctantly stand up and trudge downstairs, Secret trotting behind me, his toenails clicking on the polished wooden floor.

"How's the book?" Aunt Patience watches me as I slide into my seat.

I eye her, but there's no mischievous gleam in her face, no telltale smirk. "Uhm, it's good."

The aroma of macaroni and cheese wafts from the pot in the center of the table, and I push down the twinge of anxiety that that mix always brings. My aunt's lived across town since I was a toddler; she knows enough not to kill me.

Aunt Patience scoops the steaming food onto two plates and passes one to me. Secret's waiting by my chair, ready, and I hold it out to him.

"Check."

He gives it a few sniffs, then bops my leg, the all clear signal.

"Good boy," I croon, setting the plate back on the table and grabbing some dried beef liver from the hutch where Mum keeps her china dishes. The liver smells gross, but Secret gobbles the treat and looks up for more, feathered tail wagging.

"Thank you," I say with a little laugh. "Now you're done. Okay! Go away! Shoo." He doesn't listen, of course; he just follows me to my seat and stares at me when I sit down.

"So..." Aunt Patience raises an eyebrow, eyeing me across the table. Like every time Mum has a business trip to London, my aunt is stationed here to make sure I don't burn the house down. Sixteen is probably old enough to watch myself, but Mum's been even more protective since Dad died, and I'm definitely not complaining about more time with my favorite (and only) aunt.

"So. The book." I hesitate. "It was a surprise for me, right?"

She's silent for a long moment that stretches on awkwardly, her eyes searching my face before her gaze drops, and she sighs. "Honestly... I don't know."

"But you knew he wrote it, right?" I press.

She shakes her head slowly. "I... didn't, no."

"It's about this boy, Timmy, and his sister—they're protectors of this magic flower that can see into the future. Didn't Dad tell you about it?"

Again, she shakes her head. "I don't know, Tirana. You don't know how much I wish I did, but I don't."

"Maybe Mum knows." I stab a piece of cheesy macaroni and push it around my plate. "Or maybe Dad didn't tell anyone except the librarian. Or maybe his ghost visited her and—"

"Tirana." Aunt Patience reaches across the table and puts her hand over mine. "We'll get to the bottom of this, okay?"

I exhale slowly. "But it doesn't make sense. Why would the book end up in the library *now*?" There's nothing special about the end of May, and I would have noticed if it had been at the library when I was there last week. "How did whoever put it there know that I'd get it, and not some other person?"

Again, Aunt Patience slowly shakes her head, forehead creasing. "Don't worry. We'll figure this out. I... have a few friends who might be able to help."

"Who?" How can her friends help with a mysterious book?

She gives that small smile that says she's not telling me something, withdrawing her hand to grab her glass of water. She takes a sip. "Just... friends.

Don't worry, we'll get to the bottom of this. Can you tell me what else it's about?"

I take a bite of macaroni, thinking as I chew the creamy rice pasta. "So, there's this group of kids, protecting a flower called the Freesia. But the evil dude, Ragnar, kidnapped the Freesia and two of its guards, so Timmy, his sister Robin, and their cat need to rescue their friends and stop Ragnar from taking over the world." I nod. "Ragnar is really fixated on ruling the world. He's like a less harmless version of that *Phineas and Ferb* villain, Doofenshmirtz."

Aunt Patience chuckles, but her expression is gauging, like she's trying to mentally solve the puzzle. "A cat, huh? Dallas always did have an odd sense of humor."

"Yeah. His name is Cobie. I think half of the trouble may have been his fault." I tap my chin and shrug. "He was a stray, but Timmy and Robin took him in like a proper waif. I don't want to spoil the story, but I'm not convinced that Cobie isn't working *with* Ragnar."

"Typical." Aunt Patience exhales, gaze drifting to that faraway place her and Mum's eyes always go to when they're missing Dad.

I swallow hard, pushing around a bite of the broccoli that Aunt Patience insists makes the macaroni healthy. An awkward moment passes before I clear my throat. "This... this isn't just a joke Dad made up, is it." It's more of a statement than a question, because I can see the answer on her face.

She shakes her head, nods, then shrugs. "I wish I knew, Ana. I wish I knew."

"He wrote about secret agents. Maybe he was one," I jest. *Now wouldn't that be something?*

Her head jerks up. "Gracious, girl! Whatever would give you an idea like that?"

"Uhm..." I scan her face, but the flicker of panic that crossed her expression is gone. "I guess... nothing?"

"You're like Dallas with that crazy imagination." Her eyes crinkle, but her smile doesn't quite reach her eyes.

Secret, tired of standing next to me, heaves a sigh and trots off towards the living room, where I hear the scratch of fabric as he circles on the couch before finally settling down.

Sure I'm *just like* Dad—but I can't write like he did. He always said the little stories I wrote when I was younger were awesome, but that was just because he was my dad. Mum would normally raise an eyebrow, say "That's cute," and send me off to bother Dad instead of her.

I bite my lip and stare down at my plate, that age-old crack in my heart aching like nothing else, because I'll never get it back. Never get Dad back, never get my childhood back, and I don't even know if I'll ever get Mum back—the *old* Mum, who wasn't as distant or as consumed with work.

And if I keep thinking this way, I'll be crying into my macaroni and cheese quicker than Lucy Pevensie could vanish into that old wardrobe at the professor's house. I take a deep breath and force a smile. "I'll give you the book after I finish it, okay?"

Aunt Patience nods like she's only half listening, then seems to pull herself back into the present. She notices me watching her, and she gives me a small smile, pushing back her chair and rising. "I'll do the dishes myself tonight if you'll help me clear the table."

"No protest there. Thanks." I know she's only letting me off drying duty because *she* wants to read *The Freesia Guard*, but an excuse is an excuse.

I stack the plates, balancing them in one hand as I grab our cups, and head to the kitchen. Once the table is cleared, I go down the hall to my room and stand in the doorway, staring at the book lying closed on the arm of my chair.

I'm not sure *what* to think about this. The only way Dad could have planned to have the book appear on a random library shelf in Aunt Patience's town is if he saw into the future. Knew that he'd never return from that research trip to Florida. Knew I'd be at the library today and browse the *C*'s in juvenile fiction.

And that makes as much sense as a banana growing on a fig tree.

CHAPTER TWO
THE FREESIA GUARD

Pale moonlight fills my room, the drone of cicadas resounding through my closed window. Shadows dance on the ceiling, cast by the fan slowly orbiting the light fixture.

My mind hasn't stopped spinning either, trying to examine every possibility. Finishing *The Freesia Guard* didn't help. Somewhere, deep inside, I'd been expecting there to be answers in the book.

There weren't.

Timmy, Robin, and Cobie the Clever Cat, after a dangerous journey, managed to get back the Freesia flower and save their friends from Ragnar, and everyone lived happily ever after. A typical Dad story. I've gotta be missing something. There's no other option.

If the story and the writing aren't so obviously Dad's, I would think there's some other Dallas Caineson who wrote a random story that doesn't exist online. Or that someone stole his name, or... *something*. Anything.

Secret's warm body, pressing against my back, pins my blankets down as I try to roll over. I tug some slack in them, struggling to turn in the confines of my bed. The pinpoint of light from the alarm clock glares a harsh 12:43.

I sigh and close my eyes, but it does nothing to quell my pinballing thoughts. Dad was just a writer. A writer, father, husband... I bite my lip, focusing on the pale white blades of the fan. Something seems so *wrong* about this whole thing. Something that nags me, like an itch that won't go away.

How can a book be published nearly a full year after the death of the author... without me or Aunt Patience knowing?

Maybe that weird, something-more feeling is only because of Aunt Patience's reaction. I bite back a groan, shaking my head into my pillow. She thinks we can figure it out, that she has *friends* who can help. And why did asking if Dad was a *secret agent* freak her out?

For a brief second, my mind opens a thought that I squish like a nasty bug. I know what Mum told me: Dad's car hydroplaned on a bridge, plummeting into some river in Florida. He's *gone.* There's no way that he could still be out there, planting books for his unsuspecting daughter to find.

Sure, I only vaguely remember the funeral: muted colors, tears, and the harsh glare of the frigid winter sun. But only Tom Sawyer misses his own funeral, not real-life people. Not *Dad.*

Unless he did. The service was closed-casket. The funeral home could have buried anyone—or even no one. *What if...?*

You're like Dallas with that crazy imagination. Aunt Patience's words from earlier return, like a cartoon's personal rain cloud.

Dad made that imagination his career, and look where it landed him. Where it landed *us.* There's a Dad-shaped hole in our family, one that can't be fixed. I reach up and rub my locket, the slowly-moving fan blurring as I stare up at it.

Why'd you have to go and leave us, Dad?

CHANDLER, INDIANA
SATURDAY, MAY 26

LIGHT STREAMS ONTO MY FACE, AND I SQUINT AGAINST IT, THROWing a hand up to cover my eyes. I wonder why Mum hasn't come in with her typical "Rise and shine, darling," until I stare at the ceiling long enough for the world to come trickling back. *Right.* Mum's away, and I have a very weird book that an equally odd librarian gave to me.

I sigh, squirming out of the Secret-pinned blankets. As soon as my bare feet hit the wooden floor, he's scrambling up, scruffy white fur resembling the finest bedhead.

I wonder if Aunt Patience is done with the book yet. As promised, I gave it to her after I finished, and I haven't seen her since.

After throwing on some clothes, I slip to the kitchen, Secret at my heels. I slide open the glass doors and step barefoot onto the cold concrete patio, laughing softly as Secret races across the dew-misted grass.

After he does his business, he returns with a soaked tennis ball, dropping it at my feet and cocking his head at me. I shake my head as I scoop it up and hurl it out into the yard.

If Dad's alive, I'm going to find him. The thought comes out of nowhere, like a bird thudding into a glass window pane.

Secret comes rocketing back, and I crouch down and pick up the ball that he drops. "I think I'm going crazy." *Reading too many spy books, girl.* I toss the ball again, my eyes following it as it flies through the air. *But what if—the details don't match up—it would change everything... He wouldn't...*

Seek drops the tennis ball at my feet before backing up a few steps, body poised to dash off again. I bend down and pick up the ball, holding it loosely as I stare up into the clouded sky.

There's got to be a reason this all happened. I just have to figure it out. Dropping the ball into the grass, I turn and trudge back to the house. "Let's go, Seek." As I slide the back door open, I catch sight of Aunt Patience leaning against the counter, watching us.

Concern blossoms in my chest at the blank look on her face. *Mum—?* Everything around me blurs except for her shadowed eyes as I close the door behind me and dodge an underfoot Secret. "What's wrong?"

She shakes her head, dropping her gaze to the tiled floor. My breath catches, waiting—

"It's about the book."

Not Mum. Not another accident. I cross my arms, biting my lip.

"What... uh, what about it?"

"It's..." She gestures vaguely before tucking a wayward stand of honey-brown hair behind her ear. "It's complicated."

I wait silently for her to go on.

"Your father's miss—his last trip—" She breaks off, shaking her head. "When we were growing up, your dad and I—we were always playing pretend. His favorite game was secret agents, better yet if he could get magic in there." She pauses, eyes taking on a distant look as she gazes somewhere over my head. "There was this one game... we'd be the protectors of a magical spying flower that the bad guys were always trying to steal."

"You mean he based Timmy off of himself?"

Aunt Patience smiles, but her eyes shimmer in the light streaming in from the window over the sink.

"... and you're Robin." Biting my lip, I look down at Secret, who's nosing around the floor for crumbs that don't exist in this extra-clean house.

"Tirana."

Caught by surprise by the severity in Aunt Patience's voice, my head snaps up. Her gray eyes lock with mine.

"There's more to this than a simple story." Clearing her throat, she shakes her head. "You—you need to call your mom, okay? Tell her about the book."

"But *why*?" I can feel my brows scrunching. "You didn't say anything about it last night..."

She hesitates, as if not sure what to say. "Tirana... there are things that you don't know. That I can't tell you." Another pause, then she looks up from the granite counter to meet my eyes. "Do you trust me?"

"Of course."

She shakes her head. "No, I asked 'do you *trust me*.' Not 'do you *think* you *might*.'"

I resist the urge to bite my lip. "Uhm..."

"Good answer."

Aunt Patience must see the confusion on my face, because she grins wryly, though it doesn't meet her eyes. "Trust is something earned, Ana.

You'd do well to remember that." She pushes away from the counter and leaves the kitchen.

What in the world...? I blink, staring after her, before looking down at Secret. He's nosing his bowl like kibble will magically appear if he wishes hard enough.

"You getting the feeling she's not telling me something?"

He stares up at me.

"Call Mum. Right," I mutter as I open the lid to the container of dog food. *Maybe she can tell me what's going on.*

THE DAMP, WOODEN SLATS OF THE PORCH SWING PRESS INTO MY back as I lean into them, squinting slightly in the sunlight. Secret sniffs across the backyard, chasing a bug here and there. Birds chirp, a neighbor's car revs to life, and a train whistles.

C'mon, pick up...

It goes to voicemail. I don't leave one.

"Six-hour time difference," I mutter into the morning, "which makes it afternoon over there. She's probably just bus—"

My phone rings, the screen lighting up with a call. I swipe it quickly, heart rate accelerating. "Hey?"

"Is everything all right?" Mum's concerned voice sounds closer than whatever the distance is between Indiana and England.

"Uhm... trying to figure that out." I hesitate.

"Did something happen? Are you okay?" There's a murmur in the background, then the thud of a door shutting, and Mum speaks again. "Tirana?"

"Yeah, no, it's fine. I just—found a book, and Aunt Patience said I needed to talk to you."

Silence.

I shift, the dampness from the wood seeping into my capris. *Please tell me this is all a joke...*

"A book?" Mum's words are clipped.

"Yeah. It's called *The Freesia Guard*, and… and Dad wrote it." I bite my lower lip, all the questions from yesterday rising like an ocean wave driven by a sea demon.

"Brilliant. What is it about?"

"Uhm…" I lift my eyes from the screen, focusing on Secret, who's lying in the grass, panting in the sun. "There's no blurb or anything, but it's about this kid and his sister, trying to find a stolen flower and their friends. But, Mum—"

"Is there a cat?"

I bite off the question about the dates, pressing my eyes shut. "Uh, yeah. Cobie the Clever Cat. How—"

"Tirana, I need you to listen to me. Tell your aunt it's time you learned the truth. I'll try to wrap things up here and return as quickly as I can. Whatever you do, don't let that book out of your sight. Do you understand?"

"Yeah, but—"

"Good. I'll explain everything later, all right? Stay safe." With that, the call drops.

What in the…? I stare down at the phone for a full ten seconds before I straighten, whistle for Secret, and go off in search of Aunt Patience.

She's not in the house. She *should* be here, but she's not. After checking every room twice, I push back the curtains of the living room window.

Mum's Chevy is parked under the basketball hoop, but Aunt Patience's truck is gone.

I'm alone… and something is *very* wrong.

CHAPTER THREE
OPERATION RIDE OF
THE ROHIRRIM

Blake Hession runs a hand through his hair, cursor hovering over the email message in his private inbox. The sender's address is the kind that vanishes within an hour, leaving no trace of the person behind it, but it's the subject line that slowly turns his blood to ice: "Mauve Herring."

Apprehension churning in his gut, he clicks open the email.

> Agent Grizzled Fox,
>
> There is no time or security for explanation, but please be aware that I am calling a Code Mauve Herring. This leaves Frodo unprotected, and if things go according to plan, she will find her way into your custody. Things have changed, and I can no longer respect Bel Ria's wishes.
>
> Please note: Dove is in the possession of Frodo. Operation Ride of the Rohirrim has been set into motion. Proceed accordingly.
>
> ~Agent Mute Starburst

Blake leans back in his desk chair, rubbing the bridge of his nose. *Shades.* Nearly two years of useless searching, and now Dove's being dropped into his lap like a neatly wrapped package by "Frodo"? It's suspicious, and a

Code Mauve Herring—especially one being called by his old friend—means something isn't right.

But if Starburst wants to enact Operation Ride of the Rohirrim after all these years, then Blake won't stop it. Once upon a time, he made a promise, and he can't let Dove fly the coop. Not again.

I guess it's time for Frodo to see the world.

CHANDLER, INDIANA

"I don't like this," I whisper to Secret, letting the curtain fall back into place. If my life was a movie, there would be creepy music playing right about now. "Maybe she left a note? But where would she *go*?"

Back in the kitchen, I check the dry-erase board on the side of the fridge. "Cue the creepy music all right," I mutter, resisting the urge to glance over my shoulder. The shopping list is gone, replaced with Aunt Patience's neat writing: "Looks like the orcs won the battle with your room. You'd better pick it up before I return."

I read the words again, biting my lip. We've always had the safety measure of writing a cryptic message on the dry-erase board in case something happens, but this is the first time the orc code has been used outside of games.

Secret trots after me, nails clicking on the hardwood floor of the hallway, as I head to my room. On my desk, I find *The Freesia Guard* with a creamy envelope resting on top of it.

Unease pricks my spine, and I plop down on the desk chair with a frown. *This would make a lot more sense if it were my birthday.*

The flap is tucked into the envelope, per Aunt Patience style, and the white paper inside is filled with neat, familiar handwriting.

Tirana, if you're reading this, I'm sorry. So very sorry. If there was anything I could do... but there isn't. It's too late for that now. It wasn't planned this way, but as you must learn, things often don't go as we want them to.

First, you might have noticed that I am gone. I know it's probably not something your mom would be happy about, and your dad would have my head if he could, but I'm afraid it's out of my control.

I cannot tell you everything in a place where it can be so easily compromised. I'll just say that those books you like so much aren't complete fiction. There is more truth to them than one might expect.

Your task will not be an easy one, but you must protect The Freesia Guard until it's in the hands of those who will use it as it was intended. You will know who those people are.

I know you're capable. With that dog of yours, you can do anything. Remember that.

Find Agent Grizzled Fox. He has the answers. Trust him, and no one else.

Don't let me down, and more importantly, don't let down your parents.

Check your piggy bank, stay safe, and remember, Grace Tirana Caineson, that I love you. Forever and always.

~Aunt P.

I turn the page, but the other side is blank. "I don't understand," I mutter to Secret. "This sounds like we got sucked into, I don't know, a *spy* novel or something."

Secret gives my leg a lick, and I reach down and scratch behind his ears with a sigh. "Yeah, boy, I know. Okay... she said something about a piggy bank."

The problem is that I don't *have* a piggy bank. But Mum does.

Her room is darkened, the blinds pulled closed. I flick on the lights, and Secret jumps on her bed, tail wagging. "Very funny," I mutter, since we both know that Mum would have a few choice words to say if she knew my dog was on her bed.

The pale-pink piggy bank that's been around for as long as I can remember sits on Mum's dresser, staring at Secret with tiny black eyes and a painted smile. I'd asked Dad about it once, why the bank was in their room when it looked like a child's, and he'd said I'd find out someday.

I guess today is that someday. I pick up the piggy and shake it, and something papery wisps inside. There's no stopper on the bottom, and it looks like one solid piece. How is anyone supposed to get it open?

I take it back to my room, careful to shut off the light and close the door as I leave Mum's, and look around.

Hmm... I eye the heavy dictionary on my desk.

The piggy doesn't break. The dictionary just bounces off and lands on the floor with a huge thud that gets Secret barking.

"Hush," I order once I have my voice under control again. "*Hush*, Seek." He stops, and I take a deep breath. "Okay, good boy. Now I just need to figure out how to get this thing open."

In the garage, I find a hammer. I set the piggy bank on the dusty concrete floor and tap it. Nothing, so I put more force behind my swing. Too much, apparently, because the piggy goes rolling. I groan and set it back onto its feet. This time, I hit it as hard as I can. The hammer flies out of my grip, and I jump back just in time to avoid getting hit.

"This is crazy!" I put my hands on my hips and glare at the piggy bank. "Just *break* already!" I bend over and pick it up, examining it. All my efforts have left are a few dents and nicks in the pink paint, revealing the silver metal underneath. "Great. Just great." Maybe if I throw it hard on the floor... Just as I raise the piggy to try it, something Dad used to tell me flashes through my mind. *Take a closer look at things. There's often more than meets the eye.*

I take a deep breath and turn the piggy over, running my fingers along the bottom. Sure enough, there's a tiny hole—it almost looks like a keyhole. *Oh, come on! How did I miss that?* It seems so obvious now.

I eye the drawer of tools where I'd found the hammer. *Hmm...*

The drawer's a mess, but I manage to dig out several different kinds and sizes of screwdrivers. Tongue sticking out in concentration, I try a

Phillips-head, then a smaller one. Neither work, so I grab a tiny flathead and wiggle it into the hole. Something clicks, and the piggy separates into several puzzle-like pieces.

I'm not sure what I was expecting—a bunch of money? A note? Certainly not a single two-dollar bill.

"Huh?" I hold it up to the light, scanning the intricate details: the portrait of Jefferson; the signing of the Declaration of Independence; the optical illusion-like wave designs that border both sides.

Aunt Patience obviously had a reason for wanting me to find this, but what in the world does a two-dollar bill do? I check each piece of the piggy bank carefully, but there's nothing else there.

Maybe I missed something in the letter. I put the tools away, gather up the pieces of the piggy bank, and slip back into the main part of the house. Secret is there as soon as I push open the door, jumping around like I've been gone a whole lot longer than—I glance at my watch—less than twenty minutes.

"Any idea what this is for?" I ask him, holding up the bill. He jumps for it, and I pull it back with a laugh. "No, sir, not yours. Come on, let's go see what Aunt Patience said."

I click my tongue for Secret to follow me and head to my room, where I drop the piggy puzzle pieces on my bed and bite my lip, surveying the room. The letter's on the desk where I left it, and I pick it up, reading it carefully. *"Check your piggy bank, stay safe, and remember, Grace Tirana Caineson, that I love you. Forever and always."*

"Oh, where did you *go*, Aunt Patience?" I mutter into the stillness, blinking back sudden tears. If it weren't for the whisper of something being terribly wrong, I might have enjoyed this whole scavenger-hunt thing—but something isn't right.

There's nothing that I can find that remotely correlates with the two-dollar bill, other than the "check your piggy bank" line, and I sigh softly, resting my chin in my hand. "What'd' ya think, bud, hm?"

"Find Agent Grizzled Fox. He has the answers. Trust him, and no one else."

An agent.

"I'll just say that those books you like so much aren't complete fiction. There is more truth to them than one might expect."

An... agent. For what? For whom? The CIA? FBI? With a name like *Grizzled Fox*? How am I supposed to find a man with only a weird code-name and a two-dollar bill?

Unless... he's supposed to find *me*? Then why wouldn't Aunt Patience say, "Be found by Agent Grizzled Fox"?

The sheer insanity of my mental dialogue makes me snort aloud. I'm thinking about agents and who's supposed to find whom, when I don't even know what he's an agent *for*.

This morning, Aunt Patience asked me if I trusted her... and I do.

I'm pretty sure I have to.

I don't know what's coming next, but I have a feeling that I'll find out soon enough. I quickly pack my backpack with a folded change of clothes; toiletries; *The Freesia Guard*, Aunt Patience's letter and the two-dollar bill, tucked between the pages of a blank notebook; Secret's things, and my e-reader. At the last minute, I grab Dad's navy Dallas Cowboys cap off the dresser and set it on my head.

In the kitchen, I stick two slices of bread into the toaster and scour the pantry. At the toaster's ding, I drop my armload of various kinds of bars on the counter and make myself a peanut butter and jelly sandwich. Between bites, I fill the remaining space of my backpack with the bars, wedging in a plastic baggy of Secret's kibble and some dog treats.

Then I'm ready. For what, I'm not completely sure.

Just when I think I'm going to go crazy just sitting here, having no idea what to do, my phone buzzes. I yank it out of my pocket, hoping the text is from Aunt Patience, but my heart freezes when I see it's from Dad.

What—but—how—that's not possible!

Swallowing against the pounding of my pulse, I open the message.

DAD

George Rogers Clark National Historical Park.

"I... I don't understand. This—it just—*no!*" Willing my hands to stop shaking, I type out a quick response.

ME

Who is this?

DAD

George Rogers Clark National Historical Park.

I press my eyes closed, reminding myself to breathe. *A joke It's gotta be a joke.* I bite my lip so hard it hurts.

ME

Excuse me?

DAD

George Rogers Clark National Historical Park.

This is going nowhere. I do a quick internet search. Apparently, the park's located in Vincennes, Indiana—about an hour from here.

ME

Who are you?

DAD

George Rogers Clark National Historical Park.

"A *park* is texting me?" I stare down at the screen, blinking against the rising panic. "From *Dad's number?*" I need Aunt Patience—or better yet, Mum.

My phone dings, and I flinch. A notification pops up from an unknown number: *"Your Ride-Hailing Services number is 92225."*

What in the world...? Confusion surpasses the fear that's spiraling down my spine, and I will my hands not to shake as I send another message to the number claiming to be Dad's.

ME

Did you call a car?

Pressing the palm of my hand into my eyes until colors swirl across the darkness of my vision, I rest my elbow on the kitchen table, sucking in a deep breath and letting it out slowly. Panicking won't help anything.

When I glance back down at my phone, "Dad" has replied: *"Gray Honda Accord. Plate number GRY415,"* along with a string of numbers.

So it's not automated like I was beginning to suspect. Frowning, I stand and make my way to the living room window. Pushing back the curtain, I peer out into the street.

Nothing.

What was I expecting? A Honda Accord to just come rolling up as if beckoned by—

My breath catches as a small gray car with tinted windows enters my field of view, driving slowly down the street. As it nears, I can make out the distinctive silver *H* logo above the Kentucky license plate... the plate that reads "GRY415."

The car pulls to a stop, idling in front of the empty driveway.

"You've *got* to be kidding me." Letting the curtain fall back into place, I pace away from the window, hands going up to my face before falling limply to my sides. Secret materializes at my feet, tripping me, and I groan as I grab the back of the couch for support. "I'm not going with some random *stranger*!"

Aunt Patience's letter. Maybe there's something in it that I missed; something that'll tell me what to do. Hurrying to the kitchen, I unzip my backpack, dig around for the notebook, and slide out the letter.

Unfolding it with shaking hands, I smooth it down and skim Aunt Patience's handwriting. My eyes linger on the sentences near the end, and I mumble them aloud. "'Find Agent Grizzled Fox. He has the answers. Trust him, and no one else. Don't let me down, and more importantly, don't let down your parents.'"

Don't let down your parents.

I close my eyes, my hand going to my locket and fisting around the warm metal. *I've got this.* I have to.

"Okay, Seek, let's go." Ignoring the tremor in my voice, I shove everything back into the bag, zipping it up with a finality I don't feel.

I clip on Secret's leash, let out a deep breath, straighten my shoulders, and slip outside.

The tinted window rolls down as I approach, revealing a young woman with a pale strip of pink in her dark hair. She grins at me, her left cheek dimpling. "Code?"

For a moment, I stand there awkwardly before remembering the random string of numbers "Dad" sent me. I pull out my phone and read them off, and her grin widens, showing teeth so straight she must've worn braces as a kid.

"Climb in, and let's be off!"

I take a step forward, reaching for the back door handle, before hesitating. "Uh... excuse me... but... who are you?"

"Ivy Kander, ma'am. I'm with Ride-Hailing Services."

"And... uhm... who sent you?" I nibble my lip before I realize what I'm doing and spit it back out. I've never even heard of "Ride-Hailing Services" before today. This could be *anyone.* Too late I realize I should at least have looked them up.

"Mr. Grizzled Fox, ma'am."

My breath catches. *This has gotta be the right person.* I climb into the back, scooting over and setting my backpack beside me. Secret settles by my feet, but I don't take my hand off his lead.

Ivy has hardly pulled away from the curb before she glances back in the rearview mirror at me. "You're heading to Vincennes?"

I nod, playing with Seek's lead. *Of course she would know that, if... agents sent her.* "Yeah," I mutter when I realize she's waiting for a verbal answer.

Ivy's voice is bright, her smile almost creepily cheerful. "Vincennes is such a nice, quaint place, chock-full of history. My grandpa lived there, in a cute little house right by the river. He loved showing us kids around—the country is ever so different from big ol' Evansville, where I was raised—and we always had the most *delightful* time. The military museum was Grandpa's favorite place to take us, and then we'd have a nice little picnic in the park." Ivy pauses, a light smile on her lips even as she sighs. "Those days were truly the best. But surely you didn't come just to hear me ramble on and on! Oh! Forgive me. I've yet to even ask your name! Mama would be downright appalled at my manners." She tuts.

"Uhm..." My name. *Right.* "Grace." My legal first name offers a margin of privacy—Tirana is technically my middle name, even though it's what I've always been called.

"What a pretty name! I knew a Grace back during fourth grade. She stole my lunch once. Baloney and tuna—I pity her."

As Ivy chatters on, a grin quirks the corner of my mouth. She reminds me so much of Martha, the maidservant from *The Secret Garden.*

Maybe... maybe this isn't such a bad idea after all. Maybe I'll find this Grizzled Fox, and Aunt Patience.

I wonder what Mum would think if she knew I was in a car with a perfect stranger.

If Aunt Patience's an agent, does that mean Mum is? What about Dad? What else were they hiding from me? What is going *on*? And where is my aunt?

The rest of the drive passes in relative silence. Ivy tunes into a country station, lapsing into a silence that I'm grateful for as I try to comprehend everything that's going on. The miles pass in agonizing slowness until, finally, we're in Vincennes.

"The park, right?" Ivy asks, glancing at me in the rearview mirror.

I nod slowly, gather my bag, rouse a drowsy Secret, and then she's pulling to a stop before a wide path. It's lined with spring-green trees that lead to a pillared stone dome towering into the blue sky.

Hand on the door handle, I pause and give Ivy a small smile. "Uh, thanks for the ride. Do I need to pay you...?"

She shakes her head, cheeks dimpling with her grin. "It was no problem at all, ma'am! Happy to be of service! And nope, you're all set!"

Maybe Ivy's also a kindergarten teacher. Mentally rolling my eyes at myself, I brighten my smile and nod. "Right, well, thanks!" With that, I push open the door, cueing Secret to wait until I'm out before I let him follow.

The late May afternoon air wraps around me as I set out for the pillared tower, clouds settling somewhere close enough to the earth to provide a nice, humid cover.

I tug Dad's old Dallas Cowboys cap further down my forehead, ducking my head as I pass a lone lady with a cane. Letting Secret sniff around the base of a tree, I look back. Ivy's car is gone, and the emptiness of the space it occupied tightens something in my gut.

Now what?

I pull out my phone, but there are no new messages.

What if they just... dropped me here? To get rid of me? *Don't be a sodden-witted fool.* I scoff, sticking my phone back in my pocket and readjusting my heavy backpack.

"Right. Let's go, then," I mutter to Secret, eyeing the tower. It's probably some sort of memorial. Maybe I can find something there.

White stone steps encircle the memorial, and each thud of my boots matches the beating of my heart. Is this where someone will tell me what's going on?

At the top of the stairs, past the pillars that surround it, is a stone building. A tall glass wall stretches high above the old-fashioned glass door, and taking a deep breath, I step inside.

Vivid murals depicting historical moments—the soldiers' uniforms mark them as the Revolutionary War era—panel the round walls, and a bronze monument stands tall in the center of the room. Words etched above the murals span the ceiling before it curves into a glass dome. Squinting, I brush back Dad's cap, and I'm able to make out "Great things have been affected by a few great men well conducted," before an unwelcome, "Dogs aren't allowed in here," breaks into my concentration.

Flinching at the unexpected voice, I turn. A large stone desk sits to my left, behind which a woman glares at me through thick, cat-eyed glasses.

"I'm going to have to ask you to leave," she continues, scowling.

I tug the cap back to shade my eyes. "Uhm, he's my service dog."

"It doesn't have a vest." Cat-Eye's scowl deepens.

"He's not wearing it right now." I clench Secret's leash in my fist, trying my best to look like I know what I'm talking about. I hate when this happens.

"It's not permitted without a vest." Cat-Eye's voice is snipped with disdain, and her hand moves to the radio clipped on her belt. "If you don't leave, I'll be forced to call the authorities."

Fight or flee.

I stand there for a long, indecisive second before choosing the latter option and escaping.

There isn't anything for me in there, anyway.

But even as I stand outside, looking over the park, I know it's just an excuse. I *should* have fought; should have educated; should have told her she was dead wrong and breaking the law.

My shoes beat along to the rhyme of *get over it* as I scurry down the steps, Secret keeping time at my left. I push the incident as far out of my mind as possible and change the thumping cadence to *mission.*

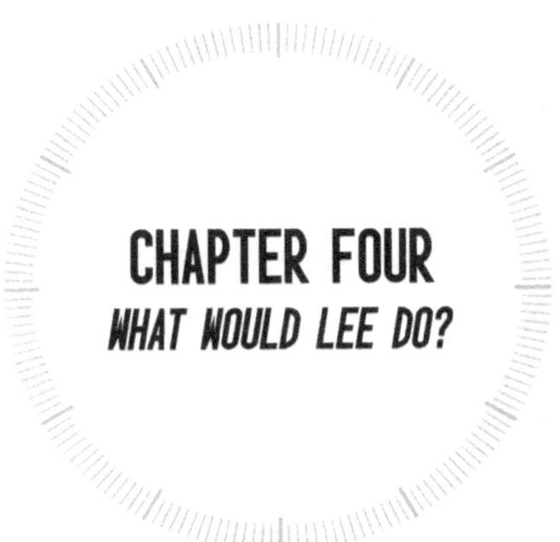

CHAPTER FOUR
WHAT WOULD LEE DO?

I'm sure Mum would have a few choice words for me, but after the experience at the memorial, I don't feel like trying the visitor center. Instead, after putting Seek's vest on him, I perch on the low wall that lines the walkway behind the memorial, staring down into the murky waters of the river. Afternoon light reflects off the surface, as if the sun is trying to make it seem more inviting. Like a siren's call before she kills her victim.

Failure hangs heavy over my shoulders, and I cross my arms over my chest, gripping my biceps to stop my hands from shaking.

I can't stand up for myself; can't figure out why I was sent here; can't do anything.

No wonder Dad left.

"No!" I whisper, my voice harsh in the quiet. It echoes in my mind, and I bite my lip before letting out a long breath.

Dad went on a research trip to Florida for his next book. I *know* that. It was going to be the sequel to *Sunglasses in Disguise*.

Or was it? Because the book in my backpack isn't connected to the dystopian world of the other novel, and if I'm right... Dad was actually working on *The Freesia Guard,* which has as much to do with Florida as Eeyore has to the hobbits.

A crow caws from the edge of the sidewalk, and another echoes its hoarse cry somewhere in the distance.

Fitting. The dove etched into the smooth metal of my locket symbolizes life as it used to be, and the crows symbolize it as it is now. Although... I might need a whole murder of crows to accurately symbolize the confusion everything is in currently.

My phone buzzes, and I jerk before fumbling it out. *Please, be Aunt Patience...* But the name that pops up is "Dad."

DAD

> To grab a seal, use pumpkin swirl muffiins.

I blink at the message, then read it again. "Huh?"

There are no *seals* at a river bordering Indiana and Illinois. There are no seals that eat pumpkin swirl muffins on the planet, to my knowledge.

But what if it's not supposed to make sense?

Brow creased, I look up from the screen, surveying the area. Ahead of me, a long white bridge spans the river—a bridge I'd tried very hard to ignore. It's far too easy to imagine Dad's car plummeting into the darkness of the water. I close my eyes, but the image of the dark chestnut coffin being lowered into the dirt fills my mind.

I tip my head, staring up into the cloudy sky. Should I have even come here? *Take the road less traveled...* But it'd be ever so much easier if I had an inkling of an idea as to what was going on.

What did you want, Dad? What is this?

"What's the best way to capture missing zoo animals?"

I jump at the voice, jerking around to see a brown-haired woman standing behind me, dressed in casual jeans and a light jacket, despite the late spring afternoon heat.

"Pardon?" I stand, resting a hand on my backpack, which I'd taken off. *Missing... what? Who is this lady? And why does she feel vaguely familiar?*

She smiles slightly. "What is the best way to capture missing zoo animals?"

I blink. "Uhm..." Nonsensical questions can only be one thing: challenge questions. "Uh... to grab a seal, use pumpkin swirl muffins?"

"Personally, I would prefer chocolate chip, but yes. Come with me, please."

Again, I blink. "Excuse me?" *How am I supposed to know that you're not going to kidnap me?*

Her expression softens into one of amusement. "I work for the same people as your aunt. You can call me Pixie."

"Uh..." Trust *her*? This random stranger? Just because she claims to know Aunt Patience?

"Let's go." Pixie turns, starting away.

Frozen with indecision, I make no move to follow. *What would Lee do?* The main character from P.D. Atkerson's AKA Simon Lee series was always getting into bad situations. *He'd probably go along and then escape if he needed to.* I nod, shaky plan in place, and follow Pixie back up the path, past the dome and where Ivy dropped me off, and up a few streets.

Finally, she stops at a small, nondescript house that blends in with its neighbors. Parked outside is a dusky-gray Honda Accord. I do a double-take, heart jumping when I spy the plate number: GRY415. *What in the...*

But Pixie's already knocking on the door, which opens immediately, revealing Ivy Kander.

I'd both expected it, and didn't. For a moment, all I can do is stare. Ivy grins. "Why, hello again, Grace! How're you liking Vincennes?"

"What... what are *you* doing here?"

Both ladies laugh.

"I'm Agent Ivy Ghost. Why shouldn't I be here?"

"And I'm Agent Respectable Pixie," Pixie adds, gesturing me into the house. "Welcome to our humble abode."

I ignore the urge to groan and lower my face into my hands. *This just keeps on getting better and better.*

THE RATTY OLD COUCH IN THE LIVING ROOM OF THE "SAFEHOUSE," as the agents call it, swallows me as I sink down at one end, setting my backpack next to me. Secret plops down on top of my feet, because, of course, that's the most comfortable place to take a nap.

Ivy takes a seat on the other end of the couch, and Pixie sits in the armchair opposite us, crossing her arms as she seems to size me up.

"Can you tell me what's going on? Please?" I bit my lip, looking at Ivy, then at Pixie, who flips her hair over her shoulder, nodding slowly.

Finally. *Answers*.

But suddenly, I'm not so sure I want to hear them.

"As you've probably figured out," Ivy starts, "we're agents. We work for an agency." She pauses, an impish grin on her face. "Or, as some might say, we're spies."

Pixie raises an eyebrow. "Don't exaggerate."

Ivy grins. "I'm just telling the truth."

I grit my teeth, in no mood for games. "What is the name of this... agency?"

"We're really not cleared to tell you much—we're only supposed to be keeping you safe—but it's the ISA," Pixie supplies.

"Which stands for...?"

Ivy raises an eyebrow. "Like she said—we're not cleared to tell you."

"Ivy..." Pixie shakes her head, snorting.

I don't have the patience to deal with this right now. I just want to find my aunt, and this Grizzled Fox person who's supposed to lead me to her— or something.

"Don't ruin my fun," Ivy huffs, but she looks like she might burst into laughter any second. "Okay, okay! We're just waiting until Agent Grizzled Fox gets here. He'll take you to... well, can't tell you that."

Grizzled Fox. My heart leaps.

"Yes." Pixie nods. "It's pretty hard to tell someone something you don't know."

I take a deep breath, weave my hands together, and lean, just a little, towards Ivy. "So, Agent Ivy Ghost, what *can* you tell me about this mysterious ISA?" *And Grizzled Fox*.

"Ah, the young interrogator." Ivy smirks. "I see what they mean when they said you had potential."

"Ivy..." Pixie shakes her head again, narrowing her eyes at the other agent, who shrugs.

Potential? Who would say that? But before I can dwell on it any longer, Secret raises his head, his eyes trained on the door. *Great, someone's here.* I hope it's a friendly party.

A knock sounds less than a minute later, and Ivy jumps up. "That'd be Agent Grizzled Fox."

Finally... maybe someone who can tell me what's going on here. I stand, shadowing Ivy as she opens the door. An average-looking, brown-haired man in his late twenties or early thirties stands on the porch, hands nonchalantly tucked into his front pockets. Like the other agents, his clothing is casual: jeans, a plain t-shirt, and work boots. I could swear I've never seen him before in my life, yet something about him seems vaguely familiar.

"Foxy," Pixie says from behind me, and something I can't pinpoint crosses between them as they exchange glances.

Then he turns to me, tipping a nod. "Tirana."

I nod back, slightly unnerved that all these people know my name—and that he knows enough to call me Tirana, instead of Grace.

He smiles, but it doesn't quite reach his icy blue eyes. "Pleasure to finally meet you."

"Uh, same here." Even if I'd only learned of his existence this morning.

"I'll be taking her from here. Thanks." There's another long, meaningful look between him and Pixie, then he tilts his head towards the door. "Let's go, Tirana. We don't have much time."

I hesitate, glancing down at Secret, who sniffs Grizzled Fox's pant leg, before squaring my shoulders. I can do this. It's new and scary, but I'm Mum's daughter; I can be brave. "Sure thing... let me just grab my bag." I duck into the living room, snatching my backpack from where I'd left it on the floor. But when I turn back to the entryway, I pause, listening to the low murmur of voices I'm probably not supposed to overhear.

"She's so grown up," a woman's voice murmurs–Pixie, I think. "This will be hard for her... If Dallas hadn't kept her away... have to understand... I'm so sorry... It's been so long... Mya and the twins... Can't imagine... please don't pretend this isn't hard for all of us..."

Grizzled Fox's answer is too low to catch, but when I step out of the living room, Pixie is hugging him. She steps away when she sees me, offering me one of those too-big, trying-to-look-happy smiles. "Are you ready?"

Ready—for *what*, exactly? I shrug, fiddling with Secret's leash. "I guess so? Seek, c'here, buddy." My dog trots over from where Ivy had been loving on him and shakes himself, looking at me with his up-for-anything expression. I clip on his leash and channel my inner Mum. As I follow Grizzled Fox out of the safehouse, I know I'll need all the strength I can get.

Next to Ivy's "Ride-Hailing Service" Honda is a black Nissan, also with a Kentucky license plate. Grizzled Fox's already opening the driver-side door when I clear my throat.

"Uhm... so... Who are you?" I don't really want to get in a car with a strange man, even if Aunt Patience *did* tell me to find me.

He glances at me, eyes meeting mine before flickering away. "I'm... I was—a friend of your father's."

I cross my arms, the way he uses past tense hitting me like a punch in the gut. *Please, no...* "Do you have proof?"

"Proof?" He levels me with an inquisitorial stare, like I'm an alien specimen who just asked for an orange lollipop before eating the wrapper.

"Yeah." I nod. *Proof that you're not a villain, or that Dad's gone, or...* "Proof that you're who you say you are."

Grizzled Fox's slightly terse expression doesn't change as he reaches into his back pocket and pulls out what looks like a small black wallet. He flips it open with a flick of his wrist, revealing an official-looking badge. The outline of an eagle perched on a branch sits above "ISA," and a maroon line borders the top, where five tan stars stand out, and the bottom, where the words "Salvis Mundi" are printed.

On the opposite side, an ID card is tucked into a laminated pocket. The same logo as the badge is printed next to a younger-looking headshot of the man standing in front of me, underneath which is "Agent Grizzled

Fox." A barcode spans the bottom, and an ID number sits above that.

He snaps the wallet closed, slipping it back in his pocket with a practiced motion. "Good enough?"

Not really, but I nod, and despite an overwhelming feeling of impending doom, I slip into the Nissan's back seat, settling my bag by my feet and Secret in my lap. Dad always said you could tell a lot about someone by how they keep their car, but the interior is neat and clean—not freshly vacuumed, but not a pigsty. The only real personalization is a small Batman symbol hanging from the rearview mirror.

I don't know much about Batman, but he's a hero, isn't he? If Grizzled Fox likes heroes, then maybe he's not a terrible, evil person.

I hope.

CHAPTER FIVE
WHERE THE LOST
THINGS GO

Blake doesn't know what to say as he pulls away from the curb. Tirana's watching him from the backseat, and he gives her a tight smile. With those speckled, blue-hazel eyes and a slightly upturned nose, she's certainly Dallas' daughter. Just like those photographs Dallas had loved sticking in his face, only older.

Over shoulder-length, straw-colored hair, she wears one of Dallas' signature ball caps turned backwards like a wannabe gangster's. *Great.*

"What's going on? Aunt Patience said you had answers." Tirana's voice is full of bravado, but Blake can hear the slight quiver in it.

He hums in non-answer.

"What... what about Dad?"

Blake grips the steering wheel and exhales slowly, loath to let the girl see the blow her words are. "Gone."

She's quiet, and after a moment, he glances at her in the rearview mirror. Her face is set, her hand buried in the dog's fur.

A traffic light ahead turns orange, then red, and he eases to a stop. "I need to see the book." *If she doesn't have it...*

"Now...?"

He jerks a nod, training his eyes on the small-town intersection as she unzips her bag. He should have made sure she had it before they left, but with Agent Ivy Ghost there, it hadn't seemed prudent. Not with this.

"Why's it so important?" Tirana asks, holding up a thick paperback. Blake barely processes the question as he stares at the cover: a blue-shirted kid racing through a shadowed city.

He tears his eyes away from it and back to the road. "What's the picture on the spine?" He watches out of the corner of his eye as she turns it over.

"A... dove?"

It's either what he's looking for, or a very good imitation.

"What's going on? What does it have to do with Dad?" Tirana sounds scared, and Blake grits his teeth. *This was not in the job description.* Then again, most of what he did—what happened—wasn't.

"That book has the power to wreak havoc on certain people." A vague way of putting it, but the less she knows, the better.

"But... what does this have to do with Dad?"

Bitterness bites Blake's laugh. "Who do you think wrote it?"

"I don't understand. It... just... doesn't make *sense. Nothing's* making sense."

Yeah, he's doing a poor job of explaining. And it's not just because of the headache beginning to throb behind his temples. *Sorry, kid.* Pixie should have been the one to pick Tirana up and bring her to Wonderland, but Blake's old friend has been in the area for a different mission and could only spare the time to make sure the girl was safe until Blake could get there.

Like Tirana was suddenly so much more protected the second Blake walked into that safehouse, instead of the opposite.

The engine's humming is a background to the tense silence that falls. If he could only find the words... but the right ones decide to make themselves scarce.

If there are any at all.

Blake bites back a sigh, glancing at the Batman emblem dangling from the rearview mirror. Bruce Wayne wasn't much better with kids, but at least the billionaire-by-day-and-vigilante-by-night was one of the best detectives in the world. If Batman were here, this case would have been solved two years ago—before Dove vanished the same night that Dallas was killed.

Movement in the mirror draws Blake's attention to the road behind him, where a menacing black truck is steadily gaining ground. *Shades and*—Blake cuts himself off, his grip tightening around the wheel as he grits his teeth.

They've found her.

IF I'D KNOWN THAT GOING WITH AGENT GRIZZLED FOX WOULD END up in a car chase, I don't think I would've gotten in.

My hand tightens on the smooth fabric of the seat as the car lurches forward, and I squeeze my eyes shut. *This can't end well.*

I clench my teeth, hoping desperately that the man knows what he's doing, as Grizzled Fox turns onto a bumpy red-dirt road. Trees pass in blurs of green, and I crane my neck to look behind us. The road is empty, devoid of creepy trucks.

For now.

Secret leans against me, bracing against the acceleration, and I hold him steady as Grizzled Fox takes a hard left down a side road.

If this was a P.D. Atkerson book, that truck would try to ram us off a cliff. Or into the woods, since there aren't exactly a lot of cliffs around here. Maybe even into a river.

I shudder. *Fiction, Tirana, that's just fiction.* Yet so much of the current state of events ought to be fiction; words printed on the pages of a book, able to be set aside if it gets to be too much. *Not... this.*

Not bumping along potholed roads in the middle of nowhere, having no idea who's after us and why, bracing against the door as Grizzled Fox takes turn after turn. Is this my fault? Do they want *The Freesia Guard*?

More twisting turns and holey roads lead nowhere fast, rattling Grizzled Fox's car so hard I'd have to yell to be heard. Finally, the sailing seems to smooth down. We're back on a main road, passing the occasional house, neighborhood or farm.

I clear my throat, breaking the almost-tangible silence. "Who *were* they?"

Grizzled Fox doesn't even spare me a glance. "Assume it's the Suns of Liberty."

I blink. Somehow, trucks, backroads, and the Boston Tea Party don't seem to mix. "Who?"

"The people who have your aunt."

"*What?*" My voice rises into what's almost a screech, and my hand freezes on Secret's head. *No! A joke. This is all one terrible joke.*

"Woah, kid." Grizzled Fox shoots me an unreadable look in the rearview mirror. "We're working on getting her out."

"But—"

He sighs, shaking his head. "I have a different duty: getting you and this book safe."

"But—Aunt Patience!" Why won't he *tell* me anything?

"She'll be fine."

Grizzled Fox's impassive reassurance does nothing to quell my racing heart. I clench my jaw and glare, but he doesn't even seem to notice my existence anymore.

At least the truck seems to be gone. I'm surprised it was so easy—if that could be called "easy"—to lose them.

Was Aunt Patience kidnapped? But that doesn't even make sense. If she was nabbed by the Suns of Liberty, how could she have left on her own terms, as her letter seemed to say?

Is it my fault these truck-driving crazies apparently have her now? I bite my lip, staring down at the backpack at my feet. *I wish I'd never found that stupid book.* But... what if Dad's alive? *And what if he's not? You've sure made a mess of things, Tirana.* A low whine interrupts my thoughts, and I sigh, looking down at Secret. "What's the matter, little man?"

He looks up at me, whimpering again.

Oh... Seriously? "Uhm, Secret needs to... do his business."

Grizzled Fox glances at me and mutters something I can't make out—nor do I think I want to. "Now?"

"Well..." I bite my lip. "Within the next few minutes would be best."

"No can do."

"Uhm..." But I really don't know what to say. There's nothing for me to do but bite the inside of my cheek, ruffle Secret's head, and hope he can hold it.

More long minutes, then the scenery starts changing from middle-of-nowhere woods to suburbs, then a city.

"Where are we?" I ask, glancing behind us yet again—still no sign of the truck.

"Evansville."

More of an answer than I'd expected, even if it's terse. The buildings blur by, and I sink into my seat, stealing a glance at Secret. His chocolate eyes stare at me imploringly, and I bite my lip. "Sorry, boy."

"What?" Grizzled Fox snaps his gaze to me, then back to the road.

"Uh... I told you. He needs to... go out."

Grizzled Fox's hands go white-knuckled on the steering wheel, but he turns into the parking lot of a small park. "Hurry up."

I clip on Secret's lead, grab the roll of waste bags from the side pocket of my backpack, and hop out of the car.

We find a nice grassy place, where I let him take his time sniffing the short, prickly grass and the bases of trees. Maybe we should hurry, but I don't want to return to the car and Grizzled Fox's silence any sooner than I have to. Once Secret's found the perfect spot, I pick up after him and cast a glance at the car. "Better head back now..."

Secret looks up at me, tongue lolling, and I shake my head, yet a little smile tugs at my lips.

The sun's warm on my back, and after I pull it around, Dad's cap shades my eyes. Birds twitter in the trees, and a cool breeze freshens the city air.

For the first time in hours, I can let myself think. Try to process everything that's happened in the last few days, especially the chaos of today.

"Dead, Secret," I mutter, scuffing my sneaker on the dirt. "Always was. And now Aunt Patience is missing." My throat tightens, and I swallow. *If only I'd never picked up that book...*

I glance again at Agent Grizzled Fox's spy-black car, halfway down the parking lot. Through the tinted window, I can make out the agent staring down at something, like he forgot I exist. The rumble of an engine blocks out the song of the birds and the friendly brush of the wind, and I sigh. "Let's go, Seek."

We only take a few steps before Secret pauses, turning to look at something behind me. I follow his gaze, and my blood turns to ice as a dirt-splattered, midnight-black pickup rolls up with all the elegance of a lumbering black bear crashing a child's playdate.

Or like the Wicked Witch of the West. I back away slowly, my eyes fixed on the truck as the doors burst open and two figures sporting fancy black tactical gear leap out.

Run. I need to run. But my legs are frozen to the pavement, like this is some kind of terrible nightmare in broad daylight. If I could tap my shoes and float away—but before I can even finish that thought, hands are grabbing at me, pulling me away—

"Hey!" A rough yell cuts through the air, and a figure hurtles into my captor. Next thing I know, I'm lying in the grass, staring up at the too-bright sky, the air knocked out of my lungs. Something cold nudges my neck, and then Secret's bright eyes are looking down at me. I grab his collar, fighting into a sitting position.

One of the black-suited guys is slumped on the asphalt of the parking lot, and his buddy seems pretty occupied not meeting the same fate, courtesy of one mad Agent Grizzled Fox.

"Get in the car, Tirana, *now*!" he shouts as he circles the goon, playing some dangerous version of keep-away.

Snapping my gaze to his black Toyota, I scramble to my feet, grab Secret, and army-crouch a mad dash towards the illusion of safety. Rounding the back of the car, I yank open the door and tumble in, slamming the door shut behind me as I throw myself to the dark carpet of the floor.

My gasps fill the air as I lie there, trying to catch my breath, heart pounding in my throat. "What *was* that?" I rasp to Secret, who's standing heavy on my chest, looking down at me with the most curious expression of "I don't know what just happened, but can we do it again?"

At least *he's* not scared to death, if trying to eat my huffed breath is any proof.

I push him away from my face with shaking arms. My backpack cramps me in here, but I'm too afraid to sit up to try to get more room.

Footsteps pound the ground; the driver's door is thrown open and the car shudders and sinks as someone slides in and slams the door.

The engine roars to life, and I'm still frozen on the floor of the backseat, bracing myself as the vehicle jerks away. I'm terrified to roll over to see who's there, terrified that a goon will be there—

"Strap in."

Grizzled Fox's harsh order unfreezes me, and I claw my way up to the seats, fumbling for the seat belt. My hands are shaking so badly that it takes a few tries for me to get the apparatus to click, but finally it's in. I hold Secret tightly in my lap, not letting him wriggle his way out of my grasp.

Grizzled Fox stares fixedly out at the road, clutching the steering wheel so hard his knuckles are white. And red—his blood, or one of the goon's?

Biting my lip, I crane my neck to look behind us. The park is already out of sight, replaced by buildings, traffic, and just plain old city views.

No black trucks.

Grizzled Fox turns into a side street, then another, and another, until I've completely lost track. Until we're out of the city, on some highway with woods surrounding us. Until I sag against the seat, letting my eyes partly close as exhaustion drapes over me like an ornate curtain

Secret's sprawled out next to me, his head half on my lap, and I smooth the fur along his back. He raises his head, looking at me with those soulful bright eyes, and I bite my lip, everything suddenly hitting me full in the face.

Clearing my throat, I eye Grizzled Fox, who's not said a word since we left.

"Who... were they?" My voice trembles, and I look down, scratching behind Seek's floppy ear. "What... Why... What was that all about?"

No response.

I glance back at Grizzled Fox. He's stoically staring at the road, but a muscle in his jaw twitches.

After a moment, he sighs. "The Suns of Liberty."

But... who? I bite my cheek, leaning my head on my hand, and I'm suddenly aware that my cap—Dad's cap—isn't on my head. And it's not on the floor of the car.

A mixture of feelings swirl together: confusion, fear, and who knows what else, brought to a head by the empty pang of loss. Then a strike of alarm when I remember something Dad once told me about the use of objects in foreshadowing; there was this movie where the older brother rushed into a burning school, and his cap flew off as he ran in.

He didn't return.

Your life isn't a story, Tirana. Yet still I swallow, fighting a frightening sense of impending doom.

Hogwash. Everything's going to be just fine.
Right?

CHAPTER SIX
WONDERLAND

"Where are we?" I eye the parking lot that Grizzled Fox has turned into. Trees, a welcome break from the rolling flatlands of green corn stalks and endless sky, shield the looming office building from the main road.

"At our destination." Grizzled Fox glances at me before pushing open his door.

Annoyance stirs at this man's stubborn vagueness, but I push it down as I swing my backpack over my shoulder and slide out of the car, squinting in the afternoon sunlight. The greenery lining the sidewalk in front of the building is freshly pruned and well-kept, with stone benches and the occasional birdbath.

Grizzled Fox starts for the building, and I hurry to follow him, juggling Secret's lead as I readjust my backpack. What are we doing here? Is this the ISA headquarters? It's pretty nondescript, with lots of tinted windows and a boxy look... It doesn't scream "spy lair." *Which is probably a good thing.*

Grizzled Fox doesn't slow his pace until he reaches the glass doors that front the building. They slide open, and I follow the agent into an average-looking foyer.

Another set of tinted doors loom before us. Grizzled Fox pulls the black billfold from his pocket, and, flipping it open, scans the card against the reader on the wall. The device flashes green, and the doors slide open, revealing dark carpeting, white walls, and a desk with a heavyset man sitting behind it.

"Afternoon," he calls over to us. "Welcome to Wonderland!"

Grizzled Fox nods, crossing over to the desk. "I need a guest pass for her."

Wonderland?

Mr. Secretary turns his attention to me, and I get the distinct feeling that he's sizing me up. A name badge is pinned to his shirt—Agent Newline Acrobat, it says, with the same logo as Agent Grizzled Fox's badge.

"Sure thing. I.D.?" Newline Acrobat's gaze shifts to Grizzled Fox, who produces the billfold and slides it over to the agent.

I'm asked my name, my birthdate, and then my reason for being there. At the last question, I glance at Grizzled Fox, and he doesn't even bat an eye before saying, "Asset."

Well, *that's* news. How... touching.

Newline Acrobat enters the info into his computer, then taps the small camera lens attached to his monitor. "Smile!"

I look at the camera, suddenly feeling self-conscious—and naked without Dad's cap. Though dull pain spirals through my heart, I keep the smile fixed on my face until Newline Acrobat nods, clicking away at his keyboard.

"All right... give the system one moment, and you'll be all set."

Grizzled Fox remains impassive. "And the dog?"

"Dog?" Newline Acrobat frowns, leaning over the counter.

Secret, sitting by my feet, looks back up at him, while I hide a smile. One of the biggest compliments a service dog team can get is the dog's existence being unknown.

Newline Acrobat shrugs and points his camera down before asking me the same questions again, this time for Secret. I'm duly impressed.

We wait a few minutes longer, Grizzled Fox's fingers tapping impatiently on the counter, before Newline Acrobat swivels in his chair and pulls two cards from a printer, slipping them into clear card holders and pushing them over to me, along with a black lanyard.

"Keep it on you at all times," he warns, and then looks at Grizzled Fox. "You know the rules."

Grizzled Fox tips a nod, pushing away from the counter.

I hastily pull the lanyard over my head and clip Secret's card to his vest before scurrying to catch up with Grizzled Fox.

He pushes another set of doors open, and we step into... color.

Light streams in from an assembly of stained glass windows, each depicting a different fairy tale and casting rainbows across the tiled floor. A wall-to-wall shelf of books, complete with rolling ladders, adds a Lemoncello Library touch, while agents linger around a stone fountain. Colorful hues speckle the water and spread across an eagle's stone body, dancing in the sunlight and catching the cascade arching from the open beak of the raptor, whose wings are outstretched as if frozen mid-swoop.

It's like a confetti bomb met an early demise, exploding into something out of the pages of *The Gollywhopper Games* or *The Wonderland Trials*.

The opening of a slide—a gaping dragon's mouth—spills out from a wall of patchworked murals. I squint at the pictures. Is that Jack and Jill and their infamous pail of water? There are three grinning pink pigs high-fiving, a proud raven with a crown, and a lion licking a lollipop tucked among an overwhelming spread of pictures.

A chuckle turns my attention to Grizzled Fox, who's watching me with an amused look breaking that expressionlessness in his eyes.

"They don't call this place Wonderland for nothing." A grin lifts up one side of his mouth. "Like it?"

I turn slowly, trying to take it all in. "It's *awesome*."

WONDERLAND IS HUGE, AND MY INITIAL IMPRESSION IS FURTHER confirmed as I follow Agent Grizzled Fox down a maze of twisting and turning halls. The walls here are muraled with mice in blue overalls, moose with muffins, and pigs with balloons, making it feel like we've walked inside my favorite picture books of old.

Grizzled Fox stops at a closed door, whose frame is painted to look like a bright blue building block, and gives the wood a rap. The door swings open, and he steps in. After a moment's hesitation, I follow him, nervously tugging at the straps of my backpack.

It's an office, simple but efficient, with a short, waiting room–style couch, a potted plant in the corner, a desk, and a curtained window that brightens the place. A woman with cropped, brilliant blue hair looks up from her computer as we enter.

"Grizzled Fox, Grace," she greets, standing up and circling around to shake my hand. "How was the trip?"

I glance at Grizzled Fox, and a muscle in his jaw ticks.

"Eventful," he says at length.

The blue-haired lady raises an eyebrow, but when he doesn't expound, she turns her attention back to me. "Grace, I'm Agent Tilted Showdown, the case leader for this job. It's nice to meet you."

"Tirana." I clear my throat, offering her a smile as I finger Secret's leash. "It's—Tirana. That's what I'm called. I go by my middle name." I can feel my face heating up at my eloquent speech, and I bite my lip, glancing from Agent Tilted Showdown to Agent Grizzled Fox.

"Well, nice to meet you, Tirana." Tilted Showdown's friendly smile doesn't waver. "I hear you have the book we've been looking for?"

"Uh... yes?" I pull off my backpack and set it on the desk, rummaging around for *The Freesia Guard* and handing it to the agent.

She examines it with a thoughtful frown, flipping through the pages before looking up at Grizzled Fox. "This is the one?"

He shrugs. "As far as I know."

He hasn't mentioned the car chase or the fight at the park. Is he supposed to? Did he forget, or is he just omitting those oh-so-insignificant details? I catch him rubbing his knuckles, and I know he hasn't forgotten.

"All right." Tilted Showdown nods firmly. "All right, then. Good job, guys." She and Grizzled Fox discuss the book for a few moments, talking about terms that fly above my head, and I stare at the framed portrait on the wall, a kingfisher with a small fish flapping in his beak.

I'm here, and I've delivered the book... but Aunt Patience is gone, and what am I supposed to do now?

"Are you hungry, Tirana?" Tilted Showdown's voice draws my attention back to the agents, and I turn back towards them with a nod.

"Yeah—but I've got some sandwiches in my bag." The banes of having food allergies; I always need to pack my food unless I know there's something gluten-free where I'm going, even with Secret.

"Nonsense. Grizzled Fox, bring her down to the food court, won't you?"

I open my mouth to explain that I'm good, really, but Grizzled Fox beats me to it.

"She can't. Allergies."

I look at him, surprised. This man doesn't even know me, so how does he know that places that serve food might kill me? Secret's vest is a dead giveaway with "allergen detection" printed on it, but most people don't really know what that means.

As if reading my thoughts, Tilted Showdown glaces at Secret. "Okay, so Juke's. They have the allergen-safe foods."

"I don't think—" Grizzled Fox starts, eying the *The Freesia Guard* on Tilted Showdown's desk, but she crosses her arms, giving him a measured look.

"Eat first, then work—it's way after lunchtime. And that's an order."

Grizzled Fox still looks like he wants to protest as Tilted Showdown ushers us out of her office. "Don't come back until you've eaten. I mean it," she says, closing the door in his face.

Jaw tight, he turns away and marches down the hall. "Let's go."

I swing my bag back on my shoulders as I hasten after him. "Really—I'm fine. I have food."

He glances back at me and keeps walking.

Great. Just great.

The murals switch from mice and cookies to other storybook scenes as I follow Grizzled Fox down a maze of halls: I spot Little Bear, Madeline, and the Little Engine That Could, among others.

Grizzled Fox doesn't say a word, and it's pretty obvious that he doesn't want to be the one babysitting the "asset." I don't blame him. Wonderland is beyond cool, but I'm not sure I want to be here, either... especially with Aunt Patience missing.

Noise, clatter, and food smells fill the air as another agent swings open a set of Grinch-green industrial doors, and I catch a glimpse of pure chaos before the doors fall shut and I hurry to catch up to Grizzled Fox. "This place has an *actual* food court?" I wasn't sure what I'd expected with what Tilted Showdown said, but a college-like food court was not it. Even standing outside the doorway for a moment has my eyes itching, and for the first time, I'm grateful for the surly agent's long strides as we hasten away.

"Yeah." He glances over his shoulder at me. "But we're going to Juke's."

If it's anything like the giant room we just passed, there's no way I'm going to be able to step foot in there, let alone *eat*. I tighten my hand around Secret's leash, the colorful walls blurring past as I focus on not getting too far behind Agent Grizzled Fox.

Secret might be a gluten detection dog, but that doesn't mean I can be in a place where airborne particles of poison are floating around like invisible pixie dust. Having him just means I know that what I'm eating won't land me in the hospital or an early grave.

Morbid much, Tirana? I grimace, and almost faceplant into Grizzled Fox's back since apparently he randomly stopped walking in the middle of the corridor. Awesome.

I'm about to ask what he's doing when he shoves his phone into his back pocket—when'd he take it out?—and turns into one of the branches offshooting the main corridor, currently Pooh Bear–themed. There's a single swing door at the end, with a glowing neon sign above it: *Juke's*.

Immediately, I feel like I've stepped into a '70s café straight out of an old film. And like everything else I've seen of the ISA, it's definitely colorful. Red lower walls match the red-and-white tiled floor, and a green stripe circles the large room like a ribbon on a Christmas present. The upper walls are tan, while the booths and tables complete the red-and-green theme.

My gaze wanders to the counter, with its sparkling soda glasses, glass ketchup bottles, and plates of ready-made food packages waiting to be taken to tables. There's a coffee station and a glass-doored refrigerator nearby. A platform rises up on the other side of the room, topped with chairs and more tables.

Old movie posters and black-and-white photographs line the walls, along with the mandatory Coca-Cola sign. An antique jukebox squats by the fridge like a neon blast-to-the-past.

Though we're not the only ones here, it's not anywhere near the rush and bustle of the other dining hall.

Grizzled Fox strides towards the counter, and I stop gawking and hurry after him.

A large sign on one end of the counter, hanging over one of those enclosed bakery display racks, proclaims "Allergen Friendly." Under that are subcategories, each item pre-packaged and the ingredients clearly listed.

"Well?"

I force my eyes away from the lavish spread—there's more gluten-free options than I've seen anywhere else under my very *nose* right now—and turn to Grizzled Fox, who's staring at me with his arms crossed.

I gesture to the shelves, half super excited and half unsure I didn't walk into a dream. "This is all... *safe*?"

He shrugs.

I glance down at Secret, then back at the array of foods, and I grin. The expression falls almost as soon as it comes, though. Why did my parents keep the ISA a secret all these years, especially since it seems to be so well-equipped for food allergies? It makes no sense, and a glance in Grizzled Fox's direction only confirms that he isn't the one with the answers... or if he is, he won't provide them.

Biting back a sigh, I linger over the pastries, finally settling on a mouth-watering cinnamon roll and skimming its ingredients. It looks great for a late lunch that Mum would have a heart attack over, and I palm it, turning to view the microwave near the coffee bar. Is it worth it to have a warm cinnamon roll...?

Yes. Clicking to Secret, I grab a paper plate from the bottom of the stack on the counter, hurry over to the microwave, and follow the instructions on the back of the cinnamon roll wrapper before stepping back to watch the nuker work its magic.

Sugary cinnamon smell wafts out when I yank open the door, and yes, I am excited about this simple pastry. It feels like the best thing that's happened since I found that book at the library, and somehow, it helps me believe I'll be okay.

"Check," I tell Secret, carefully holding out the slightly soggy plate. He sniffs it closely, nose working—he wants to lick it, but knows that's against the rules—before he bops my leg. Safe.

"Yes, good *boy*," I mutter, setting the plate on the counter and rummaging in my bag for a treat, which Secret accepts. Although going by the sniffs he directs at my lunch, beef liver is lacking today.

Dad should have told me about this place. It's not just the cinnamon roll cooling next to me, it's... everything. This entire world—*his* world—that I never even knew existed.

What other secrets did my parents hide from me?

Agent Grizzled Fox turns, balancing a black tray with his own early dinner on it, and watches me with those icy eyes, not saying a word.

I glance away, grabbing a brown-spotted banana from the basket at my elbow like that was my intention all along. A balanced diet, right?

My guardian, or whatever he is, tips his chin forward like he's Luke Danes from *The Gilmore Girls*. "Pick a seat."

"Uh, sure... Where?" I glance around the mostly empty tables, frowning. "What about up on the stage thingy?"

He gives me a weird look, but he shrugs and follows me when I begin to weave past chairs, tables, and the occasional agent. Balancing the banana, cinnamon roll, and Secret's leash, I finally make it up the smattering of stairs to the balcony area. I slide my food onto a table, scanning for crumbs before I take a seat.

Settling Secret under my chair, I feel, rather than see, Grizzled Fox sit down across from me. I straighten, unwrap the plastic fork I'd pocketed, and finally ask the question that has been burning inside of me. "Why am I here?"

He doesn't look up, slowly stirring a plastic spoon through his bowl of chili. "Because your aunt sent you."

And isn't *that* informative. "Can't you—start at the beginning or something? Because I've literally never heard of the ISA before in my life, and now I'm here, and—" I bite off my next words, shaking my head. *And nothing makes sense anymore.*

The agent doesn't respond right away, and I nibble at the cinnamon roll. It tastes even better than it smells, if that's possible; the sweet flavors melt in my mouth, and the texture isn't even that dry or gummy.

"You're a lot like Dallas, you know." One side of Grizzled Fox's mouth curves up into a rueful smile that doesn't quite reach his eyes.

"That's not what I asked." I poke at the cinnamon roll with the fork, watching the plastic tines bend and then bounce back when I relieve the pressure. "Do you know where Aunt Patience is?"

He's silent, and when I glance up, I can see the muscle in his jaw ticking.

"*Do* you?" I hate the way my voice wavers, but I swallow past it, narrowing my eyes at him.

"No."

I can't decipher the emotion in the low, single word, or the almost haunted look in his eyes, so I cross my arms. "So who does?"

He shrugs, taking a bite of his chili... so he doesn't have to reply? What is it with this guy and his apparent inability to give a straight answer?

Fine. I'd play this another way. "Okay, so... what *is* the ISA, exactly?"

A low exhale, and Grizzled Fox sets his spoon down. "You want the long answer or the short one?"

"Um... anything? Either?" It's my turn to shrug, and I take another bite of my cinnamon roll before it gets cold.

He clears his throat. "Fine. The ISA started as an agency devoted to spreading smiles and laughter a couple dozen years ago. Then it got tangled up in investigating some nasty plots against the government. Now we save the world, you might say." He gives a humorless laugh. "Your dad was one of those guys who'd protect his country, no matter the cost."

"I... I don't understand. What—happened to him?" I stare at the agent, but Aunt Patience's letter is in the forefront of my mind. *Please...*

"He infiltrated the Suns of Liberty, his cover got blown, and they made sure he'd never be an issue again."

That implication in his tone... I swallow hard, shock tingling through my hands. "They *murdered* him?" My words really don't need to crack, nor does my imagination need to conjure up a picture of some midnight-black truck chasing after Dad, dropping his body into dark, churning waves... The look on Mum's face when she stepped into my room... The walnut casket being lowered into the dirt...

I blink, and the cafeteria comes back into focus. Grizzled Fox says something that I can't make out over the buzzing in my ears.

Secret presses his nose into my knee, and I automatically smooth the fur between his eyes. *They... killed him?* A hundred new questions buzz around my mind, but I need time to process *this* first, to turn the flood of emotion into coherent words. "What... what about Aunt Patience?"

At least he actually answers this time, crossing his arms and leaning back in his chair. "She sent me—us—a Code Mauve Herring."

"A... what?" It sounds like something out of A Series of Unfortunate Events... which would be awful, since those books were nothing but tragedy after tragedy.

"Mauve Herring." Grizzled Fox runs a hand through his hair, glancing away. "It's when an agent tries to fix something on their own. Like leaving to be a decoy."

"Decoy?" So it's *my* fault Aunt Patience left? "Where *is* she?"

"We'll—they'll—find her."

"What's that supposed to mean?" I try to sound fierce, but my voice wavers, betraying me.

"It means that we're understaffed, have far too many problems to fix in the country, and certain apexes think other matters are more important." The sudden hardness in Grizzled Fox's voice makes me flinch.

"But—"

"It is what it is." His voice is no more than a snap, reminding me of a rattlesnake, and a nearby couple glances at us.

Warily, I draw away from Grizzled Fox—but no. I'm too close to figuring this out. I swallow, hoping he won't actually explode. "Why am I here?"

He levels me with an icy glare, and I feel myself deflate. On second thought, I should really learn to keep my mouth shut.

Without a word, he pushes up from his seat and grabs his tray, not even looking back as he stalks down the stairs and away from me. He drops the tray on the tray return, then shoves his way out the door, and I'm alone.

CHAPTER SEVEN
A STUDY IN CRIME

Despite the clinking of dishes and murmurs of voices, it feels like silence fills the cafeteria. I slouch back in my seat, biting my lip. "Now what, Seek?"

Maybe he'll come back. I eye the door. *Or... maybe I'm stuck here forever.*

Dramatic. I almost smile before a sigh catches up with me, and I look down at the few bites left of my cinnamon roll. Neither Mum nor Aunt Patience would applaud my choice of lunch, would they? Suddenly, I want nothing more than to hear Mum's tuts and see her raised eyebrow, or even listen to Aunt Patience's low laugh and her suggestion of something a bit more healthy.

Slowly, I peel the banana, tears pricking my eyes.

Why? Why did any of this happen? Why did Dad have to die? Why did Mum have to go on that business trip? And *why* did I ever have to find that book at the library?

A groan threatens to escape, but I tamper it into a low exhale, conscious that I'm not alone in here; I keep getting concerned glances from the couple a few tables down.

I *feel* alone, though.

Taking a bite of the overripe banana, I stare across the room for a moment before standing and heading to the fridge labeled "drinks." I scan the faces of the eating agents as I pass, listening to snippets of conversations, trying to sort out the best one to approach if Grizzled Fox doesn't return.

Grabbing a container of orange juice from the fridge, I have Secret check it—never can be too safe—before mentally going over what I know so far. A top-secret organization. Their nemesis, the Suns of Liberty. A random book—bound and printed, but not technically published. Written by *Dad*.

I rub my eyes, a headache slowly forming as I head back to my table. "I wish someone would just *tell* me," I mutter to Secret.

The melody of "The Christmas Song" filters through the room as I re-take my seat, and I frown, looking around for whoever dares play Christmas music at the end of May. Bing Crosby's unmistakable voice bursts out, tinny, and my eyes fall on the jukebox by the food counter.

A brown-haired girl around my age, wearing an oversized gray hoodie and black Converse, leans against the wall next to the bulky antique, tapping the toe of her shoe on the tile as the far-too-Christmassy lyrics play.

Despite a few murmurs and looks around, none of the agents seem to pay much heed to the music, even as Bing Crosby wishes us all a merry Christmas. Again.

Just great. Agent Grizzled Fox has abandoned me, and there are lunatics here. What could possibly be better?

I stare down at my juice as the song ends, dull longing spiking my gut as I realize that I might never have a "Merry Christmas" again. The past one was hard enough, without Dad, but without Mum or Aunt Patience?

No, they'll be okay.

"Hey! Can you stand on your head?" a cheery voice asks, and I look up with a start. The girl who played the Christmas music stands by the seat that Grizzled Fox has left vacant, holding a plastic tray with a mug and a single, soggy waffle balanced on it.

"I... excuse me?"

"I said, is this seat taken?" A grin quirks her lips like she's holding back a laugh, and her brown eyes sparkle.

I slowly shake my head. "That's... not what you said, and no. To both."

"Tragic." She slides her tray on the table and claims the seat. "It's great fun."

"Unless you drink tea while doing it." I squint at her. *Who are you?*

"Tea? I prefer coffee," she says, gesturing to her steaming mug. "And they're right."

Either she really is a lunatic, or I'm going daft. "Pardon?" And coffee... after three in the afternoon?

After taking a swig of the offending drink, the girl sets down her mug and wipes a hand across her mouth. "You're Tirana."

"Uh... y—why would you think that?" I swallow, glancing around for an escape. This went from weird to creepy in about a fraction of a second.

"Because it says so on your nametag." She looks at me like I really am stupid.

"Oh." Maybe my orange juice contains a potion that will make me shrink, like Alice. *Even Wonderland would be better than this.* Although, isn't this place *called* Wonderland? "Uhm..."

"I'm Agent Celestial Flicker. Figure since I know your name, you might as well know mine." She shrugs, but there's still a gleam in her eyes that makes me suspicious.

"Nice to meet you?" *I think?* And the ISA has kid agents?

She cocks her head at me, squinting as if in thought, then nods. "What's Simon Lee's sole purpose in life?"

I blink. "Simon... Lee?"

She waves a hand, nearly upsetting her mug. "Y'know. The main character from the Simon Lee Universe."

"You—know Lee?"

"Simon." She narrows her eyes at me. "What's his purpose in life?"

Why do I feel like this is a test? And I'm going to fail miserably? "To... uh... save the world...?"

"Nope. According to P.D. Atkerson herself, and I quote, Simon's purpose in life is 'to be a perfect little angel.'" Celestial Flicker smirks. "But I'll take pity on you. Bonus question: which kind of food does Simon avoid now?"

"Uh..." My mind is blank, successfully frozen with a spinning loading sign. "I... uhm... food? Like... uh... alcohol? Or... popcorn?"

"Ding, ding, ding!" She claps. "Never trust fair food."

I glance down at Secret, settled under my chair with his head on his paws. I wouldn't trust *any* food, if not for him.

"And your grand prize," Celestial Flicker continues, "is... drumroll, please... Aurora!"

I blink at her a few times. "... Aurora?"

"Yup! It's what they call me when I get into trouble. Which occurs a number of times, the amount of which I won't disclose to you." She grins. "Great, now we know each other. So, where's Agent Grizzled Fox?"

"He... uh... left." I glance at the cafeteria doors, which swing open as two ladies walk in, chatting. No sign of Grizzled Fox. "I think he got upset or something."

A shadow flits across Celestial Flicker's—Aurora's—face as I turn back, but before I even begin to decipher it, a grin has taken up residence instead. "You're new here. Probably have a bazillion questions that my uncle didn't answer. So, fire away." She leans back in her chair, finishing off the last of her coffee and setting the mug down with a clink.

"Your... uncle?" I feel as lost as Alice when *she* fell into Wonderland.

"Uncle Blake is his name, 'stubborn agent' is his game." Aurora shrugs. "My uncle. Your temporary handler. And guardian, since you're still a minor. My mom would have been your guardian, but she's out on a mission right now."

"Oh." *Great.* His previous words wash over me; that carelessly thrown out "asset." Is that all I am?

"I can see that brain of yours working." Aurora raises an eyebrow. "Shoot. The worst I can do is tell you that it's redacted. Which plenty of things are, cuz you're a guest, but still. Fire away!"

I'm starting to really doubt that the girl actually needed the coffee she'd downed—hopefully, it's decaf, but at this point I wouldn't be surprised if it wasn't—, but I'm not about to pass up this opportunity. "Do you know where my aunt is? Agent... Mute Starburst?"

Aurora hesitates, a frown crossing her features, and my heart falls.

"Well, she called a Code Mauve Herring. We can't go after her until she clears it, or twelve hours pass." Aurora's expression is grim. "Sometimes the rules suck."

If she called this "Code Mauve Herring" to keep me safe, then is it my fault she's probably in the hands of an evil organization? I stare at my half-full bottle of orange juice, fingernails digging into my palms.

"Who are the Suns of Liberty?" I sneak a glance back up, and Aurora's face brightens.

"That one's easy. They're this top-secret, far-right extremist, anti-government, paramilitary, libertarian group that strives to return America to her former glory!" Aurora's too-bright expression drops after a moment. "AKA our nemesis. They're behind too many scandals to name, and we've... we've lost a couple agents to them." Her eyes drop, and I know she means Dad.

"They made sure he'd no longer be an issue..." What does it feel like to drown? I gulp, twisting the lid off my juice and taking a sip to quench my suddenly dry mouth.

"Well!" Aurora straightens. "That got dark quick. My turn." Her brown eyes turn intense, boring through me. "What's the dog for?"

Not what I was expecting, and a real smile touches my lips. "Seek? He's..." I pause, searching for the right words. "You ever heard of bomb-sniffing dogs?"

She nods, eyeing him. "He sniffs... bombs? But his vest says..."

I shake my head. "Not quite. He's trained to detect gluten." At her slightly confused look, I add, "A protein in wheat, barley, and rye. I'm allergic."

"It makes you sick?"

I shrug. "Anaphylaxis—so more like semi-instant death."

"So, he, like, smells all your food? And he doesn't eat it? That's better than my brother."

"Your brother is a dog?" I feel a smile twitching on my lips.

Aurora taps her chin. "He was quite possibly raised by wolves. And he's in the doghouse often enough."

"Maybe Secret can teach him a few things," I offer. "Hey, maybe your brother can even give him some howling lessons in return."

"Funny." Aurora slaps herself in the face, then winces, rubbing her forehead.

"Did you seriously just *hit* yourself?"

"Oh, this is nothing. You should try banging your head against a wall." She leans back in her chair and crosses her arms. "Dare you to."

"You're crazy." I shake my head.

"Double dog dare."

"One Secret isn't going to make me, and neither will two." I glance down at my dog, then back at Aurora. "If you're so intent on giving someone brain damage, do it yourself."

"That a dare?"

I shrug, suddenly feeling mischievous. "Sure."

She jumps up, heads to the nearest wall, and bangs her head against it.

I put my hand to my mouth, trying in vain not to laugh. "You're crazy."

She comes back to the table, rubbing her forehead. "Man. That was a very, very bad idea. I am never going to do that again."

"Famous last words," a new voice says. I jump and whip my head around to see Agent Grizzled Fox lounging against the wall behind me. I look from him to the door and back to him. *How in the world did he do that?*

"Uncle Blake." Aurora puts her hands on her hips and glares up at him, like a Labrador puppy chastising a full-grown Belgian Malinois. "You were *not* supposed to leave her alone."

He shrugs as if he doesn't care.

I narrow my eyes, pushing away a lingering sense of frustration. Just who does this guy think he is?

BETWEEN GRIZZLED FOX, AURORA, AND WHO KNOWS WHO ELSE, I'M "handed over" to Aurora so she can "babysit" me.

I can't quite shake the feeling that Grizzled Fox is trying to get rid of me, but trailing after Aurora as she leads me up a few flights of stairs and then down a maze of halls, I find the prospect of making a friend is not entirely repulsive.

After Dad died, most of my friends seemed to vanish into thin air. Mum said they were afraid... like the loss of a parent was something contagious. *Rubbish.*

The use of one of Mum's favorite terms sends a pang into my heart, awaking that ever-present swirl of questions. *Is she okay? Where is she? Is she going to come back early? Will she know where to find me? They'll tell her, right?*

We turn into a door-lined hall, whose mirroring sameness is almost disconcerting after the crazy wall art everywhere else.

"Home, sweet home," Aurora says, stopping at a door and scanning her card before pressing her palm onto the scanner. It blinks green, and she opens the door, gesturing me inside.

The entryway opens into a living room, with a kitchen leading off of it. Aurora drags me down a hall lined with family photos I only can catch a glimpse of—Aurora, a boy that must be her brother, their mom and dad, Grizzled Fox, and some other people I don't recognize.

There's a yellow and black "Enter At Your Own Risk" hazard sign on the door Aurora stops at. Hand on the knob, she turns to me, glancing down at Secret.

"Is he good with rats?"

"Rats?" I echo.

"Rattus norvegicus domestica," Aurora says, like it's perfectly normal to spout out gibberish as clarification. In this world, I'm starting to think it is. "Not to be confused with rattus rattus or rattus villosissimus, of course."

"I... beg pardon?"

"You're pardoned." She rolls her eyes. "Okay, does he chase squirrels?"

"Uh... not when I tell him not to?" I think I left all sane and logical conversations back in Chandler. "You have... rats?"

She grins, shoving open the door. "Best pets ever. No offense to Secret. Meet Anakin, Solo, and Mando," she says, gesturing to a large, three-tiered cage set up against a wall.

An intricate cardboard maze is pushed to the side of the room, almost as large as the twin bed shoved against the opposite wall. The bed, complete with galaxy covers, is positioned under a window framed with matching curtains, and a fuzzy, moon-shaped rug hugs the hardwood floor. A vintage Star Wars poster hangs over a messy desk.

"I *love* your room," I say, though a pang of homesickness slices me. Dad and I decorated my room in a *Lord of the Rings* theme when I was nine. What if I never see those tan walls, the framed map of Middle-earth that's half as big as my bed, or my prized bookcase library again?

"It's okay, but c'mon, you've gotta like the rats." Aurora grabs a container of peanut butter from the shelf next to the cage, and Secret snaps his head from sniffing at the rats to the spread.

I stifle a grin, watching his nose twitch like a rodent's. "Leave it, buddy."

Aurora dips a finger in the peanut butter, then sticks it through the wire bars, clicking her tongue.

A little pink nose peeks out of a plastic hut, followed by a white, whiskered head and beady black eyes blinking sleepily. The nose twitches a few times, and the rest of the rat emerges, followed by another rat, white except for a dark hood that covers his head and shoulders.

"The white one's Solo," Aurora says. "His tag-along is Mando, and Anakin's black. And grumpy."

Solo starts sucking the peanut butter off Aurora's finger, but Mando has stopped and is staring at Secret, whiskers twitching.

"They haven't ever seen a dog before," Aurora explains. "Anakin's the smartest out of the bunch, followed closely by Mando, but poor Solo here can be a bit slow at times."

The white rat has polished off the food and backs up before he starts grooming himself. He pays no attention whatsoever to me or Secret. Mando, after staring up at us, comes to the bars of the cage and sniffs again. Aurora gives him some peanut butter, which he licks off her finger while still keeping an eye on Secret, who stares back, intrigued by the rodents.

At least my dog's not wanting to play with them, like I was half afraid he would. Good thing Aurora doesn't have canaries or parakeets—Seek's biggest weakness is birds.

Another nose peeks out from the plastic hut before retreating back to the safety of the inside. Solo, after taking a drink from the water bottle hooked to the wire, ambles back to the hut. But Mando is settling in to watch us, it appears.

After Aurora ducks into the bathroom to wash her hands, she perches on her desk chair and gestures for me to have a seat. I plop down in a large bean bag in the corner, next to the oversized cardboard maze.

"Rats are better than dogs, you know," Aurora says, leaning back in her chair and crossing her ankles.

I stare at her. "Are you kidding? No way."

Any trepidation I'd had falls away as we spend the next half hour debating the best pets. Somehow, dinosaurs, falcons, hedgehogs, pigs, wolves, and octopuses end up in there, too. I stand firm in "dogs rule, everything else drools."

"But c'mon, a T-Rex would be a great addition to your life," Aurora is arguing, when, without warning, the bedroom door bursts open.

Secret jumps to his feet with me only a second behind, images of men in tactical suits flashing before my eyes.

But when my vision clears, I see a teenage boy standing in the doorway, mussed brown hair and a smattering of freckles across his nose marking him as Aurora's brother.

"Agent White Egret, at your service," he says, bowing dramatically. "But please, call me Genius, for like the mad scientist they call the Joker, I shall discover the finest ways to ruin your life!"

CHAPTER EIGHT
NEVER SAY GENIUS

"Seriously?" Aurora frowns, standing up and planting her hands on her hips. "Are you kidding me?"

"Aww, what'd I do now?" the boy asks, pouting slightly before lifting his head proudly. "I'm older; I can do no wrong!"

"Very funny," Aurora says dryly. "Three hours does not give you any superiority."

"Ah, but it gives me more than you have, dear sister. Oh, and it's nice to finally see your ugly mug, Tirana! Although I'm not sure why Rory let a *dog* in here."

Aurora huffed. "It's a service dog. Better trained than *you*."

Normally, I would have taken that as a compliment, but... why does this random guy know my name? I glance down at my nametag, but it's turned around backwards, so only the side with the ISA logo and "Guest Pass" shows.

"And '*Genius*'?" Aurora snorts. "You're about as close to a genius as Bruce Banner is to Hulk."

"Bruce Banner *is* the Hulk. And a genius," Maybe-Genius says, raising an eyebrow.

"No, he's either Banner *or* the big guy." Aurora shrugs. "They hate each other, remember?"

"See, this is what I have to deal with on a daily basis, Tirana," Genius groans, turning to me. "She always thinks she knows *every little thing*!"

"Har, har." Aurora rolls her eyes. "I *do* know that her name's not Tirana."

"What?" His gaze snaps to me. "Of course it is."

"No, it isn't," Aurora counters smugly. "I'm right and you're wrong."

"Rory Pory." Genius shakes his head. "Always thinks she's so smart. But I know things, Tirana Caineson, daughter of Dallas Caineson and Isabelle Dalton." He pivots to me with a grin. "Like that you were way cuter as an infant."

"I... what?" Sufficiently creeped out, I squint at him. How does he know my parents' full names? And "*infant*"?

Aurora snorts. "First off, you were literally only a few months old when you last saw her, and second off... you're wrong and I'm right; right, *Tirana*?"

"Uh..." I give a little laugh. "I am *so* lost. You guys knew me as... *babies*?"

"We played together while our parents went off and saved the world." Aurora flips her hair over her shoulder.

"Okay, so..." I cross my arms, biting my lip. "What happened? Because I don't know you. I didn't even know the ISA *existed* before today."

Aurora and her brother exchange glances, and he plops down on the bed, resting his chin on his hand. "You wanna tell her, or should I?"

"Maybe we should wait for Mom—"

But he's already talking. "So, okay, our parents were all really good friends. They had this super cool team and everything. Then one of the apexes at their base turned evil—like, hardcore Suns of Liberty evil—and tried to take over the world. Your dad faked his death—technically, the evil apex thought she killed him, but boy was she wrong—and he took her out. It would make such an epic story; someone should totally write it. Anyways, Uncle Dallas thought—"

"He moved out to Indiana a little while after you were born," Aurora interrupts, giving her brother a look.

I furrow my brow. "'Super cool team and everything'?"

Aurora winces. "They were... tight."

"So what changed?" I cross my arms, looking from Aurora to her brother. "Because I've literally never heard this story in my life." Just how messed up is this world that my parents never told me about?

Genius opens his mouth, but Aurora speaks first. "It's... complicated."

"What isn't?" I mutter, exchanging a glance with Secret. His calm eyes remind me that he's still here, even if my entire world has been going topsy-turvy lately.

"Your name isn't complicated." Genius raises an eyebrow. "It's Tirana. *Everyone* knows that."

"Oh, really?" Aurora matches his expression.

They're not telling me everything, I can feel it, but now they're staring at each other so intensely that I'm afraid to interrupt. I bite my tongue and mull over what I just learned—their parents, best friends with Mum and Dad? And I never knew they existed? The betrayal stings more than I'd care to admit.

"You blinked!" Genius says suddenly, breaking the competitive silence. "I win."

"This time." Aurora huffs, not breaking her glare. "And you still don't know her name."

"It's so secret, huh?" Genius scoffs.

"No," I say, forcing a lighthearted tone. "*He's* Secret." Evidently my babyhood is, too. Which isn't fair—since I wasn't exactly old enough to remember some apparently very significant things, shouldn't these people fill me in?

Genius glances at his sister. "You'd protect those stinky rodents with your life, but you're letting a secret canine in their presence?"

"First off, they are *not* stinky. *You* normally smell worse than they do." Aurora's glare deepens.

"Do not! And who would name their dog Secret? Come, Secret! Tell me a secret, Secret!" Genius rolls his eyes.

I want to grill them, to figure out this mess, but at the same time, I've heard enough. I definitely need to talk to Mum, but right now, I force myself to smile and play along with the twins.

And it can't hurt to show off, right? "Hey, Seek, tell me a secret." I kneel, and my dog jumps up to lick my ear.

The twins laugh.

"Good boy." With a grin, I scratch Secret's back, and he wiggles in delight. "I've been working on that one for a while. Took him forever to understand I didn't want him eating my hair."

Aurora snickers.

Genius laughs, then straightens, eyes gleaming suspiciously. "Okay, how about this, Miss Tirana? I declare a race. Whoever gets each other's real name first—no technology—wins."

I tilt my head, considering. Yeah, he's certainly got an advantage—but how's he ever going to know my first name without technology? It shouldn't be *that* hard to get his. "Deal."

He sticks out a hand, and after a second, I shake it.

They say you can tell a lot about a person by the way they shake your hand, and Genius' grip is exactly like I'd expect—firm, brief... and slightly sweaty. Gross.

Aurora's shaking her head like I've joined their private wacko party and I'm crazy for it, but I don't mind. Won't it be fun to show this way-too-competitive boy I can hold my own?

"Until then, you can call me Genius," he says, smirk broadening. "You shall be..." He taps his chin, brow furrowing as if he's deep in thought. "... Dog Girl."

Aurora snorts. "Wow, so *unique!*"

Maybe not, but no one except Dad has ever given me a nickname other than "Ana" before, and I duck my head to hide my idiotic grin, giving Seek a wink. *"With that dog of yours, you can do anything..."* And just like that, the fun of the moment vanishes. How can I be joking around while my aunt is being held captive somewhere? My *lying* aunt. I cringe internally.

"Why, thank you." Genius bows low. "Now, goodbye, Secret Dog and Dog Girl. Don't eat her precious rats." With that, he slips out of the room, leaving the door open behind him.

Aurora groans. "I apologize for my brother. He really is the craziest person I know."

I nod mutely, staring down at Secret, suddenly feeling drained. "Yeah, no, it's fine. Uh, is there somewhere I can exercise him?"

"Yeah, of course." Aurora rattles on about the rocket ship–themed playground, the ball field, and the trails surrounding the building, but I'm only half listening.

It's been a whirlwind of a day. I pull out my phone, but there are no new texts from Mum or Aunt Patience.

My eyes linger on Dad's contact. The ISA people must have taken it over to send me those messages yesterday, and that feels like a violation, somehow. Resisting the urge to bite my lip, I slide my phone back into my pocket.

Why did they need me that badly? But I know the answer almost before the thought is finished: it's not me they wanted, it was Dad's book.

Maybe the two-dollar bill is important for the case. Maybe I should have given it to Agent Grizzled Fox, too. Aunt Patience said the bill was important, and that I could trust Grizzled Fox, but I don't know.

I don't know anything anymore.

It's not that long until Agent Grizzled Fox returns to collect me, despite Aurora's pleas for a sleepover, and shows me to my room. Because apparently, this place has everything, including quarters for guests.

Hot-air balloons are muralled onto the sky-blue walls of the hall that Grizzled Fox leads me through. The elevator is designed to look like a teleporter, and it opens up into a corridor that suspiciously resembles Unikitty's Cloud Cuckoo Land... if Cloud Cuckoo Land was a mix between a cartoon reunion and a fancy hotel.

"This'll be your room," Agent Grizzled Fox says, stopping at a door with the number 18 printed on a plaque shaped like a mouse head. "Your card should work as a room key. If you need anything, just call the front desk." He seems to hesitate, pushing a hand through his hair, then gives me the bare bones of a smile. "Someone will be back in the morning." He pauses another moment before walking away, leaving me alone in the hallway.

I reach up and finger the warm metal of my locket, then take a deep breath and square my shoulders. *I've got this.* "Let's see what's inside, yeah, Seek?"

There's a card reader next to the door, and I hold the barcode on my guest badge up to it. There's a slight beep, the click of a door unlocking, and then I push my way inside.

A half-curtained window lets in fading daylight, which falls across the red-and-black rug on the floor. I flick the light switch, and the overhead light flips on, highlighting the life-sized Mickey Mouse grinning from the wall. His cheery expression is rather disconcerting, and I glance away quickly. A white, glove-shaped lamp sits on the end table next to the bed, which sports a mouse-head comforter.

"This place is weird," I mutter to Secret, dropping my backpack onto the bed.

The digital clock on the lamp glows a blue 20:49, and I sigh, flopping down next to my bag. I dig through it until I find Seek's kibble and his collapsible bowls. The sound of his crunching fills the room as the light slowly fades outside the window.

Aunt Patience is missing—taken by the Suns of Liberty, whoever they are. I was nearly *kidnapped*, taken to a secret agency base, and introduced to people who definitely know more about me than I do about them. Now I'm sitting in this Mickey-dominated room, and I still don't know what's going on.

Was Dad's whole life a lie? And what about Mum? And Aunt Patience?

Mum, who's supposed to be on the first flight over. It's after midnight in the UK; otherwise I'd call her. Instead, I just text her—telling her where I am, and that Aunt Patience is gone, and I'm pretty sure Mum has a lot to explain to me.

Midnight-black trucks flash in my vision, and I pull in a shuddering breath. *You're okay, Tirana... you have to be.*

But half an hour later, lying under the unfamiliar covers on the unfamiliar bed, staring up at the ceiling, I feel anything but okay. Lamplight bathes the room in a golden glow, casting shadows across the walls. It would be peaceful, even with the grinning mouse gazing at me, if not for the unrelenting buzz of my thoughts.

Dad is dead. Really, no-doubt-about-it dead. I'd known it for two years, but that single day of hope reopened wounds I'd thought mostly healed.

Sighing, I reach over and switch off the lamp. Through everything that has happened today, I've tried my level best to be strong—for Mum, for Dad, and for Aunt Patience. But now, in the cover of darkness, that faked strength fails me. I close my eyes as my nose stings. Secret worms his way to my front, and I bury my face into his curly fur and stop holding back the tears. *Why, Dad? Just... why?*

CHAPTER NINE
THE PINK PANTHER THEME SONG

"*You might have thought you won, but you will never win. You may have what you sought, but you have nothing*"

Blake growls a curse as the ominous words glare at him from the screen. Do the Suns of Liberty not have better things to do with their time than torment him?

Gritting his teeth, he clicks the email closed. Best not to let them get inside his head—that's what they want. To get him off his game.

As if he hasn't been "off his game" for the past two years.

And for those long years, he'd been on a personal mission to find Dallas' book, tracking it down from one location to another, just for it to fly the coop before he could close in. Just as hard to catch as Loki, the god of mischief from the comics.

Now, Dallas' book rests on Blake's desk, staring up at him. Accusing him. His failures written on the somehow pristine cover.

Despite Blake's insistence that the information Dallas tucked in the manuscript was highly important and could bring the Suns of Liberty down, Blake's supervisor had just brushed him off. "Not enough agents," he'd said. "Take what you've got."

Two agents to help him. That's all. Agent Tilted Showdown to be the official case leader, and a rookie Neophyte-level agent to do... something.

It's not enough.

If only his old friend Agent Respectable Pixie could help. She had been able to—had *begged* to—help pick up Tirana, but Michelle has other responsibilities right now. And everyone else that Blake would have turned to... well, isn't here to turn to anymore.

Even Dallas' own sister has given up the chase of his killers—and yet she's the one currently missing. Patience should have known better than to mess with the SoL by herself. Typical reckless Caineson—but Blake can tell her how stupid her plan, and Code Mauve Herrings in general, was when she returns.

Leaning back in his desk chair, Blake studies the vintage Green Arrow poster tacked on the wall. The Emerald Archer wouldn't just stand around and let the terrorists do what they wanted, and he wouldn't wait for the team to save his friend. The superheroes never had it easy—wouldn't make for a good story—but they won in the end.

They always won.

Blake rubs a hand down his face, turning back to the book. How many times had Mya told him that life wasn't like the comics? How many times had he argued back that the core values were the same?

But there were differences. The dead stayed dead... and sometimes, the bad guys won.

If Dallas were here, he'd get that flinty look in his eyes and say something like, "Well, not today they won't." He'd tell Blake to stop overthinking and to get down to business.

But Dallas *isn't* here. And what can Blake do when he's the only one around to decode the stupid manuscript that got his best friend killed? A manuscript that the Suns of Liberty will try anything to retrieve—including kidnapping Patience and trying to nab Dallas' daughter.

And they'd almost gotten Tirana, because of Blake's incompetence.

Somehow, they know that the ISA has Dove. Stupid codename for a book, but Dallas had seemed to think it fit. Blake stares down at the novel, ignoring the beginning twinge of a headache that matches the throbbing of his knuckles.

There's probably a leak, which Apex Agent Silent Herald will be thrilled about.

Can't get any better, can it?

He'll have to press his team harder, press himself harder, to find out Dallas' secrets. Hours have been wasted already—too many hours.

Blake leans back in his chair, closing his eyes. *Man, Dallas .. why didn't you just make it simple?*

SUNDAY, MAY 27

I wake up to a cold nose and dog breath in my face. "Really, boy?" I mumble, pushing Secret away and squinting at the Mousekedo-er-shaped clock on the wall. *8:12.*

Resisting the urge to burrow back under the warm covers, I slide out of bed. *Time to face the day...*

I'm ready, and Secret is fed, as the clock inches towards 9:00.

But this time, I'm not about to let Grizzled Fox drag me around with no answers. I don't quite trust him—there's something *off* about the man. I wish I could put my finger on what. Is he a double agent, perhaps? Working for the Suns of Liberty or some other enemy organization?

Yet he said he was my dad's old friend. Aunt Patience's words come to mind. *"Do you trust me?"*

Do I?

She said I could trust Grizzled Fox... but can I?

Biting back a groan, I sink down on the neatly-made bed and rub a hand over my face. It's too early for this.

I need to talk to Mum. She hasn't replied to the text I sent last night, and I don't know what that means, so I call her. It's already afternoon in London, so it's not like she's asleep. *C'mon, pick up...*

Nothing.

I close my eyes, trying to remember when I'd last called her. Was it only yesterday morning?

Hey, Mum... where are you? Aunt Patience disappeared yesterday, then I got this mysterious text, and ended up in a car with strangers. And then another car, and then a car chase, and now I'm... here. And apparently you lied about my childhood.

I swallow, dropping the phone onto the bed and grabbing the blankets in my fist. *Why can't anyone just... tell me what's going on?*

The opening strands of "An Englishman in New York" plays, and I dart into a cross-legged position, fumbling for my phone and swiping up to answer the call.

"Mum!"

"Tirana? Is everything all right?" Mum's voice emerges tinny, her British accent more pronounced after weeks of separation.

"I..." I close my eyes against the stinging tears. "Not... really?"

There's a moment of silence, and I'm almost afraid the line dropped, then she speaks. "Are you in danger at the moment?"

"I... no. I don't think so." *If I said I was, would you come over?* But her job as some sort of consultant—or that's what she'd always said it was— has typically seemed more important. She never missed a birthday, but it was mostly Dad who was there when I scraped a knee or elbow; Dad who made my stuffed animals "talk" when I was little; Dad who made sure my lunch was packed whenever we went on a daytrip, before I got Secret and could eat out.

"What's wrong, darling?" Mum's voice has softened.

I blink open my eyes, squinting at Seek's blurry form curled up at the foot of the bed. "What isn't?"

A pause, then, "Tirana..."

"No, Mum." I bite my lip too hard, and a metallic tang fills my mouth. "Do you even know what happened yesterday? Some guys wanted to kid-nap me—and they have *Aunt Patience.* All because of a stupid *book*! Why... why didn't you and Dad ever tell me your real jobs?"

I scramble off the bed, push away the thick red curtain framing the window, and stare out into the morning woods. Phone in one hand, I clutch the windowsill with a white-knuckled grip, upended by the feeling of being unrooted.

Silence is the only answer from the other end of the line. I want so badly to be able to see Mum's face, to know what she's thinking, to be *with* her. Instead, I'm stuck in this Mickey-dominated room, with Secret the only family member left, and a hundred questions threatening to make my head—or heart—explode.

"This... isn't a conversation to have on the phone," Mum says finally, voice tight.

"Please, Mum!" I'm so close to at least *some* answers, and she's just going to... what? Disappear again?

What if something happens, and she's gone forever?

No.

"It... I didn't want you to find out like this." Mum's sigh carries over an untold amount of miles. "This wasn't supposed to happen."

Was it ever? But I bite my lip—more gently, this time—and wait, staring out into the trees.

"I'm sorry, Tirana. I should have told you everything after your father's death. I was going to, but..." She pauses. "Your father and I decided when you were born that you were better off not knowing. We wanted to give you a normal childhood."

"Didn't work." I try to keep my voice from betraying the tears that threaten to choke me. Another beat of silence, then I ask, "Mum... where are you?" I feel like a baby, crying for my mommy, but I don't care right now.

There's an exhale that's audible over the phone. "Still in London. There are still some loose threads to tie up, but I have a flight booked for tomorrow. I'll talk to you then, all right? There's... a lot for you to learn."

The pauses in her normally articulate speech worry me. I tilt my head up, gazing at the blue expanse of sky. "You... you promise?"

"You know what your dad always said," Mum replies, voice filled with forced lightness.

Yeah. I do. "Don't make a promise you don't know you can keep," I mutter, turning away from the window and dropping back onto the bed.

"I shall do everything in my power to get there soon, that I can promise."

I nod, though I know she can't see me.

Something beeps on Mum's end, and then a faint voice, like someone walked in and Mum put her hand over the phone. Muffled talking, then Mum again. "I'm sorry, Tirana, I have to go again. Don't forget I love you."

"Love... love you too, Mum."

Then she's gone. I lean back in the bed, Walt Disney's words staring at me, colors bold against the white of the wall. *"If You Can Dream It, You Can Do It."*

Dream what? Of my past? When Dad was still alive and my family wasn't spread out across the world? When I didn't know that I was raised by secret agents?

Secret jumps down from the bed, and I roll over to watch him sniff around the floor until he finds his rope pull toy. He hops back up and drops it on my stomach, cocking his head down at me.

"You're right. Enough lying around." I push myself up and grab the toy. "Let's do something fun."

Mum had better come. I don't want to consider what will happen if she doesn't.

A few minutes later, a rap sounds on the door. Squinting out the mouse-eared peephole, I see a blur of blue that morphs into a shirt, then the profile of Grizzled Fox.

Blowing out a breath, I open the door. "Can you... can you please tell me what's going on?"

"Good morning to you, too." Shadows smudge under his icy blue eyes and stubble darkens his jaw, but a smile quirks his lips.

Great. He finds me amusing. "I'm not going wherever you want to take me until I know what's going on." Bold words, but I'm tired of being in the dark.

"My sister wants to meet you."

I blink. What does that have to do with anything? "Your sister?"

"Yup."

Like that tells me everything. I sigh and grab Secret's lead and vest. "Fine. But I'd really appreciate it if *someone* had some answers around here..."

Either he doesn't take the hint, or he ignores it. How thrilling.

At the stairs, he takes the flight down, and I have to trot to keep up with him. The stairwell looks like a scene from a butterfly-filled fairy tale, but I don't have time to study it. Grizzled Fox leads the way through another maze of color-filled hallways, and soon I find myself stepping out into the clear morning air.

Aurora runs over from the playground—because of course there's a playground behind Wonderland. "Tirana! Hey!"

"Morning," I return, letting Secret's leash out so he's free to sniff. For a moment, the feeling that this isn't real washes over me. That I'm not standing with a group of virtual strangers behind the headquarters of a secret agency, the dew-misted grass polishing my boots.

Genius' shout of "Top of the morning to the Secret Girl and her dog!" breaks me out of it, and I give him a smile as he sprints over. The only other person out here, a lady with rusty red hair who must be their mom, comes over to us, although at a more adult pace than the twins had.

"Tirana," she says when she reaches us, an expression on her face that I can't place. Just my name, and nothing else.

I shift uneasily. "Aurora says that they knew me as a baby?" Too late I realize I probably should have said "hello" or something polite like that.

Still wearing that odd look and staring at me, she nods, then seems to shake herself out of whatever daze she was in. "Yes, yes they did." Her smile is warm, if not a little tight. "You've gotten so big in the past fourteen years, girl! Look at you, all grown up. I'm Mya, an old friend of Dallas and Patience." Something flickers in her eyes, but her smile stays fixed on her face. "It's so great to see you, Tirana... I'm glad you're finally here."

Okay, there's something I don't get here. Some underlying story I don't know about, which only strengthens the feeling of being dropped into somebody else's life. But Aurora pulls me away towards what she says is "The coolest trail *ever*," and her mom—it feels weird to call her Mya—has to leave for another mission.

A million questions burn my brain, but I shove them away and follow the twins to a trailhead that peeks out of the woods. When I glance behind me, I see Mya and Grizzled Fox talking. Mya's still watching me. I turn around quickly and hurry after the twins.

There is definitely something going on here.

MANDO'S LITTLE PINK NOISE TWITCHES FROM HIS PERCH ON AURORA'S shoulder, and the rat that Aurora'd been hiding in her pocket so her mom wouldn't see seems to be enjoying the fresh air as much as the rest of us. Aurora's hair is pulled back into a ponytail, and I can't help but watch Mando as we walk down the paved pathway behind Wonderland. He's tiny, but looks completely at ease, like a king upon his chariot.

Genius taps me, and I turn to him, raising an eyebrow.

"Hey, Dog Girl. I got a question."

I raise my other eyebrow, pausing to let Secret sniff at the base of a tree. "Yes?"

"What happens if you drop a piano down a mine shaft?"

I blink. "*Why* would you..."

"A flat minor!" He hoots, then sprints towards his sister, reaching out and touching her arm as he dashes by. "Tag!"

"Hey!" Aurora retorts, but he's already twenty feet down the path, where he stops and turns back towards us, grinning.

Aurora rolls her eyes. "No tag when I have a rat!" she calls to him. She sighs, falling a few steps back to me. "He knows the rules, he just doesn't know how to *follow* them."

"Right." I eye Genius. "Does he get his jokes from the Worst Dad Jokes Ever manual?"

"I think he gets them from his own brain." Aurora makes a face. "Which makes them even worse."

I laugh, and we fall into silence as we walk. Tucked away in the woods behind the building, the sounds of civilization are muffled by trees and nature.

Secret is happy to get a break, too. He's free to sniff and mark and just be a dog here. Maybe I'm free to be a girl. Maybe I can forget about this whole mess for a bit.

"Penny for your thoughts?"

I glance at Aurora. "It's... nice here."

She nods. "I know. I love this trail."

Up ahead, Genius is crouching by the edge of the pond, hands cupped in the water. I watch him sit stock-still, then suddenly dart a hand out.

"Any luck?" Aurora calls as we draw near.

He shakes his head, rocking back onto his heels and brushing his hair out of his eyes as he looks up at us. "Lots of minnows, but they're fast. Hey, does Mando want a swim? The water's nice!"

Aurora snorts. "Last time we tried that, it took a fishing net to get him back. No thanks."

"But he had the time of his life!" Genius protests, standing and drying his hands on his shorts. "Isn't it every rat's dream to have epic adventures?"

Aurora holds her hand to her shoulder, and Mando scurries onto it, beady eyes taking everything in calmly. "Perhaps, but not today."

Genius grumbles, but we continue on. The path curves away from the pond and into a patch of trees, the pavement turning into a sandy trail. Our footsteps crunch on the pebbles and dirt.

"So," Aurora says after a moment, turning to me. "Do you have any more questions?"

I watch Secret investigate a pile of leaves, his tail wagging. A squirrel chatters at us from a branch overhead. I chew my lower lip, then sigh. "I guess... *why*?"

"Why?" Genius taps his chin. "'Why'... hm... what a profound questioning of the world's deepest reflections. For instance, why did the chicken cross the road? Was it in mortal danger, or—hey!"

Aurora elbows him, and he sticks his tongue out at her.

"Why what?" she asks, giving me a small smile. "Ignore him; he's been trying to figure out why the chicken crossed the road since we were five."

"Four, actually," Genius corrects. "But proceed."

They're both waiting, and I scuff the toe of my boot against the sandy gravel. "Why is *The Freesia Guard* so important?" I need to know so much more, but nothing else is formulated into words yet.

The twins exchange a glance.

"Well," Aurora begins slowly, "your dad was writing it while he was on a mission in Florida."

"Or he'd already written it and just brought it along." Genius shrugs. "Either way, he had it. And Uncle Dallas being Uncle Dallas—"

"Uncle?" I repeat, frowning. "Why—?"

"Honorary," Aurora provides, setting her rat back on her shoulder. "He'd come over sometimes. Tell us all kinds of stories about you."

I shake my head, pushing away the pang of hurt. "Okay, so what were you saying about the book?"

Genius tosses an acorn from palm to palm, then begins to juggle with the handful he's collected. "Uncle Dallas put his case report into it."

"Put his case report into it?" I echo, frowning. "How does someone..."

"Codes." Aurora watches her brother, then looks back at me. "We don't know how yet, exactly—but now that we've found it, it shouldn't be long before it's decoded."

"What was in the case report?"

Aurora shrugs a shoulder. "Top-secret info about SoL operations, I think? I mean, that's what he was sent to retrieve. Stuff the SoL *really* doesn't want to get out."

"But after the accident, the manuscript went missing." Genius, having given up on juggling, tossing an acorn at a branch. "The SoL didn't have it, the ISA didn't have it, and the river didn't have it."

"So... who did?"

Genius shrugs. "Who knows? A dwarf? Maybe a gnome thought it looked tasty."

"Uncle Blake's been tracking it," Aurora explains, "but it kept popping up and vanishing before he could get to it. Until now." She gives me a smile. "Until you brought it in."

"Tirana, our hero!" Genius sweeps into a low bow, removing an imaginary hat. "How would we ever have fared without you, lovely madam?"

I laugh along with Aurora, but my mind struggles to understand just how serious "top secret info" has to be if it got my father *murdered*. And if SoL knows that we have *The Freesia Guard*, just how far will they go to make sure this information doesn't get out?

CHAPTER TEN
THE SECOND STAR TO THE RIGHT

What am I missing?

Blake stares at his computer screen, on which is the image of *The Freesia Guard*'s cover, with the running kid, his cat, the dark city alley, and the starry night sky.

Maybe if he looks long enough, he'll see it. Some detail that tells him where to look, what to do, what Dallas hid.

If Dallas had even designed the cover. Blake lets his throbbing head fall into his hands, the blur of sounds from the cubicles around him only amplifying the ache in his temples.

There's so much he doesn't know, so much he's expected to find out.

Maybe it wouldn't be such a problem for his old self, but he's a different person now. One that probably shouldn't even be an agent, never mind the temporary guardian of his best friend's teenage daughter.

Yeah, and he'd handed the kid off to his *niece* again. The oh-so-responsible Aurora, infamous for getting into all sorts of sketchy situations. He'd told Mya that both Tirana and Aurora could use a new friend, and ISA rules prohibited an asset from wandering the base without an escort. But mostly, it was for his own sake. That stricken look on her face, the incredulous "they *murdered* him?" that still runs through his head...

Mya seemed to buy the claim that he couldn't be babysitting Tirana and working on *The Freesia Guard*, but his sister's like a bloodhound if she senses that something amiss. How long can he keep up the ruse? At least she's away on a mission—that stupid Code Mauve Herring has finally worn off, and Mya won't return until she has Patience.

A knock ratt-tatt-tatts on his cubicle's wall, and he straightens quickly. "Yes?"

The kid agent assigned to the case pokes his curly head into the cubicle. "I think I might've found something, sir!"

Mixed feelings accompany Blake as he allows the dude to lead him down the hall to the small case room the ISA gave them to work in.

Agent Tilted Showdown, the apex who's supposed to be the "case leader," looks up as they walk in, giving Blake a nod. Her short blue hair is mussed, giving the impression she's been running her hand through it. "Agent Grizzled Fox."

Blake can't tell if it's a greeting or a reprimand, so he just gives a short nod back. The smart board on the wall is on, displaying articles on J.R.R. Tolkien's *The Lord of the Rings*.

"See here?" The kid jabs a chunky finger at the screen. "The favorite book of *The Freesia Guard*'s main characters—well, Robin's favorite, since Tommy likes *The Lord of the Rings* better—is *The Hobbit*. You said to look into anything at all, so I decided I might as well research the book and see if I could find anything, right? And look! In *The Hobbit*, they have this map that's supposed to lead them through a secret tunnel into the Lonely Mountain, which is the dwarves' original home before it got taken over by a dragon. But they have trouble reading the map because it doesn't come with instructions. Then Gandalf takes them to see Elrond, the lord of the Rivendell elves and an *expert* at reading these kinds of things. Elrond said that these things called Moon Runes were written on the map, and they could only be read on Midsummer's Eve under the light of a crescent moon. Cool, right? So, I was thinking, what if Agent Bel Ria hid the list in plain sight—something like that? Like, with invisible ink, or maybe in some paperwork or even a different book somewhere?"

Blake regards the boy silently, not willing to admit that most of what he said had gone in one ear and out the other. What can *dwarves* with an unreadable map have to do with a story about two kids trying to rescue their friends?

"Well? What do you think?" The younger agent slides into one of the chairs, tapping his fingers on the wooden surface of the table.

That you're a nerd. Blake clears his throat, working up some semblance of a smile. "I'll look into it."

"OKAY, SO YOU'RE SITTING IN THIS PARLOR OF A BIG FANCY HOUSE— visiting a rich friend," Aurora begins, leaning forward in her desk chair. "And you've just drunk a cup of tea, and on the bottom of the cup is a message that says, 'You've been poisoned.' What do you do?"

I stare at her from the depths of the overstuffed bean bag. "Uh... scream and run away? Pinch myself and wake up?"

She laughs. "Nope."

"Die?"

She shakes her head, grinning like she knows something I don't. I narrow my eyes at her. *All right... so it's a trick question.* "Laugh?"

"Now that would just be weird."

"So I got it right." A smirk spreads across my face. "If you say it's weird, you've probably planned it that way." That much I've learned about her in the less than two days I've known her.

She huffs. "Oh, come on! I'd check the calendar. If it's April first, I'd laugh. If not, then I'd call poison control."

I shake my head, but laughter lurks somewhere close by. She really is crazy, as proved by our first meeting, but it's a good kind of crazy.

I'm about to say something about *Alice in Wonderland*'s usage of tea, but a knock raps at the door before it flies open.

It's Genius, of course. I still haven't learned his real name, though not for lack of trying. Aurora's as tight-lipped as Secret is when he grabs something he knows isn't his, and I'm not sure who else to ask in this land of strangers.

"Your presence is requested by Agent Grizzled Fox, Dog Girl," Genius reports before turning on his heel and striding away.

"What does Uncle Blake want?" Aurora asks, scrambling after him.

I follow, wondering the same. I haven't even seen the agent since this morning. What can he want now?

"How would I know?" Genius retorts to his sister, turning to walk backwards down the hallway. "Ask him yourself."

Grizzled Fox is standing in the living room, talking to a man I assume is Aurora's dad, who glances at me before saying something to Grizzled Fox and ducking out of the room.

Is there news on Aunt Patience? Mum's supposed to be here sometime tonight; did she come early? Or did something happen?

Stopping at the doorway of the living room, I silently cue Secret to stay beside me, but Aurora pushes past.

"Why do you want her?" she asks, crossing her arms as she stares at her uncle. She sighs when he doesn't answer. "Well, can I at least come? I won't be any trouble."

Genius snorts. "Yeah, remember what happened last time?"

"What? When *you* managed to set off the smoke detectors during the bomb class?" Aurora huffs.

"Guys." Grizzled Fox holds up a hand. "Have you done your homework today?"

The twins exchange glances with each other. "Almost," Genius says, at the same time Aurora says, "Come on, it's *summer*!"

Grizzled Fox frowns at Aurora, and she rolls her eyes.

"Fine, I'm going, I'm going." She trudges back towards her room, muttering something about bombs and tea.

"Going," Genius mumbles, and I turn to see that Grizzled Fox's icy stare has fallen upon his nephew.

This would be humorous, except with everyone gone, I'm left alone with a guy who can make the twins do their homework with a single *look*. And I still don't know why he's here.

"Let's go," Grizzled Fox says, hardly sparing me a glance as he turns and heads towards the apartment door.

I grab Seek's lead from the rack next to the door and clip it on his collar, then hurry after the agent, a bad feeling steadily growing in the pit of my stomach. "Where are we going?"

He doesn't reply.

Down three flights of stairs, through the ballerina hallway, through another door, down yet another hall, and another... I'm almost dizzy by the time he stops at an unmarked glass door leading outside.

He pushes it open, but I cross my arms and set my lips. "I'm not going until you tell me why." It's too bold and makes me feel sick, but I need to learn to stand up for myself, right?

Grizzled Fox slowly turns to face me, his eyes meeting mine for a half-second before they shift away.

My suspicion levels rise. "Where are we going?"

"Tirana, it's fine." His voice sounds weary, and his shoulders slump ever so slightly. "There's just—something you should... that you need to see."

"What?"

Silence. Grizzled Fox is still holding the door open, letting in the humid, late-May air. He stares at the ground like it's a complicated algebra equation, then slowly raises his head and mutters, "The memorial."

"The memorial?" I echo, but he doesn't wait for me. I barely catch the door before it swings shut. I step out and hurry to catch up. Secret sniffs at a patch of grass, but I tug his lead, almost running to keep up with Grizzled Fox's strides. Is he *trying* to lose me or something?

I hustle across the length of freshly mowed grass to the five-foot hedge wall, finally catching up to the agent where a stone path, leading from a different door in the building, intercepts the hedge. There's an opening in the shrubbery, a curved wooden doorway that makes it feel like the entrance to a fantasy story.

It's easy to imagine there being another world hidden behind there, complete with pixie dust, talking trees, and rabbits with bows. I'm not even sure how many books I'm smushing together, but it still sounds cool.

But behind those green walls... it's not what I was expecting.

A tall cylinder stands in the center of a circular concrete ring, bordered with granite walls maybe four feet tall—obviously a memorial of some kind. Trees overhang the structure, creating patches of shade in the afternoon sun.

"What... *is* this?" I ask, squinting. I might as well be talking to the memorial itself for all the answers I'm getting.

Grizzled Fox stands under the trees at the edge of the clearing, hands in his back pockets and a bored, pensive look on his face.

Letting out a deep breath, I walk into the ring, eyeing the tall, bluish cylinder. Under stars and what looks like fairy dust or sparkles, hollow words are carved into it, and I circle slowly to read them.

"Superheroes may only exist in imagination, but true heroes have laughed with you, have eaten at your table, have put their lives on the line.

"Let us never forget."

Like the dawn of a new day, it's occurring to me what this place is. I lean down to scratch Secret's head—mostly to hide the tears that spring to my eyes. Blinking quickly, I straighten, taking in the structure with more attention to detail.

Names are etched into the shiny surface of the granite, angled towards the cylinder.

Too many names.

Just how dangerous is this spy world?

Maybe there *is* a reason my parents kept me away from it, for all the good that did.

I reach up and pull my locket from under my shirt, running a thumb along the raised surface of the dove. Then I step forward and skim the names on the granite wall until my eyes rest on *"Dallas Caineson."*

Drawing a deep breath, I unclasp the chain from around my neck, setting the locket next to his name and opening it.

My family smiles up at me: Mum, Dad, Aunt Patience, me, and Secret.

Whole.

Back when there wasn't a gaping hole in my heart.

I quickly wipe my eyes, hoping that Grizzled Fox doesn't notice, but not daring to turn around to look.

Then I pull out my phone and snap a few photos before replacing my locket to its rightful spot—hanging by my heart.

THE EARLY-AFTERNOON SUN IS HOT ON BLAKE'S BACK AS HE STARES off into the tree-lined distance, thinking of everything and nothing. Trying not to think. Mentally going over any possible missed angle, any anything, in *The Freesia Guard*. What has he missed?

There's *got* to be something.

He closes his eyes against the familiar ache in his temples, willing the answers to just show themselves.

But, no. They have to remain hidden, just as stubborn and headstrong as Dallas himself.

It was that same stubbornness, that loyalty, that got Dallas killed. Him and Damian both.

"Everyone wants to be the hero. No one wants to do what it takes to be the hero. Everyone wants the glory. No one wants to die." Blake can't remember who said it—Dallas, maybe?—but the quote too aptly describes the perfect picture of grief that Tirana makes as she stands, head bowed, over her father's name. She doesn't even know that Damian was once one of them, back when the 6-Some still existed.

Blake grinds his teeth together, closing his eyes. *Dallas* should be the one showing his daughter around Wonderland, not the reason Tirana's crying now. "Damian Shepherds" shouldn't be the name written on that wall only a handbreadth away from Dallas' name.

Should've been me. If he hadn't been so weak—

But enough of the self-pity. Blake has a case to solve. It's ironic. He didn't sign up to be a detective. No, he was young and naive and thought he could save the world, that he could keep innocents from the same fate as his parents'. He tried to play Batman, but failed more epically than Red Hood.

Swallowing, he turns away from the memorial. Tirana deserves privacy. She deserves more time here than he can afford to spare, but Agent Tilted Showdown forced him to take a break, threatening to remove him from the case if he didn't.

And Tirana needed to come here.

It's not hard to remember the first time Blake laid eyes on the memorial, over a decade ago. The lead agent on some SoL case Blake and guys had been brought in to help with had taken them here. Damian had vowed to stop the SoL—they all had—and look how *that* had ended up.

"Why...why are there so many names?"

Blake jolts around. Tirana's walking back towards him, that unmistakable pain of grief written on her face. She's like Dallas in so many ways, but holds an innocence that Blake's best friend had lost long before Blake knew him.

He sighs, rubbing the back of his neck. "Because the world isn't a big fan of people trying to get rid of evil."

"But... *why?*"

Patience or Michelle would've had an answer, but Blake just shakes his head, starting at the ground. *Why.* That's what he'd like to know. Just... *why?*

The "whoo whooo who whoo" of a bird comes from somewhere in the trees, and he resists the urge to hunch his shoulders like a child. If he were with Dallas, the nature geek would have certainly named the bird, just by the sound of its call.

"Mourning dove," Tirana mutters.

Blake's head snaps towards her. "Dove, huh?" he mumbles under his breath. He shoves a hand through his hair, staring up into the foliage as if he could possibly locate the bird in the dense leaves.

"Does it have anything to do with the book cover? The dove on the spine?"

His gaze snaps back to her. "What?"

She shrugs, looking down at her dog. "I mean, I was just wondering.

Dad liked doves, so it's not surprising. But there weren't any in the book itself—I thought it was kinda weird. Anyway." She shrugs again. "But he put doves in weird places anyway, like on my locket."

Doves.

Dallas' daughter.

Her... locket?

Like a missing piece of a puzzle, it slips into place. Blake freezes mid-step, turning slowly to face Tirana.

"I need to see the locket."

"You... what?" She takes a step back, shaking her head.

Don't scare her, man. He exhales slowly, softening the urgency tightening his features. "I want to check to see if he—" How to explain what he doesn't even know? "He used it. We'll just take a look at it and give it back."

Her hand strays to the piece of jewelry, something Blake can't decipher shadowing those blue-hazel eyes. Then she gives a sharp nod and unclasps the necklace, handing it over.

"Just... be careful with it?" She bites her lip, but it's him who looks away first, glancing down at the fine jewelry in his hand.

"Yeah. I will." It's the least he can do.

CHAPTER ELEVEN
LEGACY

I touch my empty neckline, a sigh leaking out. It feels like I'm missing an important part of me, and I don't like it.

"What's wrong?" Aurora frowns, expression deepening as her eyes follow my movement. "Hey, where's your necklace?"

"The boogeyman took it? Or a super spy?" Genius suggests, turning to walk backwards down the hall. These ones are painted with mice riding motorcycles and golden hamsters with notebooks, and I'm distracted for a second by the cartoonish rodents before I snap my focus back to Genius.

"What? No. Not unless your uncle's the boogeyman... or a spy." I knit my brows, glancing down at Secret before looking at Aurora. "*Are you guys spies?*"

"Yup," Genius says, still walking backward, a goofy grin on his face. "Super-duper spies. Isn't that right, Rory Pory?"

"When we need to be," Aurora answers, but she sounds distracted. She shakes her head. "Why did Uncle Blake take your *locket*?"

"Uhm... something about doves and codes and—" I stop so short, Secret gets to the end of his leash before he realizes I'm no longer walking.

"What's wrong?" Aurora's eyes are wide.

"Nothing..." I shake my head, biting my lip. "Only... do you know why a two-dollar bill might be important?" I can't *believe* that I nearly forgot about the bill that was in Mum's piggy bank.

"You stopped because you're worried about ole' Jefferson's importance?" Genius squints, tapping his head. "Are you sure all the lights are on up there?"

"Shut up, tomfool." Aurora doesn't spare him a glance. "What do you mean, Tirana? What sort of two-dollar bill?"

I quickly rehash the piggy bank fiasco as we resume walking towards Juke's. "And then I pretty much forgot about it, with everything else going on," I finish with a sigh. "But Aunt Patience must have thought it was important for some reason."

The twins exchange glances.

"Are you sure it was the bank she was talking about?" Aurora asks.

I nod. "Positive. The bill's in my room here, if you wanted to look at it." Hopefully, the twins can figure out this mystery.

"A mysterious Thomas Jefferson or lunch..." Genus frowns, tapping his chin. "Hm, what do you think, sis?"

She swats him. "Money, then lunch."

It can't be this easy. All this time, has the key been hidden right under their—more accurately, Tirana's—nose? Blake sighs, sending a longsuffering look to the ceiling of the case room. Only Dallas would slip the microchip in the last place anyone would ever think to look: behind the picture in Tirana's locket.

"What are you doing?"

Blake jumps, almost knocking the locket off the table as he turns. The curly-haired kid—Flame something-or-other—stands in the open doorway of the case room.

"Is that a necklace?"

Yup, Blake's peace and quiet is definitely gone. "Go find a microSD card reader," he orders, carefully prying the card out of the locket with a flathead screwdriver.

Flame quickly returns with the requested device, and Blake slips the tiny card into the adapter, then turns to the computer on the desk in the corner.

"What's on it? What is it? Why was it in a necklace?" Flame's breath is hot on Blake's neck.

Don't punch him. Blake's knuckles are still sore from punching out the guys who tried to kidnap Tirana at the park. So instead, he slowly turns and gives Flame a long look. The overeager neophyte backs away a step with a sheepish grin, and turning back to the computer, Blake inserts the card.

The cursor hovers over the file app for a long moment before he double-clicks the mouse and the pop-up opens. Numbers scroll across the screen, a mess of ones and zeros that make his head spin.

"Binary!" Flame breathes, rubbing his hands together. "Can I have a look?" He leans over Blake's shoulders, utterly unconcerned that he's invading Blake's personal space. Again.

"Have at it." Blake shoves out of the chair, and Flame plops down in his place, fingers flying into a blur over the keyboard.

"Just gotta run it through the program," Flame mumbles, "and it should decode it for us…"

So what was the point of Flame taking over? Blake shakes his head. Back when he was the boy's age, they painstakingly decoded everything by hand. Dallas' favorite part, and something Blake never really cared for.

Feeling about as useful as a boomerang in space, he hovers over Flame's shoulder as the program runs the code.

They're so close to a break on this mission, and Blake's pulse throbs, yet another brutal reminder he's no longer the adrenaline junkie who jumped at a chance to run headlong into danger.

Theirs is a life of risks. The Neverland Memorial confirms that, if nothing else.

And is it worth it?

"All righty," Flame mutters, jiggling the mouse, and Blake refocuses on the screen as the neophyte clicks open a file.

Shades and sunglasses. Skimming the words, Blake can feel the blood drain from his face.

It's an obituary from a newspaper bulletin.

"Lawrence Klassen, 57, of Fort Myers, Fl., peacefully left us on Monday, following a severe bout of pneumonia. He is survived by his two children, as well as three grandchildren and numerous nieces, nephews, and cousins. A funeral service will be held in his honor at 4 PM on Sunday at Friendship Baptist Church."

Under that is a notice of changed status from the ISA itself, dated for the same day: *"Agent Swift Boar; status: deceased."*

The words blur, and Blake blinks, stepping away from the computer and grabbing the edge of the table. *How...*

Flame highlights the obituary. "What's so important about a dead person?"

Blake ignores him and calls Tilted Showdown in.

"We need any info on Lawrence Klassen," he tells her and Flame. "Where the service was held, where he's buried, his relatives—everything."

Then he escapes to his cubicle, where he sits with his head in his hands—hands that *shouldn't* be shaking just because of the mere mention of a city.

Because of memories that shouldn't have such an unrelenting hold on him.

Of course it makes sense that this case would bring him back *there.*

Of course nothing can be simple.

Things never are.

SITTING CROSS-LEGGED ON THE MICKEY BED, I HOLD THE TWO-DOL-lar bill up to the light. "See, it looks perfectly *normal.*"

"Nothing suspicious is ever 'normal,'" Aurora mutters, and I hand the bill to her.

"Well, I hope you can figure out what's up with this one."

"Or we'll die trying," Genius says breezily.

I stare at him.

"Or we'll *not* die trying." Aurora scans the bill. "Looks legit. Tomfool, what do you think?"

Genius takes the bill and runs his fingers over it. "Definitely Jefferson. I'd say try for a microdot."

"Maybe..." Aurora says, hovering over his shoulder. "But why not invisible ink?"

"We'll check for both, and everything else." Genius starts for the door. "To the lab for testing!"

The "lab" turns out to be his bedroom. Dinosaur posters plaster the walls, the unmade bed sports a teddy bear bigger than Secret, and junk litters the floor. The only clear surface is the desk, which Genius plops down at.

"First things first," he says, pulling a flashlight out of one of the drawers. A fluorescent blue light illuminates the bill as he waves the beam over it, and I lean in, excitement catching my breath.

"Nothing," Aurora mutters, shaking her head. "Try your theory."

"Righto." Genius turns off the flashlight and rummages in the drawer, pulling out a magnifying glass. He clicks on the desk lamp and begins to examine both sides of the bill.

His earlier words about being a "super-duper spy" might not be that far off. Especially when he yells "Score!" and fist-pumps the air, almost punching his sister.

"Well? What is it?" I hover over them, just out of hitting range.

Genius doesn't look up from the bill. "A microdot. Right under George Washington's nose."

"What's a microdot?" I ask.

"Text or an image that's shrunken so it's easy to hide," Aurora explains. "Tomfool, move over."

"But I haven't read it yet," he protests.

"Move, or I'll tell Mom what really happened to her china horse."

"That wasn't even my fault!" But he scoots over, leaving enough room for me to squeeze in.

"See this tiny black dot on the book?" Aurora taps the bill with the magnifying glass.

I lean in, scanning the picture of the signing of the Declaration of Independence on the back of the bill. "I guess?" Nothing *seems* special about the small book centered in a smattering of papers.

"Okay, now look at it." Aurora hands over the magnifying glass, and I hover the lens over the section.

There are letters on the book. Blurry letters that hurt my eyes as I squint, but they're definitely words, white on a dark background. "Oh, *wow*."

"Yeah." Aurora sounds awed. "You can fit *so* much text on those things. I've never seen one used like this before."

"You said your dad put it there?" Genius asks me.

I'm about to say that I don't know when I find the magnifier's sweet spot and the words leap out at me. *"Hey, Ana-girl. If you're reading this, then I guess I'm not around anymore."* My breath stalls, and I swallow hard. "Uh... yeah, I guess so. It's a message... from Dad."

"Woah, really?" Genius crowds me, and I shift away from him. "Lemme see."

No... I don't want to be rude, I really don't, but—

Aurora saves the day by shoving him. "Dude, let her do it. Come on." She grabs his arm and drags him from the room. I can hear a muffled "Let her read the message from her *dead dad* in peace!" through the closed door, and I nearly laugh, but I'm too choked up.

My hands are shaking, and I'm almost more terrified than I was in Agent Grizzled Fox's car, speeding away from that midnight truck.

Secret comes over, and I rub his head, closing my eyes. I can't do this. Can't read this. It hurts so much. But... I can't *not* read it. For Dad—I have to.

Here goes nothing. Taking a deep breath, I pick up the magnifying glass.

Hey, Ana-girl.

If you're reading this, then I guess I'm not around anymore. Man, I hope that you never read this, that someday when I'm old and gray we'll find it in the junk box and laugh about it—but if life's taught me anything, it's that I can't control the future.

Right now, you're "reading" your favorite book, *Harold and the Purple Crayon*. You have the whole thing memorized, yet you still make me read it to you every single night before bed.

Mum's out, and I'm on baby-sitting duty. She's on a case, actually. Both your parents are agents, and, well, it's dangerous work. There's always a chance that one of us won't make it home. Home to you.

I grew up without a dad, and it was rough. I never want you to go through that. You're the most important thing in my life, Grace Tirana. And if I'm ever not around to tell you myself, I want you to know: It's not your fault. You're more loved than you'll ever know. And I'm *so* proud of you.

I'm not nearly as proud of the decision your mother and I made to keep the ISA from you. A few years after I had to go underground to shake a corrupted apex, one of my best friends was killed... because this world is dangerous, Ana-girl. I don't want to even imagine you in it, facing the same threats we've faced, and that we'll continue to face.

Mya thinks we're ruining your life, and sometimes, I wonder if she's right—if by keeping you away from the twins and the ISA, I'm also keeping you away from your family. But last time we were all together, it ended with a very long night in the ER because you somehow got a hold of a single cracker. You're so small, Tirana. So fragile, so innocent. If anything were to happen to you...

So we'll wait until you're a little bit older. I know you can't be kept away from the 6-Some forever—they're your family, after all. I know you might hate your mom and me for keeping you away, but I promise, baby girl, that we did it to protect you. Keeping you safe is the most important thing.

I hope you never have to read this, that it'll stay in the piggy bank, money forever untouched (remind your aunt to tell you the story behind that puzzle bank someday), but I can't promise that I'll always be around. I wish I could—I wish it so much it hurts—but I can't. And that kills me inside.

You're gonna go far, Ana-girl. One day you'll be all grown up, and your mom and I will look at you and wonder where the time has gone. The other day, you said that you wanted to be a race-car driver, an elephant doctor, or a kitten, and while I'm fairly certain you'll be none of those things, I know that you'll be the best at whatever you decide to do (you do make a very convincing kitten, though).

You're asleep now, your book open next to you, looking like an angel and not the little terror you really are. Your mom will have my head if I don't pick up the house, do the laundry, and play Mr. Dad, so I'd better get to it.

Always take the road less traveled, baby girl... and never, ever give up.

Love, Dad.

A single hot tear slips down my cheek as I sink down on the edge of the unmade bed.

They didn't tell me about the ISA, about Aurora and Genius and the SoL, because they loved me. Maybe it wasn't the *right* decision, but... he's gone now. The truth that they hid from me stole my dad.

I bury my head in my hands, warm tears slipping out between my fingers. *No, no, no...* this isn't fair, the name etched into the cold stone of the memorial isn't fair—and my dad is proud of me.

I sense rather than hear Aurora come in, feel her hand on my shoulder. "I'm sorry," she says softly.

"It's not... it's not fair," I whisper, giving a shuddery exhale. I don't hate them—I can't blame my parents for protecting me. But now Dad's gone and I'm stuck here with the people Dad called "my family," but they're strangers.

"I know." Aurora wraps an arm around me, pulling me into a hug. "I know."

I press my eyes shut against the tears. Secret jumps up, paws on my lap, and tries to nose my hands away from my face.

Aurora sits next to me until my tears are spent, the saddest look in her own expression when I finally straighten and glance at her.

Because my parents' choice affected her, too. And maybe when Dad died, I wasn't the only one who lost someone.

I was wrong, I realize as she squeezes my arm and stands up.

We may have grown up in different worlds, separated by a decision beyond our control, but that doesn't mean we can't be there for each other now. Because Dad was right.

She *is* family.

SHADOWS CREEP ACROSS THE WALL OF THE MICKEY ROOM, THE trees outside the window tossing and turning in the wind.

It's useless to try to sleep.

I sit up with a sigh, fumbling for my phone on the bedside table. I power it on, then open my photo gallery.

Today, two years ago... May 27. There are a few photos from that day: a flower, a blurry picture of Secret photo-bombing another flower, and a random page in a book.

I bite my lip, swiping up the gallery.

Dad's last birthday celebration. He holds up a pair of goose gag socks that I'd given him, sticking out his tongue as if they were the ugliest things he'd ever seen.

Tears prick my eyes as I swipe further up, flying over fall leaves and pumpkins, beaches and sand castles and running through sprinklers, until I reach the spring, when I got Secret.

There are dozens of pictures of Dad, of us, of our family.

I scroll down again, stopping at the last photo of us all: it's dated mid-September. A month before Dad left. Before our lives fell apart.

I squeeze my eyes shut, letting out a shaky breath. Mum and Dad had so many secrets. And Dad *knew* it might take him away forever. If I was really the most important thing, like he'd said on the microdot, why'd he still do it? Why'd he stay an agent? Why'd he leave me?

I'm crying again, and I'm terrified Mum might get killed, too, and it's past midnight and she's supposed to come soon—but what if she doesn't?

Right before Dad drove away for his "research" trip, he'd hugged me and whispered, "I'll be back before you know it." And he came back in a casket.

Rubbing away the tears that only make my head ache, I stare mindlessly at the ceiling. I reach to clasp my locket, but it's gone. Of course it's gone. Just like everything I love, except for Secret.

If I were a writer, like Dad, then maybe I'd try my hand at some poetry or something. Or journaling. Or... *something*.

Instead, I just wipe my eyes and slide out from under the too-warm covers, rummaging around in my bag until I locate my e-reader.

Back in bed, I push the blanket over to one side and scroll through my books. For once, I'm not in the mood for spy stories. There's too much of that in real life. So I opt for *Through the Looking-Glass* instead—a book so confusing it ought to make everything else make sense.

If only it works like that.

CHAPTER TWELVE
SECRETS AND SURPRISES

I'm up bright and early, bag packed, ready.

Mum's coming today.

If I say it enough, maybe I'll start to believe it. But I know I won't, not fully, until I see her with my own eyes.

Staring blankly at the words stenciled on the wall above the bed, I can imagine the reunion. Mum walking through the lobby door, shoulders back like they always are, strides brisk. She'll have her carry-on rolling behind her, the fancy black one Dad got her for Christmas years ago because it was on sale. Then she'll see me, drop whatever she's carrying, open her arms, and I'll rush into her embrace.

And *then* I'll know she's real.

A knock raps at my door, and I start, jumping to my feet. I almost trip over Secret as I hurry to the door, squinting out the mouse-head peephole.

My heart falls when I see Agent Grizzled Fox standing in the tunneled view, then my pulse begins to race. *Something's wrong.*

Did Mum's plane crash? Her car? Before I can let myself think too much, I swing open the door.

"Yes?"

The agent hesitates, and my heart falls into my socked feet. *Please...*

"Your locket... it's... what we were looking for."

I blink, my brain scrambling to catch up with the fact that my world is not, in fact, utterly shattered. "It... is? Can I have it back?"

"Should be able to."

I nod, more than a little relieved they won't need it forever. But... is Mum still coming? It's on the tip of my tongue to ask, but something holds me back. Fear of the truth?

Maybe if I cling tightly enough to my fantasy, it'll come true.

"You ready?"

I glance back at Grizzled Fox, who's looking at me expectantly. For the first time, I notice the dark shadows under his eyes—he looks downright exhausted.

"Uh... for what?"

"Thought you said you wanted it back."

Yeah, of course I do. Though I'm not quite sure what he has in mind, I nod, shrugging. "Okay, give me five minutes."

Closing the door, I stand there for a moment, a whirlwind of emotions hitting me at once.

No news that something's wrong. No "I'm so, so sorry," and pitying looks. *Everything's fine.* Mum will come today, and she'll fix everything. But right now, I need to focus.

"Right. Seek, where'd I put your vest..."

A couple of minutes later, we're ready. Grizzled Fox is waiting, and when I step out of my room, he leads the way down the hall.

"Where are we going?" I ask.

He pauses for a moment, then gives a one-shouldered shrug.

I grit my teeth against a flare of frustration, but follow him down the corridor. I do want my locket back, after all, and maybe I can learn something. The walls are painted with characters from a picture book I vaguely remember—brightly colored dogs doing all kinds of non-doggish activities and politely not liking hats.

I trail Grizzled Fox into a room full of cubicles, the soft gray carpeting a stark difference from the crazy colors everywhere else. As we walk through the maze, I almost inadvertently peek into the cubicles as I pass. Like in a library, glass-doored rooms are off of the main area, with "*Case Room*" and a number listed above each door. Grizzled Fox stops at the one labeled "17" and unlocks it with his keycard.

A conference table sits in the center of the long room, with a computer desk on the end opposite us and a smart board set into the wall. Grizzled Fox skirts the table and takes a seat behind the desk, using a physical key to unlock one of the desk drawers.

I stand back with Secret, watching silently. Did Dad have a cubicle here once? Did he work in a case room like this one? If he'd told me about the ISA, would he have brought me here on take-your-kid-to-work days and shown me what he did?

I run my fingers over Secret's leash and bite my lip, because I honestly have no idea what Dad did here. He always told me he wrote books for a living—but I should have known better. Should have realized that I was being lied to.

A soft thunk brings my attention back to Agent Grizzled Fox and the black jewelry box that wasn't there before.

Great. Now I don't know what to do—take it? Stand here awkwardly until the agent gives me a weird look like I'm supposed to *know* I should pick it up?

Luckily, before the moment gets too awkward, Grizzled Fox gives the box a nudge towards me. "It's not... harmed. And it's not going to blow up in your face."

"... Right." I eye the unassuming box for a moment before grabbing it. My locket rests inside, tucked into the cushion. I slide it out, running my fingers along the smooth metal. It doesn't *look* any different. Clicking it open, I examine the photo inside, but it also looks the same. "So, uh... why did you need it?"

He studies me for a moment, and I try to ignore the uneasy specimen-under-a microscope feeling it gives me before he seems to make up his mind to answer. "The dove is—was—your father's... code. That's why it was on the cover of *The Freesia Guard*."

"But... why my locket?" I thumb the engraved dove, searching Grizzled Fox's face for what he's not telling me. Why does no one ever *tell* me anything?

"He put a microSD card in it."

An SD card? "So you took it out?"

"Yeah."

This is like talking to a wall. If walls talked. Which would be creepy. I blink away the thought. "Well... so what was on it?"

He takes a moment to consider this—probably trying to figure out how much he wants to tell me, a simple *asset*. "An agent's obituary," he says at last.

Dad. But—no, that's not—

"Someone who died—unrelated causes—about the same time as Dallas was undercover," Grizzled Fox continues, and I nod slowly, looking down at the locket.

How can something so small have been the key to something that seems so much bigger? And have been literally right under my nose the entire time?

I feel a bit selfish for it, but it occurs to me that I'm not totally useless here, after all. But... does that mean Dad intended me to know more than Mum let on? I make a mental note to ask her when I see her later today.

Grizzled Fox shifts, rubbing his leg with a hand as he frowns. "What does that quote mean? On the back."

I flip over the locket, though I know what it says by heart. "'Take the road less traveled'? It's from one of my favorite songs. Something... uh, something that Dad liked to say. And... it's also in the dedication of *The Freesia Guard*," I offer, not sure if that information is at all helpful as I fasten the chain around my neck. The locket's heavy and solid against my skin, where it belongs, and I offer Grizzled Fox a small smile. "Thanks. For giving it back."

It's almost all I have left of Dad, and I can't lose it, too.

WHAT DID YOU THINK WAS GOING TO HAPPEN?

Blake struggles to keep his face emotionless, even as panic spikes through his gut. *This... but also not this.* Not sitting in his apex's office, trying not to have a panic attack, just because Blake can't shake the hold of the memories.

Apex Agent Subliminal Pawn frowns slightly. "Is there a problem, Agent Grizzled Fox?"

Yeah. Too many to count. "Did you... see the note in my file?" He knows it's there, the warning that he's no longer fit for "active missions."

The apex glances at his computer screen. "I hardly see why a trip to Florida would be an issue, agent. Especially since you have the most experience with this particular case."

Which is, of course, why Agent Tilted Showdown was appointed case leader. *Right.*

"If you have a problem with it, bring it up with Agent Silent Herald," Subliminal Pawn says with an apologetic look.

Yeah, no. Blake tips a nod, though the constant referral to agents higher up on the totem pole is getting old. Apex Agent Silent Herald runs the domestic terrorism task force, and his main goal is to shut down the Suns of Liberty through any means necessary, with little regard to the collateral damage left in his wake. He's part of the reason Damian and Dallas are now just names etched into the memorial.

No, Blake's mind whispers, *you're the reason.*

"You understand what this mission entails?" Subliminal Pawn taps the file set on the desk in front of Blake.

They both know that Apex Agent Silent Herald won't care if this mission bothers Blake. Which means Blake has no choice but to go, unless he just... doesn't. But as delusional as the ISA is, he doesn't favor getting kicked out. Mya would have his head. "Yeah."

He flips through the file; there isn't much. Nothing that he doesn't already know—although having it all written down in one place is probably not a bad idea. Especially to brief the others on his "team," which he'll be expected to do since he's been working on this for almost two years.

Pushing back the hard chair, he stands, tucking the file under his arm as he turns to leave. He's almost to the door when Agent Subliminal Pawn's low "Grizzled Fox?" stops him, and Blake slowly turns back.

Subliminal Pawn gives him a rueful smile. "Good luck out there. Kick some terrorists for me."

Sure—if they don't kick me first.

I'M SPRAWLED OUT ON A COUCH WATCHING SOME SHOW THAT Aurora swears is great—MacGyver something-or-other—when a knock sounds on the door. Genius springs up to answer it as Aurora grabs for the remote.

"Dog Girl! It's for you!" Genius hollers down the hall.

Heart leaping, I push up from the couch and hurry towards the entryway. *Mum's here?*

Almost tripping over Secret, I stumble to a stop when my eyes fall upon... not Mum, standing in the open doorway. Unless Mum cut her hair, dyed it blue, and shrank four inches.

I hold Secret's collar, eyeing Agent Tilted Showdown wearily.

"Good afternoon, Tirana. How are you?"

"Uh... good." A stock answer, and since I'm afraid I'm about to hear something bad, not exactly truthful. "Wh—"

But she's already talking. "I assume Agent Grizzled Fox informed you that he's your guardian for the time being, as your parents requested?"

"Uh... yeah." *My parents... requested? Huh?*

"Perfect." The agent nods. "And did he mention that his case calls him to Florida?"

"Florida?" That's where the accident happened. I look down at Secret, trying to make sense of this mess, before shaking my head as I meet Agent Tilted Showdown's eyes. "I... don't understand."

"In due time, Tirana." Again, she gives me that small smile, one that says she knows more than I do.

"Do you know when my mom's coming?"

Her smile tightens. "That's why I'm here, actually. She's been delayed, we're afraid, and you'll be going with us to Florida."

"Pardon?" It comes out as an embarrassing squeak.

I can't tell if her smile is gentle or full of pity as she looks at me, gaze unflinching. "We're leaving early tomorrow."

"Can we go, too?" a voice pipes up from behind me, and I turn around so fast I can feel a breeze. Aurora stands there, looking suspiciously innocent, Genius at her side.

How is this my reality? I fight the urge to rub my forehead... or hide under the nearest blanket and bury my head under a pillow until life makes sense again.

"Would your parents let you?"

I turn back to Agent Tilted Showdown, who regards the twins in a more serious way than I've seen anyone look at them, including their mom.

"Maybe," Aurora says, just as Genius says, "Sure!"

Agent Tilted Showdown nods. "You talk to them, and I'll talk to your uncle. If everyone agrees..."

"Florida, baby!" Genius whoops. "*All right!*"

"T-Boy, don't forget: this is a mission, not a vacation." Aurora elbows him hard, glancing at Agent Tilted Showdown apologetically.

He huffs. "I know, *Rory.*"

"Okay, then!" Agent Tilted Showdown claps her hands, as if she's perfectly aware this will turn into a fight of wits if left to carry on. "Tirana, someone will be at your room at 8:30."

I nod at her unspoken "Be ready."

Florida. The twins. A delayed mom and a missing aunt, parents who put the mysterious Agent Grizzled Fox in charge of me, a book, and a pack of secrets that no one will explain to me...

I let my eyes close for a brief moment before pasting on a smile. "Got it."

Please... But I don't even know how to finish that thought. *Just. . please.*

"You want me to... what?" Blake stares at the phone screen, but his sister just smiles in that "I've-got-a-secret-plan" way that's almost gotten them both killed before.

"Bring the twins on the mission, yup," Mya says easily. "It would be good practice for them."

"And... *why* would I do that?"

A video call to talk about this isn't the most ideal, but Mya's still trying to track down Patience, and it's not like his sister can just swing over to Wonderland so Blake can knock some sense into her.

Mya flicks a lock of red hair away from her face. "Because I said so." Her laugh comes in tinny over the speakers. "Really, though. It'd be good for them. They've wanted to do something in the action since forever, and what's the worst that could happen?"

You don't want to know. He blinks away the blurriness that fogs his vision, shaking his head. Of course she knew—Mya saw what happened to their friends, too. Which makes it all the crazier that she wanted *him* to take *her kids* to *Florida*.

"Look," Mya says, her voice softening. "They're good kids, old enough to take care of themselves. They won't be much trouble."

Blake scoffs, picking at a piece of fuzz on his bedspread. "You're delusional."

"Okay, fine. But how could I convince you to take them if I admitted how much trouble they are?" After a moment, she sighs. "Blake. You were supposed to laugh."

He glances up, only then realizing he'd half zoned out.

She gives him that assessing look he's known only too well since their childhood and beyond, the one that says she can tell something isn't right.

Blake resists the urge to squirm like a kid, instead meeting Mya's eyes through the screen. "They're not coming." Not more charges, along with Tirana and the other agents. Not more responsibility he can't deal with. Not... there.

Mya purses her lips. "If I could, I'd go along, but I'm a little busy here." She waves her hand to encompass the interior of her car. "But really, think about it! It would be a great experience for them. Wouldn't we have loved to have gone on a trip like that at their age? And it would be nice for Tirana, too. Poor girl keeps leaving everything she knows. The twins would be good for her."

Blake levels Mya with a glare. "They. Are. Not. Coming." He bites out the words as a low growl. His sister never did know when to let something drop.

"Blake." Mya's tone is gentle, the one she always used when one of the twins would get upset. "What's wrong? You're..." She shakes her head, auburn hair framing her face like fake angel wings.

Oh, he could fill in that unsaid blank a dozen ways. *Angry. Different. Broken.*

"The twins *do* know how to behave, you know. What's it about this mission that's got your tail in such a frenzy?" Mya cocks her head.

Potential answers flit across Blake's mind, but after a moment, he simply shrugs. The truth lodges itself in his throat, and he looks away. "Any luck on finding Pay yet?"

Mya sighs, her face blurring on the screen for a second before coming back into focus. "Don't think you can get out of my question that easily," she says, voice backed by the steel of a mother.

"What question? Didn't I just ask a question?"

Mya harrumphs. "First off, we already talked about Patience. Second, why are you afraid to go on this mission?"

"I'm not—"

She gives a knowing look, like she's caught him red-handed. "I know you better than that. They're gone, you know. There's been no recorded SoL activity there for over a year."

Blake closes his eyes. He's really starting to regret calling her, despite Mya's "urgent need to talk." Who does she think she is, a psychologist? He doesn't need a shrink to tell him that his head's messed up, and he's not about to spill his guts to his sister, especially on a stupid *video call.*

"Blake." Frustration laces her words now. "You can't live your entire life not talking about it."

But what's there to talk about? How he failed? How his best friend drowned and Blake couldn't save him? How the prospect of going back to Florida makes him so afraid he might be sick?

That stupid murky water fills his vision, the choking illusion of tightness squeezing his lungs.

"Blake..."

"It's fine." He doesn't meet Mya's eyes. "I'm *fine*. The twins are not coming. It's too dangerous."

She doesn't believe him. Heck, he doesn't even believe himself.

Mya shakes her head. "No, Blake. You just don't want to deal with facing that place again, and you're trying to protect the twins from absolutely nothing. Fort Myers is clean."

No, he's trying to protect the twins... from himself. Too bad Mya will never accept that.

"I'm sure they'll be on their best behavior," she adds lightly.

"*Shades*, Mya Brinley Harrison," he growls, resisting the urge to hang up. "I said *no*."

"*Sunglasses*, Blake Riley Hession. I asked *why*."

"Because—" He shoves a hand through his hair, blowing out a hard breath. If he tells her what a mess it was in his head, he'll be called off the mission and it will never be solved. He won't—*can't*—let Damian's and Dallas' sacrifice go to waste because of his own stupid weakness. "Because it's not *safe*!"

"Blake, look at me."

He clenches his shaking jaw, glaring at her through the screen.

"I know it's not easy to go back there, but you can't let it take over your life. Brings the twins—for Tirana's sake. They can take care of themselves, but Tirana's not familiar with any of this. It will help her to have a friend or two."

"Or *she* can stay here, too. Did you consider that?"

Mya tsks. "You know that Agent Tilted Showdown wants her to go."

"Well, it's stupid!" Blake grinds his teeth, forcing himself to take a deep breath before he throws the phone across his studio apartment.

"And it's stupid that you're refusing to even consider making it easier on Tirana. Her entire family is gone right now, Blake. We're all she has."

And whose fault is that? Damian, Dallas... even *Patience* is MIA now—

Blake throws up his hands. "You know what? Whatever. Let them." *I'll deal with it.* He'd have to.

Mya grins like he'd consented to co-host a Christmas party for the entirety of Wonderland, but then again, is taking the twins much different?

Once the call ends, Blake stares blankly at his wall. Maybe Mya was right; maybe there wouldn't be any trouble. But what if there is?

He groans, tossing his phone onto his bed. *What on earth did I just agree to?*

CHAPTER THIRTEEN
CURIOUSER AND CURIOUSER

I haven't even been here for long, but already I'll miss this wacko Mickey room. It's familiar, and whatever we're going into now... isn't. Am I even coming back?

Seek jumps onto the freshly made bed and bows at me, shaggy tail wagging. He adds a low whine for good measure.

"Well..." The alarm clock on the bedside table reads 8:05. I glance at my bag, packed and ready by the door, and shrug. "Okay."

He jumps down and tries to stick his face in my backpack as I rummage through it, and I push him away with a laugh. "Hm... play or training?"

He sits, looking from me to the bag.

I pull out a blue tug toy and toss it across the room, and he darts after it. Soon a vigorous game of tug is going on, his play growls as fierce as a baby tiger's.

Another glance at the clock reveals that thirteen minutes have passed, and I let Secret have the toy. "All done, mister."

He shakes it a few times before jumping back up on the bed and settling down to chew on it.

Five minutes to 8:30, I repack the toy, gear Secret up, then lace my boots before perching on the edge of the bed.

"Where's Mum?" I whisper into the empty air, as if the grinning Mickey painted on the wall will have an answer. *Where's Aunt Patience? And what about Dad?*

Are "assets" not important enough to tell them about the status of their own family?

A rap on the door shatters my thoughts, and I sigh as I stand to answer it. *And here we go again. More getting dragged around like an ailurophile to a dog show.*

"Good *morn*-ing!" Aurora crows as I crack open the door. "Ready to hit the road?"

"Uh... sure." *No.* I swing my backpack on, clip on Seek's lead, and follow her out into the hallway, where Genius waits.

Both the twins are dressed to travel. Aurora has her hair in a tidy braid, zip-off khaki pants, fancy hiking boots, and a t-shirt with the words "We're all mad here" written on a whimsical top-hat. Genius also wears zip-off pants, but his shirt reads "The thing that separates you from a genius is the space between us," which I snicker at.

The twins lead me down a hall I haven't seen before; this one is criss-crossed with colorful chutes and ladders on the walls and ceiling, as if we've stepped into a children's game.

What would it have been like to grow up here? If Dad and Mum had been honest about their work, would that have been possible? Could I have spent my childhood with Aurora and Genius, instead of with friends who drifted away after Dad's death?

Maybe I'd even know what was going on.

But no, they'd decided to keep it from me, this world of the ISA. My steps falter when I realize I don't even know what it stands for. The Intentionally Silly Agency? The Imaginary Serious Agency?

"I know your name," Genius says in a mock threatening tone, drawing my attention back to the twins.

I cock my head, raising a brow. Took him long enough. "Yeah?"

He nods, turning to face me, walking backwards without breaking a stride. "Yup."

"So... what is it?" I steal a glance at Aurora, but she's actually facing the right way, and I can't see her face.

"Tango india romeo alpha november alpha." A smirk breaks his dead-panned gibberish, and he spins to walk forward again, leaving me blinking after him.

"That... is not my name."

"Yes, it is." He throws a glance over his shoulder.

"No, it's not," Aurora cuts in.

"But—"

"You're wrong, and that's that." Aurora hikes her backpack up higher on her back, then turns to face us both. Does walking backwards as if it's normal run in the family? "Look, guys, we don't have time for pointless dares or jokes. You want Uncle Blake to send us back?" This is directed to Genius, who scuffs the toe of his shoe on the carpet. "And... you're also just wrong, T-bone."

He groans. "I'm never wrong!"

"Oh, yeah? Like that time when—"

"Fine!" He cuts a glance at me. "That was *once.*"

"Or the time when Dad—"

Genius glares at her. "Oh, look, we're here! Ladies first!"

I'd been too interested in their exchange to look around much, but we've stopped next to a wooden picket fence, behind which is... the mouth to a slide? A kaleidoscope of colorful light streams in through tinted windows around us, casting rainbow hues on the red carpet, Secret's back, and even the twins' faces.

Genius, wearing what's quickly becoming clear is his signature smirk, unlatches the gate and pushes Aurora through, despite her protests.

"No fair," she grumbles, even as she grabs a large brown sack from a barrel next to the slide's mouth and slips into it. She hops the two feet to the mouth, where Genius ever-so-helpfully gives her a mock salute.

Her only response is a roll of the eyes, then she's gone, whisked away down a tunnel of plastic, and leaving me alone with her way-too-suspicious brother.

"So, what *is* your name?" He narrows his eyes at me.

I cross my arms. "It sure isn't anything to do with 'Tango.' What about *yours*?"

"It..." He shrugs. "Has something to do with tango."

"Wait—"

"Your turn! Don't want to keep them waiting, you know."

"Uh..." I don't want to seem that easily distracted, but he does have a point. "What about Secret?"

"What about the secret canine?"

By the gleam in the boy's eyes, I have a feeling that I'd better hold on tight... a feeling that doubles as I hurtle down the slide after my backpack, Secret in my lap.

And I can't help but grin, because this is what it feels like to be a kid again. Free, caught up in the moment, colors swirling around me, laughing when I finally emerge into the lobby, slowing to a stop and scrambling to get out of the way before Genius rams me.

Friends... and fun.

Two things I once thought I'd lost... and two things I think I may have found again.

FORT MYERS, FLORIDA

A FEW HOURS AND A PLANE RIDE LATER, WE TOUCH DOWN IN FLORI-da. Palm trees, humidity, and a clear blue sky don't agree with the clouded, gray-scale vision I'd always imagined, but that's what we step out into.

I inhale slowly, tasting the sea in the air—we must be close to the ocean. For a brief moment, I close my eyes. The *scree* of a gull... a light breeze and the hot sun on my face... and a tap on my shoulder.

Turning, I see Aurora standing behind me. "You planning on standing there forever?"

"Sorry." I bite my lip, looking around the private airstrip. Genius is goofing off with Agent Pale Flame, a young man with curly hair and a high-pitched laugh. Agent Tilted Showdown is talking to Agent Grizzled Fox a ways off, their serious faces contrasting the boys' antics.

"I guess we're waiting for our ride," Aurora says, shading her eyes with a hand.

Tipping a nod, I check on Secret, who's panting in the late-morning heat. After offering him some water, which he accepts eagerly Aurora suggests that we stretch our legs.

"Don't know about you, but I hate being cooped up for so long. Mom always says that the only way she can get us to be still is to plop us in front of the TV." Aurora laughs, but only a ghost of a smile tugs at my lips.

"You... you wouldn't happen to have heard anything about my mum, would you?"

Her brow furrows. "Not recently."

"What about... ever?" I give her a side-eyed glance, heart beating faster.

"Ever?" Aurora frowns, lacing her hands behind her back as she begins to walk forward. "Like, literally ever? Uh... she's an Ignis agent. Was married to your dad, of course... I'm sure it wasn't easy for them to juggle both agencies. Ignis is, like, the opposite of the ISA." She shrugs. "But Mom said they loved each other enough to make it work."

Biting my lip, I nod again. Love that kept them together... and love that kept me away? A dull pain spirals through my heart, sharpening as the vague impression of the life I could have had collides with the memory of the coffin being lowered into the cold ground.

"What's Ignis?" I ask, attempting to keep myself in the present.

"A private agency based in London. We don't work together with them that often, but that's how your parents met."

"They always told me they met in London. Dad was on holiday... at least, that's what I was told."

Aurora nods. "They were on a mission together." She snickers. "I wonder if it was love at first sight, and they were chasing each other around London like lovesick fools, or if they hated each other."

I choke at the thought of my sensible mother chasing after a young

Dad. "I think it was more enemies-to-lovers. Mum always said she thought Dad was a 'half-witted fool.'"

"Aw."

I can't tell if she's making fun of it, saying that's cute, or actually disappointed. And trying to figure it out is better than letting the tears choking me up win. How does Aurora know more about my family than I do? It's not fair.

None of this is fair.

"Hey, guys!" Genius calls over to us as a black van pulls up. "Ride's here!" And my chance to learn more is over.

GREEN. THAT SUMS UP THIS PLACE, ALL RIGHT.

Blake stares out at the bright foliage rolling by, but his soul is as empty as when he'd woken up in the hospital and been told that Dallas hadn't made it.

Mission failed.

Now he's back, not at all ready to face his demons.

There's too much water here—rivers, neighborhoods built on swamp lands, swales, canals, and the ocean. There's no escaping it.

And it'll be the bane of his existence if he doesn't get his head on straight. The least he can do for Dallas is to finish this mission, and having a mental breakdown won't help anything.

Besides, he needs to keep Tirana and the twins safe. Having his niece and nephew tag along is bad enough, but adding the daughter of the man he failed? Mya might think that Fort Myers is SoL-free, but terrorists are like cancer. You can never be certain that they're completely gone.

Yes, this mission is going to be *so* fun. With Isabelle and Patience MIA, Tirana and the twins to babysit, and an overwhelming sense of dread, what can go wrong?

As the van turns into the drive of the too familiar "Wilson, Inc."—

the business front Base Buckleberry is hidden behind—Blake's hands curl into fists. His childhood heroes, Batman and Green Arrow and the others, faced trials. In the end, they always came out on top. But nowadays, those heroes feel as far away as peace on a terror-ridden, sleepless night.

Shades, it's hard to walk into that weatherbeaten business front. Everything is the same: the dreary reception area, the colorful halls and murals of bad weather.

Does everything have to be a reminder?

Those long weeks, barely in touch with Dallas as his friend dug himself deeper into the SoL. Watching, waiting, ready to extract Dallas at a moment's notice. And when the time came... Blake had failed.

He deserves the ghosts. The memories. The fear.

Stepping into the dorm room he'll be sharing with his nephew and Flame, Blake drops his bag on one of the beds and stares at the muraled wall. Golden beams of sunlight stream through thick, gray clouds, like a promise of painted hope.

Lies.

And that's only the beginning.

Not one to wait around, Agent Tilted Showdown calls a meeting to discuss the plans, and it's not long until Blake is sitting in a conference room with a misfit group of agents.

"We," Tilted Showdown starts, pointing a laser beam at the map on the wall-screen, "are here. For those who don't know, the smaller ISA bases often operate under the cover of business. Wilson, Inc., tests the durability of phone cases. Our target location is here." She laser-points a circle northeast of their location: Fort Myers Cemetery.

Tilted Showdown drones on, outlining the mission, but Blake hardly listens. He knows this already—he planned it with her.

Books. Codes. Graveyards.

What else can be expected from Dallas? "Simple" and "Dallas" had never worked well together, something that Blake had learned early on, when a rescue mission turned into a fight for survival because Blake couldn't figure out the code Dallas had left in a photograph of a rubber ducky.

No, this graveyard wild-goose chase isn't a bit out of Dallas' style. But as Agent Tilted Showdown gestures to a large-scale map of the cemetery pixelated on the screen, Blake wishes once again that Dallas was a little less... Dallas.

"It shouldn't be complicated," Tilted Showdown says, tracing her laser pointer over the route they'll take through the cemetery.

Not complicated. What world does she live in?

Get in. Get out.

No getting ambushed by the SoL, attacked by a killer croc, or freaking out over nothing.

Blake can do this.

He doesn't really have a choice.

FORT MYERS CEMETERY
FORT MYERS, FLORIDA

A TREE SHADOWS THE SOLEMN, DARK WOODEN "FORT MYERS CEME-tery" sign, and the van turns from the potted road into the fenced-off graveyard. I gaze out the window, sadness lingering in me at both the fresh flowers on some gravestones and the total disrepair of the others.

Who loved these people? Who missed them? Who felt like their whole world was shattered when they learned of their loved ones' deaths? Who visited every week, or month, or never, because now they're gone, too?

Morbid thoughts, but we are at a cemetery. Why would Dad hide it—whatever *it* is—here?

I nibble my lip, my eyes falling on a hooded figure bent over a grave-stone a ways into the cemetery.

Who's he missing? What's his story?

Then he turns, perhaps at the sound of the approaching van, and ice shoots through my veins. *No way...* But he has the same square jaw, the same nose—I can't see more because of his gray hoodie.

Dad...?

"LOOKS LIKE IT MIGHT RAIN," TILTED SHOWDOWN REMARKS, turning down another road as they snake their way through the cemetery.

The sky is pure blue, no clouds in sight. Blake glances at her, but she laughs lightly.

"Weather is finicky, you know."

Maybe she says more, but Blake stops listening when his eyes fall on a figure in a gray hoodie stooped over a gravestone. Something about the figure seems familiar, and Blake squints.

He's about to glance away, chalking it up to nerves, when the figure turns, facing the van.

Blake blinks, and the man has turned away, leaving a bouquet of blue flowers by the headstone before he climbs into a silver GMC and guns it away.

You're going crazy, Hession. There's simply no other reasonable explanation.

Because Dallas Caineson is dead, and ghosts don't exist.

"It should be right up ahead." The voice seems to come from far away, and he blinks again, his vision narrowing before clearing.

He can't let his broken mind render him unable to complete this mission. If he can dream up ghosts, he can dream them down.

Because that's all that guy was: a ghost. Simply a figment of his imagination.

Get over it, Grizzled Fox.

Agent Tilted Showdown pulls over and hops out, the kids scrambling over each other, and Blake forces himself to push open his door and step out into the humid, too-warm air. Stupid humidity—why can't the air be cold and crisp and fresh? Let him get a real breath in?

He leans against the van as the others swarm over the plot. Good thing this mission doesn't call for inconspicuousness.

"Here it is!" Flame calls, gesturing wildly to a tall headstone looming over the other stones on the plot.

Everyone crowds around the grave, yet Blake doesn't make a move towards it. Not yet. *Just what was your plan, Dallas?*

He glances over his shoulder, but no gray-hooded figures linger, waiting to spring, to say the past two years were nothing but a cruel joke.

"Aren't you coming, Uncle Blake?"

Aurora's watching him, her youthful face alight with excitement. Maybe Mya was right. Maybe this is good for them. If they don't get gunned down by the SoL the second Blake lets down his guard.

Just get this done, man. He pushes away from the van and joins the group by the grave, standing back in order to get a full view of Klassen's headstone.

It's a granite pillar maybe three feet tall. A dove, wings outstretched in flight, is carved into the glossy stone, with the words *"Liberabo tandem"* etched in script above it. Below is *"Lawrence Klassen,"* the dates of his birth and death, and the words *"Gone But Not Forgotten."*

Yeah, it's hard to forget a guy whose grave is used as the hiding place for a treasure hunt. What *was* Dallas thinking?

"So... what now?" Thomas asks, dropping back to stand next to Blake.

Aurora joins him, followed by Tirana and the dog.

Fighting a clingy sense of claustrophobia, Blake backs up a step, eyeing the headstone. They're all looking at him like he's supposed to know, but he doesn't.

Not like Dallas' here to tell us. Blake clenches his jaw as the hooded guy flashes before his eyes. It's disconcerting what a mind can dream up under stress.

The dove on the headstone marks a picture of innocence that doesn't match the rest of the scene, which is also disconcerting.

"Do you have any ideas, Agent Grizzled Fox?"

He glances up to see Tilted Showdown looking at him with that particular expression in her eyes, and he gives a one-shouldered shrug. "Nope." Being Dallas' partner doesn't mean he knows the man's mind, as this mission is continuing to prove.

He steps away, letting the kids close in on the headstone again. Maybe they'll find something, maybe not. But whatever they're looking for can be anywhere, although the date of death on the headstone aligns with when Dallas and Blake were down here.

Shaking his head, Blake walks away, listlessly inspecting the headstones. He doesn't have a clue what he's even looking for, no clue why he's even there. It's not like he's any use to the team.

Names and dates etched in stone—wasn't the pain supposed to ease with time, like the weathered graves?

He bends down, traces a finger—stupid, shaking thing—over words so faded in the limestone he can't even make them out. Bridget, maybe? Why does it even matter?

Why a graveyard, Dallas? Some sort of cruel foreshadowing?

"Uncle Blake!"

He turns at Aurora's shout, half expecting there to be trouble, but his niece is messing around with something on Klassen's gravestone. As Blake draws closer, he can see she's tugging on the dove.

"That's insane," Thomas mutters as his sister pulls the dove straight out of the stone. It slides out with a bit of give, and Aurora holds it up silently.

Blake steps over, and she hands it to him. A small drawer is attached to the back of the stone dove... empty.

Are they too late? He inspects it closer, ignoring with difficulty the five people breathing down his neck.

He can't have come this far just to fail again.

Yet... something looks off about the drawer. He gives it a light shake, and the low rattling from inside confirms his suspicions. He presses the bottom, and with a pop, it loosens. Concealed underneath is a USB drive.

Exclamations come from several directions, but all Blake feels is a profound sense of relief that they've finally found it. Almost two years, and the game is over.

I SIT ON THE EDGE OF MY BED, STARING OUT THE WINDOW AT A PALE blue sky and palm trees. Secret is a warm and comforting bundle, fast asleep with his head in my lap.

Aurora and Genius are discussing, with the occasional laugh, what the thumb drive might contain.

How much do they know about this mission? Do they know that Dad hid it? That he got whatever information's on it? I sigh, running my fingers through the curly hair on Secret's head.

"The blueprints for all the Suns of Liberty bases?" Genius suggests, tapping his chin.

"No, a recipe for the newest bomb," Aurora counters.

Genius laughs. "You and your bombs. I'm honestly surprised you haven't blown anything up yet... although, not for lack of trying." I can hear the smirk in his voice.

Aurora huffs. "That's so funny, I forgot to laugh."

Genius gasps. "Really? Aurora, *forgetting* something? What is the world coming to?!"

Aurora smacks him with a pillow.

A tiny grin quirks the corners of my mouth, but I turn my gaze back to the window. A small bird flies across the sky, alighting in one of the palm trees.

Was it really Dad I saw? But... surely not. It's not *possible.* He'd never pretend to die, then return to haunt us. Not Dad.

I pull my locket out from under my t-shirt and open it, staring down at my father's smiling face.

Was it the same face that looked out from under that hoodie?

I close my eyes, trying to picture the stranger in my mind. But the image is blurry and unclear, giving no hints to whether I'm just imagining it or whether it really *is* him.

Even Grizzled Fox said that Dad was gone, and from what I can gather, the surly agent was one of the last people to see him before... everything.

"There was an accident."

That's how Mum had said it, leaning on my door frame like it was the only thing keeping her upright. That was the day the world stopped turning.

Only it hadn't stopped. The sun still shone, the birds still sang, the condolences and casseroles piled up, until I was more than sick of both—I couldn't eat most of the food well-wishers brought over anyway, since it wasn't gluten-free.

Did we mourn a person who never died?

The bird flies out of the palm tree and off into the distance with short bursts of wingstrokes, like "I'm falling! Up! I'm falling! Up!" Again and again, until it's out of sight.

I sigh softly, smoothing back a curl on Secret's head. It's all so *confusing*. Agents, ghosts, spy gadgets hidden in gravestones...

I glance up to see Aurora watching me curiously, her head cocked.

"Is something wrong?" Her brow furrows. "You're awfully quiet."

I stare down for a few moments, biting my lip, before looking up with a swallow. "How many stories have you read where the dead person isn't actually dead?"

She cocks her head, thinking. "I don't read a lot, but there sure are a bunch of movies like that. Star Wars, for one."

"And... what about in real life?"

Genius ambles over, and he puts his hand on his chin like that thinker statue. After a moment, he proclaims, "Nope! Never met a dead person."

Aurora nods. "I have to agree with him on that one. At least, I don't think so. Why?"

"Because I think I saw Dad at that cemetery."

CHAPTER FOURTEEN
THE ROAD TO DOOM

Codes, cyphers, and secrets.

What else can Blake expect from the ISA other than headaches upon headaches?

He pages through the *The Freesia Guard*, not sure exactly what it is he's looking for. A PIN to access the drive, yeah, since of course Dallas would use one with a keypad. But it's not as if the numbers will just be posted in the front. No, of course they'd be hidden. Woven into the story, if they're there at all.

"Any luck?" Tilted Showdown walks over, not quite hovering over Blake's shoulder.

"No. You?" He lets the book fall shut, glancing up at the blue-haired agent.

She shakes her head. "Nothing. Agent Pale Flame is attempting algorithms, but we only have so many tries."

Yeah. His gaze falls back on the cover of *The Freesia Guard.*

"Do you think Tirana's locket might have it?"

Blake shrugs. "Probably not." He's honestly surprised that Dallas used the locket at all, but then again, Dallas wasn't exactly planning on not making it back. Certainly, he wasn't counting on putting his daughter in danger. "We'll check if nothing turns up here."

She hums, as if agreeing with his reluctance to drag Tirana into this any more than strictly necessary. Which, since Tilted Showdown is the reason Tirana is down in Florida with them, is hogwash.

And thinking of Tirana... "Any updates on Isabelle?"

A frown creases Tilted Showdown's eyebrows. "I'm afraid not. I've heard nothing."

Nothing. That doesn't mean anything... but Isabelle always did know what she was doing. Blake sighs. He can only hope she has a plan in all of this.

Tilted Showdown takes a seat in the chair next to his and slides *The Freesia Guard* over to herself, cracking it open. "Help me out here. What have you tried, and what would Agent Bel Ria have done?"

Blake leans back in his chair, crossing his arms. "There's no section for 'secret passwords' in the table of contents, and the blue light didn't turn anything up."

She chuckles, paging through the book. "That would make things easier, wouldn't it? And the page numbers or chapter titles aren't anything special?"

"Nope." A moment passes, then he frowns, leaning forward. "Hey, let me see that for a second."

"Be my guest." She passes it back, and Blake opens to the index, setting the book face-up on the table.

Road... road... road... There. His finger stills on "*Chapter 14: The Road Less Traveled*," and he looks up to meet Tilted Showdown's expectant gaze. "How good are you at codes?"

"What do you have?"

"Look." Blake gestures to the page. "I bet that this is a connection. Dallas used 'take the road less traveled' as a theme, and it's engraved into the locket."

Tilted Showdown nods slowly. "Worth a try. Agent Pale Flame?"

The curly-headed kid spins around in his chair. "Yeah? What?"

"We have a code for you," Tilted Showdown says, gesturing to the book lying between her and Blake.

Flame's eyes light up as he pushes out of his chair and hurries over. "Oh, cool! So, what's the deal?"

"Connections," Blake mutters, but leaves it up to Tilted Showdown to explain. *Take the road less traveled, sure, unless it leads to a pile of nothing but dirt...* or a storm-tossed river. Blinking quickly, he focuses on the mission at hand. Tilted Showdown's expounding on what Blake said, Flame mumbling to himself as he scribbles on the piece of scrap paper.

Watching him, Blake wonders vaguely why the kid was assigned to this mission... and without a partner. Most neophytes, the joining rank of an agent, are paired with a rook-level agent, but Flame's alone.

At least when Blake officially joined the ISA after the whole "rescue-a-little-girl-and-find-your-missing-sister-and-avenge-your-dead-parents" thing, Dallas, then a rook, accepted him as his neophyte, like he'd promised. *"I'll watch out for you, and you'll watch out for me. Deal?"*

A deal that got Dallas killed in the end.

"Okay, I think I got something." Flame straightens, and Blake blinks himself back into the present. "Try... 14168. Chapter fourteen, page 168."

"Are you sure?" Tilted Showdown palms the locked drive, leveling a serious expression on Flame. "We don't have tries to waste."

"Yeah, I think so." Flame looks down at his notes before nodding. "We have to try something, don't we? And it won't explode, right?"

Both Tilted Showdown and Flame turn to look at Blake, who raises his hands, palms out. "How would I know?"

"Does it work?" Flame turns to Tilted Showdown, who lets out a breath before punching the number in on the tiny keyboard.

Blake leans over to watch. The light on the drive blinks orange twice, then flashes green. He stares at it for a long moment, tension creeping up his neck. *Let's see what you've got for us, Dallas.*

"OKAY, DOG GIRL, I'M GONNA NEED EVERYTHING YOU GOT ON YOUR dad." Genius waves the tablet. "I'm a pro at evil twin finding, trust me."

"Hardly." Aurora snorts. "Have you ever won a game of hide-and-seek against me?"

He sticks his tongue out at her.

"He doesn't have a twin, for one." I shake my head. "He and Aunt Patience are a couple years apart." *Are? Where?* I don't even know anymore.

"You never know." Genius types something onto his tablet before glancing up again. "Okay, codename?"

Aurora moves to hover over his shoulder. "You seriously don't know?"

"You're worse than a yappy Chihuahua in a rap band." He glares at his sister, but she only crosses her arms. With a huff, he turns back towards me. "So. Codename?"

"Uh... I don't know." I bite my tongue with a little shrug. "I don't really know much of... well, anything."

"She has a point." Aurora taps her chin, looking down at Genius' tablet. "It's Agent Bel Ria."

I blink. "Like the dog from the book?" *How did he end up with that?* I can picture Dad's old dime novel copy with the scrappy white dog and monkey on the cover. It's a perfect codename for him.

By the twins' shared blank looks, they're lacking in literature. I might not understand this spy world, but hey, at least I know books.

"Bel Ria..." Genius mutters, typing away on his tablet. "Ah, here we go. Dallas Caineson, Regent, KIA..."

"How do you even get all that?" I squint at him, ignoring the last part. "What does 'regent' mean?"

Aurora scooches closer to breathe down her brother's neck. "It's a ranking. There's neophyte, rook, regent, and apex. Mom and Uncle Blake are regents."

"Oh." *Only the ISA.* "What are you two?"

Aurora shifts. "Uhm..."

"Neophyte." Genius doesn't look up.

"That." Aurora doesn't seem particularly thrilled. "We don't normally go by rank, though."

Maybe she's concerned about being the lowest, but I'm pretty sure "asset" is even closer to the bottom. I nod, turning to Genius. "And... does it say anything else?"

"Huh?" He glances up. "Not really. Any relatives, people who might be around here?"

I shake my head. "I... don't know. He was ousted by his family—he and Aunt Patience were—so..." I give a little laugh. "Sorry I'm not much help. He never talked about them, really." Always said that what he had now was enough.

But were we really enough for him? If I'd been a better person, a better daughter, would he have decided to stay home instead of drowning in some river? I shudder, trying not to think about the fact that I'm in Florida... the very state that he was murdered in.

Secret stands up and trots over, wagging at me like he wants to play.

"Hi, dog." Genius eyes Secret. "You wanna help?"

I shake my head, as if the motion will dispel the air of sadness lingering over me. Pushing to my feet, I cross to where I'd left my backpack. Unzipping it, I call Secret over and toss him the ugly stuffed plague doctor. "All yours, bud."

"What *is* that thing?" Aurora stands, taking a step towards Secret, but he darts away, tearing around the room.

"Plague doctor."

Her nose crinkles. "Like... from the bubonic plague?"

"Yup! It's great, right?" I glance down at Seek, who's paused his wild dash and stands a few feet away, an unmistakable "chase me!" plea in the tilt of his head. "Well, at least he thinks so."

Aurora makes a move towards him, and he darts away again, full-out zooming around the room.

We play with him for several more minutes before Genius clears his throat. "Ever heard of an Alan Westcott?"

I shake my head slowly, but freeze as Genius holds up the tablet. A grainy, security-camera image of a clean-shaven man in his mid-forties stares at me through the screen, his dark blond hair, blue eyes, and square jaw making me feel like I'm seeing a ghost. The time stamp reads from several months ago.

Air locks itself in my lungs, tightening my vision until a cold nose on my hand reminds me to breathe. This doesn't make sense—nothing makes sense anymore. One thought pounds in my brain, over and over, sending a tidal wave of destruction through everything I believed I knew.

Did my own father fake his death?

OF COURSE NOTHING CAN BE SIMPLE. OF COURSE THERE HAS TO BE codes hidden inside codes inside codes. Of course it can't just make *sense*.

Slowly, the numbers listed in the file on the screen are finding matches in the words of *The Freesia Guard*.

"76, 1, 5," calls out Tilted Showdown, and Flame flips to the page, counts the line and word, and replies, "Doom."

Blake writes down the word, hand already cramping less than halfway down the page due to the effort of making his writing readable. The gibberish on the notebook page in front of him doesn't help the vise in his head, and the steady drone of new letters and words don't have an end in sight. *"Minions in secret sections implement official nickel rest embedded pouring ocean timber against gentle enemies never trust bacon ensue letdown Ragnar is anchor indigo never fills identity leading to absolute tarradiddle in operation November oxygen finagles many octagon robots doom."*

Utter nonsense.

"41, 9, 18."

"Offers."

Yup, this is about as exciting as watching an icicle melt. But the words are forming actual words, no matter how absurd, which is better than their first several options using other methods.

Dallas could never make anything simple, could he? It'll be Blake's downfall. That, or this headache.

A knock, one soft and two harder, gives him an excuse to take a break. He's not fully sure what he was expecting on the other side of the door, but it's not his niece, fist raised as if to knock again.

"Am I interrupting?" Aurora glances around the room, a look of hesitancy on her face.

"Yes."

She grimaces. "Are you almost done?"

Is it just him, with his brain too jumbled to make sense of anything, or is she acting strangely uncomfortable?

"Who's there?" Tilted Showdown's voice materializes to Blake's right, and he flinches and steps aside.

"I—" Aurora starts.

"Agent Celestial Flicker." A rebuke is sharp in Tilted Showdown's tone. "What are you doing here?"

She shifts slightly, then squares her shoulders. "Well, Tirana says she saw her dad. And I thought that you might want to know."

Blake can't stifle his sharp intake of breath as the ground sways dangerously. *You can't mean...*

But the sincerity and concern on Aurora's young face says otherwise.

In a voice that somehow stays level, he orders Flame and Tilted Showdown to continue working on the code, then follows Aurora down the mess of halls to Tirana's room.

The girl's description of the figure at the cemetery matches what he so willingly passed off as a fluke of his broken imagination.

It's not *possible...* but evidence doesn't lie, only the interpretation.

And ghosts don't exist.

"You'll find out what's going on, right?" Aurora asks in a low voice, following him out to the hallway.

He pauses, then nods. "Gotta try." For the confused strickenness Tirana's eyes, and for his own racing mind.

"You'll figure it out." Aurora offers a small smile. "And we'll help. We codenamed him Baskerville."

Again, he can only tip a nod. It's nice of them to offer, but what can his niece and nephew do? No, this is his case. His ghosts. His battle.

Rather than returning to the case room, Blake ducks into the men's room. It's empty, and he braces against the cool stone of the countertop, trying to force air into unyielding lungs.

Someone is playing a game with him… but who? The agent he watched die, or some miserable excuse for a hoax?

With shaking hands, he turns on the faucet, cupping his hands under the stream of icy water. Cold slithers up his arms, wrapping his pounding heart in a frigid embrace, freezing his limbs, dotting his vision with gray.

No.

Sucking in a rugged breath, he smacks the faucet off with an elbow, sagging against the counter as his head spins.

Com'on…

His breath shudders, and he blinks open eyes he didn't realize he'd closed, the bright fluorescent light fading the phantomous murky water lingering just below the surface.

"Never trust bacon… leading to absolute tarradiddle… doom."

Dallas' mission revolved around fires throughout recent years that the ISA suspected were arson, despite the lack of evidence. All were connected by a thread of laws and politics. Connected to the fire that killed Blake's own parents.

Doom.

It sounds like ruin. Destruction.

And Dallas, the man who's *supposed* to be dead, is linked to everything.

CHAPTER FIFTEEN
BASKERVILLE

"So Baskerville plays Roblox." Aurora snickers, leaning over Genius' shoulder. "Lame. His username is *Imascreaminggoat.*' I betcha he screams like my brother here—like a girl."

Genius huffs. "Yeah, yeah, Miss Smarty-Pants. Believe what you wish."

I side-eye both of them, unsure if I even want to know what this is about. Aurora doesn't leave me the choice, though: she wrestles the tablet from Genius and starts tapping around.

Since when do goats scream, anyway? The twins have been finding random details on Dad's-maybe-evil-twin, or "Baskerville," as they call him, but I can't see how his gaming profile helps us at all.

"That is *mine*, thank you very much," Genius says, grabbing his tablet back from his sister before glancing at me. "Looks like Baskerville is pretty active in partaking in brain-rotting activities... Roblox, Fallout 4, Call of Duty... Was your dad a gamer?"

I shrug. "He wrote books. He didn't play games like that."

"Are you sure?" Genius taps the screen. "Hey, dude's got some good taste."

Aurora smacks him. "Don't you dare let Mom hear that. She hates shooter games. Anyway, people going into hiding often change."

"Hiding?" I echo. The thought of Dad hiding from his family cuts me to the bone.

Aurora nods. "Disappear from the grid. If you have enough cash, it's not impossible."

"But... why?" *Why* would Dad do this?

"More to the point, if this is Bel Ria, then he's made it remarkably easy to track him down." Genius frowns. "I mean, I'm good, but this is just too easy."

"Almost as if he wants to be found..."

Chills race up my spine at Aurora's mutter.

"But... *why*?" I repeat.

"Remember, we don't know that Baskerville *is* your dad," Genius points out. "Evil twins and all that shebang."

But what else—who else—could that picture have been? And Agent Grizzled Fox had looked... scared.

Maybe that's what makes me the most uneasy. Or is the uneasiness due to the total disappearance of my entire family? With a sigh, I pull out my phone, as if a message from Mum will appear if I wait long enough. Only my own line of unread texts meet my gaze, but I send her another one anyway.

ME

> Hey, where are you? There's a lot going on over here...I'd really like to know if you're okay.

She's delayed. There are many, normal reasons for a delay. But if Mum's an agent... well, then "normal" doesn't fit, does it? Maybe she just lost her phone, or it was stolen. And she's on her way home right now.

If only I can believe that.

Baskerville. The codename of the man-who-can't-be-Dad, taken from Arthur Conan Doyle's *The Hound of the Baskervilles.* Aurora and Genius' choice. If Bel Ria the dog is the hero of Bel Ria the book, then the hound of the Baskervilles is the villain—or, rather, the puppet—of the Sherlock Holmes story.

But Dad's the hero. He's *got* to be the hero. I refuse to consider that he might not be, but doubt is slowly creeping in, and I hate it.

What had Frodo said? That he wished the ring had never come to him? And then Gandalf responded with his famous quote about using the time given to us.

The Freesia Guard isn't a ring to rule them all, or even a magical flower, but it's certainly led me on an adventure. And it's the reason Dad's dead.

Or supposed to be.

Nothing makes sense anymore.

Spies. Secret agents. Secret organizations. Secrets upon secrets... and the only Secret I'm fond of is my dog, who's currently donuted on the floor, fast asleep.

A few minutes pass in silence before a rap sounds on the door, then Agent Tilted Showdown's unmistakable head of blue hair pokes in. "Is anyone hungry?"

Genius is on his feet in a flash, tablet tucked under his arm. "Heck, yeah!"

Aurora taps him before he goes more than a few steps. "Leave it here."

He scowls. "Why? I can look more—"

"Leave it, T—Tomfool." She crosses her arms, giving him a look that makes him sigh.

"Fine, whatever."

I'd almost forgotten about the name game, but Aurora's blunder—she never stutters—tells me his name really does start with a T. *Timothy? Titus? Tommy?*

Not like it matters anymore. Why play a trivial game like that with everything else going on? Biting back a sigh, I push my feet, rousing Seek from his dreams.

Back to work, little man...

After a pit stop for Secret outside in the unnatural warmth, I trail the others into a well-lit cafeteria. The tile floor is blue-and-white checked, with chairs and tables scattered around, and paintings of sea turtles, dolphins, and boats hang on the whitewashed walls.

"We caught the tail end of the lunch rush," Tilted Showdown explains, leading the way to a counter. "They serve from 11:00 to 2:30."

Serve? I don't remember that at Wonderland; it was all self-serve there. Then again, I never went to the main cafeteria, only Juke's.

Anxiety, unbidden, rises up as I near the counter. Seek's leash in my hand reassures me, and I glance down at him. Geared up in his vest, he looks like a proper service dog, ready to save the day once again.

I can handle this. As long as they're not serving steaming macaroni or pizza, anyway.

Slowly, I let out my breath, listening carefully as first Tilted Showdown, then each of the twins, orders from the blackboard menu over the counter. And when it's my turn, I'm ready.

Because with Secret by my side, I really can do anything. Even ordering food, a concept that was foreign to my younger self.

THE PHOTOGRAPH ON THE COMPUTER SCREEN STARES AT BLAKE like an accusation. Those familiar blue eyes are a plea, the question of *why*; the mischievous smirk a reminder of the fragility of life.

Blake presses his eyes closed, but the image doesn't fade. It morphs into a dusky watery grave, into a nightmare that neither man, living or dead, seems to be able to escape.

Letting out a hard breath, he tilts his head back as he stares at, only half seeing, the white tiles of the ceiling as a headache throbs behind his eyes.

He *should* be able to do this. Compare the pictures of the two men. Figure out which one is a hoax.

Even if, by some feat, some denial of logic, Dallas is alive, why would he still be in *Florida*?

He would have gone home. The Dallas that Blake knew would never have let his family suffer needlessly.

Right?

Blake clenches his jaw, but a mangled groan escapes as the old ache in his thigh throbs, a phantom pain. Trust, when his whole life was one betrayal after another, is a joke.

Hadn't Dallas said to trust him when he showed up at the rendezvous point in that ridiculous Volkswagen Beetle, the SoL hot on his tail?

In the end, neither man could win against the terrorists. And Dallas' trust in Blake had gotten him killed.

Blinking bleary eyes open, Blake resumes staring at the screen. There's remarkably little about the imposter, but Blake had managed to dig up a badly-lit photograph and an address.

This can't be a coincidence.

In the photo, the imposter—reportedly a banker named Alan Westcott—is in a suit and tie, looking off to the side with a serious expression.

Dallas, on the other hand, dons a colorful Hawaiian shirt and a Cowboys baseball cap, smirking directly at the camera.

They can't look more different, and yet they're so alike. They're the same general build and height, but there's something off about the faces. Blake squints, but the photos blur slightly as his headache intensifies. Frowning, he blinks them back into focus. Plastic surgery? It could account for the differences.

But why would Dallas want to get his face remodeled? So he could hide? The ISA would have tracked him down. *Isabelle* would have tracked him down.

It makes no sense. He doesn't have very long to figure it out, either. They're leaving tomorrow. The codebreakers at Wonderland will have a field day with Dallas' codes.

And Mya was right. Blake sighs. Maybe Fort Myers is clean now. After all, anything can happen in two years.

He'll have to track down this Alan guy, see for himself that Dallas doesn't have an unknown twin. What had Aurora codenamed Alan? "Baskerville," according to Blake's notes.

It's not surprising—neither Aurora's idea of a codename, nor the fact Blake will have to face his demons head on; but he had hoped that he'd find some solid proof that this imposter could *not* be Dallas.

And except for that little detail that Dallas is supposed to be dead, there isn't any.

"I ONCE ATE A CUP OF ICE CREAM WITH A KNIFE BECAUSE THERE weren't any clean spoons," Genius says, leaning back in the cafeteria chair.

Aurora groans. "We were talking about *shrimp*, Mister I'm-Always-Listening."

"Right, and that led to ice cream," Genius says, pushing back his chair. "I'm getting some."

Flame and Aurora jump up after him, and after a moment's hesitation, I make a move to follow when Agent Tilted Showdown shakes her head at me.

"Tirana..."

Worry creeps into my gut like a tendril of black mist. "Yes, ma'am?"

She looks at me, her gaze deadly serious. "How much do you know about your father's death?"

Um, that's such a great question to lead with... I glance down at Secret, lying under my chair with his head on his paws. "Is this about the..."

"No." There's an expression on her face that makes my heart sink. "I think it's time you see something."

"See... what?" I swallow, rubbing suddenly sweaty hands on my capris. I feel sick, dread rising so thickly it coats the roof of my mouth.

Again, her smile doesn't reach her eyes. "I'd like to take you on a little drive."

Like that doesn't sound suspicious in the least. I glance across the room, where Genius is goofing around with Flame. Aurora turns away from them and catches my eye. She must see something on my face, because she slips away from the boys and heads over.

"What's up?" she asks when she reaches us, glancing from me to Tilted Showdown.

Agent Tilted Showdown regards Aurora for a long moment, but my friend doesn't back down. She just looks a bit confused.

Finally, Tilted Showdown tips a nod, standing. "There's something that Tirana should see, Agent Celestial Flicker."

Aurora's brow creases. "What?"

I glance back at Agent Tilted Showdown, who flashes that half smile. "The bridge."

"That's *here*?!" Aurora's eyes widen, then something akin to understanding slides across her face. "Where's Uncle Blake?"

"He can take care of himself," Tilted Showdown tells her gently.

Aurora nods, but she doesn't look pleased.

I look from Tilted Showdown to Aurora, feeling as if I'm missing something important. What does Grizzled Fox have to do with this, and what bridge?

Surely, they can't mean... But their matching solemn looks tell me all I need to know. *Oh. Oh, no...* That heavy, sickening dread settles in my gut.

"Come, Tirana," Agent Tilted Showdown says, and I slowly stand, releasing Secret from his tuck under the chair.

But before I follow the blue-haired agent as she strides away, I glance at Aurora. "Is..." *Is this safe?*

The cheerful spark in her eyes is replaced by stark graveness, but she nods and gives me what I think is supposed to be a reassuring smile but looks more like a constipated grimace. "Go with her."

And why does that remind me of the librarian back at home? *"Go with God."*

The start of everything.

Will this—visiting the bridge, coming out to Florida to look at gravestones—bring it to an end?

Thoughts whirring, I hurry to catch up with Tilted Showdown. And almost before I know it, we're in an ISA-issued car, heading down the bright roads of Florida.

The miles pass in silence. The surroundings change from the business center to the city, the roads shrouded with palm trees seemingly stretching on forever.

The questions gather like brooding storm clouds, but I can't open my mouth to release them. How does Tilted Showdown know about this? If she's taking me to the *bridge*, then what about Baskerville? Was I just seeing ghosts? Or...

Or what, Tirana. Or what?

Maybe Dad really does have an evil twin brother.

The drive is an endless loop of houses and trees and skyline views. At last, the car slows down as we approach a drawbridge over a river. Agent Tilted Showdown pulls over onto the grassy shoulder and opens her door.

I realize I'm shaking as I release Secret and step out after him, following Tilted Showdown over the cracked asphalt towards the bridge.

There are stop lights, like the ones for school zones. "Stop here on red," one sign reads. "Speed limit 20," another says. Two tall posts stand on either side of the bridge. Looking closer, I realize they're arms that come down when the drawbridge is in operation.

The asphalt turns into a sidewalk, and Tilted Showdown slows down until I'm by her side.

"This is the Caloosahatchee River," she says, gesturing to the dark waters.

"What... what happened here?" I ask, my voice barely a whisper as I stare at the river snaking away into the trees in the distance. It reminds me of the river back in Vincennes, but this one feels sinister, like an evil wizard cloaked in a mask of peace.

Like a murderer.

"Some you know, some you might not," Tilted Showdown begins slowly. "The Suns of Liberty had a cell around here, and that's where Agent Bel Ria was stationed. His task was to gather information on the SoL's involvement in several seemingly accidental fires, each planned to make a mark but be untraceable. That's where your dad came in. It was a no-contact mission, due to the secrecy and the need for cover, but as his partner, Agent Grizzled Fox was placed at Base Buckleberry to keep an eye on him.

"Something went wrong—we're not sure what, but Bel Ria called a Code Crimson Flounder. Grizzled Fox went in to extract him, but the SoL picked up their trail. Bad weather made things worse, and they were going too fast when they came through here. The SoL thought to head them off by raising the bridge, but they didn't stop." Walking slowly, Agent Tilted Showdown gestures to the blue metal section of the road ahead of us. "They tried to jump the gap. Grizzled Fox rolled his window down as Bel Ria struggled to keep the vehicle in control. That was what ended up saving his life when they hit the river."

We're almost at the control building now, where the blue metal road meets the concrete.

"The car hit the water at an angle, knocking Bel Ria unconscious on impact. Grizzled Fox was knocked out for a time himself, and when he came to, he managed to pull Bel Ria out through his opened window, but..." She pauses for the first time, shaking her head. "It was too late His injuries were too severe."

The world blurs, dipping, and I clutch Secret's lead like it's the only thing keeping me upright. *But... Dad... No...*

"I was one of the team sent to recover them," she goes on, her voice dropping. "Tirana, I saw your father's body, right there on the banks of the Caloosahatchee."

FORT MYERS, FLORIDA

THE SUN IS BLAZING IN THE BLUE EXPANSE OF FLORIDA SKY AS BLAKE makes his way down the pale sidewalk that curves along cropped grass. Humidity sinks heavy in the air, like lead weighing down on his shoulders as he checks house numbers against the address on his phone.

Should he have gone alone? Probably—most definitely—not. But he's a grown man. Not a kid needing looking after.

His left boot finds an uneven patch of sidewalk, and he stumbles, jerking to attention. What *is* he doing here? Going on a fool's errand, that's what. Just asking for trouble; "stirring up the hornets' nest," his mother would have put it.

The line of houses in this neighborhood are never-ending, stretching off into a tree-obscured turn in the distance.

The roar of a lawn mower fills the air, and Blake flinches before letting out his breath, hard, ignoring the scent of freshly mowed grass that meets his nose.

Everything he'd hoped to put to rest seems to be biting him in the back, sneaking up on him when he can least deal with it.

The Caloosahatchee River, while several miles away, is too close for comfort. Too close to get a decent breath. Too close to escape the shrouding memories—the pain, shame, and guilt.

The only blessing, perhaps, is that no one on his team knows about what happened in Alva, the next town over. Not even the twins know the exact details.

"Focus," he hisses to the empty air, but his steps slow as he draws closer to the house that matches the address he seeks.

No car in the driveway. No obvious signs of anyone being home.

He walks past the low-set house, taking in the details, before continuing and passively examining other houses along the way. No need to look like a spy, though he probably does.

Or a stalker.

Oh. His stride falters when he realizes he missed something important: to figure out why the imposter was at the cemetery in the first place.

What other important information had he inevitably missed?

And this is why I'm cleared to do missions, right? Did they not look closely at his reports? Did they think he was faking it? All those tests, and he was still put back on active duty.

As if the issue is in his mind. Which makes him scoff, because it is.

And with Agent Silent Herald in charge, it doesn't surprise Blake. That man will do anything to get the job done... including risking the lives of his agents.

"You lost?"

Blake starts at the voice, turning quickly enough to make the world spin. When his vision clears, he's face-to-face with an older man dressed in shorts and sweat-stained t-shirt, who's watching him with a raised eyebrow from behind a lawn mower.

"You've been standing in that spot for nigh to three minutes. You lost?" the man repeats, a touch of amusement in his tone.

"No." Blake looks past the man to the imposter's house. *That long?* Just how bad of an agent can he prove himself to be?

"He's not home." The man jerks his head towards the house, and Blake berates himself for being so obvious.

But he might as well roll with it. "Oh?" He keeps a nonchalant tone.

"Yep. He left a few hours ago. Told me to feed his cat; said he'd be gone for a few days."

That certainly doesn't convince Blake that something isn't amiss. "Mind telling me a little about him?" To help convince the guy to speak, Blake flashes his badge.

The man's eyebrows rise. "Is he in some sort of trouble?"

"That's what I'd like to find out."

CHAPTER SIXTEEN
CLOUDY WITH A CHANCE OF DOPPELGANGERS

Darkness shadows the dorm, the heavy breathing of my room-mates indicating that they're fast asleep. I sigh into my pillow. The covers are stiflingly hot, but the heavy form of Secret pins them to me.

Closing my eyes, I imagine myself in my bedroom at home, sitting at my desk with my journal. *"I had the oddest dream,"* I'd write. *"Books of secrets, dads that are dead then aren't then are but still might not be, aunts and mothers that are probably kidnapped…"*

No. Mum *cannot* be kidnapped. She—she's *Mum.* And no way would the mother I know, spy or not, let herself be taken hostage.

Aunt Patience called a Code Mauve Herring. She turned herself in to give me a fighting chance of getting *The Freesia Guard* safely to the ISA. And now what? It's here, I'm here, but she's not.

If this is what the spy world is like, no wonder Mum and Dad kept me in the dark.

And this is hopeless.

I slip out from under the covers of the unfamiliar bed, wincing when it squeaks a protest. Slipping past the beds' shadowy forms in socked feet, I'm glad that my normal choice of sleepwear—soft shorts and a t-shirt—

doubles as everyday clothes.

As I turn the doorknob, a soft jingle meets my ears, and I almost smile, turning to ruffle Secret's ears.

We sneak out under the cover of darkness, my dog and me, down dimmed hallways and eerily quiet corridors. I don't know where I'm going, but that's okay. I don't have all the answers, but for once, I don't feel lost.

A glowing red "exit" sign catches my eye, and I make my way towards it. The door doesn't *look* like it will scream if I open it...

"Whaddya think, Seek? Should I try?"

He just sits, yawning, then stands and gives himself a shake that jingles his collar.

With a shrug and the courage of being alone in the darkness, I push the bar, testing. No alarms blare, so I carefully step forward. Cool night air blows past in a light breeze, the loud hum of cicadas assaulting my ears.

She sneaked out under the cover of darkness, into a secret garden where her father would meet her, wrap his arms around her, and swing her up into the air as if she were still a little girl.

I bite my lip, blinking away sudden burning tears as I let the door fall shut behind me. Like Harley Keene, the main character from *Stop the Rain*, said... it's easier to cry at night.

And Dad isn't here.

Do I want him to be? Yes and no. Because if he was... if he hadn't actually died... how could he possibly explain the fact that he's been missing for nineteen months?

If I close my eyes, will this nightmare of a new life vanish? Will I find myself in my bed at home, Secret standing on my chest, staring at me?

But the night air, edged with a promise of rain, blows in. In the darkness of the woods, frogs sing and crickets chirp. There's the occasional "who cooks for you!" of a barred owl, with an echoing response from another deeper in the night.

Fireflies flicker around me as I step forward like a movie character. All I need is the music. Soft, emotional—like one of those important scenes, right before something big happens.

Good thing I'm not *in a movie.* Even so, I can't shake a deep sense of foreboding that has no place in such a beautiful night.

I crouch down, an invitation for Secret to jump up and rest his front paws on my legs. He gives me a few licks on the cheek as I scratch his back, his solid warmth a reassurance.

"Why am I here?" I whisper. "What does the ISA want from me?" It might have been my locket that led them here, but I don't know anything they don't. "I just wish..." But I trail off, because what *do* I wish?

Frodo wished he'd never become the Ring-bearer, but if he hadn't, where would that have left all of Middle-earth? Bilbo didn't want to set out with the dwarves on their quest, but if he hadn't, The Lonely Mountain would never have been reclaimed, and the dwarves would still be prisoners. Even Rafi Tetrani ran from his true identity for years before owning up to it and becoming who he was born to be.

And me? "I just wish this was over."

"Be careful what you wish for."

I lurch to my feet, heart in my throat. A shadowy figure stands against the darkness of the building, arms crossed.

Secret trots over, trailing his lead, and gives the person a greeting sniff before returning to my side.

"Who—" I choke out, then clear my throat. "Who goes there?"

"Hark, I bring tidings of crickets and bugs," the person says, gravely voice deep and unfamiliar.

"What are you, a frog?" Or a twin? Maybe a stranger Secret decided he likes?

"Ribbit." The figure steps closer, cloaked in a dark hoodie.

I back away, tripping over Secret, and time freezes before I find myself lying flat on the cold ground, the air knocked out of my lungs.

Not-Frog hurries to my side. "You okay?"

I blink up into Aurora's face and shove an arm under me, pushing to a sitting position. "Think... so." I gasp for breath as Secret clambers into my lap, the wetness of his paws nothing compared to the damp seeping into my shorts.

Aurora shoves the hood off her face. "Didn't mean to scare you, not really—I mean, kinda, but not... hurt you..." She trails off, looking sheepish.

"It's fine. I'm okay." Yet I don't move to stand up. "What are you doing out here?"

"Could ask the same from you." She holds out a hand. After a moment, I grasp it, and she pulls me to my feet, much to Secret's dismay.

A few cautionary steps tells me nothing is broken, maybe just a little bruised and wet.

"You're not supposed to go anywhere alone," she continues softly, looking at me. "And the door's locked from the outside."

"Oh." Standing there, suddenly cold in my shorts and t-shirt, I feel rather foolish. "Thanks."

"Tirana..." She says my name much the same way Tilted Showdown did earlier. "Are... are you okay? Really?"

I start to nod, but change it into a shrug, blinking my eyes shut against a sudden swell of tears. "I..." *How could I be?*

"My dad's not around that much, but I can't imagine what it would be like to lose him. Or Mom, or Uncle Blake, and everyone at once..." She rests a hand on my arm. "We'll get to the bottom of it, okay? I promise."

I can only nod. *I hope so.*

INTERSTATE 75 NORTH, FLORIDA
WEDNESDAY, MAY 30

Hues of pink and orange light up the sky, illuminating clouds that speckle the still-dark expanse stretching far above the highway.

Dimly, it registers as pretty, but Blake keeps his eyes on the road, not some lying promise of a good day.

Here, no days are good. It's a constant battle, always with the lingering sting of water, the darkness ready to spring over his vision at a moment's notice.

Yeah, Agent Tilted Showdown will probably have his head when she finds out. Silent Herald could very well go as far as to kick Blake out of the ISA—something that Blake is surprised the man hasn't done yet.

It's high time that Blake pays for his mistakes. And if he goes down, at least he'll go down fighting.

Lives lost pointlessly. Children made parentless, women widowed, families shattered. At what cost? For what gain? It's all a political dance, a war for power, and innocents are caught up in the middle. Like Tirana, and like his own niece and nephew.

Blake scoffs, remembering Mya's words when she was trying to convince him to take the twins along. She'd said it would be safe, but could she be more wrong?

They'd all known the dangers of Dallas going into the SoL. But Dallas had accepted the challenge, had vowed to avenge the lives the fires had destroyed. He'd wanted to prove Damian's death wasn't for nothing, but in the end, it was Dallas who was destroyed, too. One of the ISA's best agents, now a name etched in stone.

It should have been Blake.

With no distractions, memories arise.

The youthful innocence, the recklessness, the love for all things whimsical—that was Dallas. Always there to offer a hand, even if it meant trekking through the wilderness or taking a recently orphaned neophyte under his wing.

They'd been partners, but more than that, they'd been friends. Brothers.

Blake, along with Damian, had been the man of honor at Dallas' wedding, and one of the first to hear there was a baby on the way. Man, Dallas had loved that kid. He'd loved his wife, too, but it was the girl that he'd show pictures of to anyone who even showed a shadow of interest.

And now...

Blake's grip tightens on the wheel, and he flips on the blinker to pass a slow BMW, whose driver is suspiciously peering down at the passenger seat, as if checking a phone.

"Idiot," Blake mutters, merging into the left lane. But he's not even sure if he's referring to the driver or to himself.

They said it wasn't his fault, that there was nothing he could have done—but that's an idealistic lie.

Dark frames his vision as the railings of a bridge rise up before him. A tangle of overgrown trees cluster in the dropoff, blocking anything past them from view, until a flash of the dark water glistening in the sun breaks any defense he was able to build, tossing him back into that stormy night with breath-stealing clarity.

The truck closing in behind them, the determined concentration on Dallas' face, the drawbridge seeming to come up from nowhere, a lowered arm glaring white in the headlights.

It morphs together, the bright morning and the moonless night, blurring into a roar in Blake's ears, like the rush of wind howling through the open windows into the car, whipping everything around and sucking any other sounds away. The jolt that shuddered the Volkswagen Beetle as they slammed into the arm, as they sped on, and then the water.

The dazzling paleness of the street, the sidewalk, the dumpy roadside plaza, the sun shining off the metal of an enclosed cargo trailer does little to ground him as his vision fringes with gray. Then the road is slowly rising, ramping up, and the short, chain-link fence boarding the railings can't obscure the bay underneath.

Thunder rumbles, clouds haze the sky, wind howls, and the sickening feeling of weightlessness freezes his heart even after palm trees, as still as death, replace the dizzying openness.

"Turn left onto Barefoot Beach Boulevard." The artificial tone of the GPS on his phone snaps him back to the present. The wide open sky shines a clear blue, the bright glare of the sun sending spirals of pain behind his eyes.

A peaceful, tree-lined road turns to red brick, a low-set sign welcoming him to the residences at Barefoot Beach.

"Turn right onto Barefoot Circle," monotones the GPS, and Blake woodenly follows the instructions, because no matter where he looks, sun reflects on the glistening surface of water. Because no matter how hard he tries, he can't stop the numbness from seeping into his arms, his hands, his brain, turning him into a human icicle.

He must've stopped, shut off the engine, because when a knock raps on the car door, he's parked on the side of the street, under the shadow of a tree.

Another knock, louder, and Blake flinches, slowly rising his eyes towards the window. A blurry figure stands there. A few blinks sharpen the image, yet it takes longer for his brain to process what he's seeing.

Not Dallas, no Dallas impersonators, not even Mya... no Instead his eyes are met by cropped blue hair and a displeased expression that darkens deeper into a frown.

With effort, he shoves open the door, yet words refuse to surface—only a feeling that something must be wrong, very wrong, for her to be here.

"What in the world do you think you're doing?"

He can only blink at her, the sound of waves crashing and the salt-scented breeze reaching him over the haze of his mind.

"Agent Grizzled Fox." She snaps out the words, demanding attention, and he slides his gaze back her way. "Explain yourself."

But what's there to explain? Maybe he says it aloud, maybe Tilted Showdown just guesses his thoughts.

"You drive out here alone, not telling anyone—you owe an explanation, agent." She crosses her arms, brow furrowed, eyes troubled.

"The guy at the graveyard." The ghost. Blake swallows against the rasp in his voice, nodding to the set of row houses next door.

Tilted Showdown's brow creases. "The man who walked out with a fishing pole a few minutes ago?"

Blake frowns, trying to look past Agent Tilted Showdown towards the row houses.

"Pink flowered shirt? Cargo shorts? Bright orange beach chair?" She gestures out past the houses, towards where the ocean lies in terrifying closeness. "I checked him out before I came to talk to you."

"And?"

She shakes her head. "He's not Bel Ria, Agent Grizzled Fox."

Blake stares out the open car door into the bright blue sky. Gulls screech, waves crash, a dog barks somewhere off in the distance. "Did you talk to him?" His voice is so weary, he hardly recognizes it as his own.

"Not yet."

"Then go." He climbs stiffly out of the car, an ache catching at his thigh, world tipping before it steadies. *Get it together, man.*

He runs a hand over his face—a shaking hand. Curling his hands into fists, he crosses his arms over his chest. "Well?"

"You, agent, are staying here."

Any protest is silenced by firmness in her voice, and he watches her walk away down the street, towards the ocean. She disappears around the corner of the row houses. But he can't—won't—stay here.

He's come this far. If this is a trap, Tilted Showdown will need backup, and as little as he has to offer, standing here is like being a sitting duck in the middle of hunting season.

Pushing away from the car, he starts to slam the door but stops and closes it more gently, then starts after the other agent.

The ocean grows louder as he rounds the houses, the thud of his boots almost drowned by the rush in his ears. Every instinct screams to run, but he trudges forward, eyes fixed on the sand-coated sidewalk, on his shadow stretching out before him.

Then a familiar voice breaks into his concentration, and he pauses, glancing up—a mistake. The ocean glistens before him, not two hundred paces away, as calm as a sleeping tiger. It steals any remaining breath, narrowing his vision and threatening up the coffee he'd had on the drive down.

"... have a few questions for you, if you don't mind." Tilted Showdown's voice grounds him back to the present, and Blake wrenches his eyes from the ocean. Her blue hair is easy to spot, the orange beach chair of the man she's talking to even more so. *Shades and sunglasses*, for a second, it's Dallas sitting in that chair.

Just like it was Dallas standing in the cemetery. Ghosts, both of them.

He needs to see Baskerville's face, but his legs are rooted to the sidewalk, his hand clenching the railing he'd hardly noticed was there.

"...don't know what you're talking about." The words are edged with a stubborn whine, and the man stands, facing Tilted Showdown with a combative scowl.

Tilted Showdown says more, but her words are drowned out by the pounding in Blake's ears, the rush of something—because this man is not Dallas Caineson.

She was right all along.

Only his grip on the railing keeps Blake from falling as his knees give out, the world churning into a dizzying rush of sounds and colors.

Then why was this guy at the graveyard? A random fluke, or—words rush back with startling clarity.

"It wasn't my idea!" Imposter has advanced closer to Tilted Showdown, his voice raised. "They offered me two grand just to put some flowers on a gravestone, and it ain't no crime!"

Tilted Showdown says something in reply, voice low, but something about Imposter's explanation sits about as right as a snowman in the summer.

The Suns of Liberty have been nothing but cunning. So why... *this*? Why a jabbering loose end?

"Good luck with the fishing!"

Blake looks up to see Tilted Showdown starting back across the pale sand, expression unreadable. Her sigh is visible when her eyes land on Blake, although he has a feeling she knew he was there all along.

"Didn't I tell you to stay back?"

He clears his throat. "This is back." Still far too close to the unpredictable waves, but too far to have caught most of what was exchanged.

She scoffs. "Of course. And is it also your car?"

Blake shrugs, falling into step next to her. "What did he say?"

"His name is Alan Westcott. Claims to never have known a Dallas Caineson in his life. For all intents and purposes, he's just a doppelgänger."

"And you trust him?"

"You and I both know that this man cannot be Agent Bel Ria."

Blake tips a nod, because what is there to say to that? Admit he went on a wild-goose chase for nothing?

But Tilted Showdown seems to misinterpret the motion, and her voice drops. "He was identified at the scene."

The scene? Blake turns to her, something falling into place. "You were there." *Shades*, how had he missed that?

It's her turn to nod, and her eyes shift towards the trees obscuring the street, more water shining beyond it.

So she knows, then.

Weariness arrives, a consequence of the emotional rollercoaster of the morning, taking an edge off the raw panic still lurking just under the surface.

"Keys?"

He looks at her, uncomprehending, as she holds out a hand.

"The keys, Agent Grizzled Fox."

He fumbles with them, hands them over without a protest. Doesn't meet her eyes as he does as she says and gets into the passenger seat. Doesn't ask how she got here, or how her car will return.

All he thinks as the houses and trees blur past is that she gets to explain everything to Tirana.

CHAPTER SEVENTEEN
CASTLING

Skreeee! Skreee! Skreee!

Panic jolts me awake, an eardrum-blowing alarm the first thing I'm aware of, then barking.

"Seek!" Pushing back the covers, I'm striding across the cold floor before my mind catches up, towards the door where my dog stands, barking his own alarm. "Secret, hush!"

He lets out a few more barks, then jumps on me. I pick him up, turning. Aurora's also standing, hands pressed to her ears, eyes wide.

Secret tries to wiggle out of my arms, but I tighten my grip, trying to think over the sound of the alarm. *Something's wrong.* Very, very, wrong.

Suddenly, the noise cuts off, the silence that replaces it making my ears ring. Sagging onto the nearest bed, I loosen my arms, and Secret jumps to the floor, giving a last bark for good measure. "What..."

"I don't know." Aurora scans the room. "Where's Agent Tilted Showdown?" For the first time since I've known her, I hear real fear in my friend's voice.

"I... I haven't seen her." I hadn't even noticed the agent wasn't here, but her absence is now a gaping hole that does nothing to quell the fear rising in my own gut.

"Zoinks!" Aurora groans.

I watch her pace between the beds in her fuzzy blue-and-white polka-dotted pajamas, tension drawing her face, until my own feet itch to move. "I need to go check on my brother," she says suddenly, starting for the closest door.

"Aurora—"

A crackle of static freezes us both. "Attention all ISA agents: Base Buckleberry is under lockdown under Code Magenta Serenity. Please remain where you are, stay calm, and await further instructions."

For a long moment, I sit there, staring blankly at the colorful, cartoonish fish painted on the wall. *Code Magenta Serenity?* Swallowing, I turn to Aurora. "What—"

A knock on the door cuts me off, and Secret gives a single bark that I hush.

Aurora and I exchange a glance, then she wordlessly walks over and peers through the peephole. A frown wrinkles her brow as she turns towards me, mouthing, "It's Flame."

Agent Pale Flame?

Another knock, and I stand up. "Aren't you going to open it?"

Aurora hesitates, hand on the doorknob. "Promise me something, Tirana. Whatever happens... don't trust him." Her voice is just above a whisper, her brown eyes serious.

Fear spiking again, I nod, scooping up Secret, and she opens the door.

Sure enough, Pale Flame stands there, face even paler than its normal hue. His hair is a wild mess that he digs his fingers into, and his eyes dart around, finally settling on me.

"Tirana. I... we need to go."

"She's not going anywhere with you, *neophyte*," Aurora interrupts, inserting herself in between Pale Flame and me. "And where is my brother?"

"Even if the Suns of Liberty are here for her?" The young man crosses his arms, narrowing his eyes for a moment before jerking his head towards the hall. "They already got him. I escaped just in time to warn you two."

"Did you, now?" Aurora cocks her head and taps her chin, oddly calm despite just being told her brother is in the hands of the enemies.

He looks past her towards me, urgency tightening his features. "Tirana, if you value your life, you'll come with me."

Glancing down at Secret's white curls, I swallow.

"No, neophyte. If you value *your* life, you will come with me. Both of you." Aurora shakes her head, then she abruptly turns and heads towards the back of the room. I step to follow, Secret growing heavy in my arms, but Pale Flame's low "You're seriously going with *her*?" pauses me, and I glance back at him.

"Why not?" *I have more reason to trust her than you.*

"I'm concerned about you! She's as reckless as her—"

"Are you two planning to come, or do you *want* to get left behind?" Aurora's scowl is as thick as Rabbit's when Tigger threatens to damage his garden.

"That would just make my day," Flame mutters, but I ignore him and head towards Aurora.

"You." She points at Pale Flame. "Bathroom, now."

"What—!" He gives an outraged squawk.

Aurora glares. "Now, or you'll be as dead as a slayed orc."

"Or maybe you'll be as dead as a poisoned mouse!"

"You guys are seriously having a battle of wits when the base is under lockdown?" I set Secret on my bed and grab his lead, surveying them. Pale Flame, in yesterday's t-shirt and shorts, looks like he rolled out of bed and his hair was attacked by an angry bird. His cheeks are red, his mouth set in a scowl. Aurora, somehow fierce despite her pajamas, glares at him, arms crossed.

They both turn to me, and some of the battle goes out of both faces. Aurora dons a stone-hard scowl, and Flame looks down as if abashed.

"Right. Bathroom." He runs a hand through his hair, leaving it even more of a mess, then slinks into the offending room and shuts the door.

"Throw on some clothes, Tirana," Aurora mutters, staring at the closed door. She abruptly shakes her head and turns towards me, a half smile on her face. "Sorry about that. I just…"

"Yeah." I offer her a matching smile and grab yesterday's clothes from where I'd piled them next to my backpack. Unzipping it, I hunt around for a new pair of socks when my fingers find the notebook, with a tip of creamy paper sticking out.

Aunt Patience's letter.

Ignoring the pit opened up in my gut, I grab the socks and quickly change. "What now?"

"Now?" Aurora's laugh is a hard scoff as she walks towards the bathroom. "We're going to play hero."

I'M BEGINNING TO THINK THAT AURORA, ON TOP OF BEING CRAZY, doesn't value her life. Standing in the shower, pressed like a sardine between Aurora and Pale Flame, I am seriously considering taking up Flame's offer of going the *normal* way.

Secret stands by my feet, and I coil his lead in my hand, watching as Aurora messes with the dials on the faucet... or rather, behind them, since she already pulled the faucet off.

A low whirring rises up suddenly, and Aurora straightens, a smirk replacing the scowl she's worn ever since Flame walked in.

With a jerk, the whole bottom of the shower begins a slow, steady descent. My hand flies out to a tiled wall, steadying me as Secret falls against my legs and scrambles for footing.

"How's this?" Aurora leans against a wall, full-out smirking. "Better than your way, neophyte?"

"Whatever you want to believe."

Where are we going? In the Accidental Cases of Emily Abbott, Emily was brought to the spy headquarters through an elevator shower, but we're *leaving* the base.

Why would the Suns of Liberty want Genius? Why would they want *me*? Are they here for Dad's book?

Ruthless. Wasn't that what Agent Grizzled Fox had said about the Suns of Liberty? At that thought, my blood runs cold. If the Suns of Liberty are trying to get the twins and me, doesn't that mean they'll also try for Agent Grizzled Fox?

The gray walls of the shower chute seem to close in, the light slowly fading, and I tighten my grip on Secret's lead, trying to ignore the spike of panic at being trapped with Flame and Aurora.

Then the shower grinds to a stop, and Aurora pushes open the frosted glass door and steps out, not waiting to see if Pale Flame or I follow.

I wait for Flame to exit, but instead, he looks at me, expectancy on his face. "Well?"

Wordlessly, I narrow my eyes at him. *Get out, dude.*

"You don't have to go with her. This thing goes up as well as it goes down. I can get you to safety, no harebrained, reckless plans included in passage."

Shaking my head before he's even finished, I click my tongue for Secret and push out past the agent, only to feel a hand snag my arm. Resisting the urge to jerk away, I slowly look up to meet Flame's green eyes. I'm close enough to see specks of hazel in them.

"You have a choice."

"Let me go." My voice is deadly calm.

After one last moment, he does, his hand falling back to his side. "You don't know what you're doing, Tirana."

Do I? The question haunts me as I hurry after Aurora, who's halfway across the dimly lit room. My boots thud on the concrete floor, and I glance at the doors and openings—some clearly other shower chutes, some not—as I pass.

Is this really the best choice? Following Aurora who-knows-where? The scream of the alarm still wails in my memory; fear curls in my gut. Aurora knows what she's doing.

She'd better.

I steal a glance behind me. Pale Flame is tagging along. If he's so sure his way is better, why is he still here?

If Aurora is certain he's not trustworthy, why would she leave first, giving him the opportunity to... do what? Talk to me?

Trying to shake aside the doubt, I quicken my pace as Aurora vanishes through a door marked "Crossroads."

"You have a choice, Tirana..."

My stride falters, Secret going a few steps forward until he realizes I've stopped. I glance at the door Aurora left open, then back at Pale Flame, coming up behind me.

Yeah, and I hope I'm making the right one.

FORT MYERS, FLORIDA

Buzz. Buzz. Buzz.

Blake blinks, slowly registering that the annoying sound is coming from his phone. Tilted Showdown hasn't said a word since they left the beach, which is completely fine with Blake. He fumbles for the phone, about to hang up, when Tilted Showdown glances over with a frown.

"Better answer that."

He doesn't have the energy to argue. "Hello...?"

"Well, hello there, Riley. Long time no see—I mean hear—huh?"

It takes Blake's brain way too long to figure out the voice, or the use of his middle name, but suddenly he's thrust back into the past, into a crazy "adventure" through the woods, being hunted like Green Arrow was in *The Hunt for the Red Dragon*. "What do you want, Jet?"

"Ah, so you do remember me." A chuckle, tinny and warped, reminds Blake of a deranged witch.

"Hard to forget someone who put a bullet in your leg." And tried to burn Blake and his friends alive by locking them in a convenience store.

"Petty boy, it's been what, over a decade? You still haven't gotten over that?"

"What. Do. You. Want?" Blake grinds out, clenching the phone in his fist.

"You."

Beep. Hanging up the call, Blake runs a hand over his face. Going from pesky emails to threatening phone calls...? Not good.

"What was that about?"

Dropping his hand from his face, he glances at Agent Tilted Showdown, who's side-eying him.

"Ghosts." Or lunatic traitors. "Doesn't matter."

Fortunately, she doesn't press. Just wordlessly drives, the road stretching on, busy with morning traffic.

Another buzz breaks the stony silence. After a moment, Blake sighs, picks up the phone, and glances at the screen. *Shades.* It's the same unknown number—a text, this time. No words, just an image file.

A blurred photograph of a thumb.

Blake blinks.

Then a new message flashes, and this time, it's zoomed out. It's Thomas, bound with duct tape, standing with his back pressed against a wall painted with a rainbow bolt of lightning. His chin is lifted defiantly, jaw set, and a dunce cap is on his head. Before Blake can even begin to process it, another text appears:

> It has come to this, Blake. If you value his life—and those of your nieceand her little friend, who are next—then you will arrive in the lobby of the base I'm sure you were so glad to see again. If you want to see them again alive, no tricks. Come alone, and unarmed.

And then Jet sends a GIF of an animated Joker laughing evilly, mouth bobbing like a nutcracker impersonator.

"Agent Grizzled Fox?" Tilted Showdown's voice snaps him from his icy haze, and he slowly turns to meet her concerned eyes. "What is going on?"

He opens his mouth, but nothing comes out. He clears his throat. "I... he... they..." He trails off, his head falling into his hands. *Can't be...*

He's vaguely aware of the motion of the car pulling over, then the weight of the phone vanishes from where it had dropped into his lap. Tilted Showdown inhales sharply.

"Well, Fox... what are you going to do about it?"

With effort, Blake straightens, staring out the windshield at an unfamiliar warehouse-style building. "Whatever it takes."

"Are you sure?"

Nope. But it's time he pays... for everything.

CHAPTER EIGHTEEN
SMAUG'S LAIR

Worry swirls through my gut, but Aurora's brisk pace leaves no room for questions as she strides away, walking deeper into the underground labyrinth. Several twists, turns, and halls later, she stops at a solid-looking wooden door, hesitating a brief second before scanning her card under the dragon-head brass knocker. There's a barely audible click, and she swings the door open.

Darkness shadows the room, but Aurora doesn't seem to notice as she steps forward.

A sudden flash of light blinds me, and I freeze, fully expecting a shout to ring out, or running footsteps, or some equally ominous sound paired with our discovery, but when my vision clears, a strong beam of light is illuminating the room beyond the doorway... only, it's not a room.

It's a tunnel.

The walls, pale blue corrugated metal, curve upwards, and the beam of Aurora's flashlight reflects off the shiny tiles of the floor. Sea murals with coral reefs, schools of tropical fish, lone sea turtles, stingrays, and a dozen other creatures ornament the walls, giving it the illusion of stepping into the middle of the ocean.

"Great blue snails of Eden," Pale Flame, coming up behind me, breathes.

"And we're going down *this*?"

"Unless you want to fly down it." Aurora doesn't turn, nor does her beam waver. "And unless you can, I suggest keeping quiet and following me."

Gone is the fun-loving joker, leaving no trace of the girl who followed me outside last night pretending to be a frog. Instead, Aurora's tone is all business, reminding me strangely of Agent Grizzled Fox.

Ignoring the unease churning in my gut, I scuff the tile with the toe of my boot. Our footsteps echo as we walk down the tunnel for what could be minutes or hours, the sea murals seeming to move before my eyes, before the end comes into sight: three wooden doors, each identical to the one that opened up to this tunnel.

How does Aurora not get lost in here?

She walks right up to the door to the far left, scans her card under the dragon's head, and pushes it open.

A wall of musty darkness meets us before consuming everything.

"Who turned off the lights?" Pale Flame is the first to speak up. "Agent Celestial Flicker! This isn't funny!"

Silence.

I grip Secret's leash like the worn leather is the only thing keeping me grounded in this world of darkness. Is this what it's like to be blind? Lost in terrifying nothingness, with the world falling away at your feet? The fear of making the wrong move keeping you utterly still?

"Behold!"

With an echoing *boom*, brilliant light sears my vision. When the kaleidoscope of spots and stars cease their dancing across my eyes, I squint them open, and a scream wedges in my throat.

Razor-sharp teeth glisten in a narrow, gaping mouth, and a forked tongue snakes out towards me. I stumble back, tripping over Secret, and end up half sprawled on the floor, the monster towering over me.

This is how it's going to end, in a blaze of roaring fire.

But the beast closes its massive jaws, sniffing at me with oddly small nostrils set into a scaly face. Its eyes gleam dark, the spiky crest behind them folding back across its dusky-colored skull.

Smaug.

When Aunt Patience said there was truth to fiction, I hadn't expected to come face-to-face with a Third Age–era dragon.

"He's not real, you know." Aurora steps past the dragon, resting a hand on its scaled shoulder. "Unfortunately."

Pushing Secret off my chest, I stand with a wince, coiling his lead with an unsteady hand. With all this tripping over my dog, I'm going to be awfully sore, but that's the least of my concerns at the moment.

"Great blue sea… dragons," Pale Flame breathes, stepping closer to the beast. "It's alive!"

"Then you need to consult a dictionary." Aurora crosses her arms, eying me before abruptly turning away. The dragon trails after her as she ducks around piles of miscellaneous junk waylaying the sweeping room.

"I thought it was just a rumor," Pale Flame says, following them, his wide-eyed look more akin to awe than the fear of almost being scared to death by a dragon. "The Scrubb Security Securer, model D16-81, said to be a failed operation."

"My father doesn't *fail*, neophyte."

As Aurora glares daggers at Pale Flame, I take the time to get a good look around the room. Light streams from bare bulbs strung across the shadowed ceiling, and the circular walls are dark stone, giving it the impression of a castle… or a dungeon.

With that thought firmly in mind, the dragon parked next to a large TV screen suddenly doesn't seem so out of place, though the TV itself does.

"What's this place for, anyway?" Pale Flame asks, and I look up from a cluster of bike tires and metal bars in time to see Aurora frown.

"A junk yard, of course. Why else would a bunch of random stuff be down here?"

Glancing back at the now-closed door we'd come in from, my unease redoubles. Lockdown. Attacked. Wanted.

A low, hissing grinding jerks my attention back to Aurora, then to the dragon slowly rising towards the ceiling, batlike wings outstretched and smoke billowing from its open mouth.

The wooden platform it's standing on jerkily grates its way up, and then the ceiling drops open, swallowing both platform and beast from sight.

Apparently, Agent Tilted Showdown is an ace-of-all-trades. For all his time at Base Buckleberry, Blake doesn't remember knowing about a secret entrance through a supply closet in a neighboring supply warehouse.

A single dusty light bulb illuminates the crowded interior of the closet. The dim light shows piles of neatly organized tools: brooms along one wall, ladders and hand dollies lined along another, random odds and ends stacked around.

After setting aside a ladder, Tilted Showdown crouches in front of a child-sized door in the wall, latched with a padlocked apparatus which looks normal enough. She draws out a large skeleton key to rival any pirates', and after a bit of tugging, the padlock falls open. Grunting, she yanks at the door, and with a squeal that makes Blake wince, it gives.

"There you go," she says, standing and brushing off her khakis.

Blake eyes the darkness beyond the mini doorway. Light filters in from the bulb overhead, but does little to diminish the shadows.

"Well?"

He glances at Tilted Showdown, running a hand through his hair. *You've got to be kidding me.*

She holds something out, and he squints before accepting it. A heavy-duty flashlight that weighs cold and heavy in his hand—one that Tilted Showdown certainly hadn't been holding when they came in.

"It's hard to get lost." Tilted Showdown gestures towards the opening. "You'll go down a couple tunnels, but the doors should all be marked. I'll call for backup, and they'll meet you in the lobby in ten minutes."

Blake frowns, fingering the flashlight.

"And Agent Grizzled Fox..." Hesitancy laces her words, and she offers a grim smile when he looks towards her. "Please don't do anything foolish."

Something in her tone conveys that wasn't what she intended to say.

Eying her for a moment longer, he tips a nod and starts towards the opening. Closer up, he can see that beyond the doorway is a pit, with the metal rungs of a ladder stretching down into the gloom. *Shades*, that darkness… but his nephew's face and the Joker's maniacal laughter spurs him onwards despite his whole being protesting at going down there.

What choice does he have? This is all his fault, and he's got to figure out a way to fix it. No matter how much it costs him.

So when the chill of the underground closes in as he descends, he refuses to panic. The metal is cold under his grip, slick with sweat and awkward with the flashlight, and forever or a second might have passed before his boots land on something solid, jolting the flashlight out of his hand.

It clangs on the ground, echoing, and the light shuts off, bathing the tunnel in darkness. His breath raps in his ears, the sensation of being buried alive clouding his senses with ice-cold panic.

He drops to his knees, groping blindly for the flashlight. His fingers scrape rough cement, knuckles chafing painfully on what must be a wall, reopening the scabbed-over scrapes left by punching the operative in the park.

The sting stills him, the icy fire of panic ebbing away into a numb cold spreading through his veins.

He lets his eyes close as he sags against the wall, trying to think. Without light, he'll be groping around aimlessly, probably lost down here forever, and utterly useless.

Mya and Dallas both would have brought a backup. The twins themselves would have had enough foresight for that, even if they didn't expect to be locked in an underground tunnel under a random building in Florida.

Great agent you are.

A frown settles, and he feels for the tactical pen the twins had given him last Christmas. It's hooked on the pocket of his cargo shorts, and he feels along the top, concentrating…

A sudden flash of light in his eyes jerks him back to bang into the wall, then the glare changes to a wild strobing. Another click, and the world falls back into blackness, the spots dancing across Blake's vision gradually vanishing.

More carefully this time, he clicks on the penlight, the beam small but strong enough to illuminate the solid concrete walls surrounding him. The broken pieces of Agent Tilted Showdown's flashlight are scattered around, no doubt rendered unfixable by the concrete floor. Coolness seeps through the walls, engulfing him in a chill that he grits his clattering teeth against as he shines the light down the tunnel.

Out of reach of the beam, the empty gray walls fade into gloom. He closes his eyes and lets out a breath. Ignoring the ache in his thigh, the tightness of his lungs, and ever-lingering memories, he makes his way into an adventure he never wanted.

He has a job to do, a mission to accomplish; and for once, he's not going to fail.

His friends and family depend on it.

THE DUNGEON
BASE BUCKLEBERRY
FORT MYERS, FLORIDA

Pale Flame shoves a hand through his curls. "Do you really think—"

"Yes." Aurora doesn't even spare him a glance. "Either shut up or you'll be his next meal."

Watching the TV screen, filled with black and white static, I'm not sure if that's a dangerous threat or not, but it does manage to shut him up.

Was this really the right choice? I glance down at Secret, lying with his head on his paws. Maybe going with Flame would have been safer. If anything happens to my dog because I made the wrong decision...

The screen flashes from static to a burst of colors, then darkness.

Do you know what you're doing? I want to ask Aurora as she concentrates on the thingy that looks like a game console, which she hooked the screen up to. *Do any of us?*

"Reckless." That's what Pale Flame called her, and he's right. But there's more to the girl I want to call a friend than just recklessness.

"Go get 'em, Edward," she mutters, and the screen changes to show a hallway, the rainbow lightning bolt mural vaguely familiar.

"How do you know where to go?" I ask, wondering how Aurora thinks the dragon can save us. Breathing fire and turning the Suns of Liberty into a crispy roast? Scaring them away with pure intimidation?

Smaug slips through more hallways and corridors, some with murals I recognize and some I don't. There's no sign of anyone: no ISA agents, and no Suns of Liberty.

If Base Buckleberry is so close to the Suns of Liberty base, they ought to have a better practice than just hiding in their rooms. But what do I know?

The screen stops flashing as the dragon halts in front of an unmarked door. Smaug backs up, then rams the door, which flies open.

The first thing I see is Genius, staring at the dragon, eyes wide and hands duct-taped in front of him. He jumps out of the way as a burst of flames erupts from the beast. In the smoky haze, Smaug wheels around, spinning into the room. When the screen clears, the dragon is standing in a wood-paneled office, a gun pointed at its chest.

Three guns, in fact, each belonging to a man decked out in a tactical suit. They all look equally freaked out.

The dragon roars, the cameras blurring as he springs forward. Smoke blurs the screen, but a Genius-sized shape slips into Smaug's field of vision before vanishing from sight. When the haze clears, the dragon is racing down the hall, two men pounding hot on its heels.

The camera shudders as if hit by some sort of impact, but it doesn't seem to faze the dragon. The walls blur by in a flash of blues and greens, and I have no clue how Aurora keeps track of where to direct the dragon.

Finally, Smaug is back in the little elevator room. Right before the door closes behind it, I catch sight of dark tactical gear rounding the corner.

The screen goes dim, and a low grinding fills the room as the platform lowers the dragon back into the dungeon... alone.

No goons. No Genius.

"Wow." Pale Flame is the first to break the silence that's settled. "*That* was your epic plan?"

Aurora ignores him, stepping towards Smaug.

"Are those... *bullet* holes?" I ask, stopping several feet away and eyeing the beast.

"You think he got caught in an asteroid shower?" She gives me a small smile, as if to make up for the bite in her words. "Yeah, those are from bullets."

I swallow. "What did it *do* up there? Other than getting... shot up."

"Distraction." Giving the oversized fake reptile a pat on its scaly gray neck, she lets her shoulders slump for a brief moment before she turns back around, expression determined. "Let's go."

CHAPTER NINETEEN
NEVER TRUST A HEFFALUMP

In the gloom of the tunnels, Blake doesn't register the muffled gunshots until several more rounds echo. *Shades.* This really can't get much worse. And if it can, he doesn't want to be around for it.

His light illuminates the tunnel, but does little to ward the chill from his heart as he heads towards everything he's tried to run from since he was a kid. It hadn't ended well then, and it won't end well now, of that he is grimly certain.

The concrete falls away to a small room with walls of stone, like a miniature wannabe castle. Solid metal doors line the walls, each marked with a wooden sign bearing crude writing. "Lobby," reads one; "Playroom," says another; "Cafeteria" and "Lower Offices" are the next two. "Dungeon" is the last, and his light lingers on that door, foreboding deepening its claws in his soul.

Get a grip. Tightening his fingers around the penlight, he turns to the door marked "Lobby"—where a team of agents, if Tilted Showdown has succeeded, will be gathering.

So instead, he opens the door to the offices and slips into a closet-sized room, another metal-runged ladder reaching up into the darkness above. Clipping the pen to his shirt collar, he begins the ascent.

Once in the halls of Base Buckleberry, it's not hard to know which way to go: even a person as unskilled in the art of sleuthing as Blake is would have little trouble following the sound of men's raised voices.

The murals get increasingly familiar, until he has no doubt where he is or where he's heading.

A yell freezes Blake in his tracks, then he hastens towards the office where he'd so irresponsibly left both *The Freesia Guard* and the drive, all for a wild-goose chase. He forces his steps to slow as he nears the open doorway of the office; still, the voices, three or four arguers, approach loudly, unaware of his presence.

A good thing, perhaps, since his plan isn't complicated. Just throwing some gasoline on the fire; nothing much. Just like Damian did, and years later, Dallas did.

Blake can only hope he won't suffer the same outcome as his friends, but in the end, it would be more than fitting.

But when he rounds the corner, two things happen at once: they see him, and he sees Thomas.

Shouts burst out, but through the ringing in his ears, he doesn't register them until his vision snaps clear and searches his nephew's pale face, lingering on the stain of red that seeps out between the boy's fingers, which are pressed to his shoulder.

Thomas' eyes find Blake's, glazed with pain, before the boy lurches to the side and vomits.

No, no, no… For a second, Blake is back in that abandoned house in the woods, clutching his leg, thinking *this is the end* as Jet walks away.

This is all Blake's fault. He rushes towards Thomas, but a masked operative steps in his path, pressing the muzzle of a Glock into Blake's chest. "*You.* We have business with you."

Blake eyes the man coolly, even as anger burns deep within, over the pounding of his heart and the throbbing of his temples. "Business" has been the cause of his parents' deaths, of Damian and Dallas' deaths, of the fact Thomas *has been shot.*

"Grab the kid," the operative calls over his shoulder to his two companions, waving his gun at Blake. "You, walk."

"Do you really want to do that?" Blake struggles to keep his voice level. "The charges against you are already higher than you can dream of escaping: breaking and entering, shooting a minor, threatening an agent—the list goes on."

The man gives Blake a glare that would rival any of Aurora's on her worst days, but he waves his men away from Thomas. They flank Blake, and he offers no resistance as he's herded down the corridor, like a man marched to execution.

And really, isn't he?

It will take nothing short of a miracle to save him now, and miracles are saved for those worthy of them.

THE DUNGEON
BASE BUCKLEBERRY
FORT MYERS, FLORIDA

"You really are as crazy as they say," Pale Flame says, staring at Aurora as she fastens the leather satchel she'd dug out of a pile of costumes over her shoulder.

She flashes him a grin. "Even the grumpy ones can compliment?"

"I don't think he meant it as a compliment," I mutter.

Edward—that's what Aurora claims the dragon's name is—rests on his lowered platform, looking worse for the wear. I'm starting to think Pale Flame's right: nothing even came out of that perilous trip up to the main floors. Maybe Aurora *is* wacko.

As Aurora rummages through another stack of junk, a pot clatters to the floor, followed by a wooden rolling pin and the head half of a hobbyhorse. *Okay, that's just disturbing.* She straightens, tossing something first to me, then to Pale Flame.

Fumbling, I catch the small object, holding it up. It's a silver flashlight, small but heavy. When I click it on, I can see the strong beam even through the light of the dungeon.

"First handy thing down here," Pale Flame mutters, pocketing his flashlight. "What is your plan, O Wise One?"

"What plan?"

"Ugh! You're as intolerable as your stupid dragon!"

"My 'stupid dragon' has more brain cells than you do." Aurora gives her bag one last pat and heads towards a cluster of doors along the wall we entered through. With a glance back at Pale Flame, I trail after Aurora. He doesn't look happy when Aurora chooses the door on the far right and unlocks it with her badge, but he follows us into the dankness of the tunnel.

Unlike the last one, these walls are made of solid concrete, and no paintings decorate them.

If anything happens, we'll be buried alive. And that, after everything I've already been through, would really be an awful way to die. I shake my head, dispelling such notions. Death does *not* lurk around every corner.

I hope.

Where *is* Aurora taking us? Does she even know?

The confidence in her strides says so, her set shoulders, the proud tilt of her head. But the fear I'd seen in her eyes when we first entered the tunnels challenges that, and with Pale Flame's nearly constant attacks, I'm not sure what I should do. Defend her, ask Flame why he's such a jerk, or wonder if he's right?

I feel like I'm just along for the ride... again.

Even with our flashlights, the way is dark and dreary, and I find myself wishing for the clear air and blue sky—anything but this never-ending maze of tunnels. It's like the Mines of Moria, but instead of the orcs coming from below, they're above us, doing who knows what kind of mischief.

If they're after *The Freesia Guard*, isn't Agent Grizzled Fox in danger? *Please, no...* He's the one of the last connections I have to Dad, and the story I've been piecing together about Dad's secret life isn't even close to completion.

The tunnel spills into a room that's even more like a dungeon than the one we just left. It's lined with doors, each marked with a wooden label.

"Now what?" Flame asks, gesturing around the round room. "I vote we go to the lobby."

"Did I say we were to cast votes?"

"Did we say you were the leader?" Flame retorts.

Aurora shrugs. "My mission and your mission might be different, neophyte; if that's a problem, then here our company parts ways."

And doesn't that sound ominous?

"What *is* your mission, Aurora?" I turn towards her, frustration building. "You've led us down here, sent a random dragon up to do nothing, and..." I shake my head slowly. *And I don't like this.*

"Girl's gotta do what a girl's gotta do," she says simply, offering me the bare bones of a smile.

Frowning, I eye Pale Flame. "And you?"

"To keep you safe. That's what I've been trying to do all along, if you'd just *listen*."

"*Two roads diverged in a yellow wood...*" What would Dad do? Quote poetry and know what it means? Take down both Aurora and Flame and run for his life? Go with the most suspicious of them and try to save the world?

But you're not him. I don't know which road leads to where. I'm just a useless "asset," getting toted here, there, and everywhere like a purse puppy.

Both agents are looking at me, Aurora's expression troubled and Flame's drawn. Aurora has proven, time and time again, that she's crazy. Unsafe. Reckless. I don't know what she's doing—I want to believe she has a good reason for her dragon stunt and for not telling me anything—but I'm tired of being in the dark.

At least Flame seems to care if I live or not.

And before anything else, I need to keep Secret safe.

So, fingering my locket, I swallow, resolve hardening. "I'll go with Agent Pale Flame, then."

Aurora's eyes narrow, her features darkening. "Fine, go throw your life away. But at least take this." She yanks the satchel over her head and pushes it towards me. Inside, I feel the bulk of a book.

"Is that—"

"A heffalump? No. But treat it like one." With that, she turns on her heel and stalks through the door marked "lower offices."

"Wow, and I thought she was looney before," Pale Flame mutters, staring after her before grinning at me. "No matter; she's out of the way now. Wha'd'ya say we get out of here?"

"Yes, please." I've had enough of secret tunnels and crypticness. I don't know what's happening above me, but it feels right to make my own decision for once—and I hope Dad, wherever he is, would be proud of me.

ONCE, BLAKE WOULD HAVE FACED THIS WITH A YOUTHFUL NEED FOR vengeance. Once, he did. And once, he almost bled out on the floor of that abandoned cabin, Jet slipping away without a second glance.

Now, Blake is marched forward, prodded and poked by the cold barrels of the operatives' guns whenever the ache in his thigh, the throbbing of his temples, or the exhaustion that clouds his mind causes him to stumble.

He shouldn't have just left Thomas there, but it was surprising enough that they'd listened to Blake at all. His nephew can take care of himself well enough. After everything that happened with Mya and Blake when their parents died and they were on the run from the SoL, the twins had no chance of avoiding a course—or ten—of survival and safety, even if they hadn't been raised at the ISA headquarters.

Thomas will be fine. The SoL have what they came for—Blake—and as soon as they leave, Thomas will get medical attention. He isn't helpless.

Blake doesn't know why Tirana pops into his mind next, with her scared eyes and "They *murdered* him?" The maze of murals and halls blur as the operatives prod him along, offering no escape—not for him. But Tirana... has she had any kind of training? While Blake has respected Dallas and Isabelle's wish to keep their daughter out of this world, it's one thing to hide a secret life, and another to leave your kid protectionless.

The ramble of thoughts comes to an end as they near the lobby, the operative who's clearly in charge hissing, "Don't try any funny business."

What, or they'll shoot him? Not while they think they still have something to gain. Blake wonders how long that will protect him, once they destroy *The Freesia Guard* and the drive.

An operative pulls open the doors to the lobby, and Blake stumbles as he's pushed forward onto shiny tiles. Regaining his balance, he's none too gently pulled along. There are no ISA agents here—no team Tilted Showdown managed to get word to—no help.

Only the vaguely familiar form of the man who had once called himself Blake's friend, before shooting Blake and leaving him for dead. The man who's played cat and mouse with Blake and his friends for years, and still thinks of them like toys, like puppets in his own sick game.

"How *nice* to see you again, Riley," Jet says with a menacing grin. "Or should I say Agent Grizzled Fox?"

AGENT PALE FLAME LEADS THE WAY UP THE LADDER INSTALLED IN the wall, then I hand Secret up to him, following closely behind. We come out through a trapdoor installed in the wall of a narrow, shadowed staircase.

"Now what?" I ask Pale Flame, who stands silent.

His face is wreathed in shadows as he points his flashlight up the stairs, but he seems to frown before giving a shrug. "Up, I guess."

Fingering the warm metal of my locket, I trail him up the narrow steps, trying to keep from stepping on Secret's paws. Aurora's satchel bumps against me. The desire to see what's inside burns in me, but I don't dare to look.

Heffalumps are dangerous creatures, after all.

The stuffy air is stifling as we climb up the never-ending stairs, until at long last, the dark wood of a door reflects off of Pale Flame's beam.

It's unlocked and opens into a narrow room, a long, dark strip stretching along one side, the other wall painted a solid blue.

"What is this?" I ask, stepping into the room. As if triggered by the motion, overheard lights snap on, and the dark strip turns into a window that overlooks the lobby.

"Tirana—" Pale Flame starts, glancing back towards the doorway, but I ignore him, edging closer to the window.

Slight awe gives way to fear as I realize it's not empty down there. Several dark-suited people speckle the room, one at each doorway, and near the dolphin "fountain" that uses light instead of water, four men cluster.

Three wear the same cargo pants, dark t-shirts, and camo armor plate thingies that seem to mark them as Suns of Liberty, but the fourth has on jeans and a light gray t-shirt, the slight hunch of his shoulders familiar.

Oh, no, that's not...

The man shakes his head slowly, shifting just enough that I can make out his features. Agent Grizzled Fox.

Why is he the only ISA agent down there? Why isn't he fighting, or... something? I know he *can* fight; he took down the goons in the park. So why's he just standing there?

It's like watching a silent horror film: their mouths are moving, but there's no sound. All I can do is to study their expressions and try to piece everything together.

The man directly in front of Agent Grizzled Fox has dark hair and olive skin hinting at Italian descent, and his smirk reminds me of a cat cornering a mouse. "Creepy Villain" is the description that seems to fit him almost as well as his tactical suit.

Something is going on, but I can't tell *what*. Only that it can't be good.

Villain steps forward, face hardening, but Grizzled Fox doesn't move. He just stands there, almost unnaturally motionless.

If these men *are* from the Suns of Liberty... does that mean they're the people who killed Dad and kidnapped Aunt Patience? This isn't a Disney fairytale—this is straight out of *Grimm's Fairy Tales*, and it makes about as much sense as *Through the Looking-Glass.* I feel sick.

Pale Flame clears his throat, drawing my attention back to the room I'm standing in. He looks nervous. "You think we should... go?"

I wave a hand towards the window. "Are you serious? It's swarming out there. And they're killers!"

"Tirana, we really need to go."

Something in his face makes me back up a step, almost tripping over Secret for the third time in twenty-four hours. "I don't think so."

Without warning, he jumps forward and yanks at the satchel. I try to pull it back, but he's stronger than I am. With a release of tension that sends us both reeling, the worn strap snaps, and Pale Flame disappears down the stairwell.

I scramble after him, only pausing to order Secret to stay and to close the door, then I'm tripping down the stairs after Pale Flame. My heart pounds in time with my boots on the wood, and I don't know what I'm doing, only that I can't let Flame take the satchel.

He passes the trapdoor we came out of, beating down the steps like Smaug himself is after him, and not Aurora's toy, either.

If I had wings, I could fly and easily take the agent down, but I can only follow like a lame ostrich, the beams of our lights sending crazy shadows skittering around the stairwell.

Abruptly, Flame rams to a stop against a wall, then veers off to the side and vanishes out of my line of sight. Light spills into the stairwell, then recedes.

My pace slows as I near the bottom of the stairs, the vision of what I saw from the viewing room in the forefront of my memory. They tried to kidnap me once, and isn't that what Pale Flame said they want now?

But he stole my—*Aurora's*—satchel.

Cautiously, I walk towards the door Flame must have used. It's slightly ajar, letting in a sliver of light... and voices.

I click off my flashlight and slip it in a pocket, then slowly pull open the door just enough that I see out of it.

Pale Flame is hurrying towards the group of men by Agent Grizzled

Fox, and my heart falls so low I think I may be sick.

"Dimitri!" Villain turns towards Flame, crossing his arms over his vest. "What—do you have her?"

Flame shakes his head. "Yes and no—but I have *this*." He flips open the satchel and draws out the familiar form of a book.

CHAPTER TWENTY
WORMTONGUE

"*The Hobbit?*" Jet says incredulously, glancing from the green-bound volume to Flame—yet another traitor in their midst. A frown creases the boy's brow, and he shoves a hand through his curly hair. "I—"

"Where did you get that?" Blake hasn't seen that particular copy since... since *when*? All he remembers is that it had been Dallas'.

"Good work, Dimitri." A slow smile spreads over Jet's face.

"But—"

A roar fills the lobby, cutting off Flame's protest, and Blake turns in time to see a dragon burst through a pair of swinging doors.

Edward.

His next thought is, *Aurora.* Because if Thomas is down, then only Blake's niece can be behind the remote-controlled dragon's antics. Edward blows a puff of "fire" that makes the operatives cower, but next to Blake, Flame merely snorts.

"Why, the little... Sir! It's fake!" Flame whirls towards Jet, but Blake catches the kid's arm and draws him back.

"I'd suggest you keep quiet," Blake growls, not losing his grip on Flame's arm even as the traitor scowls fiercely at him.

Wailing alarms join the fray until the lobby is a mess of chaos. Some trigger-happy operatives let loose their rounds, and in the middle is Jet, facing off with Edward, gun raised in a two-handed stance.

Pulling Flame along with him, Blake edges away from the light fountain. His pulse hammers in his temples. The alarm shrills, and no ISA agents are in sight, save for him and Flame—if the traitor counts.

He's doomed.

"Let me go!" Flame wrenches his arm away and sprints towards the mess of chaos.

It's at that moment that Edward, as if prompted by some unseen force, spins around, breaking away from the operatives. The dragon makes a fast retreat the way it came, and at Jet's yelled command, the operatives check themselves and regroup.

All but Flame, who races after the dragon. They both disappear behind the swinging doors, alarms still wailing.

The attention turns to Blake and the satchel laying on the tiled floor near the fountain.

He's not far enough away to make a break for it, yet he's too far to say it was an accident, and there's nothing he can do as the same operative from the office hauls Blake back to where Jet stoops to pick up the book and satchel.

"Once again, you have failed, *Riley*," the man hisses as he stands, tucking *The Hobbit* underneath his flak vest. "We have what we came for. Men, let's get the heck out of here."

WORMTONGUE. THAT'S WHAT PALE FLAME IS. A TRAITOR FIT TO BE burnt to a crisp by Smaug. And not a saga crisp, either.

I consider chasing after him, but who's to say the goons won't return? Instead, I turn and make my way to the viewing room, where Secret acts like I've been gone for hours. Swallowing, I sink to my knees on the cold floor and let him lean into me, closing my eyes and stroking his curls.

I'm so, so sorry. For so many things. Trusting Pale Flame instead of Aurora. Doing nothing and letting them march Agent Grizzled Fox away. And most of all, getting us into this mess. If I had never found that stupid, codswalloped book, none of this ever would have happened, and we'd all live happily ever after in our fairytale lives.

As if fairytales don't have their fair share of traumas, deaths, evil stepmothers, talking wolves, and other such questionable things.

"Tirana?"

I start at the low voice, hastening to my feet. Agent Tilted Showdown stands in the open doorway, running a hand through her kingfisher-blue hair, her face lined with wariness.

Fumbling with Secret's lead, I don't look at her.

"I..." The agent lets out a low breath. "Let's go."

"Go where?" I glance up, my voice sounding empty to my own ears. She might be a wormtongue herself, for all I know.

Maybe the whole world is.

"You remind me a bit of my daughter." Tilted Showdown's head is cocked ever so slightly, her expression softening into something akin to sadness. "Brave. Resourceful." Her gaze lingers on Secret, then she seems to snap out of it, giving me one of her small smiles.

"You have a daughter?" I don't mean to ask, not really, but it takes me by surprise.

She just smiles, her eyes filled with a sorrow of regret. "It's unfortunate you had to witness any of that," she says, gesturing out the viewing window, "but it's who we're facing. The Suns of Liberty—and others—are ruthless. They don't care about the collateral damage, the innocents, or anything other than their 'cause.' That's what the ISA is for." She turns to fully face me, something in her expression I haven't seen there before.

Passion.

"And it's my job, right now, to keep you safe." She offers another miniscule smile, but the intensity in her eyes burns fiercely. "Grace, I know you've been through a lot, but we can't stay here. Will you come with me?"

My fingers curl around the worn leather of Secret's lead, and my eyes prick. I've already messed up. Why is she offering me the choice? At least if she ordered me, it won't be wholly my fault if something goes wrong.

Aragorn, no matter how many wrong choices he made, never gave up. Even though it burdened him heavily, he continued on, through weather, the wariness, and the doubt.

The riddles in *The Lord of the Rings* seem far-fetched compared to the ones facing me now, but Tolkien was Dad's favorite author for a reason.

Agent Tilted Showdown is watching me patiently, and slowly, I take a deep breath and straighten my shoulders, giving her a smile that I hope comes across as brave.

Maybe I don't fully trust you, and maybe I can't, but I'll go with you. Because I don't want to be a coward, and I think that's what Dad would have wanted.

THE MURALS ON THE WALLS BECOME VAGUELY FAMILIAR AS I TRAIL Agent Tilted Showdown deeper in the base. Other agents pass by, urgent and tight-voiced, but at least the base is moving again instead of being frozen on lockdown.

Tilted Showdown stops at the same office door Smaug entered so dramatically not even an hour ago. The door is ajar, but Tilted Showdown doesn't hesitate before pushing it open and scanning the office.

It's a mess. Papers are scattered around, the computer monitor is on the floor, and it basically looks like a dragon interrupted a band of thieves, minus any burn marks on the wood paneling or the maroon carpet.

Not daunted, Tilted Showdown steps inside, but I linger in the doorway. Why does she want me here? Why is *she* here?

She goes straight to a wall print of a path weaving through misty mountain trees, hanging on the wall above the desk, and twists it so it's upside down.

Behind it is a safe. The sliding door is open and the dark insides are empty.

"What was in there?" I ask, stepping carefully into the room, cueing Secret to stay close.

She sighs, turning to me. "Exactly what we *didn't* want the Suns of Liberty to get."

Words fall on the tip of my tongue, but I bite them back. *I thought Agent Grizzled Fox was what we didn't want them to get?*

The lead jerks in my hand, and I look down to see Secret pulling towards a mussed-up pile of papers, nose twitching. "Hey—no, sir," I say quickly, pulling him back. "Leave it." But, as I eye the mess that he's so interested in, I notice rusty blotches darkening the cimmerian carpet. "Uh, Agent Tilted Showdown...?"

"Hm?" She glances over, frowning when I point out the suspicious blotches. Her eyes narrow, and her face is pinched when she straightens.

A bad feeling stirs in my gut. "This is the room where Aurora's dragon..." I trail off, because I'm still not sure what Smaug/Edward did here—other than apparently cause a mess. "Where did—" Again, I don't finish, because I don't even know Genius' real name—Thomas, maybe? But I haven't seen him since his form blurred across Edward's screen, and the uneasiness in my gut grows.

Tilted Showdown doesn't answer. She takes another look around the room, then leaves, pushing past me. I step aside, moving to follow her down the hall. I want so badly to ask what's wrong, but the sick feeling is just growing stronger, until I'm not sure I can speak at all past the balloon of stress.

Secret pulls towards one of the slightly ajar doors we pass, tail half wagging as if he's happy, but hesitant, about something. I'm about to call him back to me, but I pause instead. "What's up, little man?"

Agent Tilted Showdown stops too, sighing. "Tirana—"

Secret sniffs at the doorway, tail speeding up, and I glance at Tilted Showdown. "I think... I mean, *he* thinks there's something in there—"

"Tirana, it's an empty case room." She shakes her head like she's annoyed, pushing open the door.

Secret trots inside, looking back at me plaintively when he reaches the end of his lead, but I don't let him go any further. Because half-leaning against the wall across the room, eyes closed, sits a very pale Genius.

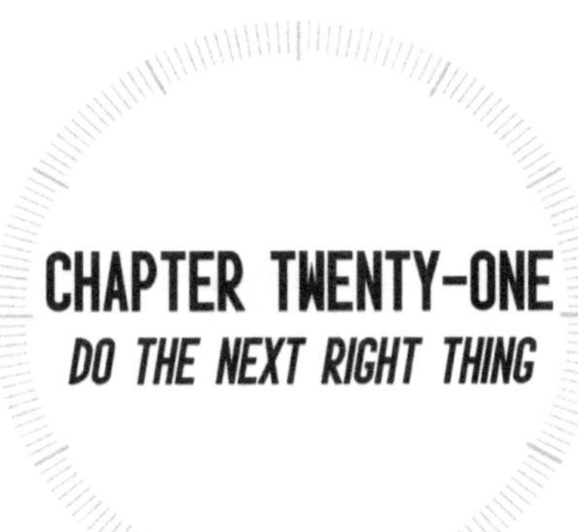

CHAPTER TWENTY-ONE
DO THE NEXT RIGHT THING

Everything after that is chaos.

"We have a Code Rainbow Orca at case room 23; I repeat, Code Rainbow Orca at case room 23," Tilted Showdown says into the radio clipped onto her belt, then she kneels down next to Genius. "Thomas? Thomas, can you hear me?"

Red seeps through his shoulder, and my stomach turns. I back away slowly, mind reeling. The shots—the dragon—somehow that led to this.

Aurora did this.

I pull Secret close to me, kneeling on the floor, the carpet biting into my legs, as I watch Agent Tilted Showdown try to wake Genius up.

The Suns of Liberty did this. The dragon did this. But so did I, by bringing that book to the ISA in the first place. By letting the twins help me. Now Agent Grizzled Fox has been taken captive, Genius might be dying, and it's my fault.

Secret perks up, craning his head around my shoulder, and I blink quickly before checking to see what's caught his attention.

A team of medics are hurrying down the hall towards us, and I stand, sinking into the shadows of a doorway opposite the room Genius is in.

Genius is loaded up on a stretcher, and I only get a glance at him as they carry him away—but it's enough to see his pallid face tense with pain, his eyes squeezed shut. My gut churns.

"He'll be fine, Tirana."

I swallow, glancing up at Tilted Showdown. "But…"

"Come on." She squeezes my shoulder. "An ambulance is on the way." Then she turns and briskly walks after the medics and Genius. I trail behind them.

Maybe this is why Dad kept the ISA a secret. Maybe… maybe he was right to.

AURORA BURSTS OUT OF THE BUILDING AS THEY'RE LOADING Genius into the ambulance. "Thomas!"

Tilted Showdown catches her, grabbing her by the shoulder. "Agent Celestial Flicker, calm down."

"Calm *down*?" Aurora struggles in Tilted Showdown's grasp, trying to get to the ambulance. "But—my *brother*!"

"Will be fine." Tilted Showdown releases her. "You can ride in the ambulance; I'll drive behind."

Aurora nods, taking off for the ambulance. The last thing I see before the medic closes the doors is her perching on the black bench inside and clutching Genius' hand.

Tilted Showdown turns to me with a grim smile. "Let's go, Tirana."

I nod, numbness slowly taking over like the icy fingers of a supervillain. The ten-minute drive to the hospital seems to take a lifetime yet flashes by, the ambulance blaring ahead of us, cutting through traffic until it vanishes from view.

He'll be okay, I tell myself, repeating it in my head until it drowns out any other thoughts. *He'll be fine.*

Tilted Showdown parks, and as I climb out of the car and stare at the sprawling, bright-white campus of the hospital, I suddenly realize that

Secret doesn't have his vest. The blue-haired agent is already seven steps ahead when I catch up, anxiously rolling Secret's lead around in my hand as he trots next to me.

"Uhm... Agent Tilted Showdown...?"

She turns, a frown pulling on her brow. "What's the matter?"

"His vest—he doesn't have it—it's still at the base." The words rush out in a jumble, and I try to catch my breath. Panicking—especially over *this*—won't help anyone.

"It's fine, bring him anyway." She turns and hurries towards the hospital, and I swallow hard before running to catch up again.

It seems stupid to worry about my dog's vestlessness when Genius is maybe—possibly—*dying*, but I feel like everyone is staring and silently judging me for bringing my pet into an emergency room.

Aurora's already in the waiting room, pacing. She rushes over as soon as she sees us, relief easing a bit of the worry from her face. "He's in surgery right now," she says, fingers twitching like she struggles to keep her hands still.

Agent Tilted Showdown nods. "Why don't you go wait outside, girls? I'll talk to the receptionist, but it's all waiting at this point."

Aurora opens her mouth to protest, and I bite my lip. "Can we, Aurora? Secret needs the time off."

"I promise I'll contact you the second I hear anything." Tilted Showdown gives Aurora a gentle smile.

"Promise?" Aurora lets out a shaky breath, and when Tilted Showdown nods, she swallows and turns back to me. "Okay."

It's warm outside, the humidity as thick as melted ice cream, the open sky and palm trees reminding me once again just how far I am from home. Aurora and I walk slowly, letting Secret be a dog and sniff around. The cries of seagulls, slamming car doors, and our footsteps ground me.

Genius will be okay. Agent Grizzled Fox is fine. Pale Flame isn't a liar.

Mum and Aunt Patience are in no trouble whatsoever.

Dad's at home, arms wide open, waiting for me to find my way back.

Take the road less traveled... but what if Dad was wrong? I finger my locket, glancing up at the blue expanse of sky. What if it's not worth it?

What happens when the cost is more than the gain?

"It's the darkest just before dawn."

I don't know what dystopian fantasy worlds or traumatized orphans who find refuge in the color blue have to do with the world crashing down around me... but everything was crashing down for Jay, too, in *The Colour Red*.

For everyone.

For Alice, when she fell into Wonderland. For Dorothy, when she landed far from Kansas. For Rafi and Ceridwen, when their worlds turned against them. For gallant Frodo, for steadfast Sam, for Gandalf and Aragon and the others as they fought against the destruction of middle-earth.

But unlike them, I'm not a hero. I'm not fictional. Alice woke up and found it was all a dream. Dorothy tapped her heels and found her way home. Rafi changed the tides, and Ceridwen emerged from the ashes stronger than ever before. "And Frodo changed the course of the world," I mutter.

Aurora glances at me. "What are you talking about?"

I sigh, shaking my head slowly. "Just... thinking aloud. Pale Flame... he took the satchel. He... that *wormtongue*. And I trusted him, just like you told me not to."

"It's okay." Aurora looks back towards the hospital looming behind us. "Flame's locked in the dungeon... I should probably let someone know about that," she adds as if an afterthought. "And I'm sure they really enjoyed *The Hobbit*. I bookmarked the page where Thranduil captures the dwarves."

"You..." I stop walking, staring at her, and almost laugh. "Seriously?"

She nods. "When I sent Edward into the case room—" her expression twists "—Thomas was able to sneak *The Freesia Guard* into his mouth. I left it there to fool Pale Flame, and gave you *The Hobbit* instead."

"So you knew that I was going to go with him?"

She glances away. "I... had my suspicions."

"But you *let* me go with him?" I bite my lip, scuffing a boot against the asphalt.

"I'm sorry," she whispers, rubbing a hand over her face. "I just couldn't think of a better way."

A part of me wants to be mad—but I understand. I'm only an asset, after all. Expendable. "They have Agent Grizzled Fox," I say, voice low, watching Secret sniff the base of a palm tree.

"I know." She clears her throat. "I messed up, and now everyone's—" She breaks off, turning away.

"Hey. It's **not** all your fault." I nibble my lip. "It's the SoL's. They stormed the base—they shot Genius—they took your uncle." They *killed* my father—and unlike Inigo Montoya, I can't do anything about it. My hand tightens on Secret's lead as I suck in a deep breath. "We can't let them win completely, can we? Blaming ourselves—that's not helping anyone. It just... hurts us. And the people around us." I squeeze the warm leather of Secret's lead, forging on. "Sure, we messed up, but we can't let that stop us. We have to be brave, and to do the next right thing."

Aurora sniffs, running a hand under her nose. "Who taught you how to give such good pep talks?"

"Dad." I blink away the tears. I don't know how taking the road less traveled got me here, crying in a hospital parking lot in Florida, but I muster up a small smile for Aurora anyway. "We can go back inside now, if you want."

She nods, then suddenly steps forward and hugs me. "I'm glad you're here," she whispers.

I squeeze my eyes shut and return the embrace. I don't know *why* I'm here... why any of this happened... but I *am* here. And even if I can't do much, I can be here for Aurora. I can do the next right thing.

**LEE MEMORIAL HOSPITAL
FORT MYERS, FLORIDA**

"HE'S OUT OF SURGERY, AND HE'LL BE FINE," AGENT TILTED Showdown greets us in the waiting room. "The bullet did some damage, but it missed the bone and arteries. He's in recovery now, and your mom is flying in on the next plane."

Relief floods me, and a glance at Aurora reveals that she feels the same way. "Can I see him?" she asks, hands twisting.

"Soon." Tilted Showdown gestures for us to take a seat. The waiting room is half full of people, some watching us, some pretending not to, some zoned out or on their phones. No one seems to notice Secret, other than the single "cute puppy" mutter I heard when Aurora and I walked in.

"*How* soon?" Aurora presses, dropping into an empty chair.

Agent Tilted Showdown shakes her head. "When they're ready for us to, I suppose. Tirana..." She pats the empty seat next to her, and I sit down obligingly. "This morning, Agent Grizzled Fox and I paid a visit to a man in Bonita Springs. 'Baskerville,' I believe you called him."

"That's where you were?" Aurora's brow furrows as she leans in. "When we were attacked?"

"Yes." The agent gives a rueful smile. "Unfortunate timing, I believe... They didn't care if we knew about Baskerville, but they did want Grizzled Fox to be on base." She frowns thoughtfully, then looks me in the eye. "Tirana... that man was not your father. He was paid by the SoL to place roses on a grave in the cemetery. I assume he was chosen because of his uncanny resemblance to Agent Bel Ria—the term 'doppelgänger' would apply here."

I nod, dropping my gaze to the floor. Secret lies at my feet, head on his paws, and I let out a long breath for something I'd forgotten about in the chaos of the day.

Of course it wasn't Dad.

I think—in a way—it's good. Dad didn't lie to us. But... it also means he's gone. Really and truly... gone. I finger my locket, absently watching the muted TV in the corner. A blue cartoon dog races down a cartoon hill in a cartoon wagon, and I close my eyes as my nose stings. I'm not a kid anymore, but I wish like anything that I was.

When Dad died, my life shattered like the snowglobe that I dropped one Christmas, pieces of a world no longer whole. Now it's changed once more, hurling me into something I'd thought were only figments of imagination.

And now, I really do feel as lost as Alice did in Wonderland.

"Ma'am, I'm going to have to ask you to remove that dog."

I jerk upright, my eyes flying open to see a bespectacled nurse in pale blue scrubs glaring at me.

"He's—he's my service dog," I say quickly, gulping as my heart races. "He's just not vested right now—we had to leave in such a rush—" This isn't—*can't*—be like at the park, where I turned tail like a coward. Here, Aurora needs me.

The nurse eyes him. "What task is he trained for?"

"Allergen detection." I swallow, trying to keep my voice from shaking. "I have—life-threatening allergies."

"Nurse—" Aurora glances at the nurse's name tag "—Crystal, this dog is my friend's service dog. Please—just tell me if my brother's going to be okay. His name is Thomas Harrison."

The nurse sighs, giving Secret another long look. "I suppose he can stay. Just know that jumping, barking, or biting are not allowed, and if he's not under your control at any time, your dog will need to be removed."

Thank you. I sink back into the chair, letting out a shaky breath.

"And my brother?" Aurora asks hopefully.

The nurse says she'll check, and returns a moment later. "He's stable and has been moved into a private room."

Aurora runs her hands over her shorts, standing jerkily. "He's not going to lose his arm?"

"No. He'll have to undergo physical therapy, but he'll probably be able to regain full use." A small smile makes the nurse's eyes crinkle slightly.

He'll be fine. The words echo in my head as we follow the nurse to Genius' room. *He'll be fine.*

As fine as lying in a hospital bed, nearly as pale as the sheets below him, is, anyway.

Agent Tilted Showdown stays in the hall, talking to the nurse. I follow Aurora into the room, but linger by the door as she steps up to the bed.

"Hey."

"Hey." His voice is weak, but... it's there. He's alive. He's maybe—

probably—sort of okay?

Aurora sinks down into the chair by the bed, giving her brother a small smile. "How do you feel?"

He quirks a grin. "Like... I've been shot? And drugged?"

"Baby." Aurora sticks her tongue out at him. "Betcha they got you so doped up on meds that you don't feel a thing."

"Well, I'm not loopy, if that's what you're after." His eyes flutter shut, but he blinks them open after a moment, scanning his sister's face. "Did we win?"

She glances at me, and I step forward to stand next to her. "We *will* win... thanks to you, T-bone," she says softly. "We may have lost the battle, but we can still win the war."

PART TWO
LONDON

CHAPTER TWENTY-TWO
SMOKE SCREEN

"Still think you're the hero?" Mockery bites Jet's words, twisting his grin as he pulls the zip ties tight on Blake's wrists, locking him to the metal bar behind the row of seats along the side of the van.

Blake keeps silent, ignoring the traitor as best he can. Which isn't exactly very well in the back of a modified Mercedes-Benz Sprinter, surrounded by people who won't hesitate to kill him if Jet gives the order.

"What? No smart retort? A dead fish would make a more exciting hostage." Turning to his goons, Jet jerks his head towards Blake. "Hollis, Ryder, keep an eye on him."

The two burly men who seem to be assigned as Jet's bodyguards slide in on either side of Blake, as if the cuffs and the operatives that pile in, filling the empty seats along the walls, aren't already enough. Even if Blake had a mind to, he'd be hard-pressed to escape.

Think. But think... what? There's no hope for escape. No hope for much of anything, except that Jet never realizes *The Hobbit* isn't what he's after.

The longer Blake can hold up the ruse that it is, the more time the ISA has to do something about it. If Tilted Showdown can solve the riddles from *The Freesia Guard*, then that and whatever case the SoL—this cell, maybe even the whole underground organization—brought against themselves with this attack will be more than enough to shut them down.

Even having friends in the government can't keep the Suns of Liberty going forever.

The van rattles to life under Blake, any small chance there had been to escape gone as the vehicle leaves the parking lot. He struggles to stay calm, at least in appearance. Bullies are like sharks, and he can't afford to give any signs of weakness. As if not fighting in the first place isn't "weak."

Three operatives sit across from him, dressed in khaki pants, dark t-shirts, and matching flak vests. With Hollis, Ryder, and another skinny-looking guy next to Hollis, that makes six. Probably all armed. Jet, of course, has claimed the driver's seat, and another operative fills the passenger side.

Two empty seats.

More prisoners they didn't snag? One for Flame? Who knows.

The plastic zip ties press into Blake's wrists, sending tingling through his arms. There are way too many bodies of water around here for this to be safe. Swallowing, he shifts, only to have both Ryder and Hollis turn to glare at him.

Minutes—hours—days tick by, the only sound the rumbling of the engine, broken by the occasional burst from the radio with some crackly update on the location of cops.

There's a fine line between keeping it together for real and keeping it together for show, and Blake is afraid he'll lose both battles before long. His arms and hands have lost most of their feeling, the ache in his leg reminding him just who holds him captive. The throbbing in his head, and the panic that hasn't gone away since that fiasco with Baskerville, swirls everything together into a mess of too-loud noises and the rankness of sweat.

"Dude."

Blake blinks the world back into focus, but the operative who spoke isn't looking at him. The kid hardly looks old enough to shave, let alone go on a mission to attack an ISA base. He gestures out the back windows, brows furrowed. "What happens if the cops come and we're found with him?" He tips his head towards Blake.

"Delmer." The guy to the kid's left groans. "The cops ain't gonna stop us."

A swear bursts from the cab, then the van is flumping and swerving, throwing Blake into the burly shoulder of an operative. Something hisses, the van seeming to sink on its axles, and Ryder shoves Blake away with a deep scowl.

"What was that?" The kid again, looking around with wide eyes. "I told you the cops would come! I *told* you!"

"Shut up," several none too friendly voices retort in unison.

The van shudders before jolting to a stop. Through the tinted windows, only trees, still in the late morning air—or is it afternoon already?—mark where they are.

Jet swings up, facing them. "I want every man out, guns drawn. Prepare for trouble."

A terse chorus of "yessir" fills the van as the operatives spring into action. Delmer alone pauses, glancing back at Jet. "What happened, sir?"

"Some idiot's playing a game, and we're not going to lose it. Get moving!" Jet turns back and pushes open his door, jumping out. The main and back doors are slid open, operatives pouring out, weapons at ready.

Blake, heart thudding, jerks at his ties, but the plastic only cuts deeper into his skin. He's not going to be able to break them from this angle.

Silence, as tense as before a hawk strikes, enfolds the world. Through the open doorway, bright sun filters in, the hot, humid air chasing away any air-conditioning. A songbird calls, answered by another, then it's only the whisper of wind ruffling the trees and the antsy shuffling of the operatives.

A sudden pop breaks the stillness, and the world explodes into a cloud of hissing white.

Gunshots ring out amid shouts and coughs, and sparks fly as a spiral of smoke rockets around like a loose balloon, dousing everything in white mist. It pours into the van through the open doors—sulfur mixed with pepper that burns Blake's noise. Eyes smarting, he jerks away, but the zip ties hold firm. Another yank does nothing but send pain lacing through his arms.

The deadly mist rises, burning everything it touches. Gray crowds his vision, and he gulps in a gasping breath, fire sliding down his throat. Coughing seizes him.

Underwater. Trapped. *Need to get out.*

Dallas. Where is Dallas? Why can't Blake's hands move? Why can't he breathe?

Burning consumes him: his eyes, nose, throat, skin. He chokes, struggling vainly, tries to call out to Dallas.

This is the end.

Something brushes against his arm, then suddenly he's free, jerked upright. The mist spins, or is it him, falling through the air?

His knees hit the floor, but he's hauled up, dragged by a force he can't fight. The ground dips and falls out from under him, and he stumbles, a hard tug sending him reeling forward.

Gasping for breath, it's all he can do to keep his feet under him as he's pulled away. Time blurs as he stumbles along, then he's vaguely aware of stopping, and dim voices. Another cough steals any bit of breath he manages to catch, then something splashes cold on his face.

Water. *Dallas.*

He chokes, jolting upright and forcing stinging eyes to squint open. A blurry form stands before him, holding something up.

What... but his voice refuses to comply, his vision won't clear, he still can't breathe, and nausea is rising.

"Blake Hession."

He turns slightly at the new, distinctly familiar voice, squinting. "Mya?" The word emerges as a hoarse croak.

"Do you know where you are?"

Blinking does little to clear the sting and tears from his eyes, and all he can see are greenish blurs that might be trees and the dark form of the woman talking to him. Another cough steals any answer he might have given.

"I'll take that as a no. Were you the only one?"

"Only..." Only *what*?

Dallas. His heart rockets, and he jerks around, trying to see past the haze of his vision. Maybe he said something aloud, maybe he didn't, but a firm hand grips his arm, bringing him to a halt.

"Blake, you need to calm down. Listen to me. Were you the only person the Suns of Liberty abducted?"

"He's gone, Agent Grizzled Fox. I'm sorry."

"Hession."

Blake blinks past the tears that aren't all from the evil mist, clearing his throat as if that will relieve the tightness and burning. "Think... so."

"Did you see Tirana?"

He failed them both, didn't he? A half shrug is the only answer he can think to give. *Might be a trap...*

"Was Tirana in one of the vans?" Her voice is sharper, impatient.

"No." He doesn't have the energy to figure out a lie. Whoever these people are, he can't stop them.

Only when she lets go of his arm does Blake realize she'd held it, and he sinks to the ground, still fighting for a decent breath. Curse the person who thought water would help. Curse the mist. Curse the broken mind that can't handle a little gassing.

The dull murmur of voices falls off almost before he's aware of it, then the woman is standing over him, arms crossed and face hard. Brown hair is swept into a windblown bun, and a dark bluish-purple bruise mars her cheekbone.

"Let's go, Blake."

SOMEWHERE IN FLORIDA

"CS GAS AND A COUPLE SMOKE BOMBS." THE MAN SITTING next to Blake shrugs as if it's perfectly normal to ambush convoys and spring prisoners with the use of caltrops and debilitating smoke screens. "Nothing lethal, just enough to give a little spice, eh?"

"They did seem rather lashed," put in another guy, leaning back in the passenger seat of the minivan and crossing his arms behind his head. "All in a good day's work."

"Lashed?" The first guy scoffs. "You have an interesting definition for that word."

Maybe twenty minutes after getting out of that deathtrap of a van, Blake's in another one, surrounded by Brits. His eyes, nose, and throat still burn, it feels like he's got a bad sunburn over the rest of him, and his head throbs, but he can handle it.

So long as the memories and panic stay at bay, and he can draw in a decent breath without choking on his own spit. Apparently, the bodily reactions to the chemical in tear gas aren't pretty.

Seeing Jet in a similar state might be worth it. A grim smile almost threatens to surface at the thought, but any fragment of humor vanishes as the vaguely familiar woman turns in her seat in the second row, glancing back at him with serious eyes.

"How is Tirana? You were her guardian?" Her words are clipped, but her accent only highlights the concern in her voice.

Blake's pretty sure he knows her, and she acts like she knows *him*, but he can't quite place her over the pounding of his head and the fogginess from the gas. He's pretty sure the group is Ignis, a private UK-based agency, but what would a group of five agents from Britain want with the ISA? Why bother breaking him out? Taking him along... wherever it is that they're going?

The agent's eyes narrow, her sculpted eyebrows drawing together. "You *are* aware you were her guardian, correct?"

The others have fallen quiet, watching them, and Blake shoves a hand through his hair. "Yeah. And last I saw, she was fine." Unlike Thomas. That kid better be okay, or Jet *will* regret it. He'll regret *everything*.

"What?"

Her sharp voice breaks Blake out of it, and pressing a hand to his thigh, he shrugs. "Like I said. She's fine." Or as fine as anyone in this mess could be.

The agent's pinched brows indicate that she isn't convinced, and Blake sighs, which turns into a cough that grates in his throat. Ignoring the revenant dizziness, he gives her what might pass as a smile. "If it's any comfort, my niece has been looking after her."

The agent's nod doesn't give away any thoughts as she turns to face forward again. Probably a good thing, if she knows anything about Aurora.

Blake clears his throat. "Who are you guys, anyway?" *And what were you doing in Florida with CS gas, smoke bombs, and tire tacks?*

"Norton," says the guy next to Blake, holding out a hand, which Blake accepts. "I'm the one in charge of chemicals and bombs. That there—" he jerks his head towards a quiet woman in the middle row "—is Kensal, our techie. Mundford's up front, and the driver's Kinsworth, the brooding butler who can double as a medic. And she's Dalton, who had to get kidnapped and get us all dragged out here to balmy Florida."

"Norton..." The lady—Dalton—sounds unamused. "I seem to recall you breaking a few rules on your heroic rescue mission."

"More than a few," Techie mumbles, arms crossed.

Blake half listens to the banter as he tries to pin down *why* this Agent Dalton seems so familiar. The ache in his head sharpens until he's ready to just give up and leave it be. Exhaustion tempts him to let his eyes close, but he's not safe here.

Nowhere is safe.

Tirana isn't safe. Patience isn't safe. Isabelle isn't—

Suddenly, it clicks.

Ignis agents. Dalton... *Isabelle* Dalton. Dallas' wife... and Tirana's mother.

CHAPTER TWENTY-THREE
THERE'S NO PLACE
LIKE HOME

Somewhere there isn't any trouble... Do you suppose there's such a place, Seek?" I mutter, coiling his lead in my hand as I follow Aurora through the parking lot. The woods are a welcome sight, even as the ISA building looms before us.

It's still as nondescriptly impressive as when I first laid eyes on it, but now, it almost feels like coming home. Secret agents, wacky headquarters, people who can't seem to avoid getting kidnapped... it sounds like something out of a novel. A crazy, fictional story that I'd rather read than live.

Agent Tilted Showdown and the agent who picked us up from the airstrip have already gone in with Thomas, but Aurora begrudgingly stayed out with me while I let Secret sniff around the greenery to let him decompress a little after the three-hour plane trip.

Now, we're heading into the place they call Wonderland, missing two of the party we left with: one a traitor, and one betrayed.

As Aurora strides towards the doors, they slide open. She scans her card on the wall scanner, the second set of doors open, and I follow her into the cool air of the lobby.

How often did Dad come here? Swallowing the ache, I smile at the woman sitting behind the desk this time around. She returns the gesture, welcoming us to Wonderland as Aurora scans her card again. As I run the barcode of my own card over the scanner on the desk, the words "Guest Pass" seem terribly stark against the surface's gloss.

An asset... but what am I now that the mission failed? Who's my guardian now?

Circus music plays from hidden loudspeakers as we step into Wonderland, the colors that burst from all directions dazzling me for a moment. A tug on the lead jerks my attention to Secret, who's politely but pointedly trying to get to something, tail whipping. I slowly look up, confusion turning to shock as I meet the familiar gray eyes of Aunt Patience.

"Ana," she whispers before stepping forward and wrapping me in a hug.

For a second, I can only stand there, then I fiercely return the embrace, tears searing my eyes. She's here.

She's actually *here*.

"I am so, so sorry, Tirana," she mutters in a hoarse whisper, then holds me out at arm's length, looking me over. She must find me passing, because she nods before kneeling down to greet an excited Secret.

"Come on, there's so much to tell, but not here." She stands, pulling me away through the lobby.

Yeah. I glance back at Aurora, but she waves me on, and I'm more than happy to go. A purple, rectangular crayon drawing turns out to be a door, and Aunt Patience gestures me through it.

She's real. If I tell myself that enough times, will this dream break and dump me back into reality?

"Look, it's Lilac." Aunt Patience pauses, pointing at one of purple crayon illustrations on the wall. The fluffy outline of the dog seems to bound after a ball, a picture of doggy happiness. "You used to love Harold."

Looking down at my own dog, I grin. "Still do." *Yeah, this is a dream, all right.* One I have no intention of waking up from.

We pass more crayon drawings, but for once, I'm not staring at the murals. Because if I take my eyes off my aunt, she might disappear. She looks different, too. Rough. I guess anyone would after facing the Suns of Liberty.

"In here." She stops at one of the purple-framed doors and pushes it open. "A friend is letting me borrow it for a bit."

Two black, padded chairs face the blocky wood desk centered before the far wall. A large, framed picture of a crayoned half-moon adorns one wall, giving the official-looking room a more personal touch.

And the other picture, hanging above the desk... I can almost recognize the young man, slightly blurred, posing next to—is that a younger version of Agent Respectable Pixie, the agent who wanted to know about seals and pumpkin swirl muffins? They're in front of a bookstore, and the guy's face is half covered in a painful twisting of scars.

"Who's that?" I ask, watching my aunt's gaze travel to the picture.

She blinks quickly, the crushed look on her face similar to the expression she wears when she talks about Dad. "Someone... someone that I loved once."

I stare at the picture for another moment before Aunt Patience clears her throat, gesturing for me to take a seat.

Secret jumps up on Aunt Patience's lap as soon as she sits, and she smiles down at him, ruffling his ears as he tries to lick her face.

There are more framed pictures on the desk. One has younger versions of Aunt Patience, Aurora's mom, and Agent Respectable Pixie, arms linked, grinning out from the photo like they'd just defeated the armies of Mordor. There's a watercolor painting of six figures on the top of a van, silhouetted against a pink sunset sky. Another photo is of a younger Agent Grizzled Fox and Respectable Pixie with the unnamed scarred guy, standing in front of some plank thingy, sticking out their tongues.

"What happened?" Turning back to my aunt, I clear my throat, shaking my head. "You were *kidnapped*? And called a Code Mauve Herring? And—"

"I'm sorry, I know I messed up. Again." Aunt Patience closes her eyes. "It's... all such a long story. If you haven't figured it out by now, you were right. Dallas was a secret agent. We all were—are."

And I never knew? *Why?* But I need to ask something else. "Do you know where Mum is?"

The shadows on her face deepen, answering before her words do. "No.

I was... only recently informed she wasn't with you." She pushes Secret off her lap, letting her head fall into her hands.

He returns to me, and I rub his ears, trying to swallow down tears that have no permission to choke me. "I... I need to know." Everything. Even if it kills me to hear it.

Aunt Patience nods into her hands before straightening, brushing a strand of hair away from eyes that glisten. "You do. We should never have concealed the truth for this long. Oh, Ana..." She draws in a breath, letting it out slowly. "Where do I begin?"

"The beginning?" I offer, but I can't hide the quiver in my own voice, and my heart's pounding like it did when those alarms jolted me into the nightmare that was yesterday. "But first—where *were* you?"

Aunt Patience sighs, glancing back at the photograph on the wall. "That's... complicated." She hesitates. "The SoL originally went after me as I'd planned, but they somehow figured out that you had the book, and decided I wasn't worth the trouble."

I frown, biting my lip as anger courses through me. "What did they do to you?"

"It doesn't matter." Seeming to draw herself together, she clasps her hands together, staring at them. "Right... so, the beginning. When Dallas and I joined the ISA. He got in trouble with the law and found out about the ISA through a community service program. We didn't look back. Ended up turning in a cousin for working with an eco-terrorist—that's why you've never met our side of the family; they never quite forgave us for that. Dallas met your mom in London, of course, on a mission. And the others... Blake, Mya, Dallas, me, Damian, and Michelle... we were the 6-Some." Aunt Patience picks up the framed painting of the figures on the van, staring down at it. "We were supposed to be the greatest team the world had ever seen, and for years, we were.

"And then Isabelle got pregnant, and Dallas got into trouble. We thought he'd died, and when he came back, he vowed to keep his daughter safe from the evil of the world. Then... you were born. A couple weeks in the NICU while we weren't sure you would make it, and then your allergy..." Setting down the photo, Aunt Patience sighs, wiping her eyes.

"Dallas and Isabelle only wanted to protect you. Our world isn't safe, and you needed time to be a child. We tried so hard to keep you safe, Ana. And when you were a toddler, Dai..." She breaks off, spinning in her chair, turning her back to me as she stares at the photo over the desk. "Damian... We were engaged. Going to get married and have kids. He... A mission went wrong... he didn't make it."

Didn't make it... Like Dad. My mind spins, and I blink back tears. Aunt Patience was going to get *married*?

But she's not done. She blows her nose, turning back to me, the pain that's etched into her eyes seeming to drown her. "And Dallas... after he died... It was just your mom and me raising you, and neither of us could bear to let you enter the world that killed your father. When I saw that book, I should have brought you and it straight here. But I had doubts; I wanted to make sure it was what I thought it was. Then it was too late. There was nothing else I could do but... but..." A muffled sob cuts her off, and she shakes her head. "Oh, Ana, I am so, so sorry."

"So you called a Code Mauve Herring." By some miracle, my voice doesn't break. "So I could get the book to the ISA."

She nods, grabbing another tissue from the desk and dabbing her eyes.

"But you didn't fail." I have to clear my throat, then I repeat the words. "You didn't fail." Samwise would have something better to say, but I'm not Samwise Gangee. I'm Grace Tirana Caineson, daughter and niece of the bravest people I know, and I say so.

Even if Dad's always been dead. Even if this wasn't the way anyone wanted it to happen. Even if they all kept secrets that have completely flipped my world.

Scooching forward, I kneel on the rug and clasp Aunt Patience's calloused hand in my own, Secret joining the sort-of-hug.

"It all happened for a reason. We just gotta believe that." I squeeze Aunt Patience's hand, and she slips it around my shoulder, pulling me close.

SOMEWHERE ABOVE THE ATLANTIC OCEAN

Seems like no matter what he does, trouble just can't let him be. Even thousands of feet in the air, in a private plane bound northeast.

Blake glances over at Isabelle Dalton as she slides into the empty seat next to him.

"We've sent word to the ISA that you are no longer in SoL custody," she begins, expression grim. "The SoL have not been known to leave the country, have they?"

"You think they'd intercept your message?"

She looks at him silently before asking, "Do you?"

Ask the supposed expert, will you? He tips a nod, a weary sigh rising. "And no, there have not been any known cases of them leaving the country. Doesn't mean much." Not when it's Jet. "Like I told you before, it will probably be some time before they realize they don't have the right book." And then it won't be just Blake that Jet's after. "Is Tirana safe?"

Isabelle's expression tightens, the shadows under her eyes as dark as the bruise on her face. "I've sent for her to come to London."

"How do you know they didn't intercept that?" If the SoL learned that either he or the girl isn't in the States, the protection of the ocean won't be much protection at all.

"You seem to think this unorganized group of ragamuffins is capable of much," Isabelle says, tone light yet deadly serious.

Blake shrugs. "Arson; dozens of murders, including of women and children; political scandals... They've tried to kidnap your daughter several times already." Not to mention murdering his parents, Damian, and Isabelle's husband, and also shooting Thomas. "Dallas..." He swallows, studying the marks left from the zip ties, that cursed murky water threatening to steal his breath. "What happened... it... it wasn't a singular thing."

"What do you mean?" Words sharp, the Ignis agent narrows her eyes at him.

"Anyone who gets in their way... You know what they do." Clearing his throat against what he tells himself is the lingering effects of the tear gas, he

shakes his head slowly, staring at his hands. "Just make sure Tirana's safe."
I couldn't.

A light hand on his shoulder jerks his attention back to Isabelle, who stands with a small smile. "Try to get some rest. We should be in England in six or seven hours."

He nods, but says nothing as she returns to her rightful seat next to one of her teammates. Why doesn't she hate him, after everything? Why rescue him from a fate he deserves?

The Ignis agents were stingy with their details when they'd grilled him on the attack. Dalton was captured by the SoL when she landed in the States, so her team came to break her out. They suspected the SoL of taking Tirana, so they sprang their own attack on the convoy, only to find the sole captive was Blake.

Something about it all grates on Blake. It just doesn't add up. Why post a random guy in a random graveyard? What person would lead an attack against an entire base with only a handful of men? What base would hold back and not stop them?

It feels like a game of puppets, but just who is holding the strings?

One of Dalton's teammates, the talkative one, says something about being "glad to be headed home," and Blake fixes his eyes on the clouds and sky spanning outside the window.

Home. A room at Wonderland, down the hall from his sister, brother-in-law, niece, and nephew.

Yet his mom's humming, as soft as a warm evening breeze, invades his thoughts. With the swish of the broom or the scrape and slosh of washing dishes—there was always the humming. *That* was home, once upon a time—the sprawling house in the mountains; the sloped, cracked driveway; the picture windows that fronted the living room; and the holly tree out back that was perfect to climb.

Dad would often hide away in his study, poring over books, but he'd emerge for a game of Scrabble or Monopoly or—his personal favorite—Risk. There would be fresh flowers on the kitchen table, and the tang of orange cleaner. And Mom, with her cheerful presence no matter the circumstance. Her staunch "never give up" attitude, her gentle smile, the way she'd smack him playfully with the dish towel if Blake inched too close to the freshly baked cookies cooling on the counter.

Blake swallows against the lump in his throat, resting his forehead against the acrylic plastic of the window.

The reek of smoke hangs heavily over the memories. The darkened shell of a house is no longer home.

The SoL took everything from him. His parents, his childhood, his friends—no, his *brothers*. And almost his nephew.

For too long, Jet and his goons have gotten away with their crimes.

No more.

WONDERLAND
HENDERSON, KENTUCKY

MIST HANGS LIGHTLY OVER THE DARKENING WOODS, AND THE air brushes humid and cool against my bare arms and legs. Crickets hum in the background, and our steps crunch on the gravel between the smooth gray stones leading towards the memorial.

Light spills from the cylinder, casting words of steady blue on the marble and granite of the structure. I hear Aunt Patience's breath catch as we near the Fallen Star Memorial, and I swallow against the lump in my own throat.

Secret meets my gaze when I look down at him, and the flickering lights of fireflies catch my eye as they rise up into the rapidly darkening trees.

Aunt Patience clears her throat, taking a seat on the stone bench by the entrance of the memorial and gesturing for me to follow suit. "It's a beautiful night, isn't it?"

I sit down next to her, taking in a deep breath that smells of summer. "Yeah... it is."

"Your mother made contact."

Relief floods through me as I turn to my aunt, trying to read her expression in the twilight. "Really?" *Mum's alive? She's okay?*

"We're going to London to meet up with her." Aunt Patience reaches over and squeezes my shoulder, a real smile on her face, her eyes glistening.

"London? She's in London?" My mind is spinning—wasn't she coming over here? "But—"

"I'm sure she tried her best to get to you, Ana."

Yeah. I blow out a shaky breath, blinking back tears that have no right to blur my vision. "She'll explain it all when we see her."

"That's the spirit." Aunt Patience gives my shoulder another squeeze. "We'll leave tomorrow morning."

Another plane trip. Another journey into the unknown. But Mum's alive.

See, Tirana? Not everything is broken.

The fireflies rise up, blinking their wordless song.

My fingers seek out my locket, and I rub the engraved metal with my thumbnail. "Is taking 'the road less traveled' really the best way?"

Silence meets my question, and I glance at Aunt Patience, who stares off into the distance.

The blue light falls from the cylinder, casting backwards words onto the stone.

"If this is what it leads to... is it worth it?"

"Let me ask you something, Tirana." Aunt Patience shifts, facing me, gray eyes serious. "If everyone decided it wasn't their problem, what would happen? If no one took up arms against evil, what would there be left to fight for? If we have the power to do something, how can we do nothing?"

Blinking quickly, I stare at the locket before popping it open. As I hold up the picture tucked inside, a beam of light catches it, illuminating the smiling faces of a family blissfully unaware of what the future holds.

"How did Sam put it? 'There's some good in this world, Mr. Frodo, and it's worth fighting for.'" Aunt Patience waits for me to meet her eyes again before going on. "We can't just sit here and let evil take over the world when we have the power to help *save* the world."

"So that's what the ISA is for?"

"Yes. The Incognito SMILE Agency isn't always as whimsical as it appears." She smiles, though her eyes remain solemn. "We can't give up, Tirana, no matter how high the mountains seem, or how dark the night. The world needs hope, and we're here to give it."

"Even when it... when it kills someone?" I don't realize I'm crying until Aunt Patience wraps her arms around me. I clutch my locket in one fist, squeezing my eyes shut as hot tears burn down my face. "Even when the bad guys win?"

Her own voice is hushed, choked, but she whispers, "Can darkness truly win unless we let it?"

WONDERLAND
HENDERSON, KENTUCKY
FRIDAY, JUNE 1

Friday morning dawns cool and misty, a fog shrouding the treetops as I stare out the window of the Mickey room.

"You ready for this?" I whisper, even though Secret is still curled up on my bed, dozing. *Will I ever return here?* Not only to this room, but to Wonderland?

To the friends I've made here?

Genius will recover, and Aurora will always need someone to keep her sane around him—although maybe it's Genius who needs to be kept sane around *her*. Or it's just a hopeless battle either way.

Once Agent Grizzled Fox returns, their family will be whole again. That shouldn't make my heart ache like it's my own family who's missing right now.

"'London Bridge is falling down, falling down, falling down. London Bridge is falling down, my fair lady...'" The memory of the melody in Dad's low voice when I was little, bouncing on his knee, only widens the gap in my heart.

"He'll come back, Aurora," I whisper into the quiet. But the promise seems worthless in the wake of my own loss. If Dad didn't, why should his friend?

No, no, that's not fair.

A gentle rap at the door makes both Secret and me jump up, a half bark rising in Seek's throat. I hush him, peeking out the peephole. Aunt Patience stands in the pinholed view, and I swing open the door.

"Good morning," she says cheerfully as she steps in.

I return the salutation, but I'm watching Secret as he greets her, jumping around with his tail wagging. Obviously, he's still a little on guard after this whole adventure—not that I can blame him. I'll have to work on that, try to help him decompress; but what can I do when we're about to travel once again?

"Tirana? Everything all right?"

"Yeah, just..." I bite the inside of my lip, perching on the edge of the neatly made bed, and Secret jumps up next to me and tries to worm into my lap. "Remember that game we used to play with Dad? Singing as many different songs as we could at one time?"

A smile quirks her lips. "Made your mom go crazy, if I recall correctly."

"That's what life feels like right now—like a dozen or two stories are squished together." And it doesn't help that Wonderland's theme is just that—murals from a quilt of a fairytale storyland.

"Ah, Ana." The bed shifts as she sits down next to me. "It's *your* story. That's what life is... a mad mix of stories, and somehow, it creates a new one just for you." She squeezes my arm. "It's different from Dallas' story, my story or your mom's... but it's yours, and all the pieces will come together to make something beautiful and unique and *you*." She winks at me. "And if we don't hurry, your next chapter will be titled 'The Time I Missed the Plane to London.'"

I stick out my tongue at her. "How about 'The Time My Aunt Made Me Miss the Plane'?"

"You'd never." She clutches her heart with a dramatic gasp, and I snicker.

"Just watch me. Or—" I slide to my feet and grab my bag "—I could call it 'I Did Not Miss My Plane'!"

Aunt Patience laughs, and for a moment, all is right in my world. The London Bridge stands tall, rebuilt by the teasing of my favorite (and only, as she's always quick to remind me) aunt.

So starts our next journey, or rather, the next leg of our journey.

EVANSVILLE REGIONAL AIRPORT
EVANSVILLE, INDIANA

CONVERSATIONS BUZZ AROUND US, ECHOING IN THE TERMI-nal, as Aurora leans back in the black plastic chair next to mine with a smirk. "Haven't you always wanted to see if dragons could get through security?"

"No?"

My friend laughs, shaking her head. "Aw, what's the fun in that?"

"How have you stayed out of trouble for so long?" I squint at her.

She snorts. "I haven't? But don't worry, Thomas gets in more." Something flicks over her expression, and she glances away, mumbling something about all the good that did him.

"So at long last, I know his name. That counts me as the winner." The joking lilt in my voice works; the smirk returns to Aurora's face, albeit smaller than before.

"I'll make sure to tell him that."

The loudspeaker buzzes another boarding announcement, and Aunt Patience stands, grabbing her carry-on. "That's us, girls."

Clicking my tongue to Secret, I swing my backpack over a shoulder and follow Aurora and Aunt Patience as they head down the dark-carpeted ramp among the other passengers.

On the plane, Aurora claims the window seat. I don't argue, letting Secret go ahead of me before I slide into the middle, leaving the aisle seat for Aunt Patience.

She hands us each a stick of gum, and Secret sniffs at my hand as I close my fist around the gum. "Check it," I mutter to him, and he boops the all clear.

"How does he not eat everything you put in front of him to check?" Aurora asks, raising an eyebrow.

"Tons of training. A lot of the time he'll want to check my food even if I don't ask him, like he just did. Then again, he also just loves gum." I make a face, slipping him a treat.

We talk for a few more minutes, about Secret and gum and, for some reason, dragons again, before a silence settles over our little group.

We'll be in London late tonight. Mum will be there; she has to be. I ignore the underlying doubt deep in my soul.

It's over, isn't it?

No. I can't let myself relax, not just yet. The flight attendant comes out and starts going over safety procedures, reaffirming the unsettling sense of danger lurking behind every corner.

Aurora, too, is unusually quiet, staring out the small window, probably lost in thoughts of her own.

I pull out my phone and snap a selfie of Secret and me. He leans into me, and I let out a slow breath as we rise into the air. *I'm not ready for this.* I haven't been ready for *any* of this.

But the choice has been to meet it head on, or to get trampled.

"And I—I took the road less traveled by." Robert Frost's poem seems to sum it up, and isn't that what Dad would have wanted? My own life—my own story. Not everything is in my control, but I've tried my best with the things I could... I got *The Freesia Guard* to the ISA, didn't I? And didn't die, and wasn't kidnapped, and...

I rest my head against the leather seat behind me, blinking away the sting of tears. Sure, a couple bad choices almost ended with disaster, but it wasn't Dad's book that the SoL ended up with. If it weren't for Aurora...

I eye her, but she has earbuds in, and we're not exactly in a place suited for private conversations anyway. But she'd insisted on coming—and perhaps more surprisingly, her mom let her.

Why?

Aunt Patience has explained a little, but it feels like the more I know, the more questions arise.

My fingers find my locket, and I close my eyes, letting the low drones of conversations and the rumble of the engine wash around me. Baskerville was a wild-goose chase, and I'm ashamed I ever fell for it in the first place. It feels like I betrayed Dad by believing, even a little, that he'd ever pretend to die like that.

"But you've got to pick yourself up, Tirana, and try again. Never let failure control you." That's what Mum always said. Or in Dad's words when I crashed my bike years ago, "If you fall off the horse, get back on, or you'll turn into a puddle of mushy spaghetti."

"You girls want to watch something?" Aunt Patience pulls open the player in front of her.

Aurora pulls off her earbuds, grinning like the Cheshire cat. "I have just the one."

NOTE TO SELF: DON'T LET AURORA PICK THE MOVIE. *NATIONAL Treasure* is not a film that improves my general opinion that books are better than movies. Neither is *The Bourne Identity*, although spies with memory loss are better than treasure-hunting fools.

One layover and more movies later (one about a superhero team that Batman forms to save the world from evil cubes, and a Star Wars one about space knights and a little boy who likes racing spaceships), we land at Heathrow Airport.

It's a huge, bustling place that seems like it never sleeps, and I'm afraid that I'll get lost as we skirt around the crowds that mingle everywhere. After we're admitted into the country, Aunt Patience leads us to a stop against a wall before stepping away to answer a call.

Between the movies on the plane, Aurora has apparently been reading up on stuff while I was dozing off, and she informs me of random things about London etiquette—like to not talk to anyone on the Tube, to stay on the right on escalators, and to never cut a queue.

I'm mostly worried about Secret, though. If it weren't for him, there's no way I'd be able to be in England right now. What if something goes wrong? Sure, I have the right paperwork, and customs let us through easily enough... so I guess the hardest part is over. But still...

I run my thumb over the worn leather of Secret's leash, longing for the peace of the woods back home. The bright incandescent lighting reflects off of the shiny white tiles; a hundred voices and the drum of rolling luggage echoes through my ears.

London Bridge is falling down, falling down, falling down...

Blinking the business of the airport back into focus, I scan the faces that pass, heart jumping at each one that even slightly resembles Mum. I keep on thinking that I see a tight brown bun, or the flash of a tan trench coat, but it's never her.

"Girls, let's go." Aunt Patience is suddenly there, grabbing her carry-on before heading into the crowd.

Secret's leash clutched tightly in one hand and my duffle bag in the other, I force myself away from the relative safety of the wall, keeping my eyes trained on Aurora's nondescript gray t-shirt.

There's a break in the crowd, and suddenly, Mum is there, embracing me in a hug so tight I can hardly breathe. I don't care. I return the embrace, closing my eyes against tears that sting my nose. For the first time in who knows how long, I feel like everything will be okay.

A train ride—and a walk down tree-lined streets under an overcast sky—later, Mum turns into the entrance for a shabby-looking inn nestled among equally shady, yet cool, buildings, all connected in a row that seems to span the entire block.

The room I'll be sharing with Aurora is small: two iron-framed twin beds with matching duvet covers; white walls; a designed maroon carpet; and a small desk. Nothing fancy, but it's homey.

I drop my bag on one of the beds and cross to the lone window, overlooking the city. We're two flights up. I brace my arms on the windowsill. The coolness seeps into my palms, the glass fogging up with my breath.

A bicyclist. Cars. A man in a dark hoodie, head down as he hurries down the sidewalk.

"Life goes on..." A fragment of some song I can't quite remember; a tune that's lost somewhere in the threat of a drizzle outside.

It's no myth that London is dreary.

A soft knock raps on the door, and Aurora slides off the other bed and opens it before stepping aside. "Oh, hey, Agent Dalton."

Mum enters, the harsh hotel light highlighting the ugly bruise on her face. Another person, a short guy in a beret, lingers behind her.

"This is Norton, a friend of mine," Mum says by way of introduction. "Norton, this is my daughter, Tirana, and—"

"Agent Celestial Flicker at your service, sir." Aurora nods at Norton.

"Pleasure to meet you girls," he says with a tip of his beret. "Which one am I taking?"

"Taking?" Aurora's eyes narrow as Mum tips her head at her. "Wait, what? I didn't do anything! Honest!"

Mum's chuckle is more wry than lighthearted. "Norton, take care of her."

"With pleasure, m'lady. Miz Flicker, this way, please." Norton steps back, gesturing down the hall outside the room.

"I—but—" Aurora stammers, looking from me to Mum to Norton, brow furrowed and eyes wide. "Zoo tigers! What is going on?"

I turn to Mum, but her face is as serious as always. Except... is that a twinkle brightening her eyes? I glance at Norton, who has a similar expression of mirth tightening his crow's feet. *Hmm...* How much will it really hurt Aurora to go along with whatever game this is?

"Tirana!" Aurora turns desperate eyes on me, and I have to bite my lip to keep from grinning.

Clearing my throat, I shrug. "I'd suggest going along with him... I've heard Ignis is pretty harsh to those who don't listen."

Is it my imagination, or does Norton muffle a snort? I knew I liked that guy. He steps forward again and firmly places a hand on Aurora's shoulder, saying in a grave voice, "Your friend here is right. Have you ever heard of Dead Man's Hole?"

"Dead Man's..." Aurora echoes, squinting at the man. "That place under Tower Bridge where they executed people? What does that have to do with anything?"

Norton raises an eyebrow. "Do you want to find out? Come along, Miz Flicker."

Muttering something about them being sorry if they hurt her, Aurora complies, and then it's just Mum and me.

"What was that about?" I ask, taking a seat on the edge of a bed. Secret jumps up and begs for pets.

"Oh," Mum waves a hand, "Norton's idea of a joke. Now, I believe we have a week's worth of 'adventures' to discuss…"

SAINT FLORIAN INN
LONDON, ENGLAND

WHAT AM I MISSING? BLAKE SHOVES A HAND THROUGH HIS hair, smacking the heavy volume of *The Lord of the Rings* shut. The resulting thud makes him jump, but gives no light to this case. It doesn't help that he doesn't currently have the manuscript or the decoded jargon with him, and the three-book volume on the desk in front of him is over a thousand pages long.

Maybe the copy of *The Hobbit* was something more than just a ruse. It was Dallas', after all, and the older agent had thought to leave it with Edward for some reason unknown to Blake.

Maybe if Blake wasn't such an idiot, he would even know what he's looking for. *Wouldn't that be the day?*

A rap sounds on the door, and Blake shoots to his feet, nearly upending the desk chair. A glance through the peephole shows one of Isabelle's teammates and… *Impossible.* Yet blinking does nothing to clear his niece from his vision.

His brain is still trying to catch up with this… *whatever* it is when the guy knocks again. "Open up, Hession."

Woodenly, Blake does, and Aurora still stands there, arms crossed.

She's the first one to break the silence. "So... they weren't lying. You really *did* get shipped off to the Big Smoke. I wasn't sure if it was a ruse or not."

Blake stares at her. "What are you doing here?"

"What are *you* doing here?" she throws back, narrowing her eyes. "Last anyone knew, you were kidnapped by the SoL, then you flee the country without even *letting us know*? It was Tirana's mom who told Mom you weren't, I don't know, *dead* or something!"

"I will leave you two to it," the man—Nor-something—says, backing away and escaping down the hall. Lucky guy. Facing an enraged Aurora who shouldn't even be on this side of the *world* really wasn't on Blake's to-do list for the day.

Rubbing a hand over the back of his neck, Blake steps back. "You'd better come in." No need to have this conversation out in the hall. *Shades*, if only Mya were here. She would actually know how to deal with this. *Wait.* Dropping his hand, Blake narrows his eyes at Aurora. "Your mother *does* know you're here, right?"

"No, I managed to sneak across the Atlantic Ocean without her noticing." Aurora steps inside the room and closes the door before turning to him, crossing her arms. "Of course she knows. I don't really feel like getting grounded until I'm seventy-three."

"Right." He probably should have contacted his sister after Isabelle had taken him along to London, or... something. The past days have been a blur, and now—somehow—Aurora is here.

"Uncle Blake..." Aurora stares at him for a moment before her expression crumples and she lunges at him.

He stumbles back, half in shock and half because a fifteen-year-old throwing herself at someone requires bracing in order to stay upright.

"I'm sorry," Aurora whimpers, burying her face in his shirt. "I messed... I messed everything up, didn't I? Thomas got shot, and... and..." A muffled sob cuts off her words.

Awkwardly, Blake wraps his arms around her. "Rora... no. It's not your fault." Someday, he'll need to hear the full story, but now isn't the time. But thrown into the ugly world that she never should have experienced at this age— "Aurora, no, this is *not* your fault."

"But I... I *knew* they were planning something! I knew it, and I did *nothing*." She shakes her head, anger biting her words even as her voice breaks.

Foreboding fills Blake, but he keeps his voice soft. "What did you know?"

"Agent Tilted Showdown... the whole base... it was all on *purpose*. They wanted a trap for the SoL, and... and that's why no one stopped them. They *let* them take you, Uncle Blake. It was... everything was *planned*. And I did nothing."

The news hits like a ton of bricks, but at the same time, it makes perfect sense. Why Tilted Showdown had gone after him and shown him the tunnel. Why all the ISA agents were nowhere to be seen. Why they didn't capture the SoL when they could have easily overpowered them.

Aurora pulls away, stalking to the lone window and swiping at her nose with the back of her hand. "I *knew* something was up. They didn't tell us, but Thomas and I figured most of it out. I just didn't think they'd actually *do* it."

Never underestimate those with power. Phantom substances—water, tear gas, who knows—tightens his throat, and he clears it against it. "Rora..."

"Thomas got *shot* because of me, Uncle Blake." She turns towards him, anger and tears shimmering in her eyes. "And Tirana almost went to her doom with the stupid *traitor* from your team! Because I needed to make sure I did my part so Thomas wasn't killed, but it just made things *worse*. They weren't—they weren't supposed to actually *shoot*! And they weren't supposed to take you!" Her voice breaks, and she shakes her head, squeezing her eyes shut.

"Aurora." He crosses the room, laying a hand on her shoulder, and waits for her to look up at him. "I'm here. I'm fine. They didn't even get the manuscript, due to somebody's quick thinking."

The hint of pride in her eyes confirms that it was, indeed, his niece who was behind *The Hobbit*'s noble sacrifice. Then she glances away, rubbing the back of her neck. "Yeah, about that... I know where it is."

Blake squints at her. "Where?"

"I, uh, may or may not have brought it."

"You *what*?"

CHAPTER TWENTY-FIVE
DOCIOUSALIEXPISTICFRAGICALIRUPUS

"'S upercalifragilisticexpialidocious,' even if the sound of it is really quite braggadocious. If you say it long enough it can become hypnosis, and nothing you can do can stop it from being velocious," Aurora warbles into her hairbrush. "Pa plays the fiddle and Ma diddley diddles... fiddles fiddle fiddles and diddles diddle diddles... hiddles, middle, riddle riddles, and gittles want for skittle skittles; if you want to sound quite mad it's 'dociousaliexpisticfragicalirupus!'"

"You *do* sound quite mad," I mutter. Not to mention out of tune, and I am pretty much certain that's not how the song goes.

"Oh, you just don't know good singing when you hear it." Aurora swats at me, and I duck away, laughing.

"No, I think I can tell the difference between singing and imitating a dying cow who watched too much Mary Poppins."

A knock on the door interrupts Aurora's comeback before she even opens her mouth, and she shoots me a "this isn't over" glare, following me as I hurry to answer the knock.

It's Aunt Patience, dressed in day clothes and looking decidedly perky, almost suspiciously so.

"Morning," I greet her, opening the door wide enough to let her in.

Secret wags up at her, and she crouches down to ruffle his ears.

Not for the first time since arriving in England, I'm struck by a sense of... everyone being together, and everything being *right*. I have both Mum and Aunt Patience, and *The Freesia Guard* isn't our problem anymore. I'm not sure where it is, although I reckon it's still at Wonderland. I don't think we can ever go back to before, but I'm starting to think that whatever comes next might not be so bad.

Breakfast is served in a small dining area downstairs, and we're just in time before they close it down—apparently jet lag from traveling five hours into the future makes everything seem way earlier than it is.

Neither Mum or Agent Grizzled Fox are in sight, and I try to tell myself I'm not disappointed as I survey the array of muffins, fruits, and cereal on the counter.

Aurora's still humming "Supercalifragilisticexpialidocious," or whatever her wacky version is, and Aunt Patience hums right along as they pile up on food. I'm last in line, skirting around the open pastries with a wide breadth till I see a hand-lettered sign reading "Gluten free" by a plate of blueberry muffins. *Awesome.*

I put two on a napkin, juggling them, Secret's lead, a banana, and a cup of tea as I follow the others to a table. Aunt Patience and Aurora are engrossed in an animated conversation about waffles or pancakes being superior, and I set my stuff down and take a seat, happy to just be there, listening to them try to out-argue each other. They're both failing.

Grabbing an extra napkin, I pick up one of the delicious-looking muffins and hold it down for Secret to check, still paying half an ear to my aunt trying to convince a doubtful Aurora that cheese on pancakes is actually delicious.

That's why I almost miss Secret's raised paw, the alert for detected gluten.

"Aw, rats," I mutter before asking him to check it again. Another paw, this time more insistent, like "didn't you see it the first time?" I sigh, setting the muffin back next to the other and treating him—it's not his fault some people don't know what they're doing.

"What's wrong?" Aurora asks, leaning over. "You're scowling."

I glance at her. "Want a muffin?"

"Sure!" She grabs the nearest one. "Are they gluten or something?"

"Yup." *Or something.* "Maybe it's something as little as cross-contamination because it was so close to the other baked stuff on the counter, or they used the same pan, I dunno."

Aunt Patience mutters something under her breath before giving me a small smile. "I'm sure your mother will have bones to pick."

"So, how does he tell?" Aurora asks, mouth full of the muffin that I try not to envy her for. "Like, he can detect anything?"

"Yup." Realizing I'm sounding like Eeyore, I laugh, shaking my head. "He needs some training anyway, to keep it sharp. Why don't we just show you?"

Cramming the rest of the muffin into her mouth, Aurora nods eagerly.

Aunt Patience grins, though seriousness still lurks in her eyes. "Never does get old watching magic."

"It's not magic. Just science." I wink at her. "Let me go wash my hands, and we shall begin. Aunt Patience, can you hold him for a sec?"

On my way to the sink, I make a little detour to the food counter, again skirting the baked stuff as best I can. Leaning in as far as I dare, I check out the muffin plate again—the sign is definitely for them. *Welp, you were getting too lax, after all.*

And I try not to think of what could have easily happened if Secret hadn't caught the contamination. A hospital visit on my first *day* in London? Mum would never let me out of her sight again.

Back at the table, we prepare a wonderful spectacle. First, I have Secret check my banana—he bops my leg, an all clear. Same goes for my tea: another clear. His wagging tail betrays that he's enjoying this as much as I'm starting to.

"What about this?" Aurora holds up the other muffin I'd taken.

I shrug. "First off, your hands are pretty dirty, but sure. Put it in a new napkin."

She does, then hands it to me. Carefully, I take it, lowering it to Secret's level and turning it slowly as he sniffs it. He raises a paw, sitting.

"Good job, buddy." I glance at Aurora, setting the offending food back on the table. "See?"

"Impressive." She grabs the muffin and takes a big bite. "Wat abob dis?" She holds up a shiny red apple.

"Hmm... wanna try, Seek?" I hold out my hand, and he nudges it with his cold nose. I slip him a treat, cue a spin, then ask for a sit and Aurora's apple, cradled in a clean napkin. "Check."

He sniffs it, then paws the air, looking at me expectantly. Grinning, I give Aurora back her poisoned apple and give Secret his hard-earned piece of dried liver. "How's that?"

"Very impressive. But I didn't think apples had gluten in them." She raises an eyebrow, inspecting the fruit.

I smile. "What did you touch before you touched it?"

"Uh... your muffins? A pastry?"

"Exactly."

Understanding dawns on Aurora's face. "So it's like gunpowder or something—trace amounts are still there, right?"

"Exactly." I ruffle Secret's head. "He's saved me more times than I can count."

"And you keep on protecting her, you hear, Secret?" Aunt Patience, who'd been silent, raises an eyebrow at my dog. "Now, if you girls are done with breakfast, Isabelle wanted to talk to you."

As we pack up and head out of the dining room, Aunt Patience falls into step beside me, squeezing my shoulder. "Proud of you, girl."

I duck my head with a smile, heart warming. It's been a long journey to get here—in more ways than one—but what she said in that letter is right.

With my dog, maybe I really *can* do anything.

"MINIONS—THE SOL? OCEAN TIMBER—DRIFTWOOD? NICKEL tickets—new kind of music? Gentle enemies?? Never trust bacon—pigs? Ragnar—evil person, SoL? Anchor indigo never fills identity (color doesn't fill

something?) leading to absolute tarradiddle in operation November (mission?) oxygen finagles many octagon robots doom (???)." The notes scrawled on the blue lines of the notebook paper are hardly legible, even though Blake wrote them himself.

He sighs, pushing away the hard-backed chair and standing to survey the array of notes, books, and other paraphernalia cluttering the small table tucked into the corner of the tiny library. Two code books lie open with *The Freesia Guard* next to them, and a small laptop sits to the side, the copy of the drive that Thomas had apparently made plugged in.

Blake had painstakingly re-decoded the first bit, up until "doom," before attempting to tackle this section, for all the good it did.

He just isn't good at codes, plain and simple. Too bad he's the only one to do it.

"Hession?"

Blake glances up to see Isabelle enter the library, trailed by Aurora, Tirana, and the dog. They crowd in, Aurora craning her neck over Isabelle's shoulder.

"How is your progress?" Isabelle crosses her arms, eyeing the table.

Blake fights the urge to cover everything up, shrugging instead. "What's this about?" Sure, she was nice enough to let him use the hotel library, but what are the girls doing here?

Aurora pushes past the Ignis agent, grinning. "Why, Uncle Blake, isn't it obvious? We're here to help you."

Help? He eyes the girls. They don't need to be involved in this—

Isa's raised-eyebrow look of "don't raise a fuss or you'll regret it" makes him sigh.

"Fine."

"Good chap." Isabelle flashes him a *charming* smile before leaving them alone.

The first thing Aurora does is pull up another two chairs and rearrange his perfectly fine arrangement, then she turns to his notes.

"That's all you got?" She eyes the latest, eyes narrowed and nose scrunched up.

He shrugs, deciding not to mention the crumpled papers that will never see the light of day. Or that he's been working for three hours straight already.

"Operation November?" Tirana glances up from the paper, looking confused. "Nickel tickets?"

"Exactly," Blake mutters, leaning back in his chair and ignoring the urge to rub his temples. Of course the strain of close-up work for so long has started a headache, but he doesn't really care. He just wants it done and over.

"You're looking at this all wrong," Aurora says, tapping the piece of paper with the end of a pen.

As if he can't figure *that* out. Why in the world would someone not trust bacon?

"Dad always liked hiding things in plain sight." Tirana fingers her locket. "So... what's the simplest thing it *could* be?"

Aurora considers the list of words. "One of the letters in each word spelling out the secret message?"

Blake bites back a sigh. Flame or Tilted Showdown would have already tried that, though anything Flame touched might as well mean nothing. Fortunately, the ISA has the traitor in their custody, according to Aurora, so he can't go blabbing everything to Jet.

"Minions in secret sections implement official nickel rest embedded pouring ocean timber... The first letters would be too easy..." Aurora mumbles to herself, tapping her pen on her chin as she grabs a blank piece of paper and sliding it towards her. "Tirana, write this down: s, n, t, s, t, l, l, t, d, g, n, r. Okay, now show me."

Tirana holds up the notebook, shaking her head. "It's nothing."

"We'll see about that." Aurora taps her chin with the pen. "Write down m, i, s, s, i, o, n, r, e, p, o, r, t..." Her voice trails off, her eyes cutting to Blake, who straightens.

Tirana gasps. "'Mission report!'"

Huh? A bunch of letters turn into words in the air? Because he didn't catch them.

"A, g, e, n, t, b, e, l, r, i, a," Aurora continues, voice high with excitement, and this time, Blake has no trouble figuring out what the letters spell.

Heart suddenly pounding painfully, Blake swallows, because *this* was what Dallas was working on during that last mission.

This is what got him killed.

And two hours later, the full report is completed.

Mission Report, Agent Bel Ria

Infiltration of Mordor cell in or near Minas Tirith, Middle-earth

Blotmath 22 to Termination

I. Primary objectives:

To gain information regarding suspected arson across Minas Tirith and the surrounding area throughout the vicennium.

To determine the rumors of an upcoming planned terrorist attack (Operation Doom).

To study and report on the techniques used by Mordor.

II. Key Observations:

Blotmath 23: Have enlisted in Isengard as Lewis Foest. Isengard meets bimonthly at Orthanc.

Blotmath 25: First meeting a success. Topics discussed were hunting dogs, a new game law, trucks, and the results of the election. Connections made with several orcs, namely Shagrat and Gorbag.

Foreyule 2: Uglúk seems suspicious and wishes to test me. Set a private meeting for tomorrow night.

Foreyule 3: Uglúk plans to send me with Shagrat and Gorbag, destination Cirith Ungol, to "see how we do things here."

Foreyule 5: Cirith Ungol a success.

Foreyule 9: Third Isengard meeting. Uglúk hinted at Operation Doom, refusing to say more upon my asking. Something large is being planned, yet only about half of Isengard are in on it.

Foreyule 11: Private dinner with Shagrat proved fruitful, as drink loosened his lips. Mentioned involvement in arson, seeming proud and saying Isengard was too good to get caught. Did not mention more.

Foreyule 15: Shagrat made contact, warning me that Uglúk is suspicious of me. Must lay low.

Foreyule 17: Secured information regarding several arsons, including: Shepherd residence, Iona, Middle-earth, Wedmath 11, reported cause kitchen fire, casualties two; Center Fire Department, Minas Tirith, Middle-earth, Afterlithe 27, reported cause faulty wiring, zero casualties; Crassus residence, Olga, Middle-earth, Wedmath 11, reported cause kitchen fire, one casualty; Huxley residence, Tice, Middle-earth, Wedmath 11, reported cause faulty wiring, zero casualties; Goodyear residence, Minas Tirith, Middle-earth, Rethe 14, no reported cause, one infant casualty. Copies of the files have been collected and stored.

Foreyule 23: Isengard talks openly of plans to attend a rally in Fangorn in Afteryule. No other talk is made, but something else is afoot.

Foreyule 27: Dinner again with Shagrat, who mentioned other "secret" meetings with orcs of Isengard. I suspect that select orcs meet to plan for Operation Doom. Must be tactful—Uglúk wields the Eye of Sauron.

Afteryule 6: Isengard focuses all attention on upcoming rally. Planted palantír in Meduseld.

Afteryule 9: Operation Doom is to enact January 14, targeting the Samuel and Lily Cotton residence, due to Cotton's involvement in the seizing of property from private landowners to build Minas Tirith Appliance Emissions Licensing Board. Palantír was discovered. Must remove myself from Isengard and contact Gondor for extraction. Uglúk will not show mercy.

KENSINGTON GARDENS
LONDON, ENGLAND

SUPERCALIFRAGILISTICEXPIALIDOCIOUS... AURORA'S STILL HUM-ming that song lightly under her breath as we stroll through the open wrought iron gates of what Mum says is Kensington Gardens. Well-pruned holly bushes border the fence line, which is brick and topped with iron bars, giving me the feeling like I'm walking into something like *The Secret Garden*, despite the traffic from the busy street we just turned off of.

I'm not exactly sure whose idea it was for us to get ice cream on this overcast day, nor why we're going to a park for it, but neither Secret nor I are complaining about either. The fresh air is nice, and walking gives me time to think.

Aunt Patience and I walk next to each other, with Mum in the lead and Aurora and Agent Grizzled Fox taking up the rear.

The silence between all of us feels more awkward than peaceful, despite the warm-but-not-hot weather, the green grass, and the towering, droopy-leaved trees boarding the wide path.

Drawing in a long breath tinted with city and park, I glance at Aunt Patience. "What did you think of *The Freesia Guard*? Didn't really get a chance to ask you before... everything."

Her head snaps towards me like I said something wrong. "Come again?"

"The book. What did you think of the plot? Who was your favorite character?" I roll Secret's leash between my fingers, hoping I'm not breaking some unspoken rule by talking about it.

"Well... the talking cat was an interesting touch." Aunt Patience smirks, getting that look in her eyes like when she's about to go into book reviewing mode. "Let's see... Timmy was a brave, kind-hearted little boy, though a bit reckless and impatient. Robin was the typical younger sister, much like *someone* I know—" she clears her throat "—and she had outstanding smarts, good looks, and common sense. The unsung hero of the story, if I do say so myself. After all, without her, Timmy never would have been able to make it to Ragnar's lair. Joseph and Harpy were a hoot, but they were very dedicated Freesia Guards, and Ragnar was a nasty villain indeed—he certainly deserved what he got."

"Sucked into the Great Black Hole of Evil Villains?" I nod. "Do... uh, what did you think—about the time when Timmy and Robin had to crack those riddles to get into the cave?" Biting my tongue, I pretend that was what I was going to say all along, and not "do you think the plot has anything to do with the report?" Because she hasn't seen the report, and I don't think that either Aurora or Grizzled Fox would be happy if I mention it.

"That it wasn't worth it, and they should have found a different way." Something in Aunt Patience's voice makes my wonder if she's even referring to the book at all.

"But... then they wouldn't have found Harpy's brooch, and wouldn't have known that Harpy and Joesy were held there. And they wouldn't have found Harpy's message."

Aunt Patience hums a noncommittal note, but says no more. Before I can even begin to figure out something to say to lighten the mood that had suddenly dropped to match the dreary clouds overhead, the path spills out into an open area, reminding me of a sort of developed crossroads.

"What's this?" Aurora asks, passing me to examine a small stone fountain with two hugging bears perched atop.

"Welcome to the Italian Gardens," says Mum, a smile playing on her lips. "Ice cream will be at the van right up ahead."

Sure enough, a boxy white antique van is parked next to a fenced-off section of garden that houses an ornate stone building. In the single window of the van, there's a small sign that I can't read from here, and only the chalkboard menu sitting on the running board indicates it's an ice cream truck.

There's no line, and pretty soon we all have some sort of frozen treat, including some vanilla ice cream for a very appreciative Secret.

"Isn't the Peter Pan statue around here somewhere?" Aurora asks, licking her cone.

"Can we go?" I ask, looking up from my popsicle.

"It's not too far from here, but perhaps later." Mum's gaze drifts towards Agent Grizzled Fox, who's staring down at the ice cream Aurora insisted he get, despite his protest of not being hungry.

What has the gloomy agent got to do with visiting a famous landmark? He'd been even gloomier than usual, even since we decoded that file.

Uglúk will not show mercy.

The last line of the report sends shudders down my spine, despite the warm weather and the sun peeking out between the clouds.

Uglúk, one of the orcs from *The Lord of the Rings.* A leader of the Uruk-Hai, a group marked with the white hand of their master Saruman. Not someone you'd want to meet in a dark alley... or ever.

Was this Uglúk behind Dad's death? My hand tightens around my popsicle stick.

And the rest of the report was coded in *The Lord of the Rings* jargon, too. People, places, times—even Dad's alias, Lewis Foest.

And somehow, that's supposed to help the ISA.

One report in exchange for my dad's life.

How can that possibly be worth it?

CHAPTER TWENTY-SIX
THE NORTH IN OUR STARS

They died.

The family that Dallas had tried to save, had given up his life for—they were dead.

"Friday night, Samuel Cotton, 43, his wife Lily, 41, and their young daughter, Rose, were killed in a fiery car accident on SR-82. They were on their way home from a church function when Cotton reportedly lost control of the vehicle, which rolled several times before slamming into a tree. Investigation is ongoing."

Only a month after Dallas had blown his cover to stop the planned arson on the Cottons' house, it was a car accident that ended them.

Blake rubs a hand over his eyes, that heavy feeling of doom settling deep in his gut. It wasn't an *accident*. Accidents are accidental. They don't happen when a family is targeted by terrorists.

Dallas' death wasn't an accident, and neither was the Cottons', but with no proof, there can be no justice.

So focus on what you can fix, Blake tells himself, straightening and clicking through the files that Isabelle's agents had unearthed from a hidden folder on the drive.

This is supposed to be what made Dallas' sacrifice worth it. Copies of the SoL's meticulous records of their evil deeds. Proof that the "accidental" fires across Florida, including the one at the Shepherds' residence that took the lives of Damian's parents, were arson.

No wonder the Suns of Liberty tried so hard to get their hands on *The Freesia Guard*. No wonder they killed Dallas over it.

Maybe Dallas' intervention postponed the Cottons' death by a month, but *shades*, it's so, so—*stupid*.

Blake drops his head into his crossed arms on the desk, closing his eyes. How was it worth this? The Fort Myers SoL cell is already gone, already neck-deep in trouble from their poorly planned attack on Base Buckleberry. This will only drown them.

No, not that. He sucks in a shuddering breath, straightening and staring at the file open on the computer screen. *"March 14—Goodyear fire a success. Robert Goodyear has revoked his opposition to the bill and will no longer be a problem."* Yeah, because that fire killed his *baby*. Because that fire undoubtedly ruined his life, just like the fire that ruined Damian's, and the one that had taken Blake's own parents.

Blake grinds his teeth. The SoL *will* pay.

There's a rap on the door, then a familiar head sticks in. "Isa said I'd find you here—"

Blake turns away from Patience, swiveling the office chair to face the wall of the borrowed office.

"Blake? Is something wrong?"

Of course nothing's wrong. Everything is perfectly fine.

"Blake, talk to me."

Seconds tick by, and he closes his eyes for a moment before swiveling the chair to face his old teammate. Patience has claimed the only other chair in this closet of an office, and her eyebrows are raised as she watches him.

"It wasn't worth it," Blake says flatly.

"Blake..." Patience reaches out like she wants to touch his arm, but she pulls her hand back and sighs. "I know he was your best friend, but he was my *brother*."

Blake bowes his head. "Pay—"

"Blake." Her voice drops to a frustrated sigh. "Stop feeling sorry for yourself."

"I'm not—"

Patience crosses her arms, something sparking in her eyes. "There's a level of grief, and a level of trauma, but Blake—you've given *up*. Don't you see? We've both lost opportunities and people, and life will never be the same, but... you have to *try*."

"Try what? To pretend it didn't happen and we're still the group of stupid kids we used to be?" Blake glares at her. "We're not. *I'm* not."

Patience shakes her head, clearly frustrated. "C'mon, Foxy, look at yourself. When's the last time you've enjoyed anything? When's the last time you spent time with Mya or the twins? When's the last time you *lived*?"

Blake freezes at the old nickname and looks away, because he can't remember when. Or maybe, his subconscious whispers, he just doesn't want to admit it.

When Patience speaks again, her voice is softer. "This isn't what they would have wanted, Blake. Are you going to *let* their deaths be in vain?"

"It's not up to *me*." He turns the computer to face her. It's still open to the news report on the Cottons' "accident."

She reads the report, lips tightening into a thin line. "Well, that's certainly despicable."

"Dallas tried to *save* them." Blake crosses his arms against his chest, staring at the wall over Patience's head. "He blew his cover to stop that fire, and that family still died. It just—took longer." Which is a better coffin... fire, or twisted metal?

Patience is silent for a long moment before she pulls the laptop to herself and clicks through the files, shaking her head slowly. "Unbelievable."

Except it's all too believable. Thanos, Darkseid, Hydra, the Joker, and all the other ultra-evil supervillains don't exist outside their fictional universes, but the SoL isn't some made-up, diabolical fantasy.

Blake watches Patience as she reads through the files, her face twisting into greater disgust the further she reads. She'd always been the strong, playful one, just as likely to offer a hug as she was to play a prank. Losing her fiancé and then her brother should have destroyed her, but here she is, still fighting just as hard as she had when they were younger.

Blake shifts, exhaling slowly. "How do you do it, Pay?"

"Do what?" She glances up from the computer with a frown.

He hesitates, but forces himself to say it. "Keep from drowning under—everything."

She considers him thoughtfully. "I suppose I just try to keep my sights on what's here, and know that Damian and Dallas both lived their lives to the fullest—so that's what I try to do. It's not easy; of course it's not easy; but I do it for them... and for Tirana." Her gaze lowers, and she fingers the edge of the computer. "If I were to vanish into the abyss, where would that leave her? I might never have kids of my own, but if anything were to happen to her..." She trails off with a half shrug. "Dallas and Damian are gone, and it's up to us to make sure their sacrifice is worth something. Even... even if it's just an extra month for a family that otherwise wouldn't have it."

But it's not fair. Blake studies the scratched surface of the desk. Mya's told him, time and time again, that he needs to move on, but it's impossible to just "move on" when a piece of his mind is stuck back in that Florida river. But maybe Patience is right. Dallas would never have let Blake close himself off from his friends and family. Dallas would never have let Blake wish that he'd died in that crash, too. And Blake hadn't died—for better, or for worse.

Maybe it's time to stop acting like he did.

"Okay." Blake uncrosses his arms, eyes flicking to Patience.

"Okay?" she repeats, a question in her voice.

He nods. "Yeah." Dallas is gone, Damian is gone, and even the family Dallas gave up his life to save is gone... but this isn't the end. Blake won't let it stop here. After all, they have a domestic terrorist group to take down.

"Huh, what's this?" Patience frowns at the computer. "Two copies of the same report?" She squints the screen. "Huh... this one must be marked wrong. And I thought all these files were about the egregious crimes the SoL *committed*."

"What?" Blake frowns, leaning forward.

"Look." Forehead wrinkled, she turns the computer so that Blake can see the screen. "This date isn't in the past, Blake. It's *next month*."

CHAPTER TWENTY-SEVEN
PLEASE LOOK AFTER THIS BEAR

"So... how are you finding London?" Blake glances at his niece as they walk. The early morning air is cool in the shade, but the sun's been warming the city for hours. The residential streets are still waking up, and it's mostly quiet, though the rush of traffic is a never-ending cadence in the background. A pigeon hops out of their path, tilting its head at Blake and Aurora as they pass.

After unearthing a bombshell like the one Patience had found last night, it feels wrong to be out and about, doing what is decidedly not mission-related sightseeing, but Aurora's wanted to see Paddington Station since she watched the movie about the bear when she was eleven. There's nothing Blake can do about the planned attack—Isabelle and Patience pretty much kicked him out of the building—and... Well, he's trying to do better by his family.

Aurora pulls out her phone and snaps a few photos of the pigeon. "Did you know the City of London is the smallest city in England?"

"Looks plenty big to me." Blake eyes the sidewalk, lined with apartments and wrought iron fences with the occasional, evenly spaced tree.

"Yeah, but the City of London is only like... one square mile. We're in the City of Westminster."

"Thought it was London."

"It is." Aurora grins. "Gotta love districts—technically, boroughs, since they're their own administrative units."

"What is it about cities making things needlessly confusing?"

Aurora snickers. "Trust me, the city Thomas and I are building in *Cities XL* is *so* much worse. It looks like the urban planners drew the blueprints with their eyes closed."

"Did they?" Blake raises an eyebrow.

She snorts. "He started it."

Of course Thomas did. Despite himself, a smile tugs at Blake's lips. "Let me guess... a dare?"

"We wanted to see how ineffective we could possibly make a city. And the best part? Mom counts it as school." Aurora smirks, then sighs. "I wish Aunt Isabelle would've let Tirana come. She'd *love* seeing the Paddington statue."

Blake gives his niece a rueful smile. "Well, if Isa wants some time with her daughter, she's getting it." In truth, the Ignis agent just doesn't want Tirana going anywhere without her, and she's too busy trying to stop a SoL attack to chaperone this trip. "Guess you're stuck with me."

Aurora narrows her eyes and looks him up and down. After a moment, she nods. "It'll do."

Blake huffs. "What? I'm an *it* now?"

"Not unless I tag you." Aurora skips away, tossing a grin over her shoulder.

"Lame," Blake mutters, shaking his head as Aurora drops back next to him, her eyes sparkling with the light that's been missing since Florida.

"Not as lame as you," she retorts.

"Okay, now *that* is lame." Blake raises an eyebrow. "What are you, seven?"

"Get in the times, old man Blake! You're, like, eight years behind. Do you even have Wi-Fi in the cave you grew up in, or did you catch the dinosaurs with your bare hands?"

"The disrespect." Blake sighs. "If you must know, we had very efficient bows and arrows."

"Ha! I knew it!"

He grunts, rolling his eyes, and Aurora chatters on as construction barriers pop up, taking up half the sidewalk and making London look like any other city—always undergoing some new project. Blake doesn't particularly know where he's going, but Aurora is confident that she does, so he lets her lead.

He should be back at Ignis, helping his sister do whatever they need to do when a major plot against the ISA is discovered. Over two years in planning, and the ISA hadn't caught wind of the fact that the SoL was scheming to attack them directly? *Bombing* their bases? Dallas' file had been scarce of details, hidden behind another file—had he even known he'd copied it? Dallas had been so intent on saving that Cotton family when he had contacted Blake. Or had Dallas mentioned it, and Blake forgot? It's all lost in a blur of panic and water.

"We're here, Uncle Blake." Aurora's words jolt Blake back to the present, and he flashes her a tight smile.

"Lead the way, Lightsaber Lady." Because he promises that he's trying. For Aurora's sake—for Dallas' sake—and maybe for his own sake.

It's busy inside Paddington Station, and the tiled floors, the echoing loudspeaker, and the commuters' rolling suitcases behind them reminds him of an airport. Overhead, the ceiling arches in sprawling white and red architecture.

"This is a security message. If you see something that doesn't look right, tell staff or text the British Transport Police. We'll sort it. See it, say it, sort it," an automated woman's voice blares over the loudspeaker. Blake scoffs, wondering how much the corny message actually helps crime in this place.

"This way," Aurora calls over the hustle, apparently knowing exactly where to go. The famous sculpture is positioned under a huge clock, and Aurora kneels on the platform next to the bear and poses. "Take a picture of me!"

Blake laughs and pulls out his phone, snapping a photo. Without Thomas making bunny or elephant ears over his sister's head, it looks unbalanced, but Aurora runs over and demands to see the pictures before Blake can worry about how his nephew is doing.

"Great, now we need a picture of both of us," Aurora says, bouncing on her toes. Before Blake can protest, Aurora turns to a passing stranger with a fancy-looking camera slung over her shoulder and waves her down.

"Hey, excuse me—can you take a picture of my uncle and me?"

The lady agrees, and Aurora hands over her phone before pulling Blake to the statue.

"Rora—" Blake objects, but Aurora shoots him a look that's identical to Mya's "do this or else" expression, and what can he do other than obediently pose? The lady takes a few pictures, gives Aurora her phone back, and after Aurora thanks her, goes on her merry way.

"Well, now what?" Aurora asks cheerfully.

A couple with three way-too-hyper little kids comes up to the bear, and Blake moves away with a shrug, nearly bumping into a businesswoman wheeling a suitcase. "Back?"

"Boring." Aurora wrinkles her nose. "We're tourists here—we can do anything!"

"Does 'anything' include coffee?" Between the jet lag and the grating, constant hubbub of the station, Blake wouldn't mind some.

Aurora brightens. "Coffee! I saw a sign for a Starbucks—I think it's this way." She takes off, and Blake hurries to not lose her in the crush of people. After a pit stop at the bathrooms, a few wrong turns, and nearly getting run over by a group of teens, they finally make it to a part of the station that reminds Blake of a food court in a mall.

The Starbucks is on the mezzanine level above the food court. The line isn't long, and soon they're settled at a corner booth with coffee and pastries.

"We're probably going to be heading back to the States soon," Blake says as nonchalantly as he can, taking a sip of cappuccino. He hasn't told Aurora about the new developments yet, because she'll be less inclined to actually enjoy their last few days here if she knows that her beloved ISA has been threatened.

She narrows her eyes at him, setting down her ridiculously large frappuccino. "Why? Did something happen? Is Thomas okay?"

She's too suspicious. Always has been. Blake offers her a smile, but her gaze hardens.

"This is a Hard Stare," she says, not breaking eye contact. "What's wrong?"

"Nothing's *wrong*, Rora." Blake rubs the back of his neck. "The case just—needs us back at Wonderland. Patience found something..." He hesitates, but Aurora is Mya's daughter; she'll find out one way or another. "Plans for a large-scale attack that's supposed to be planned for this August."

Alarm flickers in Aurora's expression, but Blake holds up his hand. "Look, we don't even know if this is still happening—it's from nearly two *years* ago. It's easily nothing."

She just frowns. "What kind of 'large-scale attacks'? What does that even mean?"

"Didn't say." Or, at least, it didn't specify... but the "blow up ISA bases" written on that report probably gives some clues.

Aurora's next question, unsurprisingly, is "Why didn't you tell me sooner?"

Blake sips his coffee slowly, meeting her gaze. "It's not your job to save the world, Rora."

She crosses her arms, leaning back in her chair and giving him another Hard Stare. "Oh? And is it yours?"

"Kinda?"

She huffs. "And that's why we're here instead of working to stop *another* attack? Or was the one at Buckleberry part of this grand plan, too?"

Blake rubs his forehead. "I don't know. I think that was just Jet. And—I don't know. Maybe I just wanted to—" He cuts himself off, staring down at his cup, slowly swishing around the bean water. Does it even matter? No matter what he does, it's never good enough.

"Enjoy our day before freaking out?" Aurora offers, always too perceptive.

He shrugs. "Pretty much." For all the good it did.

"Then let's do that."

He glances up at her with a frown.

"Let's stay here and finish our drinks and not worry about anything until we get back." There's a determined look in Aurora's eyes, backing her uncharacteristic proposition. "They've already taken enough away from us. Why should we let it take away our freedom and joy, too?"

"You're way too wise for your age." Blake huffs, curling his hands around his drink. "Your mom's taught you well."

"Dad's the one who always says that rebellions are built on hope." Aurora shrugs, taking a bite of her croissant. "And that fear is the path to the dark side. Dad also claims that quoting Yoda won't get me out of dish duty, though, so take that with a grain of salt."

Blake snorts. Mya's husband is a Star Wars superfan to rival Mya's love of the X-Men. Having *another* friend who made constant pop culture references that he didn't get had driven Damian crazy. Everything remotely popular somehow always managed to go right over his head—except, for some reason, Alice in Wonderland.

"Earth to Foxy?" Aurora waves a hand in front of Blake's face, and he blinks.

"Hm?"

"I was saying, 'Luke, I am your father.'" She raises an eyebrow. "Did you miss the entire lightsaber fight?"

"What?... *Lightsaber* fight?" Nothing on the small table resembles a weapon, and he squints at her.

Aurora laughs. "Just messin' with you." She reaches for her pocket, then frowns. "My phone's gone. I was going to take some pictures for Thomas, but..." She checks her other pockets, then the seat beside her, and the floor. "It's definitely not here. I must've left it at the bathrooms." She makes a face. "I hope no one stole it."

Blake starts to gather the bagel's he hardly touched, but Aurora slides out of her seat and shakes her head.

"I'll be *right* back." Not even waiting for a reply, she darts away like she's the Flash, almost knocking into a waiter. Shouting an apology over her shoulder, she vanishes into the station.

Blake almost snorts. *Only Aurora.* Mya's probably going to have his head for letting Aurora wander around Paddington alone, but at this point, it's probably better to just stay here and wait. That way, she'll at least know where he is.

He sighs as he leans back to wait, the café music and the buzz of talking a drone in the background. Sipping his coffee, he lets his gaze travel around the room, catching on a family a few tables down. A dad, a mom, and two kids—a girl and a boy, maybe six and nine.

"Are we going to the Tower of London today?" The boy bounces in his seat, almost spilling his drink.

The girl snickers. "Only if you don't faint again, Parky!"

He sticks his tongue out at her. "I never *faint*, Rose. Fainting is for sissies. I just—sometimes fall asleep on my feet."

"Kids," the mom warns, "be nice or we're not going anywhere. And Parker, sit still or you're going to make a mess."

"Sorry." Parker stops bouncing for about three seconds before he starts wiggling in his chair. "I wanna see the place where they executed people! Are we going there?"

"This is your fault," the mom says to the dad, shaking her head. "Your stories, your kid."

The dad laughs. "If you listen to your mom, we'll make sure to stop at the tower, Parker."

"But I wanted to go to the zoo!" Rose protests, lower lip sticking out as she begins to pout.

"Don't worry, Rosie." The dad winks. "You two are a traveling zoo. And you know what that makes me? The animal-tickler!" He reaches under the table to tickle the little girl, and she squeals in laughter.

The mom bats his hand away. "Not when we're *eating*, honey! Geez, you'd think my family is a band of hooligans!"

"Don't worry, Mom," Parker assures her, "we're the *best* band of hooligans."

It's one moment in time, one burst of laughter, one picture in a Starbucks in a city full of chaos, but as Blake watches them, he begins to understand.

In the comics, a superhero can never save everybody. The Flash can't,

Batman can't, even Superman can't. But that's not why they fight, is it? They fight because it's the only thing they can do, and because it's worth it.

Everything Dallas and Damian did, every sacrifice, every loss and fight and win... It's worth *something*. A child's laughter. The smile of a loved one. A simple gesture of kindness by a stranger. It's not useless, not meritless, because it keeps the darkness from taking over.

The dad ruffles Parker's hair, and the mom begins to clean up as the little girl chatters about zoo animals.

That family could have been Damian's, if Damian had lived past twenty-four. It could be anyone's family; anyone's beloved grandchildren or niece or nephew or sister or brother. But they're together, they're laughing, they're a *family*, because there are people out there who care. People like Blake's old friends. People willing to die for something greater than themselves.

And isn't that the greatest form of love?

Blake's phone buzzes, and he frowns as he picks it up and glances at the text.

AURORA

> meet me outside the
> Paddington Basin exit :)

"I guess she found her phone," he mutters to himself, shaking his head as he cleans up the table. Why the Paddington *Basin* exit, though? It seems odd, but he trusts his niece. She probably found another photo opportunity or... something.

It takes some time to find the right place, but when he finally climbs the stairs to exit the station, he kind of wishes he hadn't. It's not the fact that Aurora is nowhere in sight, which is worrying in its own right, but the canal can't be more than thirty paces away.

Blake freezes, turning to retreat back inside the station. Whatever Aurora's plan is, he's not doing this.

"I'm so glad you could make it," an eerily familiar voice purrs.

Blake turns very slowly to face the speaker, and the man tips the brim of his English cap.

"I was beginning to think you weren't going to make it." Jet leans casually against the side of the building, hands in his pockets and a sinister smirk on his face. "And wouldn't that be a shame?"

This cannot be happening. Blake takes a step back, almost tripping over the uneven surface of a stair behind him, and he barely grabs hold of the railing in time to keep from falling.

"Come on, old friend!" Jet pushes away from the wall with a wink. "At least pretend you're happy to see me. And I wouldn't raise a fuss if I were you," he adds in an undertone as he draws up to Blake. "If you value your niece's life, that is."

CHAPTER TWENTY-EIGHT
FOLLOW MY LEADER

"What do you want?" Blake swallows against a mouth as dry as a desert, crossing his arms and ignoring their tremble.

"Come." Jet tilts his head towards the wide pedestrian street that borders the canal. Low-set houseboats bob in the water, brightly colored floating coffins, and people walk by like it's just an ordinary day. A couple hug, their laughter blowing away in the stiff, water-scented breeze.

"What if I don't?" Blake keeps his voice low, stepping away from the stairs.

Jet holds up a phone like it's supposed to mean something.

Blake looks at it, then at Jet, schooling his expression to stay impassive, even as his heart thuds painfully against his ribs. "Why are you here? What do you want?"

"You don't recognize this?" Jet's expression twists into a confused sneer as he eyes the phone.

"Why are you here?" Blake repeats levelly, staring the taller man down. "You're a wanted man back in the States." And most certainly here, too, if Isabelle had anything to do with it.

Jet glowers. "They won't catch me. Now come on, let's go."

"You expect me to go anywhere with *you*?" There's a security guard at the end of the plaza, looking their way. If Jet tries anything.....

Jet obviously notices the guard, too, and he growls a curse under his breath. "Blast you, Hession, this is your precious Aurora's phone! If you want to see her alive, you'd better do as I say."

It would probably take the guard under thirty seconds to get here, if Blake flagged him down. Jet's jittery—unpredictable at the best of times, but he's unsettled, nervous. Had he expected Blake to go along with his schemes without proof or protest?

"And if I don't?"

Jet fumbles with Aurora's phone, pulling out what must be his own phone with a sneer. "Have it your way, then, *Riley*." He dials a number and holds it up so that only he and Blake can hear the voice on the other end. "Richard, give our little friend a voice, won't you?"

"'appily," returns a male voice laced with a Cockney accent, and a whimpering scream cuts through the phone's tinny speakers.

"Satisfied?" Jet raises an eyebrow, hanging up and replacing the phone to his pocket. "Or should I give him a call back? I'm sure there are more... *creative* ways to make a girl scream."

Jet has the upper hand, and he knows it. If Blake had a bow and an arrow, or a batarang in his pocket, or laser vision, Jet wouldn't stand a chance. But this isn't the comics, and if Jet really does have Blake's niece... "What do you want?" Blake growls.

Jet laughs. "You know full well what I want. Come, let's have a little chat, shall we?"

The security guard is gone, Jet has Aurora, and like a man walking the gangplank, Blake has no option but to obey. The stupid canal is too close, and the laughter that rings from the houseboats mocks him. To his left is a brick wall, leaving no room for escape. As Jet leads him down the cobblestone sidewalk, his bad leg aches, the limp harder to conceal, but that's the least of his worries. If they have Aurora... *No. She'll be fine.*

The walk seems to go on forever, but at least the open walkway funnels into an alley behind shabby brick buildings, pressed together like children huddling against the threat of danger.

First Thomas, now Aurora—Mya's going to kill him.

"This way." Jet makes a sharp left into a narrow alley, and Blake clenches his jaw.

"Where are you taking me?" Surely nothing good can come out of this area—nor this situation. "Where's Aurora? Why are you even *here*?"

A cackled huff of a laugh is Jet's only reply.

Blake grits his teeth, refusing to entertain the thought of what Dallas would be thinking—if this mess hadn't *killed* him.

And if it kills Blake, too—then at least he'll join his friends.

The cobblestone abruptly turns to wooden slabs several minutes later, and when they round the corner, the ripping waves of the canal explain why.

"Move, you idiot," Jet hisses.

Yet his feet are rooted on the ground, his mind frosted over with the ice sending fire through his veins. Jet can't possibly expect—

"*Move.*"

"I'd listen to 'im if I were you," a new voice speaks up as an average-looking man rounds the corner to the left and leaning against the fence, arms crossed. "And better make it look nice for the cameras." The Cockney accent matches the one that had made Aurora scream, and Blake glares at the man.

"Where is she?"

He laughs, stepping forward to give Blake a not-so-friendly slap on the back. "You sure you want to know, mate?"

"Come on," Jet growls, grabbing Blake's arm and tugging him forward. Towards the canal. Only the boardwalk separates Blake from the water, yet he forces himself to follow Jet, the stranger shadowing behind.

This is for Aurora. Blake repeats it in his head like a chant. His fight, his enemy, and his family.

They approach a houseboat docked alongside the boardwalk, and it takes everything in Blake to not break away and make a run for it. The station has security; someone could call the cops, call Isabelle—but anything could happen to Aurora in that time.

His vision blurs, narrowing as Jet slows and turns to the houseboat. The back opens into a platform and a low doorway.

"Get in," Jet growls.

"Watch your step," the stranger cautions, coming up behind Blake.

After everything... a *boat*? The irony burns. "Tell me where my niece is," Blake demands, but his voice shakes, betraying him.

Jet rolls his eyes. "Just *get in*, moron. We don't have all day."

Thomas' pained face flashes into Blake's mind, a reminder of the last time Jet and his men wanted something. No one was killed that time—but what guarantee is that? Life isn't a guarantee, but Blake will do everything he can to keep his niece safe. Even enter a floating prison.

The boat rocks when he steps down, boots firm against the swaying deck, hand clutching the rail. He knows that Jet is enjoying his fear, that Jet has caused all this, but the terror swallows the anger, rising up like a deep pit, consuming everything.

It doesn't matter. Nothing matters. Just the water and the fear.

SAINT FLORIAN INN
LONDON, ENGLAND

"I didn't know where else to go; he's gone." Aurora's panicked voice breaks into the quiet of the hotel library, where Mum has been telling me stories about Dad's old team, the 6-Some.

Mum stands as Aurora and Aunt Patience enter the room, and I follow suit, worry blooming in my chest.

"What's happened?" Mum is strictly business, but I can hear the concern in her voice.

Aurora's eyes are wide, and her gaze flits around the room. "We were at the station, and I left my phone in the bathrooms—I went to look for it, but when I got back to the Starbucks, Uncle Blake was gone. I couldn't find him anywhere! I even used one of those payphones to try to call his cell, but nothing. I didn't find my phone, either. I didn't know what to do, so I came back here." She bites her lip like she's choking back tears. "This is all my fault. I shouldn't have left him to get my phone."

Aunt Patience sets a hand on Aurora's shoulder and squeezes. "It's not your fault, Aurora. He probably just went to find you and got lost. You know how he is."

"What are you going to do?" Aurora sniffs, looking at Mum.

Mum offers Aurora a smile. "We'll sort it out. Ignis is—how would you say it? A pro."

No one mentions what we all fear. After what happened in Florida, what's the likelihood that this is a coincidence?

The "ten minute walk" to Ignis headquarters feels longer to my frayed nerves, even though I know Secret is appreciative of getting out. At least it's not raining, although clouds are blowing in.

How can a guy just... *vanish* in the middle of Paddington Station? Did he just get lost like Aunt Patience suggested, or did something happen?

Pigeons flock the sidewalks, and I can feel Secret wanting to chase them. I click my tongue, reminding him to focus. *Sorry, pup, not now.*

"Here we are," Mum says, stopping at one of the nondescript stone buildings that seem to have stood here since before the Second World War. A tinted glass door leads into a foyer; another set of doors requires her to buzz in.

Mum's agent friends meet us in the lobby, and Mum turns to Aurora and me.

"There are some pastries in the kitchen—Tirana, there's some set aside for you. Agent Kinsworth will be keeping an eye on you, so don't be a nuisance." Mum nods to a bald man who vaguely resembles Batman's butler. "Patience, come with me." Without waiting for a reply, Mum hustles away. I can almost imagine loose papers flying out behind her as she hurries down the carpeted hall, her team at her heels.

Aunt Patience gives us a little shrug and a crooked smile before following Mum. And just like that, Aurora and I are left alone with this hairless stranger who doesn't look any more thrilled about this than I feel.

"Come along, then," Agent Kinsworth says with a sigh. "To the kitchen." His English accent is stronger than Mum's, tinging his words in a way that only strengthens the feeling of being dropped into London like the little orange man in Google Maps.

After a quick breakfast that's less eventful than yesterday's, although Aurora only picks at her food, Kinsworth takes us on a small tour. The drab grays of the Ignis headquarters are the opposite of Wonderland's vibrant colours, and it makes me wonder what exactly drew my parents together.

Did Dad walk these halls? Did he compare it to the whimsical murals and decor of the ISA? Did he ever feel as homesick as I do, like his world was ripped away from him?

Oh, why didn't you let me into this world before *everything went wrong?*

"Here's my office," Kinsworth says, opening a nondescript door in a nondescript hall. "Dalton requested that you stay with me until she comes to get you. How thrilling."

The office is as nondescript as the building. A desk takes up the majority of the room, with a chair across from it and a small couch pushed into a corner. A few sketches of famous London landmarks are framed on the off-white walls.

I follow Aurora's lead and take a seat on the couch, and Secret jumps into my lap. Kinsworth doesn't say anything, so I let Secret be, rubbing his ears as he leans into me. The silence is as tense as a cricket in Times Square, and I eye the door, which is still ajar. A man can't just vanish into thin air... and that means he can be tracked.

Which is probably what Mum is doing right now. After all, according to Aurora, Mum and her team sprung him from the SoL in Florida. So they can do it again, right?

"Where's the restroom?" Aurora blurts suddenly.

The agent glances up, giving a blank stare, then he frowns. "Ah, the loo. Down the hall to the left."

"Thanks." Aurora slips from the room, and I stare vaguely after her before it clicks in my mind that something's off.

"I'll just... go with her," I tell Kinsworth, unease slithering through me. "Seek, c'mon."

The hall is empty, but it's easy enough to find the single-stall bathroom. The door is ajar, and the room is empty. *Oh, Aurora...*

"Okay, if I were Aurora, where would I go...?" I bite my lip, looking down at Secret, but he tells me nothing. To the right, we'd have to pass Kinsworth's office to get anywhere, and I know Aurora headed left when she left the office, so...

"Onwards, ho."

The hall turns into another, which leads into a corridor that spans right and left. I bite back a groan and give Secret his head. He'll have more idea than I do, even though he's not trained to track people.

He picks right, and after another turn, I see her, back towards me as she concentrates on the window before her. *What in the...*

"Aurora?"

Blowing out a breath, she spins towards me, reminding me of Aidan from the Of the Stars series. "What are you doing here?"

"I think the question is what are *you* doing?"

"I would think that would be simple to figure out." She turns back to the window and drags up the sash. A fresh, early summer breeze blows in.

"Aurora! Are you *insane*?"

"Yes?" She leans out the window, looking around, before pulling back in and turning to me. "Look, I need to find my uncle."

"But... you—you can't just..."

She crosses her arms, eyes blazing. "I can, and I will. Look, I can't just sit and wait around for strangers to do my job. So I'm going to fix this mess, okay? You can't stop me, so don't even bother to try. Goodbye, Tirana. It was nice knowing you." She swings her legs over the windowsill.

"Aurora, no, think about this! You can't just go off in a huge city— you don't even know where to look!" I lunge forward, but she's already climbing out.

There's a thunk as her sneakers hit the concrete, then the sound of running footsteps.

"Aurora!" I lean out the window, only to see her retreating gray t-shirt dart around the corner. "No... that did *not* just happen." I did *not* just let my friend jump out of a window on a fool's errand in the middle of London.

Secret jumps up and puts his paws on the sill next to me, nose working. A cool breeze blows in, the hint of rain stronger, smelling of danger and urgency.

"Oh, no, no, no. We are *not* going to follow her. No way."

CHAPTER TWENTY-NINE
PAINTING THE ROSES RED

I'm going to get grounded for life.

Dropping out of the window is not the smartest thing I've ever done, especially carrying a lanky 20lb dog. A lofty endeavor—resulting in a few scraped limbs and a jolted body—later, I set off down the narrow street.

Trees have overtaken much of the fencing behind me, giving the alley a *The Secret Garden* feel. But the pit of anxiety in my stomach isn't the stuff of storybooks; this is real life, and Aurora's heading towards trouble.

I crouch, letting Secret lean into me, and consider my options. I'm so tempted just to go back and let Aurora handle this herself, to be the good girl who obeys her mother, to do what's *safe*.

But is life really about being safe? I finger my locket. "'Take the road less traveled,'" I whisper softly, rubbing Secret's curly head with my other hand.

"With that dog of yours, you can do anything. Remember that." Even now, the words from Aunt Patience's letter encourage me.

I'm not brave... but maybe it's time to start acting like I am. Maybe I made the wrong choices before... but only a coward would back down because of that. Aragorn didn't, and neither will I.

So I stand up, coil Secret's leash, and stride down the sidewalk like I know where I'm going.

"We'll find her, Seek." I nod like I believe it. "Find her and bring her back. And who knows? Maybe we'll stumble upon Agent Grizzled Fox while we're at it."

PADDINGTON BASIN
LONDON, ENGLAND

Muted daylight shines past the crack in the dark curtains covering the window above the dinette table, dust floating lazily in the thin streams of light. Blake shifts, the metal folding chair squeaking a halfhearted protest. Rolling his shoulders does little to lessen the strain sending spirals of pain into his neck and head. Duct-taping his arms together behind the back of the chair was a vile move on Jet's part.

As if any bit of this isn't. Dragging Blake into a *boat*, of all possible places, and leaving him tied to a chair cannot be counted as pleasant. Lack of sleep, jet lag, and utter exhaustion threaten to steal the little sanity Blake has left.

Just where is that cursed traitor?

Blake eyes the single guard, a burly Russian who's slouched on the dinette bench, messing with his phone like a bored teenager. A switchblade rests on the table in front of him.

Blake nearly scoffs. What's the use? Are they afraid of him escaping? If Jet doesn't show his ugly mug soon, Blake just might try.

He tenses his arms, testing. A couple hard tugs should break the tape, then all he'd need to contend with is the tape binding his feet to the chair legs. The burning in his arms helps to distract his mind from the water he can *feel* surrounding him, from the panic that lurks all too close.

Reassuring himself that he *can* get out, if the need arises, he learns his head back. If he listens, he can hear the water lapping against the boat. The rumble of an engine starting up. A muffled shout.

"You, straighten up," the operative growls, rapping his knuckles against the table.

Blake jerks upright, pulse racing, before the sound registers as harmless. He grits his teeth, slouching back down as much as the bindings allow.

The rocking of the boat sometime later jerks Blake back to full alert. Boots clomp, then unfiltered daylight spills in the dim room. The next moment, the lanky form of a man descends fully into the boat's body.

At last, the traitor himself. Blake fights to keep his face impassive as Jet slouches forward until he looms over him.

"Looking rough, are you?" Jet has the audacity to sound like there's no other place he'd rather be. Dismissing the guard, he leans against the cabinets lining the wall. "Are you willing to talk now?"

Silently, Blake regards the man who has tormented him for so long. He can't ask about the impending attack that Patience unearthed because it would just tip the SoL off that they know, but the thought of what the terrorists have planned makes his blood simmer.

"Well?" Jet growls, leaning closer, a sickly-sweet odor of cloves, cinnamon, and minty mouthwash wafting off of him. "You have one chance. *Talk.*"

Blake swallows against a dry throat. "Where is my niece?"

Jet laughs. "Would you believe me if I told you that I took her away from everything she ever knew and loved, just like you did to my sister all those years ago?"

Blake grits his teeth. "You guys were *using* the kid as your personal spy." Blake had rescued her, and Jet will never forgive him, or any of the 6-Some, for it.

"She was my little sister!" Jet's voice rises.

"She was *eight*. Where is my niece?" Blake struggles to keep his own voice level. God help him, if they laid a hand on Aurora...

Jet glowers darkly at him. "Riley, Riley, Riley..." He tuts, shaking his head, and gives a villainous smile. "Won't you ever learn? *I* hold the cards here."

Blake returns his glare. "The very fact that I'm even here means you've failed; not once, but at least three times."

"Why, you little…" A hand snakes towards Blake, backhanding him.

Blinking the world back into focus—unfortunately, that includes Jet's looming face—, Blake ignores the dull throbbing of his cheek. "You will *always* fail."

Jet bristles like an angry cat. "If there's one thing you must learn, *Riley*, it's that I do not *fail*." He spits out the word as if it's coated with poison—one he'd take pleasure in making Blake consume.

"Oh yeah?"

"Don't play games with me." Jet's eyes darken dangerously. "Where is the manuscript? We know it's not the stupid book you tricked us into taking. We *know* you have it. You want your niece to know what it's like to hurt?"

Shades, no. Blake clenches his jaw. Jet cannot get away with threatening Aurora—but there's nothing Blake can do. Nothing but try to fool the master trickster. It's time to play a different game.

Blake scoffs. "Fine, we have it, but it's a worthless piece of junk. Dallas hadn't finished coding it, so it leads to a dead end. Is that what you wanted to hear? That all the time you spent chasing it was useless?"

Jet's expression darkens further—whether in anger, disbelief, or confusion, Blake can't tell.

"I said no games," snarls Jet, leaning closer, minty breath reeking. "That means *no games*. If you choose to make this difficult, then you will regret it."

You haven't seen "difficult" yet.

Looking Jet in the eye, Blake yanks against the tape. Before the other man can so much as blink twice, Blake's hands are free, and he punches Jet squarely in the nose.

SOMEWHERE IN LONDON, ENGLAND

"Admit it. We're lost," I mutter to Secret, standing still on the sidewalk as cars whiz past—it still catches me by surprise that they're on the wrong side of the road.

Even street signs are different here. Instead of the signposts I'm used to, there are white plaques either on stone walls or the sides of buildings. Not even the mail trucks are like the ones at home. I pick up my pace, lest the red "Royal Mail" truck driver think I've stopped to stare at him.

"I need a map." I look down the street, sighing, then freeze. "Is... that literally a map?" Sure enough, a tall, skinny sign, like something from a mall, is posted on the corner.

Unfortunately, I've no clue where we started. I trace my finger over the map. "The City of Westminster? I thought this was *London*." Oh, where is that walking encyclopedia when I need her?

This is stupid.

I bite my lip, swallowing, as the repercussions of this "adventure" hit me. Now Mum's going to have to track down Agent Grizzled Fox, Aurora, *and* me.

I've gotta find my way back. If I take a left here, it should get me back to the end of this block, then I can start retracing my steps back.

Yet all the buildings blend together, and it doesn't come out to where I'd thought it would. The Victorian-style row houses turn to green hedges on my left, with construction across the street to my right.

Finally, there's a break in the hedges as a gate comes into view. The sign on the wrought iron fence that surrounds the block reads "Craven Hill Gardens."

If the garden's public, maybe I can get in and ponder what to do there. Surely sitting in a garden won't lead to suspicion the way standing on the street like I'm lost will, right?

"C'mon, Seek," I say, stepping off the sidewalk and circling the garden, taking a berth around the parked vehicles.

The iron gate, rising up in an arch, isn't hard to locate. But as I step closer... *Of course.* A padlock and chain encircle the bars. One of the unmarked white vans parked next to the fence sports a ladder tied to the roof, but... no. Only Aurora would try to scale her way into the garden like that.

Craning my neck to see over a parked truck, I spot another fence. *May-*

be... but upon inspection, it's also locked. *Rats.*

The delicate white roses inside the garden look nice, too. It's a shame I can't get in.

Sliding down to sit on the stone at the foot of the fence, I stare out into the narrow street. "Would be hard for even more to go wrong, huh?"

Secret just licks my hand, and I scratch his head, sighing.

"A phone is useless without a working plan," I continue, muttering under my breath, "but I wonder if there's free Wi-Fi around here somewhere..." Sliding my phone from my back pocket, I turn airplane mode off and browse the available networks. Quite a few come up, but they're all locked.

This can't be good. How long until Kinsworth realizes we're gone and contacts Mum? I cringe, because it's not hard to imagine how mad she'll be. *Great decision-making skills you have, Tirana. Just great. Everything you do only makes things worse.*

I finger my locket, closing my eyes against tears that have no right to sting. *This isn't what you meant, Dad, is it? I'm sorry I failed you.* A sob threatens to rise, but I choke it back, the locket pressing into my hand as I clutch it tightly. *I'm sorry that I failed everyone.*

A wet lick on my chin makes me blink open my eyes, and I suck in a shaky breath. "Right, no falling apart." Swiping a hand under my nose, I push to my feet, giving the garden another longing glance before starting down the road.

I come out on the same street I was on before, and make for the map, studying it closely. Maybe if I can find the Italian Gardens where we got ice cream, I'll be able to retrace our steps from yesterday.

With a destination in mind and the help of the maps posted every so often along the route, I weave my way down streets that grow progressively busier as I near the park. Houses, shop fronts, and businesses line the roads, and while it's quaint, I can't help but long for the solitude of Indiana's woods, for the feeling of belonging.

Will I ever go back there? I won't be going anywhere if I don't get back to the hotel or the Ignis base.

Slowing, I eye a church primary school that screams Catholic from the red arched doors to the towering structure. The tan stones contrast with the white of the surrounding buildings, made fascinating by the fact they're all connected, yet different. *Perhaps someone there can help me...*

The aroma of coffee draws my attention to a small café tucked just beyond the school, and I pause outside, scanning the menu. They advertise several types of coffees and drinks, but only sandwiches for food. Perhaps it's safe enough... and they might have Wi-Fi. And I can get a soda or something with the $10 that I keep in Secret's vest pouch—a cold Coke sounds pretty good right about now.

The café's door is open, so I step inside, getting a feel for the tiny place. Only one of the three compact tables are occupied, and a serving counter is stationed at the end of the room.

This is either a great idea, or one of the worst I've ever had.

I step up to the counter, only half noticing how my grip tightens on Seek's leash. "Excuse me?"

A girl maybe a few years older than me turns, brushing a lock of dark hair out of her eyes. "Hullo! What can I do for you?"

"Do you sell Coca-Cola? And do you have free Wi-Fi here?" Every word and action marks me as a tourist, but there's nothing I can do but roll with it.

She hesitates, glancing back into the depths of the kitchen behind her. "Hey, Paul! What's the password for the Wi-Fi? And bring up a Coke!" Turning back to me with a little shrug, she gives a low laugh. "I always forget the password."

A tall, aproned man emerges from the back, a can of Coke in hand. "Password?" He rattles it off in a strong Cockney accent. Accepting my thanks, he sets the drink on the counter. "'ere ya go. Cheers."

I finish punching in the password on my phone before kneeling to unzip the pouch on Secret's vest, digging around until I locate the folded ten-dollar bill. *That's funny...* I don't recognize the feel of one of the small objects in the pocket; it's certainly not an ADA card. Leaving it there to check out later, I stand and straighten the bill before holding it out.

The girl frowns. "Oh, we don't accept US notes here..."

"Oh." Awkwardly, I stick the bill into my pocket. "Sorry. Well, thanks, anyway."

Paul shakes his head, sliding the bottle towards me with a smile. "Consider it on the house, lassie."

"Really? I mean… thanks!"

"Better sort the currency soon. Not everyone is as nice as us." With a wink, Paul vanishes back into the kitchen, and I'm left to find a place to sit.

Deciding it's probably not wise to stay in here any longer than I have to, even if there don't seem to be any floating particles of gluten in the air, I claim the bistro table squeezed outside next to the door, setting the Coke on the wooden slats before logging into my phone and opening the messaging app.

After shooting Mum a text briefly explaining what happened and where I am, hopefully adding "sorry" enough that I won't be grounded for life, I lean back, enjoying the just-warm-enough-to-be-pleasant air. The pale, cloudy sky still promises rain, but it's held off so far. Twisting the cap off the Coke, I have Secret check it—especially halfway across the world, one can never be too careful—and take a long swallow.

Maybe I should get lost more often, I think wryly, idly watching the passive traffic. Or not.

It's only when I shift and the ten-dollar bill crinkles in my pocket that I remember the weird thing in Secret's pocket. Bending over, I unzip both pockets of his vest and empty their contents onto the table.

"What in the world…?" I don't even know what I'm looking at as I survey the little spread. I recognize the ADA cards, stating a service dog's rights in the United States, but the two foreign black squares, one from each pocket…?

I examine each in turn, but there are no markings. They're about the size of a quarter, but that's where the resemblance ends. They're just mini black plastic boxes, as if that's not suspicious in the *least*. Frowning, I snap a photo with my phone before sliding them into a pocket of my capris. Maybe Mum will know what they are… and what they're doing in Secret's vest.

Just as I finish repacking his vest, my phone buzzes. My heart leaps as I scramble to grab it. It's Mum.

"Don't you dare move. I'll be right there."

Relief floods me, and I sag against the seat, suddenly exhausted. Mum's coming; everything will be okay.

Except that Aurora's still out there, Agent Grizzled Fox is missing, and the black boxes can't mean anything good.

There's got to be an explanation for all this... only, I'm not sure I want to know it.

CHAPTER THIRTY
AS MAD AS THE HATTER

"You *will* regret that," Jet growls, a scowl deepening his voice as he runs a hand under his nose, frowning as it comes away bloody. "Petrov, you know what to do."

The goon using Blake as a seat grunts. "Of course."

Blake hardly has enough time to process that, let alone ponder the repercussions of the statement, before a coil of rope drops from some unseen place and lands half a dozen feet away from where Blake's face is pressed against the cold tile of the floor. An expensive, well-oiled boot kicks it closer, and Petrov's bulk shifts before the weight eases off of Blake's back and his arms are yanked upwards.

"That... really... necessary?" Blake pants, struggling to draw in sufficient breath as Petrov roughly ties his hands together.

"What do you think?" comes Jet's unwelcome, smirking voice, unnervingly close. "We can't have you trying something again, now, can we?"

Blake can only grunt as Petrov jerks him upright and the world spins dangerously. A meaty hand all but drops him in the same cursed metal folding chair before getting to work with the rope, tightening it as if Blake is a mast pole instead of a human being.

"Still proud of yourself, are you, little Blakey?" Jet loafs against the cabinets, the smeared stream of crimson under his nose doing nothing to lessen his egotistical smirk. "Got to say, I didn't see that coming. Didn't think you had it in you." He feigns a yawn.

Blake glares at him, biting back a wince as Petrov jerks the rope tighter before stepping back, brushing his hands together.

Petrov's face remains carved out of stone as he looks Blake over. "That'll do, *svin'ya.*"

"Indeed, 'pig'; that will do." Jet straightens, brushing off his impeccable suit jacket. "Now that that's all over, Hession, why don't you and I have a little talk? Petrov, leave us."

Once the man has disappeared up the few steps leading to the door, Jet, tilting his head, turns his full attention to Blake. "I ask once more: Where is it?"

"Your birthday present? I didn't get you one." The snark is more up Damian's ally than Blake's, but Blake can't find it in him to bite back the retort.

Jet clicks his tongue. "You truly have grown dumber in the fifteen-odd years since I dragged your innocent little soul into that cabin."

Blake can't hold back a snort that his ribs protest. "You're a pyromaniac."

"Prove it." Jet picks up something off of the counter, spinning it around in his hands as he gazes down at it. His smirk turns into a satanic grin as he holds the lighter up, clicking on the flame.

"*Seriously?*" Blake stares, mind flashing to the fires that killed his parents and Damian's, marred Damian's face, and eventually took Damian's life.

"Going to talk?"

"No." Blake shifts, the ropes cutting into his wrists like they must have cut Damian's when his friend had been held captive by the SoL, nearly twelve years ago, on that ill-fated mission. Blake swallows hard, holding Jet's gaze. "I've got nothing to say to you."

Jet sneers, bringing the flame closer to Blake's face like a madman. "Is that so?"

"You're insane," Blake grits out, flinching as the villain clicks the flame off and on like this is a sick game. To Jet, it is.

A shrill melody rings out, and Jet swears as he tosses the lighter back onto the counter and scoops up his phone. "Yup? Oh, *really...*" A smirk replaces Jet's annoyed expression as he listens to whoever's on the other end. "You may prove your usefulness yet, Richard. Yes, bring her in... our friend here needs the incentive to talk."

LONDON, ENGLAND

"What were you *thinking*?" Mum faces me, eyes ablaze. "Do you have any idea how much trouble you've caused?"

I look up at the blue sky, blinking away sudden, traitorous tears as exhaustion lurks all too close. A British flag hangs next to a shop's overhang, the bright red stripes crossing the blue background just another reminder how *far* I am from home.

And now I've made the person I care about the most mad. While Dad was more of a gentle chider, it's always easy to know when Mum's upset.

"Grace Tirana." Her tone is hard. "You have a lot of explaining to do. First off, where is Aurora?"

I squeeze my eyes shut, unable to meet her angry glare. "I..." Yet any explanation gets mangled in my throat. I just shake my head helplessly. "I don't know. I'm sorry."

So, so sorry.

"How can you not know?" Mum shakes her head as she starts down the street, muttering something that's probably a Shakespearean insult under her breath.

"I... I got lost trying to find her." Secret presses closer to me, but I give his leash a light twitch, reminding him to heel nicely and not trip me. "She wouldn't take 'no' for an answer." *You didn't try hard enough, Tirana. You failed everyone.*

Mum doesn't respond, and we walk in silence despite the noises of the city assaulting us from every direction.

"I'm sorry," Mum says at length, and I look towards her, surprised.

I bite my lip, studying the sidewalk. "No... *I'm* sorry. I should never have tried to follow Aurora."

Mum tuts gently. "Have you ever heard the story of how you got your name?"

"Because... I was born in Albania?"

"No, the Grace part."

I frown. I guess I've never thought that much about my first name. I've always just been Tirana, unless I'm in trouble.

"When I was a young woman," Mum begins in her storytelling voice (which isn't actually any different than her normal voice), "your father and I were assigned to a case together. He was the most insufferable Yank I'd ever laid eyes on; thoroughly American in every way imaginable. Here's our stop." She nods to a clear-paneled, red-roofed bus stop. "Long story short, he mucked up our mission, and I had to learn how to swallow a lesson of mercy." When she looks at me, her eyes aren't angry anymore. Instead, sadness and maybe regret linger in their depths. "Perhaps we made the wrong decision and let the untruth live for far too long, and I'm sorry you've had to pay for that."

Things change, Tirana... Swallowing, I inch closer to Mum. Now that Dad's gone... she's the only parent I have left, and I'm suddenly aware of how much I don't want to lose her. "It... it'll be fine." Someday. When my friend isn't lost on the streets of a foreign city in search for her missing uncle, and a group of fire-hungry terrorists aren't at large.

Mum wraps an arm around me, her warmth warding off the chill of the dreary morning.

A family... maybe broken... but still a family.

My family.

BACK AT IGNIS HEADQUARTERS, MUM MAKES ME APOLOGIZE to Kinsworth, but doesn't let me out of her sight. That's how I find myself curled up in the corner of the comfy leather armchair in her office, watching Mum and Norton discuss plausible leads and possibilities. Apparently, they sent a team to search the station, and one of Mum's agents is working on gaining access to security footage.

And now they have to find Aurora, too.

Norton pages through a map, spreading it out over the surface of the desk and tracing his finger along the paper. "We know that Aurora exited the mews onto Porchester Terrace, and she could have gone either towards the park or Hallfield—not counting the endless sidestreets she could have taken. With an average walking speed of three miles per hour, the furthest away she could theoretically be is about four miles."

"Unless she took a bus," Mum adds, studying the map. "Although in all likelihood, she would have returned to the station."

Norton sighs. "This friend of yours, Isabelle—are you sure he and his problems are worth all this trouble?"

Mum gives him her signature "are you daft?" look, and he raises his hands halfway to his chest in mock surrender. "Kidding, kidding. I prefer my head attached to my shoulders, thank you very much."

Mum ignores him as her phone buzzes. She picks it up and sets it to speakerphone. "Yes, Kensal?"

"It looks like I found something for the girl." A woman's voice comes in faint and tinny. "There's footage of her walking behind Paddington Station, towards the basin. I'm sending it over now... but Dalton, it looks like someone grabbed her before the cameras lost track of her."

All the agents straighten, exchanging grim glances. Mum opens a file that pops up on her computer screen, and a grainy, half obstructed video plays. I move to stand behind Mum's chair.

A girl with a brown ponytail and a gray t-shirt walks slowly down the alley-like sidewalk, hands in her pockets. Just before she leaves the range of the camera, a dark, man-sized blur seems to grab her. There's a struggle that cuts in and out of view, but either Aurora loses or runs the other way, because there's nothing more that happens on the footage.

Oh, Aurora... If only I'd been able to stop her, or had told someone instead of following her, then this wouldn't have happened. Gulping back a swell of nausea, I return to my seat. What if she's hurt? What if she's *killed*?

Norton turns to the others, expression grave. "Anyone up for a cuppa?"

"A cuppa" turns out to mean Norton and another agent going to scope out the area. From my place on the armchair, it's about as exciting as watching Secret nap. My dog's conked out on the floor by my feet, and I wish I could drift off, too. It's early morning back in the States, and my mental clock is convinced that I've been up since 3 AM. I close my eyes, but all I can see is the grainy video feed. If I hadn't gone and gotten lost, would Mum be able to find Blake and Aurora faster?

A knock on the door startles me, and I sit up. One of Mum's partners enters, a tablet in her hand. "They've set up the surveillance as directed," she says without prelude. "We believe that this narrowboat is our target."

Mum examines the tablet's screen. "Kensal, have you—"

"It was sold on June 5 to a man by the name of Timothy Petrov. Petrov is listed as one of the chairmen of Greenlight Front. Also, CCTV footage shows several men coming and going over the past few days—and this morning, it looks like Grizzled Fox joined them."

Mum stills. "I want you to find everything you can about that man and boat... and what an American, neo-fascist organization has to do with an eco-terrorist group like Greenlight."

PADDINGTON BASIN
LONDON, ENGLAND

No.

Blake's eyes have to be deceiving him, because it looks like his niece is standing at the bottom of the stairs that lead to the door, trying to fight her way out of the British goon's arms.

Shades... just—shades.

She glares at Jet, expression fiery enough to combust a marshmallow.

So Jet hadn't been lying about having her, unless they'd used Blake like fish bait to get her.

"Let. Me. *Go*," she hisses, trying to pull away from the goon's grip. The man doesn't even have the decency to look peeved at Aurora, let alone seem taxed by her efforts.

"Is that wise?" Jet asks mildly, raising an eyebrow. "I don't think so."

"You... you..." Aurora growls, scowl deepening. "What *is* your game, wormtongue?"

Jet smirks. "Comparing me to the chief advisor to the king? Why, *thank* you, dear."

"I see even that was too nice for the likes of you," Aurora spits. "Why, even the Big Bad Wolf is too lame a title, although he's remarkably easy to kill in the end."

"Have you seen his victim count? Little girls are at the top of his list. Now, as amusing as this conversation is, I actually have business to attend to." Jet turns again to Blake. "Is our incentive *inciting* enough, Riley? Or do we need... more?"

"'The queen of hearts has lost her tarts,'" Aurora begins singing under her breath, but Blake silences her with a small shake of his head. Riling Jet up will only make this worse for Aurora... and for Blake. If there's any chance of getting his niece out of this mess, he'll have to play his cards with a different hand.

"So, Blakey," Jet drawls, "what do you have to say for yourself? Do you yield? Give up? Weigh the cost and decide that it's not worth the fight? Is your little niece more important than a worthless book, or would you like to see her... suffer?" Jet brushes his overcoat open to reveal the butt of a holstered gun that is definitely not legal to carry here.

"You're not gonna shoot anyone, Mr. No-Good, Very Dumb Coyote." Aurora's know-it-all tone stiffens Jet's stance. "The sound of the shot, even if you had a muffler, would attract too much attention. And don't you know the Road Runner always, *always* wins?"

"That's what *you* think, Miss Smarty Pants," Jet hisses, apparently having no clue how juvenile that just made him sound.

"It *is* what I think." Aurora's grin is outright savage. "How astute of you."

"Aurora..." Blake mutters a warning not to antagonize the villain with the gun, but she doesn't break her stare down with Jet.

The British goon clears his throat. "We're running out of time, sir."

Jet levels the goon with a withering glare. "*Who* is in charge here?"

"You are, sir, but if we don't—"

"We'll wait till dark, then tie the girl up and dispose of her in the basin," Jet interrupts, staring at Blake.

"That's a terrible idea." Aurora wrinkles her nose. "I am *way* too useful to be a murder victim here."

"Be a good girl and let the grown-ups handle the murder," Jet condescends, rolling his eyes. "Agent Grizzled Fox, what do you say? Do I send her to join the choir invisible, or will you talk?"

Frayed nerves and lack of sleep threaten to break through the mask of calm, but by sheer willpower, Blake meets Jet's coyoteish gaze. But before he can open his mouth, it's Aurora who cuts in.

"Mr. No-Good, Very Dumb Coyote, we both know my uncle's too stubborn to actually tell you anything. Yours truly, on the other hand..." She shrugs. "Well, I'm just a scared little girl, aren't I? But I know stuff. Maybe, just maybe, if you tell your goon to unhand me, I'll even share my secrets."

Jet scoffs. "How about... no. I don't take orders from pint-sized blabbermouths."

Aurora smiles sweetly. "Sir, don't you know that 'Pride goeth before destruction, and an haughty spirit before a fall'?" She shakes her head, tutting. "It's a real shame."

"Rora—" Blake starts, but she ignores him.

"And I'm really supposed to believe anything you have to say?" Jet scoffs. "I'm not falling for your little dramatics, twerp."

"But I know where the book is, and I know how you can get it."

Jet eyes her suspiciously. "Let her go, Richard."

The goon releases Aurora, and she stumbles forward, rubbing her arms. "You have a real death grip there, mate," she tells the goon, making a face.

Jet strokes his gun, probably thinking it makes him look menacing instead of like a toddler coddling a kitten. "If you really do know so much, missy, I suggest that you get talking."

"It's not worth it, Jet," Blake growls, tugging at the ropes that only bite deeper into his wrists. "I told you, we weren't able to decode it."

"You really want this book something fierce," Aurora says, cocking her head at Jet.

The man scowls. "*I'll* be the judge of what's important and what I want. Richard, go with Petrov and get some lunch. I want to speak to them alone."

The goon mutters an apology to Aurora—Brits—and hurries out, shutting the door with a solid click that only strengthens the sense of dread slowly building inside the boat.

Aurora sighs. "Well, Mr. Coyote, I hate to tell you this, but you're too late."

Blake clenches his jaw. By some miracle, he'd been able to convince them to leave Thomas alone after the boy was shot, but how is Blake supposed to protect Aurora when he's tied to a stupid chair in the belly of a boat?

And just where is Aurora going with this? If Blake knows his niece, she'll have a plan. He just isn't sure he likes where this is going. Jet is more unhinged and dangerous than Aurora knows.

"What do you mean, too late?" Jet narrows his eyes, picking up the lighter again and spinning it.

Aurora glances at Blake. "Please don't hate me for this, Uncle Blake... but I have to."

"Rora—" Blake grits his teeth, but she's already past the voice of reason. Jet will get *The Freesia Guard*, and everything Dallas died to protect will be lost, and there is nothing Blake can do but watch.

"We couldn't get everything off it," Aurora begins, biting her lip as she side-eyes Blake. "So... Ignis had it sent to the ISA. What time is it?"

"Just before noon," Jet says, eyes narrowed at Aurora. "Exactly what are you saying?"

"I'm sorry, Uncle Blake," Aurora whispers before squaring her shoulders. "They sent it with an agent on a plane that leaves Heathrow at 12:35."

Jet might be trying to hide his reaction, but his body tenses, and he tosses the lighter away, crossing his arms. "And why should I believe this?"

"Because you literally have us prisoner, and you're the one with the gun?"

Jet's expression is hard to read, but he seems to think that Aurora's statement is reasonable. "If you're lying, you won't live to regret it." He ties Aurora up, locks her in the bedroom, and hurries up the stairs.

Thunder rumbles overhead as the door of the houseboat slams shut, leaving Blake alone, trapped, and utterly confused.

CHAPTER THIRTY-ONE
POOL OF TEARS

"It's raining buckets out there," Norton says, smacking his beret over his head as he enters Mum's office, another agent trailing behind him. "Of all the times to plan to storm a canal boat."

The other agent shakes his head, turning to Mum. "It's done, and we've scoped out a plan."

"Brilliant. Norton, call Kensal and Mundford in here." Mum then turns to me, revealing that she hasn't actually forgotten my existence in the armchair. "Tirana, you may listen in, but please keep mum."

I nod, though there are a dozen questions on the tip of my tongue. Dad had been the one I would go to with my questions. Mum was always more likely to point me to a dictionary. But there isn't exactly a guide book titled *What Happened to Aurora and Agent Grizzled Fox* lying around.

When all four agents are collected in Mum's office, it's a bit crowded, and I inch back into my chair, feeling invisible. It's obvious this is where Mum belongs, and that this is her team. It's as far removed from the ISA as Wonderland is from the Wonka Chocolate Factory, and I feel displaced, like Dorothy after she found herself in Oz.

"We'll pass Paddington Station on A206, round the basin on South Wharf Road, and find parking on South Wharf," Mum is saying, tracing the map. "From there, Norton, Kinsworth and I will enter the boat, while Mundforth stands by. Kensal, you will stay here and do the surveillance."

"And her?" Norton nods at me.

So I'm not invisible after all... bother.

"She stays with Kensal." Mum stands, looking towards the female agent. "She'll behave."

Which I'm pretty sure is a veiled threat directed at me.

Ten minutes later, they're pulling away in an unmarked white van under a steady drizzle of rain, and I trail Ms. Kensal away from the window overlooking the back of the building to her office.

Silence fills the small room as she turns to her computers, and I shift on the couch, the lack of Aurora stark. *Is she with Agent Grizzled Fox right now? Are they with the SoL? Is* The Freesia Guard *safe? Is that really all the SoL is after?* Not that I know much about terrorist groups, but isn't following us to England just for a coded book a little... oh, I don't know, *extreme?*

I don't even really understand the code. Dad must have used *Lord of the Rings* jargon instead of the real names of people and places, but what good is that unless there's a key somewhere?

Unconsciously, my hand travels to my locket, rubbing the smooth metal before I freeze. *No... he wouldn't...* But it makes perfect sense, in some convoluted way. Slowly, I press open the jewelry, examining the picture inside. It looks perfectly normal. But it looked normal before Grizzled Fox found that chip in it.

Except that Dad wouldn't have known what the names and locations were before he left. Clicking the locket closed, I sag back into the couch. *You can't go chasing every crazy lead you think about, Tirana...* Still, I'll mention it to Mum when she returns. Maybe she'll even explain why her mouth had pressed into a flat, unimpressed line when I'd shown her the weird black boxes that were in Secret's vest. She'd put them into a locking box in her desk and said she'd look into it, though by her expression, she probably already has an idea what they are and how she'll repay whoever put them there.

What if the key is on the gravestone in Florida? Or maybe it's at the bottom of that river.

"You want to see how a rescue works?" Ms. Kensal's voice jerks me out of my thoughts, and I look up to see her smiling at me.

"Uhm..."

"Come over here."

Slowly, I stand up, step over Secret, and round the desk to her side. Several computer monitors are up, each showing a different feed overlooking what must be Paddington Basin and the surrounding area, which is full of glass-paneled office buildings and fences painted with murals.

"There's the target," Kensal says, pointing out a short-set narrowboat on the basin. The rectangularish part above the water is colored an interesting forest green with faded black trimmings. It doesn't look completely out of place among the few other boats in sight. "They should be coming in... just about now."

Sure enough, on another screen, movement turns into the familiar form of Mum descending a set of stairs, umbrella and trench coat adding to her just-walked-out-of-1990s-Britain factor.

Ms. Kensal taps her ear. "All clear, but take caution."

On another screen, Norton and Kinsworth enter from a different direction, strolling as if having a friendly chat on a lunch break. As if normal people go out walking in the rain... Then again, this *is* London.

If I didn't know better, the two parties would look entirely unrelated as they near each other; even as it is, it's easy to believe they're all just randomly strolling next to Paddington Basin in a freak rainstorm.

Speaking of freak... I eye the screens, a couple of which are slowing images so blurred that the rain must have picked up. Looking at Mum, you can't tell, but the two men hunch forward, glancing up at the sky.

"Is that... good?"

"Good?" Ms. Kensal glances towards me. "Hm?"

"The rain."

She huffs a laugh. "Love, this is London. There's no such thing as bad weather, only inappropriate clothing. Now, no more chin-wagging, please."

Right... Mum's favorite term to get me quiet. The old fears come rushing back as I watch the blurry footage. Pushing away the plans for if something *does* happen, I stare hard at the cameras. There's no sound, but I can imagine the roar of the rain beating down. The streaks of white increase until I'm pretty sure it's a downpour.

Mum nods to the men as they come up abreast to her just as she reaches the stern of the narrowboat, and as if that was some unspoken cue, the three of them turn towards the target.

"Still clear," Kensal says, tapping her earpiece. Her eyes are glued to the screens as she mutters, "They're going in."

PADDINGTON BASIN
LONDON, ENGLAND

BLAKE GROANS SOFTLY, CLENCHING HIS FISTS. THE ROPE CUTS into his wrists as the boat rocks dangerously to and fro, the wind attempting to steal the wretched craft. Just when he thought it couldn't get much worse, rumbling thunder and pouring rain proved him wrong.

The rain drums on the roof like a bunch of angry tap-dancing pigs threatening to short-circuit his brain completely and fry any fragments of sanity he has left.

Soon, Jet and his men will return. Finish what they started. And when Jet realizes that Aurora fed him another tall tale... Well, Blake isn't sure how they're getting out of this one.

Aurora... Jet had tied her up and thrown her into the bedroom before racing off to catch a plane that might not even exist, and after a few minutes of yells and thuds, it's been deathly quiet in this floating coffin.

If Mya knew where her daughter is, she'd probably steal a plane to come rescue Aurora, and to give Blake a piece of her mind for not defending Aurora. Not protecting her. Not saving her from this awful mess that he's created.

Why? The question wrenches from his very soul as a deep rumble shudders through the boat.

Why couldn't he have been stronger? Come up with a better plan, or a better ruse? The manuscript might be safe—for now—but at what cost? What about the planned attack? The blood of one man is on his hands already. He can't let his niece suffer because he's a weak fool.

The boat rocks again, harder, before footsteps tap down the few stairs leading to the kitchen. Blake's tempted to just keep his gaze down, to not look at the man he knows won't leave again without something to show for it, but he refuses to give the villain the satisfaction.

Biting back a grimace as his neck protests, Blake forces his gaze to meet Jet's... only, it's not Jet.

Slowly, the woman lowers her gun as she looks around the room, shaking her head as her gaze settles on Blake. "Truly, Hession, you're more trouble than all my agents combined. Kinsworth, you can have the pleasure of untying him, if you don't mind."

The agent makes quick work of his task, and as soon as the last of Blake's bindings fall, Blake stands, only for the world to sway dangerously under him. He manages to mumble something about Aurora, watching numbly as Isabelle and another agent head towards the front of the boat.

"You don't look so great," the agent who stayed behind says helpfully, studying Blake like he thinks Blake might topple over. Which isn't so far from the truth.

"Thanks," Blake mutters, not looking away from the hall the agents went into. He can see the back of one of the guy's shirts, but that's all. If he wasn't fairly sure he'd faceplant if he took a step in this rocking prison, he'd push past them and get Aurora out himself.

"Leave me alone!" A scream rings out, jerking Blake into motion.

No... no... no! Stumbling down the narrow hall, he prays it's not what he thinks. But standing in the doorway of the bedroom he'd watched them drag Aurora into, one hand pressed against the wall, he knows it is.

Wind and rain blow in through a wide-open French door, ghostly white curtains whipping around as if trying to escape. Isabelle and another agent stand there, but Aurora is gone.

"Over there!" The cry carries over the pounding shower, an agent pointing out the window into the wall of rain.

Crossing the cluttered room in a few halting strides, Blake squints out the window, the sight of the dark, churning canal water momentarily stunning him into paralysis.

No.

Aurora—where is Aurora? She's tied up—can't swim like that—

The pounding of his heart competes with the driving rain as he scans the water. *There.* Something bobs in the water, thrashing away from the boat, into the angry waves. He tries to call her name, but he can't even hear himself over the torrent.

Forcing feet of lead to shuffle forward, he stands on the edge of the bow for a terrifying moment before he jumps.

Water.

Burning, suffocating—

Blake chokes, gasping, as the vile substance sends fire into his lungs. It burns his eyes and throat, stripping away his breath and sanity as the dark waters morph into another storm, another night, another body of water.

Aurora.

He struggles to the surface, gasping, scanning the water through the stupid rain—*there.*

Shaky strokes bring him towards the bobbing, sputtering dark head. A wave crashes over his own head, and water fills his nose and mouth.

A silent scream fills his soul, but he emerges, fighting for breath over the panic, around the lethal water that clutches at him with its icy, mind-numbing grasp.

Aurora. The one coherent thought in this mess of insanity.

Another burst of panic shoots through him as he scans the water through a sheen of rain and waves.

No, no, no... no!

She can't be gone!

Blindly, he thrashes through the water, searching for the girl he was supposed to protect. Ice has captured his mind, stolen his breath, is trying to kill him—

Aurora.

Something solid and jerking bumps into him. He grabs her arm, anchoring both of them in this mess of stormy waves and pouring rain and half-remembered memories.

And shouts.

Shouts?

As he blinks past the water in his eyes, the city blurs into view with dark forms standing on the edge of the canal.

"Bring her here!" The voice is vaguely familiar, and he struggles towards it, towing a wriggling Aurora. The distance is seemingly endless, but he refuses to loosen his grip on Aurora's arm, even as she thrashes against him.

Lungs burning, he squints into the rain, the dark blurs moving up ahead. Suddenly, he bumps into something hard and solid, the jolt enough for Aurora's arm to slip out of his grip. There's nothing he can do as he's hauled up, something firm settling under his feet.

"That was rather unnecessary, but a touching move," a familiar British voice says, and he turns towards it, blinking until his vision clears enough to make out the blurry form of a tan overcoat and the woman who wears it.

"You really ought to stop being so much trouble," Isabelle continues, clucking her tongue. "It's starting to seem like the ISA wants to be known for heroic stunts."

"Let me *go*," a far more familiar voice sputters, infused with all the venom the half drowned teenager can muster, and Blake whips around so fast that the world spins.

"One moment, love," says the agent working on untying Aurora's hands, then he steps back, letting the length of rope drop to the rain-slicked boardwalk.

"Uncle... Uncle Blake?" Teeth chattering audibly, Aurora just looks at Blake for a long moment before her expression crumples. "I... I didn't mean to... I thought the goons had come back so I jumped. I—I'm sorry. I didn't think—"

"Rora." Ignoring the soaked state of her clothes—not like he's any better—and the rain still falling, he wraps his arms around her. "It's... fine."

If she's fine, then it's fine.

If Aurora can feel his heart pounding under his t-shirt or how much his body trembles, she doesn't say anything. Sniffing a little, she pulls away enough to look up at him.

"Where are the goons?"

Frowning, he turns, breath catching pathetically as his gaze falls on the cursed basin. *Not now, not with Aurora.* Letting out a shaky breath, he spots Isabelle a dozen feet away, talking on the phone under the shelter of an umbrella.

Hanging up, she turns to one of the other agents. "Norton, Kensal said she spotted Timothy Petrov entering a nearby pub about twenty minutes ago with another man. The police are on their way to apprehend them."

Well, that answers Aurora's question. Except... "There were three."

"Pardon?" Isabelle turns to Blake.

He clears his throat against the tightness. "Three. Those guys... and Jet Sullivan."

"Charming man," Aurora mutters. "I'd rather face an angry crocodile anyday. I told him you were sending *The Freesia Guard* on the next plane, and he hasn't returned since then, so..." Her teeth chatter, and Blake tightens his arm around her shoulders.

"Kinsworth and Mundford, stay here in case this fellow decides to return," Isabelle orders. "Norton, Hession, Aurora, come with me." Not leaving room for debate, she spins on her heel and stalks up the walkway, leading them away from that miserable place.

CHAPTER THIRTY-TWO
PETER PAN

"Now what?" I glance at Ms. Kensal, who's busy typing something on her computer.

Aurora and Agent Grizzled Fox are safe, and the whole mission didn't take more than half an hour. The freak downpour had lasted five minutes, tops—it had stopped as suddenly as it started, not long after Grizzled Fox and Aurora had been pulled out of the basin—but it felt like so much longer.

Ms. Kensal hums, and suddenly one of the screens changes from the area surrounding the narrowboat to a building fronted with glass. She pulls it up on the main screen.

"What...?" I squint at it. "Is that...?"

"A pub." Ms. Kensal nods. "Even criminals need supper. Good for us, not so much for them."

"Is anything happening?" I eye the rolling footage. Other than a strolling couple holding hands, sharing an umbrella between them, everything seems still. The sun is already breaking through the clouds.

Ms. Kensal shakes her head. "You young people, only caring about the action. This shouldn't take long."

Sure enough, only moments later, dark figures show through the glass in front of the doors. Then cops are marching two men, both handcuffed, around the side of the building. I can *feel* the detainees' scowls from here. It's rather disconcerting.

"Are they SoL?" I ask once they're pushed into a police car and carted away.

Ms. Kensal glances at me. "That's something to ask your mum. She'll be here shortly."

Sure enough, long minutes later the van pulls up behind the Ignis building. I watch from Ms. Kensal's footage as everyone piles out.

The first thing I notice is the bright pink blanket wrapped around Aurora's shoulders, which almost makes me snicker. *Never thought I'd see the day Aurora played princess.*

Aurora and Agent Grizzled Fox both look like drowned rats, unsurprisingly. Or what Aurora's rats would look like if they got caught in a downpour.

"Can I go now?" I ask Ms. Kensal, eyeing the Ignis agent. "I'll go right to them. I know the way."

"Go ahead."

With a muttered "thanks," I start for the door. "C'mon, Seek."

He scrambles to his feet, letting out a gaping yawn as he stretches leisurely before trotting over to me and giving my hand a lick.

I clip on his lead and slip out into the quiet halls. My footsteps pad softly on the carpeted floor, my capris swishing and Secret's gear jingling.

We meet the group right inside the door, and I step aside to let Mum, Norton, and Grizzled Fox pass, falling into step with Aurora, the princess-pink blanket hanging limply off of her shoulders.

"Nice dress." I raise an eyebrow, and she just makes a face, her single brown braid swinging like a waterlogged rope. A few cold drops splash on my bare arm, and I jerk back.

She snickers, and I shoot her a glare. Apparently a dip in the basin hasn't done her much harm. It's hard to think of anything doing Invincible Aurora much harm... but Genius got shot.

Norton splits off from the group, ducking into Kensal's office; then it's just Agent Grizzled Fox, Aurora, Secret, and me, following Mum down the hall like a bunch of ducklings.

I study Grizzled Fox's profile. Not much to see, with him in front of me. A leather jacket that's too large sags off his hunched shoulders, and his arms are crossed tightly.

Far cry from the self-assured guy who picked me up from that safe-house in Vincennes a lifetime or two ago. I guess the SoL can have that effect on people.

Aunt Patience meets us in Mum's office with two bundles, which she hands to Aurora and Agent Grizzled Fox, and Mum sends them away to change.

"How did it go?" Mum takes a seat at her desk, studying Aunt Patience.

Aunt Patience pulls a cigar box out of her bag, setting it on Mum's desk and opening it up. "As you suspected, I'm afraid. Your agent confirmed what they are and disabled them."

Leaning closer, I examine the two familiar small black boxes before glancing from my mother to my aunt. "What are they?"

"This," Aunt Patience says, picking up the narrower one, "is a tracking device. The other one is a recording bug."

I feel myself go pale. "But... those were in Secret's *vest*!"

Mum's and Aunt Patience's matching tight-lipped looks confirm just how bad this is.

"How is that even possible?" I groan, sinking into the armchair and burying my face in my hands. Secret is *always* with me! How could I not notice not one, but *two*, bugs in his vest?

"There's more," Aunt Patience says, and I look up to see her grimace. "I was able to get into contact with Agent Tilted Showdown. According to her, everything that happened at Base Buckleberry was a trap to catch the Suns of Liberty."

Just a few questions? This feels more like an interrogation.

Blake crosses his arms, sitting stiffly in the chair across from Hudson's walnut desk, where the Ignis agent seems to be attempting to intimidate him by staring him down.

Shades, because it's working, too.

Blake looks away first, gaze flitting around the wood-panelled walls and posh decor. "What do you want?" He's pretty sure he wasn't called into the principal's office just so the high-level brass could stare him down.

"What is your connection with Jet Sullivan?" Hudson asks at length.

Blake stills. "Is that... relevant?"

"Given the fact he thought it necessary to apprehend you from under our noses... Yes, it is."

Rubbing at the old ache in his thigh that the little swim in the basin did no favors to, Blake swallows. If they insist on grilling him about his past, do they have to do it when he's a sleep-deprived, traumatized mess? "He... we... met when we were teens. He... uh, pretended to help me with something... some information I was looking for." Running a sweaty palm over his pant leg, Blake exhales slowly. "It... ended up being a trap and he's been after me ever since."

"And how does that connect to his recent advances?" Hudson presses, because of course the brass can't just leave it there.

"My... uh, my partner and I were working on a case about two years ago, and Jet didn't... he didn't take too kindly to... to my partner interfering. I've been... working on tracking the manuscript down since then." *See, that wasn't so hard, was it?* He clasps his hands in his lap, suddenly feeling as cold as if he were still in that cursed basin.

Now would probably be a good time to get out of here. He pushes halfway to his feet. "If you're done—"

"Bear with me a moment longer, Hession, if you don't mind."

Slowly, Blake lowers himself back into the chair, eyeing Hudson cautiously. What more can the Ignis agent want to know?

"Would you mind expounding on the events surrounding *The Freesia Guard*?"

Forcing himself to concentrate, Blake frowns. "What... exactly are you wanting to know? The code, or...?"

"Everything you can tell me. It's currently in our custody until you can get it back to the States, and I would like to know who and what we're dealing with here."

Right... Blake attempts to think back to the coded report. "Da—my partner encoded his mission report into a book he was working on at the time, *The Freesia Guard.* After the mission was... terminated, the manuscript went missing. I... I was just able to get it back about two weeks ago. Some... events came up, prolonging the normal rate of decoding, but we have a mostly full report now. The SoL wasn't... wasn't happy that the manuscript still exists, and Jet thought I would be their best chance of, uh, getting it."

"I see." Hudson nods, marking something on the pad of paper next to him. "You mentioned that the mission was terminated?"

Blake's breath catches in his throat, but he manages to slowly let it out. "I... yes."

"Can you explain why?"

Please, no. But it's not really a question. "My partner's cover was... exposed, and the SoL made sure he'd—never be an issue again." The sickening feeling of the Beetle crashing past the arm of the bridge. Water pouring in. Dallas, not moving. Blake fists his hands, digging his fingernails into his palms. It's too much, too hard to draw a decent breath—

"And do you have an idea of where Mr. Sullivan might have gone?"

Blake's gaze flits to Hudson, and he forces a shrug.

"Any friends or relatives who might harbor him?"

"I..." Blake blinks, trying to keep it together as the office starts to spin. "I don't—I don't know." He blinks again, Hudson's profile blurring back into focus. "Is... that all?"

The agent frowns. "I suppose so, for now. Thank you for your time, Agent Grizzled Fox."

Blake tips a nod and stands, gripping the arm of the chair for a moment as the world tips and rights itself. The doorway seems impossibly far away, but he sucks in a shallow breath and ignores the graying at the edges of his vision. He—he's fine.

"I'll be in touch," Hudson calls after him, and Blake jerks before hunching his shoulders.

Right.

Gritting his teeth against the shaking of his jaw, Blake turns into the hallway—only to nearly bump into Tirana. The girl backs up quickly, eyes wide.

"I'm sorry," she says quickly, gaze darting to her dog and then back up. "I didn't mean to eavesdrop—honest! I was just walking by and I heard you talking and—" She bites her lip, expression crumpling. "Agent Tilted Showdown told me what happened. The mission, the crash..." Maybe she says more, but buzzing fills Blake's ears, and he presses a hand to the wall as the ground shifts.

C'mon, not here... not now... He eases in a careful breath, trying to figure out if he can just push past the girl and escape to—somewhere, anywhere—before he completely loses it.

"She said that you were hurt, too." Tirana's low voice registers past the buzzing. "I... I'm sorry." She ducks her head, playing with the dog's leash.

"Kid—" Blake clears his throat, sucking in another breath that shudders as he exhales. He clenches his jaw, torn between the girl's words and the urge to run. "It's not... not your fault." Shoving a shaking hand through still-damp hair, he avoids her eyes. "I—I'm the one who's sorry. Your dad... he... he should be the one here right... right now." Blake closes his eyes, nausea rising as he turns away. He needs to go before Tirana realizes just how weak he is. Before—before—

She sniffles, the sound driving another stake deep into Blake's heart. This is his fault—the kid crying because he wasn't able to save her dad—

"She took me there, you know. To the bridge." Tirana sniffs again. "You did the best you could."

Blake stills, crossing his arms tightly over his chest. "You... don't know what happened."

"Maybe not." Her voice is stronger now, backed with conviction. "But it's the Suns of Liberty who did it. You didn't kill Dad, Agent Grizzled Fox; *they* did. I don't care what they say—it wasn't your fault." A moment passes, then her footsteps pad slowly down the hall before halting.

Blake glances up, and her eyes meet his, her expression holding something he can't quite read. Pity?

"Are you okay? Should I call—"

"I'm fine," he interrupts, clearing his throat. His eyes burn, but this time, he has no bloodthirsty basins to blame it on.

Just a girl who has every right to hate him... but doesn't.

KENSINGTON GARDENS
LONDON, ENGLAND

MAYBE I SHOULD HAVE KEPT ON WALKING WHEN I OVERHEARD Agent Hudson's demanding tone from one of the offices when I was coming back from the restroom, but they were talking about *The Freesia Guard*—and Dad. I hadn't expected Grizzled Fox to catch me eavesdropping, nearly bowling me over as he left the office like there was a man-eating tiger in there. And I definitely hadn't expected Grizzled Fox to react the way he did, his eyes filled with unmistakable shame and guilt.

If I know one thing for certain in this land of uncertainty, it's that Dad would never have wanted his friend to blame himself for his death.

Swallowing, I raise my face to the sky. It's still cloudy, but the sun is making a valiant effort to shine through.

As I follow Mum deeper into Kensington Gardens, the scenery becomes increasingly familiar. The tree-lined paths, the pools of the Italian Gardens, the ice cream truck that's no longer there... Was it truly just yesterday we were here? It feels strange not having Secret with me, but he's taking a well-deserved nap back at Ignis.

Skirting a puddle, I hurry to catch up with Mum. She didn't say exactly where she was taking me, only that she had something to show me.

The third person to have said that in the past two weeks. Is this one connected to Dad, too?

The scene on my left turns to a wrought iron fence bordering a tangle of undergrowth. Behind that, the dark waters of a lake reflect the clouds. The path seems to stretch on forever, disappearing around a bend at the treeline. Yet the further we go, the thicker the crowd coming from the opposite direction seems to get. Couples and loners, joggers and old ladies, families with little kids, pairs of friends... All of them enjoying a nice afternoon at the park, none seeming aware of how *close* danger is, of how quickly one's world can be shattered.

The trees open on the left, providing another clear view of the water, and to the right— "Is that Peter Pan?"

"It's certainly not Mother Goose." Mum gestures me forward.

After waiting for a couple with their faces in their phones to pass, I cut across the path and up the few stone steps to the platform.

Staring at the bronze sculpture is like being teleported inside of *Dust*. If only the statue had the same effect on me as it did on Peter Pan in that book; maybe then I could begin to understand why this all had to happen.

"This is where your father proposed," Mum says, coming up next to me. "I have something for you." Her hand dips into the pocket of her trench coat, and she holds something out to me.

It's a brass pocket watch, engraved with a silhouette of Big Ben. Slowly, I reach out and pick it up, weighing it in my hand. It feels heavy, solid.

It's Mum's face when I glance up that catches me by surprise, though. Her eyes have this distant look, like she's worlds—or decades—away, and I haven't seen her look so... *sad* since Dad died.

Swallowing, I press the knob of the watch, and the cover clicks smoothly open, revealing a clock face adorned with aesthetic roman numerals. The slim, golden hands are frozen at twelve past five.

"He gave that to me the first time we met," Mum says, voice low. "Silly chap decided to go and hug a stranger on the street. I returned it to him before he left London, and then it became a sort of game, hiding it on each other wherever our paths crossed."

"I miss him," I whisper, wrapping my hand around the pocket watch.

"As do I." Mum's voice is thick as she puts an arm around my shoulders, a side hug that's somehow more comforting than a crushing bear hug.

We stand like that, under the shadow of Peter Pan, where Mum and Dad once stood so many years before, until a few noisy children run up to the statue, and Mum pulls me away. I lean against the railing overlooking the lake, watching a colorful duck dive into the dark waters.

Mum clears her throat. "The watch is yours, Tirana. You've earned it. You've proven that you can hold your own, and I apologize for not seeing that my baby girl is growing into a bright young woman." Mum squeezes my shoulder. "I'm proud of you, Grace Tirana."

"But..." I shake my head. "I made so many mistakes. I'm not..." *Someone you should be proud of.*

"That's what growing up is, Tirana. Making mistakes and learning from them. 'You have brains in your head. You have feet in your shoes. You can steer yourself any direction you choose.'"

I squint at her. "Is that... Doctor *Seuss*?"

She winks. "You know that I only quote the masters."

I look at her for a second, then we both laugh.

The Lost Boys longed for a mother, didn't they? I turn back to Peter Pan, looking at the youthful, bronze face and playful stance as he blows the pan pipes. A vague memory surfaces—Mum and I cuddled on the couch, Mum reading *Peter Pan* aloud in her lyrical, reading-aloud voice. How had I forgotten that? Dad might be gone, but Mum's not.

I look down at the pocket watch, a tangible connection to my parents and the secret life that took Dad away. It's not fair—but life isn't fair. I sigh and turn to Mum, biting my lip. "Will they be back? The Suns of Liberty?"

"I do not know." Mum's gaze drifts over the lake before coming back to me. She offers a small smile. "As soon as I tie up a few loose threads here, we'll be heading back to the States."

This is London, the city of royalty; Mum's homeland. But even in the gardens, even standing next to the Peter Pan statue where so much history was made, my heart longs for the quiet of the Indiana woods.

I was not made for the city, for the hustle, for the fast-paced life where you can't get a real breath. But soon, we'll be back in Dad's territory.

No, life will never go back to how it once was.

But maybe I can learn to love this life.

Step into Dad's shoes.

And who knows? Maybe one day, I'll save the world.

Can't hurt to try, right?

CHAPTER THIRTY-THREE
WE COULD BE HEROES

The moment Blake steps into his room at Wonderland, he knows something's off. Dropping his duffle bag by the door, he flips the light switch, and the dull gloom brightens.

Nondescript white walls, a bed and a desk shoved into their respective corners, large curtained windows...

"Don't you think that's a bit *juvenile*, Mayo?"

The hanging curtains rustle, and a certain redhead emerges with a snort. "Not a bit, Blakey. Not one bit."

Next thing he knows, Mya's wrapping him in a tight hug. He grunts. "Trying to kill me or something?"

"Always." But she lets go, plopping down on the office chair and swinging her legs up to rest on the surface of the desk. "Heard you had quite the adventure."

Thousands of possible answers flit through his mind, but he just hums and sinks down on the bed, grateful to be home. "You're not supposed to be here, you know."

She laughs. "Who says? I needed to practice my lock-picking skills *somewhere*."

"You have the key."

"And you trust me with it?" Mya links her hands behind her head, leaning back in the chair. "Sooooo...."

"You sound like a teenage girl." Despite himself, a grin quirks the corners of his mouth.

"You sound like a boring old man." Mya's green eyes sparkle with mischief. "In fact, you look like one, too."

"Har, har, har." Yet the bantering is familiar, like a pair of boots that have been broken in. He and Mya had had their fair amount of fights growing up, but they stuck together.

Always had, always would.

A twinge of guilt pricks him. Wouldn't be a lie to say he'd been avoiding his big sister, with her soul-piercing glare, for the past few years.

That gaze's settled over him now, any mirth gone from her features as she drops her feet to the carpet and picks up the small, black-and-white stuffed cat from the dresser.

"I heard what happened, Blake. Aurora told me everything. Says you're a hero." A smile tugs one side of her mouth as she looks down at the toy.

"She's a good kid. Takes after her mom." Yet his words thicken, betraying him, the memory of the storm-tossed basin lingering all too close. He jerks his head up as warmth touches his arm. The mattress sags when Mya sits, not removing her hand.

"You did good back there," she mutters.

"My fault she was there in the first place." Blake shakes his head, pushing to his feet and striding to the window to stare out over the greens of the garden behind the building. Tirana might not blame him for Dallas' death, but that doesn't change the fact that he'd dragged both girls—and Thomas—into the chaos of the past two weeks.

Mya doesn't say anything for a long moment, and when she does, her tone is thoughtful. "Remember Carrie? When we visited her in the hospital and did the whole Mission Get-A-Want thing?"

Of course he remembers Jet's little sister. He'll never forget the little girl who conspired with Damian to give Blake the stuffed cat ten-odd years ago, the last toy in that huge Santa sack they'd brought in for the sick kids, because Damian thought the plushie would make Blake's grumpy teenage self feel better.

"You saved her life, you know."

Blake doesn't respond, just stares at the trees, remembering when he was seventeen and thought that he could make a difference.

They all thought they could make a difference.

"Blake—"

"Mya, no." He turns, arms crossed tightly over his chest, looking her in the eye. "I was stupid, and it was my decisions that put everyone in danger. Including your daughter." *A miracle no one got killed... this time.* He grinds his jaw at the burning in his throat, the ever-lurking blur of the day he failed so miserably sharpening, threatening... "I'm no hero. You know that."

Mya nods slowly. "You're right. You're not. You're a human who was faced with incredible odds, who did the best he could with what he had. Sure, you've made some unwise choices, done some admittedly dumb things—same as anyone. You don't think you're a hero—and maybe you're right. Heroes are renowned for being brave, courageous, saving the day, yada, yada, yada. The keyword being 'renowned.'" She crosses her arms, raising her left eyebrow in a perfect arch. "Which isn't exactly the mission of the ISA."

"Your point?"

Mya smirks like she's won and she knows it, holding up the stuffed, cow-colored cat like the toy illustrates her words. "Superheroes are outdated. And Blake—come back, okay?"

"Back?"

"Don't be a parrot." Mya sticks out her tongue. "We miss you around here, little brother. Family dinner's at six on Sunday, and I expect to see you there. No more 'sudden missions' or 'last-minute deadlines,' or else." She wiggles the cat in his direction, giving him her signature mom look. "Deal?"

"Or else what—you'll kidnap Hope?" Blake huffs lightly. "I'm shaking in my boots."

"You'd better be." She stands, tossing the cat to him, and he catches the toy. "So, should we be expecting you?"

Blake exhales slowly, giving his sister a crooked smile. "Sunday at six?"

"We can't have you eating microwaved ramen forever. After all—outdated superheroes need more calories." Her phone buzzes, and she pulls it out, frowning as she glances at the screen. "I got to go. Hope you like the new decorations, Blakey—welcome home!" She tosses a grin over her shoulder as she heads for the door, then she's gone, the door clicking shut behind her.

New—what? Blake frowns, turning to take in the room in more detail. His eyes settle on the Batmobile-through-the-years poster tacked on the wall over his bed... Batmobiles that now sport *dashing* mustaches and eyebrows.

He laughs, placing Hope back on the dresser where she belongs. Yeah... it's good to be home. Even if he probably needs to rethink letting his sister have the key to his apartment.

THE CLOCK TICKS TOWARDS MIDNIGHT AS BLAKE SHUFFLES through the papers on his desk. The quiet is a relief after the business of the day.

With a sigh, he closes the file and leans back in his chair, exhaustion weighing heavy as it sinks in. After everything, *The Freesia Guard*'s case is out of his hands. Agent Tilted Showdown is suspended for her role in this whole fiasco. In that last debriefing, she revealed her entire plan, how she had manipulated the scales to cause the SoL to overstep their normal boundaries.

"I apologize for going about it the way I did," she'd said. "It was not preferable to allow the Suns of Liberty to take hostages, but it was necessary."

As if any of that was *necessary* to get the SoL into more trouble than they were already in. As if Blake'll ever be able to forget the sneer on Jet's face, the feeling of being tied up as a prisoner, or the deadly hazing of smoke.

But the pawns don't matter to the brass.

"We had someone working on the inside," Tilted Showdown had explained. "One of ours who risked her life to pose as a SoL operative here in the ISA. She planted a listening device on Tirana's dog and fed the SoL choice tidbits, while keeping us informed of the SoL's plans and activities.

"We let a true SoL mole stay in position, one you would know by the name of Agent Pale Flame. He, unknown to us, placed a tracking device on Tirana's dog as well. That was a slight oversight on our parts, I'm afraid, and how they were able to track you to London."

Of course, that's all the agent had to say on *that*. Letting a mole stay in position? *Shades*, sometimes Blake doesn't understand how his superiors have stayed in the game for so long. His own *friends* haven't.

Flipping open the file again, he turns to the papers devoted to *The Freesia Guard*'s code. Rather, *codes*. Dallas' report is listed in full, plugged in with names, dates, and places that the *Lord of the Rings* jargon once filled. After the book was handed over to the code breaking division, the key was discovered written in invisible ink—cobalt chloride, the file claims—on the very pages of the book itself.

Then there are the files that had been on the SD card they'd found in the headstone, not to mention the file Patience had discovered warning about an impending attack. The ISA has been scrambling, but they've been keeping it hush-hush. Last Blake heard, they were getting the FBI involved.

One thing's for certain... the SoL won't be recovering from this. The cell that killed Dallas has enough dirt piled on it to put the terrorists behind bars forever. It's over.

As over as it had been when the ashes settled over the bookstore, and Damian never emerged. As over as it had been when the VW Beetle hit that Florida river.

As over as it will never be.

Picking up his pen, Blake hesitates before signing the last paper, marking that he, Agent Grizzled Fox, approves that the file is correct.

Bang!

He jumps, pen dropping from his hand and rolling off the desk. He's trying to determine if someone dropped something or if a shooter is on the loose, when there's another bang.

Blood chilling, he shoves to his feet, ignoring the ache catching at his leg as he moves to peek over the top of his cubicle. Most of the large room is empty, but light shines from a cubicle a few rows down.

Hands itching for a weapon, he inches forward.

Bang! A deep boom like an echoing gunshot, coming from the left.

Wasting no time, Blake grabs the umbrella leaning against the thin partition wall and heads out, pulse jumping.

The dimly lit room is devoid of life, silent.

Chills crawl up his arms, and he tightens his grip on the improv weapon as he scans around.

Bang!

He jerks, hastening towards the sound. *There.* A case room door stands open, faint light spilling out onto the gray carpet of the hall.

Umbrella raised, he draws closer, every sense on high alert.

Out of everything he expects to find, books sprawled on the floor of the case room are not on the list. After clearing the space and finding nothing hidden under the table or behind the door, Blake pokes the nearest volume with the tip of his umbrella. *Matthew Poole's Commentary on the Holy Bible*, a hefty thing.

Volumes eight and fourteen of the Oxford English Dictionary and an ornate copy of *The Complete Works of William Shakespeare* lie nearby.

Letting out a breath, Blake picks up the books and sets them on the table with a heavy thud. They don't even belong in the case room. It was probably some stupid kid's prank, which he wouldn't put past Aurora or one of the new recruits. He'd better not meet anyone on the way back, or he'll have a bit of an issue explaining the umbrella.

With the accessory hanging over the crook of his elbow, he feels a bit like Alfred Pennyworth as he walks back to his cubicle. Good thing Mya isn't around to poke fun at him.

He sets the umbrella against the rolling file cabinet before turning back to his desk. It's probably time to call it a night...

His thoughts trail off as he notices the official-sized white envelope resting on top of his papers.

A quick scan of the cubical doesn't point to anything being moved. Nothing out of place. Only that offending letter.

Warily, he picks it up. His pen—the fountain pen the twins had given him for his birthday—rolls down and comes to a rest against his closed laptop.

The pen he'd dropped on the floor and not retrieved. *A conscientious invader?* Or something more?

A feeling of premonition clenches in his gut as he inspects the outside of the envelope. It's utterly blank. He slides the tucked edge of the envelope open, and pulls out a piece of folded paper.

Slowly, he straightens it. The short message is typed in a generic font. *"This isn't over."*

The penned doodle of a black cat, broken dove hanging from the feline's mouth, signs off the letter.

Of course. The traitor will never give up, will he?

Well, this time, Blake would give him no choice.

The paper crumples in his fist, more resembling trash than a threat.

If you want war, then let's have war.

There really is no place like home. Is this how Dorothy felt when she finally clicked her heels and returned to Kansas?

Squinting in the morning light that floods my bedroom, I push aside the covers and slide out of bed. I dig my toes into the fuzzy rug and smile at the framed map of Middle-earth over my bed. Just as Bilbo's journey drew to an end, so has mine. At least... kind of.

"Delivery!" The door bursts open and Aurora, still in her pajamas, which are patterned with lightsabers and Darth Vader masks, charges in and drops a package on my bed.

Secret rouses himself from the tangle of Aurora's blanket shakedown, stretches, and trots over to Aurora, sniffing her pants.

"What is that?" I eye the parcel, which is shaped like a loaf of bread and wrapped in Christmas paper. It's June; that's definitely not okay.

"Probably not a pot of honey, definitely not a white elephant... maybe a bomb?" Aurora shrugs, crouching to pet Secret. "It's addressed to you."

"It's wrapped in surfboarding *Santas.*"

Grinning, Aurora begins to sing the opening to "The Christmas Song," only getting as far as "open fire" before a pillow hits her full in the face, effectively silencing her.

Ignoring her sputtering, I pick up the offending box, frowning as I examine the tag tacked next to the fancy bow. Sure enough, "G. Tirana Caineson" is written on the tag in a neat print that I don't recognize.

"Where did this even come from?"

"It was outside your front door."

I frown. "Why were you on my porch?"

Aurora shrugs. "Someone knocked."

"And you *answered* it?"

"Well, by the time I got to the door, there weren't any people—just that package."

I resist the overwhelming urge to facepalm. "Ignoring all that, aren't you, I don't know... *concerned?*" Mum is going to be. When our parents agreed to let Aurora sleep over, I'm pretty sure the many conditions did not include letting her answer our door... if this isn't just one of her pranks.

Aurora grabs a toy and throws it for Secret. "I've been wanting to try out my bomb-defusing skills in the real world. Well? Aren't you gonna open it?"

"Your fault if it kills us," I mutter, carefully unwrapping the paper in the meticulous way that always drove Dad crazy. I might as well play along with her prank and let her have a bit of fun.

Inside, among layers of tissue paper, rests a navy-blue baseball cap embroidered with the logo of the Dallas Cowboys. My breath catches. "What..." Hands suddenly shaking, I lift it up, turning it over so the tag is visible.

The thick, black-marker initials "D.C." are as clear as they were the day that Dad slid the too-big baseball cap over my head and said that I'd make a fine cowboy yet.

"A... hat?" Aurora sounds unimpressed, but I shake my head slowly, looking up from the cap to meet her eyes.

"Where did you find this?"

"I told you—it was outside the door." She frowns. "I thought your aunt left it there. What's wrong?"

"This isn't just *any* hat, Aurora. This... this is what I was wearing when the SoL tried to kidnap me when Agent Grizzled Fox was taking me to Wonderland. This is the hat that I lost."

TO BE CONTINUED...

CHARACTER INDEX

ISA AGENT LEVELS (RANKING FROM LOWEST TO HIGHEST):

Neophyte

Rook

Regent

Apex

TIRANA'S FAMILY:

Grace Tirana Caineson

Secret Caineson

Dallas Caineson (ISA Agent Bel Ria; status: deceased)

Isabelle Dalton-Caineson (Ignis Agent Dalton)

Patience Caineson (ISA Agent Mute Starburst; regent)

OTHER IMPORTANT ISA AGENTS:

Blake Hession (ISA Agent Grizzled Fox; regent)

Aurora Harrison (ISA Agent Celestial Flicker; neophyte)

Thomas "Genius" Harrison (ISA Agent Coruscant Falcon; neophyte)

Mya Harrison (ISA Agent Unknown Number; regent)

Michelle Shepherds (ISA Agent Respectable Pixie; regent)

Damian Shepherds (ISA Agent Tempered Lightning; status: deceased)

Dimitri (ISA Agent Pale Flame; neophyte)

Jennifer (ISA Agent Tilted Showdown; apex)

REFERENCE LIST

CHAPTER 1: TROUBLE LURKS AHEAD
TITLE INSPIRED BY THE ALMIGHTY TERRIBLES' SONG *"TROUBLE LURKS AHEAD"*

Lady Shadow | Character (*Studio C* | Sketch Comedy Show)

The Lord of the Rings by J.R.R. Tolkien | Book Trilogy

Tesla's Attic by Eric Elfman and Neal Shusterman | Book

Dr. Heinz Doofenshmirtz | Character (*Phineas and Ferb* | 2007–2015 Television Series)

Lucy Pevensie | Character (*The Lion, the Witch, and the Wardrobe* by C.S. Lewis | Book)

CHAPTER 2: THE FREESIA GUARD
TITLE INSPIRED BY DALLAS CAINESON'S FICTION NOVEL *THE FREESIA GUARD*

Tom Sawyer | Character (*The Adventures of Tom Sawyer* by Mark Twain | Book)

CHAPTER 3: OPERATION RIDE OF THE ROHIRRIM
TITLE INSPIRED BY PETER JACKSON'S 2003 FILM, *THE LORD OF THE RINGS: THE RETURN OF THE KING*

Martha Sowerby | Character (*The Secret Garden* by Frances Hodgson Burnett | Book)

CHAPTER 4: WHAT WOULD LEE DO?
TITLE INSPIRED BY P.D. ATKERSON'S CHARACTER SIMON LEE

Eeyore | Character (*Winnie-the-Pooh* by A.A. Milne and E.H. Shepard | Book)

AKA Simon Lee by P.D. Atkerson | Book Series

Kipper by HiT Entertainment and Mick Inkpen | 1997 - 2000 TV Series

Batman | Character (DC Comics)

CHAPTER 5: WHERE THE LOST THINGS GO
TITLE INSPIRED BY EMILY BLUNT'S SONG *"WHERE THE LOST THINGS GO"*

The Wicked Witch of the West | Character (*The Wonderful Wizard of Oz* by L. Frank Baum | Book)

Big Hero 6 by Don Hall and Chris Williams | 2014 Film

CHAPTER 6: WONDERLAND
TITLE AND BASE NAME INSPIRED BY LEWIS CARROLL'S BOOK *ALICE'S ADVENTURES IN WONDERLAND*

Mr. Lemonchello's Library by Chris Grabenstein | Book

The Gollywhopper Games by Jody Feldman | Book

Wonderland Trials by Sara Ella | Book

"Jack and Jill" | Nursery Rhyme

"The Three Little Pigs" | Fairy Tale

Dr. Seuss's ABC by Dr. Seuss | Book

If You Give a Mouse a Cookie by Laura Numeroff | Book

If You Give a Moose a Muffin by Laura Numeroff | Book

If You Give a Pig a Party by Laura Numeroff | Book

Little Bear by Else Holmelund Minarik | Book Series

The Little Engine That Could by Watty Piper | Book

Madeline by Ludwig Bemelmans | Book

Luke Danes | Character (*Gilmore Girls* | 2000–2007 Television Series)

A Series of Unfortunate Events by Daniel Handler | Book Series

CHAPTER 7: A STUDY IN CRIME
TITLE INSPIRED BY SIR ARTHUR CONAN DOYLE'S BOOK *A STUDY IN SCARLET*

"The Christmas song" by Mel Tormé and Robert Wells | Song

The Joker | Character (DC Comics)

CHAPTER 8: NEVER SAY GENIUS
TITLE INSPIRED BY DAN GUTTMAN'S BOOK *NEVER SAY GENIUS*

The Hulk/Bruce Banner | Character (Marvel Comics)

Princess Unikitty | Character (*The Lego Movie* | 2014 Film)

Mickey Mouse | Character (*Mickey Mouse Clubhouse* | 2006–2016 Television Series)

CHAPTER 9: THE PINK PANTHER THEME SONG
TITLE INSPIRED BY HENRY MANCINI'S SONG *"THE PINK PANTHER THEME"*

Loki | Character (Marvel Comics)

"Englishman in New York" by Sting | Song

Walt Disney | Quote

CHAPTER 10: THE SECOND STAR TO THE RIGHT
TITLE INSPIRED BY SAMMY FAIN'S SONG *"THE SECOND STAR TO THE RIGHT"*

The Hobbit by J. R. R. Tolkien | Book

Peter Pan by J. M. Barrie | Book

The Green Ember by S.D. Smith | Book Series

Red Hood | Character (DC Comics)

CHAPTER 11: LEGACY
TITLE INSPIRED BY TONY GILROY'S 2012 FILM *THE BOURNE LEGACY*

The Mouse and the Motorcycle by Beverly Cleary | Book

According to Humphrey by Betty G. Birney | Book Series

Through the Looking-Glass by Lewis Carroll | Book

Harold and the Purple Crayon by Crockett Johnson | Book

CHAPTER 12: SECRETS AND SURPRISES
TITLE INSPIRED BY LAUREL HICKS AND MARION HEDQUIST'S *ABEKA READER SECRETS AND SURPRISES*

Go Dog. Go! by P.D. Eastman | Book

"Road Less Traveled" by Lauren Alaina | Song

MacGyver | 1985-1992 Television Series

CHAPTER 13: CURIOUSER AND CURIOUSER
TITLE INSPIRED BY LEWIS CARROLL'S BOOK *ALICE'S ADVENTURES IN WONDERLAND*

Green Arrow | Character (DC Comics)

Star Wars | Film Series

The Thinker by Auguste Rodin | Sculpture

CHAPTER 14: THE ROAD TO DOOM
TITLE INSPIRED BY THE LORD OF THE RINGS' MOUNT DOOM

Bel Ria by Sheila Burnford | Book

CHAPTER 15: BASKERVILLE
TITLE INSPIRED BY SIR ARTHUR CONAN DOYLE'S *THE HOUND OF THE BASKERVILLES*

The Hound of the Baskervilles by Sir Arthur Conan Doyle | Book

Roblox | Online Gaming Platform

Fallout 4 | Video Game

Call of Duty | Video Game Series

CHAPTER 16: CLOUDY WITH A CHANCE OF DOPPELGÄNGERS
TITLE INSPIRED BY PHIL LORD AND CHRIS MILLER'S 2009 FILM, *CLOUDY WITH A CHANCE OF MEATBALLS*

Stop the Rain by Kassie Angle | Book

Rafi Tetrani | Character (The Fireborn Epic by Gillian Bronte Adams | Book Series)

CHAPTER 17: CASTLING
TITLE INSPIRED BY P.D. ATERSON'S BOOK *CASTLING*

Rabbit | Character (*Winnie-the-Pooh* by A.A. Milne and E.H. Shepard | Book)

Tigger | Character (*Winnie-the-Pooh* by A.A. Milne and E.H. Shepard | Book)

The Accidental Cases of Emily Abbott by Perry Elisabeth Kirkpatrick | Book Series

Green Arrow 8: The Hunt for the Red Dragon by Mike Grell | Comic Book

CHAPTER 18: SMAUG'S LAIR
TITLE INSPIRED BY J. R. R. TOLKIEN'S BOOK *THE HOBBIT*

CHAPTER 19: NEVER TRUST A HEFFALUMP
TITLE INSPIRED BY A.A. MILNE'S BOOK **WINNIE-THE-POOH**

Grimms' Fairy Tales by Jacob and Wilhelm Grimm | Book

CHAPTER 20: WORMTONGUE
TITLE INSPIRED BY THE LORD OF THE RINGS' GRÍMA WORMTONGUE

CHAPTER 21: DO THE NEXT RIGHT THING
TITLE INSPIRED BY KRISTEN BELL'S SONG "THE NEXT RIGHT THING"

The Colour Red by Katja H. Labonté | Book

Ceridwen | Character (The Fireborn Epic by Gillian Bronte Adams | Book Series)

Inigo Montoya | Character (*The Princess Bride* | 1987 Film)

Dorothy Gale | Character (*The Wonderful Wizard of Oz* by L. Frank Baum | Book)

CHAPTER 22: SMOKE SCREEN
TITLE INSPIRED BY P.D. ATKERSON'S BOOK *SMOKE SCREEN*

CHAPTER 23: THERE'S NO PLACE LIKE HOME
TITLE INSPIRED BY VICTOR FLEMING'S 1939 FILM *THE WIZARD OF OZ*

CHAPTER 24: LONDON BRIDGE IS FALLING DOWN
TITLE INSPIRED BY THE SONG *"LONDON BRIDGE IS FALLING DOWN"*

"The Road Not Taken" by Robert Frost | Poem

National Treasure by Jon Turteltaub | 2004 Film

Justice League by Zack Snyder | 2017 Film

Phantom Menace by George Lucas | 1999 Film

The Bourne Identity by Doug Liman | 2002 Film

CHAPTER 25: DOCIOUSALIEXPISTICFRAGICALIRUPUS
TITLE INSPIRED BY ROBERT STEVENSON'S 1964 FILM *MARY POPPINS*

"Supercalifragilisticexpialidocious" by Dick Van Dyke and Julie Andrews | Song

Mary Poppins by Robert Stevenson | 1964 Film

CHAPTER 26: THE WORTH IN OUR STARS
TITLE INSPIRED BY JOHN GREEN'S BOOK *THE FAULT IN OUR STARS*

Thanos | Character (Marvel Comics)

Darkseid | Character (DC Comics)

Hydra | Terrorist Organization (Marvel Comics)

CHAPTER 27: PLEASE LOOK AFTER THIS BEAR
TITLE INSPIRED BY MICHAEL BOND'S BOOK *A BEAR CALLED PADDINGTON*

Paddington by Paul King | 2015 Film

Cities XL | Video game

CHAPTER 32: PETER PAN
TITLE INSPIRED BY J. M. BARRIE'S CHARACTER PETER PAN

Peter Pan by Sir George Frampton | Sculpture

Dust by Kara Swanson | Book

Oh, the Places You'll Go! by Dr. Suess | Quote

CHAPTER 33: WE COULD BE HEROES
TITLE INSPIRED BY MARGARET MARY FINNEGAN'S BOOK *WE COULD BE HEROES* AND ALESSO AND TOVE LO'S SONG *"HEROES (WE COULD BE)"*

Commentary of the Holy Bible by Matthew Poole | Book

Oxford English Dictionary | Book

The Complete Works of William Shakespeare by William Shakespeare | Book

AUTHOR'S NOTE

When I first created Tirana, I gave her a life-threatening allergy to gluten. I know, I'm so nice to my characters, right? Despite all the versions *Trouble Lurks* has been through, this is one of the things that hasn't changed (heck, back in that first draft, Secret was a border collie named Chance!).

Everyone probably knows about celiac disease and peanut allergies, but true allergies to gluten aren't as common. And service dogs that sniff out the allergen, like Secret does for Tirana? It's gotta be fictional, right? Nope.

Like Tirana, I was born with anaphylaxis to gluten (a protein found in rye, barley, and wheat). Unlike celiac disease, which is an autoimmune disorder that affects the small intestine, anaphylaxis is a severe allergic reaction that can affect multiple organ systems, leading to difficulty breathing and a drop in blood pressure, which can cause a potential loss of consciousness. In other words, my immune system views gluten as a foe and tries to fight it, resulting in a life-threatening, systemic reaction. Anaphylaxis can be caused by both ingested and airborne allergens, and it can be tricky to avoid, as Tirana puts it, "particles of poison [that float] around like invisible pixie dust." Both anaphylaxis and celiac disease require a gluten-free diet, and even trace amounts of gluten can cause a reaction or make someone sick for days.

There's no cure, but there are dogs that have been trained to alert to minute amounts of allergens—like Secret. The miniature poodle spent his early puppyhood with a puppy raiser, where he learned the basics—sit, stay, come, etc. Once he was ready, his training took him to a program that trains service dogs for medical alert, where he was paired with Tirana and finished both his public access and his allergen alert training.

When Tirana was finally able to take Secret home, she gained independence beyond what she ever could have had without him. She could safely eat out at restaurants, knowing that Secret would alert if her food was cross-contaminated. She could travel without worrying about her plans getting pushed aside in favor of an overnight stay at the E.R. And most importantly, Secret offered relief from the constant anxiety that accompanies severe food allergies—both for Tirana, and for her family.

If there's one thing I hope every reader can take away from my story, it's that service dogs offer disabled people the freedom and peace of mind many didn't even know existed before they received a service animal.

If you see a service dog out in public (they usually wear a vest or some other kind of identification, although it's not required by law in the United States), the most polite thing to do is ignore it. Don't stare, don't baby-talk, and don't try to pet the dog. Even if it doesn't look like it's working, it has a very important job to do.

According to the Americans with Disabilities Act, service dogs (internationally known as "assistance dogs") are not required to be a particular breed, although labs, Golden Retrievers, and German Shepherds are common choices. They are trained with at least one specific task that helps mitigate their handler's disability, like how Secret checks Tirana's food for gluten, or mobility service dog might pick up fallen items for a wheelchair user.

I would like to point out that while emotional support animals (ESAs) also can support those with mental health struggles, ESAs do not have the same training and public access rights as a service animal. The main difference between a service animal and an ESA is that a service animal undergoes a substantial amount of special training—often for years—whereas an ESA is not required to be trained. ESAs purely provide emotional support (and if you're dedicated enough to be reading this, here's a fun little spoiler for book two... Blake finds himself a pint-sized ESA doggo).

In a year or two, my own dog—who also happens to be a mini poodle—will graduate from a scent-training program and become a full-fledged service dog. I'm training him myself, under the guidance of a professional, because unfortunately, the program Secret came from is fictional, and not many programs exist that train successful allergen-detection dogs.

My hope is that by reading *Trouble Lurks*, you've learned something new, and gained an appreciation for these heroic dogs. If you have any questions about allergen-alert service dogs, or just want to chat about service dogs in general, you can contact me through my website at elisabethjoywriter.com.

ACKNOWLEDGMENTS

Writing is not a solitary endeavor. Sure, you're typing away at your laptop, maybe in your special writing space tucked away from humanity in the depths of the deepest cave... but it takes a community to whip a book into shape. Sometimes, it takes a community just to start one.

So my first acknowledgements go to the King's Daughters' Writing Camp, which is the community behind *Trouble Lurks*. I won't even try to list out all the people who have played a role in the creation and evolution of this book, and I'm no doubt forgetting some important players as it is... (If I've forgotten you, sorry, and thank you with whatever you helped with!)

Every great story has a beginning, and *Trouble Lurks* started with an innocent writing prompt. So thank you very much, Courtenay Burden, for supplying me with a main character and a random book in a random library. Without you, Tirana wouldn't have found *The Freesia Guard*... or, y'know, exist.

I'd also like to thank my "fans," who motivated me to finish the first draft in a month, always wanting the next installment. It was great fun to see where y'all thought it was going—indeed, some of the greatest fun I've ever had writing. (Yes, Genius came to ruin Tirana's life, and no, Blake is not evil.) Special thanks goes to Courtenay Burden, Lydia Jupp, Lydia Coral, Lanora May, Jewels, Vonnie, Charis, Lucy Peterson, and E. N.

Manning for providing ideas and suggestions, because it would certainly not be the same story without y'all.

Honorable mentions go to Liza Bird for everything service dog (from imaginary dogs, to Secret, to Clue); to Timothy "Fred" Wolfe for being a cool brother and my writing inspiration; to Auntie Rebekah for providing Tirana's name; to Auntie Hannah G. for help plotting some super-fun terrorist stuff; to Faith Gilliosa for help with all those medical issues that befell my poor characters, and to my epic LotR team: Jewels, Nova, Ariana, and Lucy.

I'd also like to thank my awesome team of beta-readers: Kerasia Forester, Aggie, Abigail, Tiffany, Rhys-Marie, Grace, Serenity F. Helzerman, Karen, Michelle E., and Bethany, as well as Abigail Sneed and Rebekah Allgood for volunteering to be proofreaders and reference-hunters.

A huge thanks goes to my editors, Cate VanNostrand and Katja Labonté. I would also like to give a shout-out to Rhys-Marie Whitnell for such a fantastic cover (and for being so patient with all the variations!) and to Abigail Kopp for all her hard work on the beautiful formatting (this book looks so good because she did it, trust me).

Michelle... you were there every step of the way. No, we didn't end up with ISA bases under pizza joints like your brother suggested, but I think the book is good anyway, ja? So thanks. We both know it wouldn't have been possible without you.

Lucy. Wow. I'm not sorry I dragged the Shepherds into the TLU, and I don't think they are, either (other than the whole Burning Pages thing with Dai, but we won't mention that...) Thanks for sharing your characters—it's been fun, and it will continue to be. After all, the 6-Some have so many more stories to tell. Chapter 27 is for you, Nyan.

And finally—thank *you*, reader, for giving *Trouble Lurks* a chance. I hope you enjoyed Tirana, Blake, and the crew as much as I enjoyed writing them!

ABOUT THE AUTHOR

Elisabeth Joy is a master obfuscator, an incurable daydreamer, a seeker of little-known knowledge, and a writer at heart. While furthering her characters' conflicts in a slew of different stories is one of her main hobbies, she can often be found chasing after her service dog in training, lost in the captivating world of research, or catching up on Marvel movies and shows.

Connect with her on her website (elisabethjoywriter.com), or on Instagram (@elisbethjoywriter).

If you enjoyed *Trouble Lurks*, consider leaving a rating or review on Goodreads or Amazon! You never know who you might help find their next favorite read.

THE PAST NEVER STAYS BURIED.

Once upon a time, the 6-Some was the greatest team the world had even seen, until it dissolved in the wake of ashes and death. Now only four of the original six members are left... and it's up to them to find out who is trying to dig up the past on a quest that takes them to where it all began.

The past and future collide as Aurora joins the fight that her family took up a generation ago. For too long, the terrorists have run around unchecked. It's time to stop them, once and for all.

140-5-22, 219-17-17
24-5-15, 84-10-2
238-12-6, 40-30-19
175-10-6, 6-1-2

ELISABETHJOYWRITER.COM/TOPSECRET

www.ingramcontent.com/pod-product-compliance
Lightning Source LLC
Chambersburg PA
CBHW031204310726
48969CB00001B/217